THE
KING
BETRAYED

DEBORAH CHESTER

2003
50TH
ANNIVERSARY

ACE BOOKS, NEW YORK

This is a work of fiction. Names, characters, places, and incidents either are the product of the author's imagination or are used fictitiously, and any resemblance to actual persons, living or dead, business establishments, events, or locales is entirely coincidental.

THE KING BETRAYED

An Ace Book / published by arrangement with the author

PRINTING HISTORY
Ace mass-market edition / December 2003

For information address: The Berkley Publishing Group,
a division of Penguin Group (USA) Inc.,
375 Hudson Street, New York, NY 10014.

ISBN: 0-441-01115-2

ACE®
Ace Books are published by The Berkley Publishing Group,
a division of Penguin Group (USA) Inc.,
375 Hudson Street, New York, New York 10014.
ACE and the "A" design
are trademarks belonging to Penguin Group (USA) Inc.

PRINTED IN THE UNITED STATES OF AMERICA

10 9 8 7 6 5 4 3 2 1

PART I

Chapter One

The chamber of state lay shrouded in mist and shadow. In its center stood the heavily carved throne of the king, illuminated by a burning lamp suspended on a chain. The light shone in a small, golden diameter and shimmered rich highlights across the heavy velvet robes of the man standing alone before Faldain, king of Nether. The man's face and shoulders were concealed by shadow, but his long pale hands gestured in the light with the vehemence of his words: "Send the queen away from court. It is your majesty's only chance to survive."

Anger swelled Dain's throat so much he could not speak.

The pale hands extended themselves toward him in entreaty. "Your majesty knows her influence has maligned many who would serve you willingly."

Still mute, Dain shook his head vehemently.

"How can she, a mere woman, judge the hearts of men who are eager to swear loyalty to your service? By what right has she been given such authority?"

"By my love and decree," Dain struggled to answer. "I trust her."

"Trust?" the man before him said with disdain and mockery. "She betrayed your majesty once. Will she not do so again?"

"Never!"

"And these weird changelings she bears your majesty, why, of what merit are they to a man who must have a true prince of the blood royal rule in his succession?"

An immense weight seemed to be pressing Dain down in his chair. With all his will he struggled against it and slowly rose, although the effort made his muscles and sinews tremble. He faced this man who was half-hidden in shadow, and his rage was like something alive in his chest, clawing to break free. "Get out," he growled.

"She will drag your majesty down. She will destroy your monarchy and all that you've worked so hard to gain. Already, thanks to her, you have lost the trust of the people. Soon they will rise against you and then—"

With a hoarse cry, Dain threw himself at the knave and knocked him flat. Suddenly there were several men surrounding them, shouting and trying to pull Dain back. But he straddled his enemy, pummeling him hard. Yet none of his blows landed, and the man laughed at him in triumph.

"Behold, Netherans!" he shouted. "Come and gaze on this barbarian who dares call himself your king."

The realization that a trap had been laid for him and he'd fallen into it humiliated Dain. He moved away from his laughing tormentor. Abruptly there was silence. The chamber of state vanished, as did the men in it. Dain found himself standing outdoors, in the mist, a cold rain falling on his naked body. And around him circled shadowy creatures, their eyes glowing red in the darkness. His anger died in him, extinguished by an icy rush of fear. He had no weapons, nothing with which to defend himself. Above him, out of sight, came again that soft, mocking laughter.

"A choice lies before the king," his enemy called out unseen. "Surrender the queen. Send her forth in exile, or face what will tear your majesty to pieces."

"Thod damn you a thousand times," Dain shouted, but his time had run out.

One of the Nonkind creatures sprang at him, its deadly jaws seeking his throat . . .

Crying out, Dain bolted upright in bed, his right arm fending off the monster that had already vanished in mid-leap. His fists clutched the bedclothes; he was panting and trembling as though he'd run a long distance. A dream, he thought, shutting his eyes with a silent moan. Only a dream.

"Sire?" whispered a gruff voice. A shadow crept forth from the darkness around him and came to stand beside his bed. "What require you?"

Recognizing the voice of his protector, Lord Miest, Dain fought off the tangled vestiges of nightmares and fear. "Nothing. I'm well," he said, and ground the heels of his palms against his burning eyes. He was soaked through with perspiration, and found the interior of the tent stifling. "Can no breeze be enticed inside?"

"Shall I wake your majesty's squire and have the flaps opened to the night air?"

"Nay," Dain replied. The last thing he wanted was for his servants to be roused. "Let it be."

Miest retreated, leaving Dain to sigh and rake back his tangled hair with his fingers. He realized that he slept alone.

Frowning, he leaned over to sweep his arm across Alexeika's side of the bed. Cool, with no lingering warmth of her body. She'd been gone from him a long while.

The dream would not fade. It had been weeks since he'd suffered from one so vivid. Shuddering, he left his bed, hiking his loose sleeping robe higher on one shoulder, and ventured stealthily through the large tent with its multiple inner rooms and soft carpets underfoot. Miest followed him, equally quiet.

Outdoors, the summer night lay heavy and still, yet it was cooler out there than inside the tent. Dain inhaled the fragrance of the pines and fjord and stood a moment to let his eyes adjust to the gloom.

It was nearly dawn, for night was paling to gray, and along the eastern horizon glowed the palest hint of light. Birds had begun to twitter in the trees, and from across the camp Dain heard the approaching tramp of booted feet. The guard was about to be changed. Soon the servants would be up and about their duties.

The last day of refuge, he thought bleakly and felt a surge of dismay that he swiftly checked. How foolish to dread going back, and yet, if he was honest with himself, he dreaded it more than almost anything he'd ever faced. The last day of this sojourn far, far away from his court in Grov. The last day of this blissful, lazy summer rusticating in the farthest, most remote reaches of his realm. And his decision was still not made.

In fresh annoyance, he scowled and set off barefooted toward the fjord. Miest followed him past the sentries on duty, and as Dain threaded his way through the other tents and reached the tree-lined shore, the protector fell back to a more discreet distance in his wake. Ahead, Dain saw a slim, upright shadow standing at the water's edge, staring out across the vista at the mountains on the other side.

His heart quickened, as always, at the sight of Alexeika. As he neared her, she must have heard or sensed his approach, for she whirled around with a little gasp. His arms enfolded her, and with a sigh she melted against him, her body warm and pliant.

For a moment they stood together, her back against his chest, his chin resting on her hair, both of them staring in silence at the inky expanse of water. In the distance, a bird called an eerie, plaintive cry that echoed across the waves, and was answered.

Alexeika shivered against Dain, and he hugged her closer. "I wanted to see the moon set over this last dawn," she whispered. "It's so beautiful here, so unspoiled and peaceful. I shall miss it."

A feeling of gratitude swept him for this marvelous woman who never failed to enchant him daily with her moods and passions. Although he'd made her his queen seven years ago, at heart she still remained the wild, unfettered warrior maid of mountain and wood, unspoiled by high estate and privilege, taking none of it for granted any more than did he. He kissed her temple, and she smiled.

But then without warning she stirred in his arms and

broke free of his embrace to stare at him through the shadows. "What woke you?" she asked. "I instructed Laure last night to not rouse you so early. What—"

"Hush, wife," Dain said, keeping his tone light. "Nothing roused me save your absence."

She snorted. "I have been out here for hours, my beloved. I could not sleep in that oven of a tent."

"Let's steal away into the mountains tonight and spend our last evening alone beneath the stars," he murmured.

She laughed like a girl, and for a moment he sensed her eager accord before she sobered and shook her head. "You are mad. What sport could we enjoy, surrounded by servants, protectors, guards, and courtiers?"

The truth of her words doused his mischievous mood, and with a sigh he moved away from her to kneel and dip his hands in the cold water. He bathed his face, feeling the drag of fatigue in his muscles.

A moment later, she crouched beside him, her hand gripping his shoulder. "Faldain," she said in concern, caressing his dripping cheek. "What's wrong? Not another dream?"

He considered lying to her, but surely he'd lied enough already. "Aye," he admitted, and slicked his unruly hair back with another splash of water. "Stupid, I know."

She stroked his hair with a gentleness that made him want to crush her against him in his need for comforting. "Not stupid," she said quietly. "Worrisome. I thought—it's been weeks since any troubled you. I hoped you were finally free of them."

"No," he said bleakly, thinking of last spring when the pressures and intrigues of his court had so preyed on his mind that he could barely sleep at all. His shoulders had burned from long hours spent poring over documents and dispatches. His head buzzed with fatigue, and his wits felt clouded and thick. He'd lost the ability to concentrate on matters that needed the utmost care, and he'd lived with the constant strain of fearing he would make a terrible, possibly fatal, error of judgment during the difficult forging of a new treaty agreement with Nold.

But the treaty had been signed and sealed eventually, and

although political intrigues at Grov never stopped, at last it seemed possible for him to get away. During the summer, he and his family had journeyed on a slow king's progress across the realm, enjoying the coolness of these mountains and the serene beauty of fjord country. His subjects in these remote provinces had been granted the rare opportunity to see their sovereign, and Dain had gradually found himself relaxing, growing fit, tan, and rested once more in the peaceful company of his wife, children, and a carefully selected group of courtiers.

"It's the arrival of Prince Tustik," Alexeika said with annoyance. "And I saw a dispatch pouch in his luggage wagon, so do not pretend to me that he didn't bring one. And after we agreed that you were not to be disturbed until your return to Grov. I am furious with him."

"Alexeika—"

"No, don't make excuses for the old lizard! There's no emergency, or Lord Thum would have sent a courier to you. What is Tustik doing here, interfering with our last days and already driving you from your sleep?"

"Shush," he said, putting his arm around her shoulder to calm her fierceness. She clung to him, still as responsive to his touch and proximity as when they were first wed. Her long dark hair, unbound here in the privacy of night, smelled faintly of herbs and soap. Loving the scent of it, Dain inhaled deeply. "Don't blame old Tustik," he said. "He isn't at fault."

"What then? Something is worrying you. I know it, no matter how much you pretend there's nothing. Why won't you confide in me? You always have before. I—"

"Alexeika," he said in anguish, for what could he say about the Kollegya's request that would not wound her deeply? Yet if she suspected this much, did his continued silence not hurt her in a different way? In his heart he cursed the petty jealousy of his advisers and wished them at perdition for putting him in this quandary. He gripped her hand in the darkness and, when she tried to draw away, held it tighter.

"Alexeika, it's a matter of state, a decision to be made."

"And you want no advice or counsel of mine," she said.

He heard the prickliness in her tone with relief. If she lost her temper, she was easier to deal with. "I need none," he replied.

Breaking free, she strode away. He caught up in three quick strides and spun her around to face him.

"You fool!" she said, but there was no genuine annoyance in her voice now. "It's Jonan, isn't it?"

Caught by surprise, Dain blinked and did not reply immediately.

"I knew it!" she said. Tossing her long hair over her shoulder, she began to braid it into order in the quick, impatient way he loved. "Nothing else could trouble you so much. And nothing is less worth that trouble. Beloved, why do you concern yourself so much with the wretched boy?"

Relief filled Dain, for she could not have guessed more wrongly, yet he also felt ashamed for continuing to deceive her. "I must care about him, for no one else does."

"I know. I'm sorry," she said. "A kinsman is a kinsman. All these years, you've protected him and tried to raise him into something decent and honorable. But Thod's teeth, he's hopeless!"

Dain frowned. "Tustik has always urged me to banish him. I fear he will suggest it again now that Jonan's about to reach his majority."

"Another worry. I hate them for fretting you with such things."

"My little protector," he said, his voice suddenly gruff with ardor. Catching her hand, he kissed it, then pulled her into his arms. As always, she was quick to respond to his passion, her mouth soft and sweet, her body pliant in his embrace. He wanted to lift her in his arms and carry her to one of the skiffs tied nearby. He wanted to row her far out to one of the tiny islands dotting the middle of the fjord and sport with her under the kiss of a new day. His blood roared in his ears, and whatever he murmured to her made her laugh, her voice throaty with equal desire.

"Come," he said. Hand in hand, they hurried down the bank to where the skiffs bobbed on their moorings.

"Sire!" called a voice.

Dain halted with a low oath, and when he looked at Alexeika in the improving light he saw his frustration mirrored in her features.

"Sire!" called Laure, his squire. "If I may assist you with footgear and a cloak?"

Glancing over his shoulder, Dain saw his middle-aged, spindle-shanked attendant hurrying through the dew-laden grass beneath the pines with a bundle of clothing in his arms. Dain scowled at the man in exasperation. "Thod take the creature," he muttered.

Alexeika laughed, clapped her hand over her mouth, then laughed again. Dain turned his scowl on her, but the sight of her blue-gray eyes brimming with merriment awakened his own reluctant mirth. A smile tugged at the corners of his mouth.

She leaned close to his ear, and whispered, "Imagine Laure's embarrassment, sire, if you returned for breakfast clad only in your sleeping robe and everyone saw you."

He still wanted to break the squire's neck, but the whole situation was absurd now. There was little he could do save give in with whatever grace he could find.

"And you, my lady?" he retorted. "What would our courtiers say about *you*?"

"That I'm a brazen hussy who should know better than to be in love with her husband and lord."

Dain caught her close and kissed her hard, despite Laure's approach. When he let her go, they were both breathing hard, their gaze locked with a heat that nearly tempted him to sweep her away no matter who saw them.

A sultry smile spread across her mouth, and the expression in her gaze changed to something that arrested his attention. He had the sudden conviction that she intended to tell him a very important secret.

"What?" he asked, half-smiling at her. "Alexeika?"

She looked smug. As the sun's crown blazed above the horizon and cast rosy pink light over them, she seemed to glow. Never had her beauty dazzled his eyes more. "I believe," she said softly, "that Laure wishes to remind your majesty of a very important engagement this morning."

He felt bewitched, his wits clouded by the glory of her hair, skin, and eyes in that special light.

She smiled and gave him a little push. "Go, sire. Your daughter no doubt is awake and impatiently awaiting you."

"For what?"

"Hunting."

He blinked at her, his mind still blank, before memory swept over him. Ah, yes, he'd promised to take Tashalya hawking. And later, the twins were to join them for a last outing. He'd been looking forward to the children's company, but now he wanted Alexeika to join the fun.

"And you will come with us?"

Another mysterious smile tugged at her mouth. "I have other plans for my last day here. If your majesty will permit me to go my own way?"

"Of course," he said, hiding his stab of disappointment. He glanced at Laure, hovering nearby with his garments, and bowed to her. "Until later."

She curtsied to him. "Enjoy yourself and remember to make Tashalya be careful with that bird."

"Yes, wife."

"And don't let old Tustik spoil things with his dispatches and reports." She met his gaze with keen insistence. "Jonan can wait. All of it can wait. There will be time enough on the journey homeward to inform you of all that's transpired in our absence."

Dain nodded and caught a glimpse of Laure's face as the squire knelt before him to slip soft leather shoes on his feet. The squire bowed his head swiftly, but Dain saw the look of disapproval on his pale features.

Thoughtfully Dain cast another look at his wife. She stood there, wrapped in a lightweight cloak, her braid hanging over her shoulder, her gaze confident and forceful. What he saw as wifely concern, Dain realized, others seemed to misinterpret as orders. Alexeika had never lost the habit of issuing her opinions as directives. She still argued with him when she saw the need of it. She so often commanded rather than asked. Dain understood these old habits from the days of her girlhood when she'd tried to keep her father's band of rebels united in the fight against the tyrant Muncel. She'd faced dangers no highborn lady should ever know, and she'd survived terrible ordeals. It was unreasonable to expect her to become some retiring, shy, docile creature in long skirts and a veil of modesty, sitting about passively with her hands folded and her eyes compliant.

Dain had never wanted that from her. He valued her opinions, honesty, and bluntness. But he was growing to understand that many others did not. Many members of the Kollegya thought she was usurping her place as consort and trying to rule for him. They resented her influence, especially the fact that he usually took her advice rather than theirs.

They're fools, Dain thought angrily, and stepped abruptly away from Laure's attempt to cast a thin cloak about his shoulders. "Are you mad?" he said to the squire. "It's too hot for that."

Laure looked dismayed. "Your majesty perhaps does not wish to return to camp in only his sleeping attire."

Dain cast an impatient look down at his thin linen sleeping robe. It was open to the waist and inclined to slip off his broad shoulders. He hitched it up with annoyance. "Do you fear a scullery maid will see rather more of the king than is customary?"

Laure's face turned bright red, and over beneath the trees Lord Miest fell into a sudden coughing fit behind his hand.

With his servant temporarily vanquished, Dain started up the bank, then paused and glanced back over his shoulder. Alexeika stood at the water's edge, watching him.

She schooled her features quickly, but not before he caught the fleeting look of worry on her face. He gave her a smile, false and bright. She returned one exactly the same. Lifting his hand to her in light salute, he hitched up his robe and strode away.

But as he walked, he could feel her gaze boring into his back, her curiosity and concern like barbs to his conscience. He bowed his head in self-anger. *I have lied to my wife*, he thought miserably. *I have let them drive a wedge between us, and when she finds out she will never trust me again.*

At that moment, he wanted to go back to her, taking her again in his arms and pressing his hot face to the soft comfort of her breast. He wanted to tell her everything, of that secret meeting with the Kollegya shortly before their departure, of how the archdukes wanted him to reduce her power and relegate her to the background far from state politics. They did not understand how much he needed her. From the first difficult days of his reign, she had stood shoulder to shoulder with him against intriguers, schemers, and false friends.

It was not easy to rule Nether, and during these years he'd faced pitfall after pitfall. The realm was making a slow, steady recovery from the ravages it had suffered under Muncel's rule, but although every year the crops were more bountiful and the lambing rich, poverty hung on too tightly in too many remote corners of the land. The greedy and unscrupulous still plundered and stole from the less fortunate. The ambitious still schemed and plotted. Corruption and graft flourished on all sides, and Dain's attempts to eradicate both had earned him enemies. Traitors paid him lip-fealty while planning his downfall. Although he had returned the long-lost Chalice of Eternal Life to its rightful place, defeated an invasion of Gantese forces, and forced his tyrant uncle off the throne, Dain was not a popular king in some quarters. Too many scoundrels had gained estates and wealth under Muncel's favor readily to relinquish their holdings to the rightful owners now seeking redress. Churchmen of the Reformed Faith criticized Dain for restoring the old religious ways, and claimed he sought to lead Nether back into an unenlightened age. The restored nobility grew ever more conservative, clinging stubbornly to moribund customs and resisting all change, resenting him when he tried to force through new ideas or practices. The political intrigues never stopped, never gave him a moment's peace, and now his enemies had found a weakness, a point of vulnerability to attack.

He'd given in on many other issues, too many perhaps.

Dain had learned the hard way that being a king meant making compromises, especially when he shared his power with an entity as powerful as the secret Kollegya. But although he resented their presumption in daring to attack the queen, he also understood that Alexeika fitted in no better than he did himself. Neither of them had been raised conventionally according to the position of their births. She'd grown up as more a boy than a maid, the only child of a warrior general intent on foisting the tyrant off his ill-gained throne. Dain had grown up ignorant of his royal heritage, a half-breed scrambling to survive in a cruel, indifferent land. No one else save Alexeika understood his doubts at times, or how often he still felt like a foreigner in his own realm. He trusted her more than anyone except Thum, his friend since his days as a foster at Thirst Hold. He needed her far more than he needed his official—or secret—advisers.

And they were jealous of that. Petty, cruel, and jealous. It infuriated him, and yet he understood that if they united against him, he might be forced to yield. Better to agree of his own will than to be defeated.

Resentfully he thought, was he not the king? Did he not possess the sovereignty? Who were they to make demands of him? How dare they seek to dictate what the queen might or might not do?

They had chosen their point of battle with a guile and cunning that shook his confidence. He comprehended their strategy all too clearly, although as yet he did not quite know how to defeat it. Dain preferred battles of armed combat, out on a field where one man's physical courage was tested against another's. That kind of fight he understood. But this plotting and feinting of wits wearied and sometimes bewildered him. He could defy them, of course. That's what he wanted to do, but it would force an open confrontation and political schism at court, at a time when he'd begun to fear another war might be looming with the Grethori. The savages were constant troublemakers, and recent intelligence pointed to another possible uprising. In fact, today's hunt was primarily a cover for him to ride forth to gather more information on what the savages might be planning.

No, the Kollegya could not have chosen a worse time to force this issue. As, of course, they knew. If they chose to oppose him in an open fight of political maneuvering while he was trying to quell another Grethori uprising, well, he might lose everything.

In his heart he cursed them, and as he walked away from his wife and queen, he felt already as though he'd lost.

Chapter Two

Despite an ill start to the day, the morn had turned fine indeed, too fine to fend off spies and conspiracies.

Sitting astride his black courser, Dain tipped back his head to watch the lazy spiral of a wyrn-falcon overhead. The sky arced blue and cloudless, save for the thunderheads massing west of Uthe Peak. The clouds would likely bring rain this afternoon, but at the moment the sun was warm and the air soft. The company was pleasant and the hunting lazy. Nearby, the courtiers who'd accompanied Dain on this outing chatted and joked quietly beneath the trees, while servants dispensed mead in stirrup cups of chased silver and proffered trays of sweetmeats and dainties.

Dain, however, kept his attention trained on the sky, where the wyrn-falcon sailed and circled.

"Watch her closely now," Dain said to his six-year-old daughter. "See how she drops a little in the sky with each circle? She's seen the ducks. She's waiting for the right moment."

Mounted on her pony beside him, Tashalya frowned with

concentration. "Why doesn't she hurry? I want her to strike *now*!"

As though the falcon heard the child's command, she abruptly tucked in her wings and plunged straight down, plummeting toward the fjord. Tashalya screamed with excitement, startling her pony, and the groom standing at its head grabbed the bridle to hold it still.

"Strike, Arvi. *Strike*!" the child shouted.

Frowning, Dain held back his reprimand. Early this morning, when he'd taken a sleepy-eyed Tashalya from her warm tent cot to go on this hunt, he'd reminded her that she must stay calm, letting her mind flow in companionship with her bird of prey, not in command. But clearly his instructions were already forgotten.

Tashalya was shrieking and pounding the pommel of her saddle with excitement. "Faster, Arvi!" she shouted. "Strike hard!"

"She'll ruin the bird, sire," the master falconer muttered. Standing beside Dain's stirrup, he watched in anguish. "It's got to hunt of its own will, not hers."

Dain ignored him, just as previously he'd ignored the man's respectful protests that Princess Tashalya was too young to hunt at all. A mere snippet she might be, but already she exhibited a keen intelligence and precocity beyond her years; *that is*, he thought wryly, *when she could manage to curb her impatience*.

"Sire," the falconer moaned, "I beg you to intervene. She's driving the bird, *driving* it! She'll—"

"Hush," Dain said sharply, and turned his attention back to his excited daughter. "Gently, Tashalya." He forced his voice to be calm yet forceful enough to gain her attention. "Don't push her. She'll strike when she's ready. Let her choose her own prey."

Tashalya's small face was knotted in concentration, her gaze never leaving the sky. He could tell she was flying with the bird; her mind—nay, her entire being—joined with it in common purpose.

Dain felt his heart swell with love for this small, dark-haired beauty, his firstborn and favorite, as willful as she was courageous. Unobtrusively he signaled with his hand, and the beaters slung stones across the water where a flock of wood ducks were concealing themselves among the shoreline reeds.

The small yellow-headed ducks rose in alarm, their wings whirring rapidly as they took to the air. Tashalya's wyrn-falcon struck prey on the wing, her cruel talons clutching a duck as she glided to the ground. Landing, she snapped the duck's neck and began to feed.

"Papa!" Tashalya called out, gripping his sleeve. "Did you see her? Did you? She struck first, just as I wanted. I have the first kill today!"

"Yes, I saw," Dain said, giving her a smile.

Beaming with pride, Tashalya met his look, her eyes still full of wind, sky, and plummet. She threw back her head and laughed, giddy with the exhilaration of the hunt.

With excited shouts, the other courtiers released their hawks. For a while the sky was filled with strike and cry as the wood ducks were brought down. Cheers rang out, and swift bets were laid among the men while the predator birds wheeled, struck, and sailed down with their captured prey.

"Sire!" the master falconer called out, and Dain turned his attention back to the skies. He saw his eagle far aloft, remaining high and remote from the rest of the hunt. The courtiers' hawks continued their lethal plummets, taking the fat little ducks easily, but Dain's bird sought other prey.

He sent his mind lightly to it and felt the cold, keen contact of its thoughts: *seek/seek/seek/seek.* Then it saw what it wanted and dropped with lethal speed so fast it made Dain dizzy. He closed his eyes and his mind to the eagle, rallying himself before he could sway in the saddle. Out in the middle of the fjord, his eagle struck at the water and rose with a powerful flapping of its wings, a huge fish clutched in its talons.

The courtiers clapped and cheered anew. "Well done, sire!" some of them called out.

Dain smiled in answer—having learned the odd man-custom of accepting compliments for what was none of his doing—and turned his attention back to his daughter. Shaking a leather lure back and forth, much to the nervousness of her pony, she was avidly watching her falcon feed. As soon as the bird finished, she whistled in the sharp, quick way Dain had taught her, and the wyrn-falcon flew obediently to her gauntleted hand.

Glowing, she turned to her father. "Papa, look!" she crowed.

"Hood her first," he said, alarmed by her carelessness. The falconer moved swiftly to slide a leather hood onto the wyrn-falcon's head and pulled the strings snug at the back. The bird tilted its head from side to side in patent displeasure, and lifted one foot to claw at the hood.

Dain met Tashalya's pale blue eyes. "Always hood her when she's on your arm. You forget every time."

She shrugged. "You don't hood your eagle, Papa. He rides on your arm, and you never hood him."

"That's different. I have hunted with Baz for years. He and I understand each other."

"Arvi and I understand each other, too," Tashalya said, with a toss of her head. Today she wore her curly dark hair braided tightly back, warrior-style, like her father. A delicate circlet of oldin silver glinted on her brow. Clad in doeskin leggings and a linen tunic embroidered at the neck and wrists with silver thread, she looked like a miniature vision of her mother, with all the same fiery spirit and beauty that melted Dain's heart each time he gazed at her.

He found his exasperation fading as he faced the willful self-assurance in his young daughter's eyes. It was time to try a different tactic. "Your mother granted her permission for you to hunt *only* if we are very careful," he said sternly. "That means we must obey all the rules of safety. Remember that both you and Arvi are learning the same lessons. She must be hooded when you are around others. While she might not strike you, she could harm Lord Matej or one of your attendants. Think of others, my daughter, and keep her hooded."

"Yes, Papa," Tashalya said impatiently. Turning away from him, she stroked Arvi's breast feathers and cooed to her. In response, the bird dipped her blind head and pecked playfully at Tashalya's fingers.

"Verily, sire, the bird seems to have rapport with her highness," Lord Omas rumbled from nearby. It was his duty to serve as the king's protector during the day, while Lord Miest served at night. And like the other protectors presently on duty among the courtiers, Omas was not hawking today, although his rank permitted him the right to fly a bird. With a smile, he nodded at the princess. "That's rare, with both being so young."

Dain cast a quick smile at his lord protector. "Aye," he agreed. "And both of them equally full of mischief."

"Mischief done and hard to mend," the master falconer muttered. "'Tis a sweet little hunter, this bird, sire. The finest wyrn-falcon I've trained in years. But if she's forced too hard, too soon, she'll lose her natural instincts and go sour."

"Arvi's still hungry, Papa," Tashalya announced. "I'm going to let her fly again."

She reached for her falcon's hood, but at that moment there was a stir among the outer edge of the hunting party. Matej, the princess' protector, stayed her little hand. "Nay, your highness," he said. "Bide quietly a moment."

Dain saw a horse and rider approaching from the southeast, barely visible through the thick trees. The Agya guards shouted a challenge, and received an impudent reply. Moments later, Chesil Matkevskiet was reining up before Dain with a flourish. He bowed low over his saddle.

Young and fit, with quick, gleaming eyes and a ready flash of filed teeth, Chesil was the younger son of General Matkevskiet, a fierce man who'd been a friend of Dain's father and was now an invaluable ally as well as the commander of Dain's Agya forces. Chesil wore his hair braided in multiple strands adorned with painted wooden beads, and a gold ring glinted in his ear. Garbed in vivid red and blue, and wearing the badge of royal service, the youth carried a scimitar belted around his slim middle. As one of Dain's aides, he'd proven himself to be reliable, trustworthy, and quick-witted.

"Well?" Dain asked sharply.

"They await your majesty at the appointed place."

Dain gave him a nod of satisfaction. "Twenty guards."

Saluting, Chesil wheeled his horse around and galloped off to relay the order. Meanwhile, Dain turned his attention to Lord Matej.

"Let her highness continue hunting, if she chooses," he said quietly to the man. "Two more passes perhaps."

Matej, a patient man of few words, bowed his head in compliance.

The master falconer, however, groaned. "Majesty, consider the bird!"

"Her highness must have practice if she's to improve," Dain said impatiently. "I leave it to you."

Ignoring the man's look of frustration, he gathered his reins, gave Omas a nod, and flicked Tashalya's cheek with his finger.

"Papa, where are you going?"

"I'll be back very soon."

She frowned with a quick flare of temper. "But you promised this was to be *our* day! You promised!"

"I shall keep that promise. Remember there are runes to see with your brother and sister when I return."

Delight flashed in her face. "You'll hurry, Papa? Promise that you'll hurry?"

Smiling, he plucked her from her saddle, falcon and all, and balanced her on his hip to give her a kiss and a squeeze that made her squeal.

Winding her free arm around his neck, Tashalya kissed his cheek with a big smack. "I love you, Papa," she whispered. "But do not trust the Grethori you're about to meet. They're wicked."

Startled, he gazed into her blue eyes and saw the devilry dancing in their depths. Although his eldin blood gave him the ability to sense the emotions of others, he could not see clearly into their thoughts. Tashalya, however, had recently begun to reveal that she could do exactly that. It indicated a strong manifestation of talent, too strong. He did not want to lose this child to a life of arcane mystery and sorcery.

Nor did he want her exposed to harsh condemnation from those still prejudiced against eldin blood mixed with human. The Reformed Church fomented the old prejudices, and Dain feared that once Tashalya's burgeoning talents became public knowledge, Cardinal Winnder would attempt to stir up controversy against her and the entire royal family.

But the future must manage itself. At present he found himself facing a blue-eyed imp. What else had she read in his mind? he wondered uneasily. He must remember to guard himself from her in the future, lest she delve into all his secrets.

Frowning, he said very sternly, "You are not to know the king's plans. You are not to prattle to anyone about where I'm going today. Promise?"

She shrugged, clearly enjoying her moment of power. "You mean I'm not to tell Mama."

That made him laugh. He hugged her again, then lowered her back into her saddle and rode away swiftly with Omas and Chesil at his side and a contingent of twenty Agya warriors at his back. His courtiers watched his departure in blatant curiosity, but Dain offered no explanation. He'd been waiting for this meeting for days, and had just about given up, especially since on the morrow, he, his family, and his court would be breaking camp from this idyllic spot.

Vlink, he thought with irritation, had cut things very fine in delaying until the last minute.

A fierce cry shattered the air. Dain glanced up at the shadow that sailed over his head. Thankful he hadn't thought to remove his thick gauntlet, he lifted his arm just in time, and Baz his eagle settled powerful talons around his wrist. Dain glanced into the eagle's yellow eyes and touched Baz's mind in the briefest contact. That was all the majestic bird required. Still wild at heart despite its extensive training, it leaned forward as though enjoying the ride, then without warning flew into the air again. The huge predatory bird sailed close overhead, however, as though it, too, was curious as to why he'd left the hunt.

Winding away from the shore of the sparkling fjord, the trail headed up into the foothills that grew progressively more rugged. The forest changed from gnarled, wind-twisted hardwood trees into tall pines and larches that soared to the sky. On Dain's left Uthe Peak towered high.

Shortly thereafter, Dain and his companions reached the summit of a lesser mountain and emerged cautiously into the open. On one side stretched a breathtaking vista of mountain, fjord, and sky. On the other side waited a group of ruffians mounted on shaggy mountain ponies with a rim of forest at their backs.

Waiting in silence, these scowling Grethori warriors looked even wilder and more ragged than most. Over the years, Dain had learned many of the tribal markings, but these he did not recognize.

That made him wary indeed. All Grethori were savages, no matter which tribe they belonged to, but a few of the eastern tribes had adapted to forming loose alliances with the Netherans, engaging in trade and sometimes selling their services as mercenaries. Others vanished as soon as they were sighted, avoiding civilized men, as elusive as smoke. These warriors clearly belonged to the latter group. They sat their ponies with tension evident in their bodies, their eyes as wild as feral beasts.

One individual came forth to meet Dain's party and dismounted. He was a Netheran, although he made scant effort to look like one. Garbed in leggings and a tunic, Vlink the spy also wore a sleeveless jerkin fashioned from Grethori cloth in garish geometric patterns of vermilion and yellow. Begrimed and stinking of beyar grease, he inspired no trust.

"So, King of Nether," he said without waiting for permission, "we meet at the appointed place. What payment do you bring?"

Omas stiffened. "Sire, this insolent dog needs a lesson in manners."

Dain lifted his hand for silence. He knew that a good bargaining began with indifference and disdain. This was a world apart from the throne room of state, where diplomats whispered of treaties and alliances, where every compliment held a lie, where what was promised and what was done were seldom the same. Relying on an ever-growing network of spies and informants organized by Thum, Dain vigilantly collected intelligence from all corners of his far-flung realm, for betrayal and treason swirled constantly beneath the surface of his rule.

"I bring the payment we agreed on," Dain said. "What news have you?"

"I see no payment," Vlink said. "Your hands, great king, are empty."

"And your mouth is filled with air. If I spread wealth before you, how will you be able to remember what you've come to tell me? Like a dog slavering for its meat, you will forget half of what you know. Speak swiftly. If what you say pleases my ear, full payment will I grant you."

"And if you like not my message?"

Dain shrugged.

Clearly Vlink disliked that answer, for his brow furrowed, and he shot an uneasy glance at his comrades. The Grethori grew restive. The talk was being conducted in Netheran, and although Dain doubted they understood what was being said, they were an impatient people and liked to deal swiftly. Dain, on the other hand, was prepared to spend an hour—or even a day—at this if necessary.

"You are hard, great king," Vlink muttered. "Summer is ending. Soon the game will migrate south, and the tribes must migrate with it. Winter comes cruel up here at the World's Rim."

"You waste my time," Dain said harshly, and tightened his reins to turn his horse away.

"Wait!" Vlink called out.

Dain lifted his brows.

Resentfully the spy said, "There is to be a gathering of all the tribes. The summoning is called a *reshehad*."

"When?"

"I know not."

"Why?"

"It's the command of the *shedas*, the old wisewomen. It's rare. I've heard some of 'em talk about it, but I've never been around when the summons went out before."

Beside Dain, Chesil leaned forward slightly in his saddle and hissed between his teeth.

Dain frowned. Time enough to question Chesil later. Now, however, he kept his attention focused on the spy. "Are the tribes gathering for war?"

"I know not. A *sheda* council can call for war. It can also be a time to make new alliances. Sometimes they form new tribes and get rid of others."

"Do the western tribes intend an uprising?"

Vlink stared at Dain a long time without answering. Dain stared right back, concentrating, but the man's mind was all slippery evasion, making it impossible for Dain to discover whether he spoke lies or truth. Still, Dain now sensed there was indeed something useful that Vlink knew, something he was holding back.

"Well?" Dain asked sharply.

"A king should know his enemies," Vlink replied, and fell silent. Clearly he intended to tell no more without prompting.

A quick gesture from Dain sent one of the Agyas forward. With his horse prancing sideways, the Agya pulled a cloth pouch from his saddlebag. He held it aloft, then flung it at Vlink's feet.

When it hit the ground, the pouch burst open and salt spilled out. Behind Vlink, the savages craned their necks to look, murmuring in their strange tongue.

The Agya pulled out another pouch and threw it beside the salt. When the second pouch hit the ground, the unmistakable clink of coinage could be heard.

Like dogs after meat, the Grethori surged forward, but Vlink was quick and snatched the money out of reach before anyone else could get it. Grinning, he clutched it to his chest.

"There is half your payment," Dain said. "If you want the rest, you will tell me the real information you bring."

"And perhaps we will take the rest by force," Vlink retorted.

Dain shrugged. "If you think your men can match mine."

Vlink's arrogance slipped, and he shot the Agya warriors a wary look. They outnumbered the bandits, and Agyas were fabled fighters—fierce, cunning, and ruthless. It was said that in battle a single Agya was worth four common knights. Dain went nowhere without his faithful guard of these bronze-faced, valiant men.

Vlink might be cunning and sly, but he was no fool. Hefting the money pouch, he said, "This is enough. I will talk no more."

"Look inside the pouch," Dain said.

Frowning, Vlink pulled out a handful of coins, cursed, and flung them back inside. "Trickster king!" he shouted. "You bring me brass skannen when you promised me gold pieces and silver!"

"Aye, and you'll have them when you tell me the truth. Out with it!"

"The *reshehad* has been called for spring. After thaw," Vlink mumbled sullenly. "There is a *sheda* of the Wind Tribe who calls for war against the pale-eyes. She is powerful, and her voice is heard by many. She wants an uprising."

Omas swore softly beneath his breath, and the Agyas tightened their grip on their weapons. Vlink's black eyes shifted rapidly about.

"Does this wisewoman not know that there have been three uprisings in seven years?" Dain asked harshly. "And all have been crushed?"

Vlink shrugged. "Who can say what she knows? She has called for *reshehad*, and her summons will be obeyed. If she calls for war, the western tribes will rise. Perhaps more."

"How many more?"

"I know not." Vlink held up his hand quickly to forestall Dain. "Who can say what Grethori will do? Even these men who follow me . . . I cannot tell you what they will do."

Dain said nothing.

"That is all I know, great king. It is not easy to learn the intentions of the tribes."

Another lie. Angrily Dain narrowed his eyes, wondering how to shake the truth from this sly *weasyn*. A shadow sailing overhead gave him his answer. Without glancing up, he sent his thoughts to Baz: *Come/come/come*.

The eagle dropped instantly from the sky, swooping over Vlink's head so low the man ducked and cried out. Baz landed on Dain's wrist with a powerful flapping of his wings, then settled himself and turned his yellow, predatory gaze on Vlink in an unblinking stare.

The spy had turned pale. Behind him, the Grethori bandits were muttering uneasily, and several held up amulets made of bones and hair as though to ward off something evil.

"As you see," Dain said quietly, "I command a wind spirit. If I order him, he will claw out your eyes."

Vlink dropped to his knees and held out his hands in appeal. "We had a bargain, great king. I have told you what I know."

"Wrong! You lie and withhold. Since when does a single *sheda* command many tribes? Since when does one tribe lead the others? This is not the Grethori way. What secret are you keeping from me, Vlink?"

Baz flapped his wings as though he meant to fly, then settled again. His talons—strong enough to crush Dain's wrist—pricked through the stiff leather of the gauntlet. Aware that Vlink's fear was arousing the bird, Dain lifted his arm as though he meant to hurl the eagle straight at Vlink, and said, "What else? Speak now, and quickly."

Vlink was sweating. "'Tis said this old crone's power has been strengthened by another."

"Who?"

"I know not."

Dain released Baz, who flew with an angry squawk. Vlink cringed, throwing himself flat on the ground.

"There is magic!" he babbled. "*Sheda* magic and foreign. I know nothing of such things, except this alliance has increased her power and made her much talked about among the tribes. It is forbidden for me to tell you the mysteries behind their wisewomen. I do not know!"

He lay there, calling on his gods, and Dain realized there was no more to be drawn from him. "Pay him," Dain said curtly.

More salt and the promised gold pieces were tossed to Vlink. He rose to his hands and knees, gathering his treasure and shooting Dain a look of resentment. Dain understood. He had forced Vlink to reveal his cowardice to his men, and Grethori despised cowards above all else.

As Dain wheeled his horse about and rode away, Vlink called after him, "Just wait, great king! You are cursed, aye, you and your pale-eyed brood. When *sheda* magic strikes you, no armor will dash it aside. The next uprising will be like no others you have known."

Dain rode on without glancing back. His men closed ranks about him, guarding him on all sides as they retreated down the steep, twisting mountain trail. Without being ordered, a dozen of the Agyas at the rear gradually fell back and melted their surefooted horses into the forest. They would hide and wait in case Vlink's little band tried an attack or ambush, but nothing happened, and shortly thereafter, Dain reached the foothills, topped a rise, and rode down to the flat shores of the fjord.

Ahead in the distance, he could hear the chatter and jokes of the hunting party, as yet out of sight among the trees. A burst of hearty laughter from that direction caused annoyance to knot Dain's brow. Not yet ready to rejoin the idle company of his courtiers, he reined up and sat mulling over all that Vlink had said.

"I *should* have cut out that varlet's tongue," Omas growled. "A liar and cheat, if ever I saw one."

Huge of frame, with a beefy face and luxurious mustache, Omas had served Dain faithfully in the years since he'd first sworn his oath as protector, and had proven himself to be as steadfast as a mountain. Even better, the large man had become a friend, and his easygoing ways and constant good cheer meant much to Dain, especially on dreary days when all seemed a tangle and nothing went right.

At the moment, however, there was no merry twinkle in Omas's brown eyes, and his scowl looked thunderous. "Daring to curse the king. He—"

But Dain was in no mood to waste time venting ire. He turned to young Chesil on his right. "What think you of Vlink's report?"

"Before or after he cursed your majesty?"

"All of it."

"That liar!" Chesil said contemptuously and spat. "*Aychi*, but Vlink's tongue has so many crooks in it I wonder how the man can eat. When he said a council of *shedas* is rare, he lied. The tribes meet every thaw. They trade slaves, ponies, and women. He lied, too, when he said one *sheda* could call many tribes to her command. The old crones use magic to guide and advise their chieftains, but they do not rule."

"As far as we know," Dain said. "But old customs can change."

"Unlikely, sire," Omas said. "The Grethori keep to themselves too much. They never change. They will not learn or be taught."

"This *sheda* of the Wind Tribe," Dain said thoughtfully. "Chesil, know you aught of her?"

"Nay, sire."

"Even if we discount Vlink's babble about magic," Dain said, "the rest fits in with what's been rumored all year. More trouble to come." He sighed. "Three uprisings since I took the throne, and another one planned. And this one to be different . . ."

The idea of quelling another uprising wearied him to his bones. Past campaigns had proven to be bloody and grim, for the savages were tough to kill and difficult to defeat. They fought in swarms, screaming to the accompaniment of their wild pipes and drums, and followed no rules of combat. And who was stirring up this new rebellion? Was it an agent of Gant, or some traitor in Nether?

He sighed. "Great Thod, I do not need this kind of trouble now."

"With the Grethori there is always trouble, *neya?*" Chesil said.

"Be quiet, you young pup," Omas said to the aide. "That's not what his majesty means. Sire, you place too much weight on what this blackguard Vlink has said."

"Better to worry too much and avert disaster than to ignore the warnings," Dain replied. "Foreign magic and *sheda* magic," he said thoughtfully. "If all the tribes unite with Gant—"

"Nay, sire, that's most unlikely," Omas said quickly. "Thod knows they fight among themselves more than they fight anyone else."

"But if united, they would make a fearsome force."

"Vlink's just wanting to see us squirm," Omas said. "Gant's army cannot cross our border and march unnoticed through the high plains. The Chalice protects us from Ashnod."

"Aye," Chesil chimed in. "Grethori magic is too thin to fear."

"Your majesty has all winter to prepare," Omas said, "But by thaw they'll have likely forgotten their plan. They'd rather raid than wage war."

"A *reshehad* is just a religious ceremony," Chesil said. "If I remember aright, some of the tribes believe an old legend about a great leader who will someday help them conquer the world. They gather each spring to eat blood and chant for him to come, but that is all. My father says they have no more sense than children and will never truly work together."

"There, sire," Omas said heartily. "As Chesil says, 'tis nothing. Let Vlink's lying trouble you no more."

Dain nodded, but inside he thought, *Nay, my large friend. I'll prepare for trouble now and take no ease until it's gone.* "Tonight," he said aloud, "I'll pen a dispatch to Lord Thum and set him to the task of sifting through our border reports. If Gant's up to new mischief, we'll catch it ere it has time to brew."

Omas shoved back his mail coif and wiped perspiration from his brow, for the day was warming fast. "Well and good. As for—"

"And the auxiliaries should be posted away from Grov, where they can do less harm if they turn traitor. I'll include the order with my dispatch."

"Your majesty is wise," Chesil said in approval. Like most of the Agyas, he hated the notion of using Grethori auxiliaries in the army. His father the general considered it lunacy and said so at every opportunity. "They should never be—"

The piercing sound of a child's scream rent the air. Every man's head snapped in that direction, and for an instant, as he recognized his elder daughter's voice, Dain thought his heart would stop.

"What in Thod's name was that?" Omas asked.

But Dain was already spurring his horse to a gallop. "Tashalya's in trouble. Come!"

Chapter Three

As Dain galloped through the forest with his men behind him, the princess screamed again. Terror and rage blended in her young voice, and Dain urged his horse even faster, drawing his sword in readiness to slay whoever threatened his beloved child.

What had gone wrong in his absence, he wondered frantically. Had Vlink's bandits circled around and attacked? Grethori were notorious stealers of children, yet surely the rear guard of Agyas would have intercepted any such attack. Had the wyrn-falcon turned against Tashalya and raked her with cruel talons and beak? A dozen such imaginings ran through Dain's mind as he bent lower over his horse's whipping mane.

Minutes later, he came bursting through the trees into the clearing, scattering startled courtiers, dogs, and huntsmen from his path. Through the confusion, Dain saw Tashalya, still mounted on her fat pony and bearing her bird on her wrist. But screaming and cursing like a hire-lance, Tashalya was grappling with someone three times her size—her cousin Jonan, Dain now saw. The boy was trying to wrest something away from her, and from the violence of their struggle, accompanied by the savagery of their yells at each other, 'twas no ordinary quarrel. Tashalya's pony reared up, and Dain feared his daughter would surely be thrown.

But sticking to the saddle like a small burr, she wrenched around with something clutched to her chest, and screamed again.

"You little vixlet," Jonan cried in exasperation. "Give that back!"

"Won't!" Tashalya shouted.

He slapped her, and her squall ignited Dain's rage.

There was no time to wonder what had happened to Lord Matej as Dain thundered up, brandishing his sword so ferociously it whistled scant inches above Jonan's head. Yelling in fright, Jonan dropped to his knees. Dain pointed Mirengard at his fool of a cousin.

"Jonan!" he roared, and such was his temper at that moment that the very air seemed to crack beneath the force of his voice. "Thod's bones, sirrah! Have you gone mad?"

The son of Muncel and his queen Neaglis—surely two of the most evil despots ever to rule Nether—gave no answer but instead clutched his head and rocked back and forth, moaning aloud.

By now Dain had regained mastery of his emotions. His fury faded to pity, and he frowned at his white-faced cousin. "Come, Jonan, on your feet," he said more calmly, sheathing his sword. "Explain yourself."

Gawky of limb and sometimes slow of wit, Jonan gaped at Dain with fear clouding his brown eyes. "I—I—" he gasped, but managed no other answer.

Tashalya's pale blue eyes were blazing. "Kill him, Papa!" she shouted. "Cut off his head!"

"Majesty!" Jonan gasped, looking so pale and scared that he seemed ready to faint. He stretched up his hands to Dain in appeal. "I beg you for mercy. Please spare me!"

"Papa—"

"Have done, both of you!" Dain shouted, and they fell silent.

"Great gods," he said in exasperation, "must the pair of

you squabble like guttersnipes? Remember who you are. Jonan, get on your feet."

The youth obeyed, sullenly brushing dust and pine needles from his clothing. Tashalya's wyrn-falcon, clearly unsettled by the argument, chose that moment to beat her wings violently and nearly struck the princess in the face.

Hastening up, a falconer swiftly took the bird from her. Shrieking with rage, the hooded bird slashed with her talons, but the man was deft enough to get her away before Tashalya was harmed.

"You're a thief!" Jonan said. "You've no right to my pouch. Give it back."

"I can have it if I want," she retorted. "I wish I had made Arvi attack *you* instead of just taking your silly pouch. Then you'd be sorry, gashed and dripping with blood, your eyes pecked out and your— "

"Tashalya, that's enough!" Dain said.

Her gaze flashed to her father. "You're the king, Papa. You can punish him for twisting my arm. I wish you would."

"Only because she wouldn't give back my property, your grace!" Jonan said. "I lost my temper. I'm sorry. But she wouldn't let go, and she tried to make that damned bird peck me."

"Papa," she said slyly, shooting Dain a look from beneath her lashes, "don't you want to know what Jonan keeps inside it?"

Jonan's face turned white with fresh alarm. He tried to speak and choked instead.

Dain felt a spurt of curiosity that he quelled. "Tashalya, return Jonan's property."

"He smokes tyneweed for—"

"Shut up, you little she-cat!" Jonan shouted, and threw himself at her.

Tashalya screamed, but Lord Matej appeared just then. Gripping Jonan by the front of his tunic, he shoved him sprawling on his backside.

Sputtering, the boy picked himself up awkwardly. Some of the men laughed, and Jonan's face turned bright red.

Tashalya laughed, too. "You can't do anything to me," she

taunted him. "I have a protector, traitor-spawn, and if you *really* hurt me, my father will order you destroyed."

"Tashalya, be silent!" Dain said in shock. "You go too far."

Straightening, Jonan glared at Tashalya with such hatred that Dain's brows knotted thoughtfully. The youth advanced on Tashalya with clenched fists.

Matej blocked his path, and when Jonan tried to shoulder the protector aside, Dain said sharply, "Jonan, desist at once! Do you want a flogging?"

The boy's eyes widened, and fear replaced the anger in his face. "Please no, your grace! I'm sorry. I'm sorry. I just want my pouch back. Make her give it back, sire. Please. Then I'll be good."

"Oh, in Thod's name, be quiet," Dain said.

Jonan bowed his head and began to cry in a feeble, sniveling way that changed Dain's pity to disgust. At seventeen, the boy was a hopeless mendicant and coward. Seldom was he actually punished, for usually a threat was enough to subdue his unsteady temper.

Not for the first time did Dain question his decision to adopt Jonan in the aftermath of the Battle of Grov. Merely a child at the time, Jonan had been a frail, sickly boy too young to play a part in his parents' evil. Disregarding those who urged him to execute Muncel's son, Dain had instead kept his young cousin in his household. After all, Dain reasoned, Jonan was a kinsman, however unlikable, and harmless enough. Since then, the boy had grown out of his numerous childhood ailments into this gawky, ill-favored youth who was presently wiping his nose on his sleeve like a peasant.

Revolted, Dain shot a look at his daughter. "Princess Tashalya," he said formally, "return your cousin's property."

She cast Jonan a long, calculating look from the corner of her eye, then flung the small pouch at his head. It bounced off his ear, making him flinch and cry out as he juggled to catch it.

The men around them laughed, and Jonan's face grew redder. He glared at her. "You little—"

"Jonan!" Dain said sharply. "You have the king's permission to withdraw."

Wildly, his face contorted with resentment and humiliation, the youth glared at Dain. "Sire, I want to—"

"You heard the king," Omas broke in, moving closer, with his hand on his dagger hilt.

Alarmed, Jonan shuffled backward. "At once, your grace. Forgive me, your grace. Thank you, your grace, for returning my pouch."

Hastening away, he mounted his horse clumsily, nearly falling from the saddle before he got astride. One of the servants tried to help him, and with an angry mutter Jonan kicked at the man before he rode off toward camp. The courtiers' laughter rang out anew, and Tashalya laughed, too.

"He is so stupid, Papa!" she cried loud enough for the departing Jonan to overhear. "I only sent Arvi to pluck his pouch off his saddle to show everyone how well I can command her. Jonan loses his temper like a baby."

Far from amused, Dain turned on her. "'Twas ill done of you, daughter, to pick on your cousin this way."

"But it's so much fun! I do it all the time, Papa."

"Then you are much in the wrong."

"But he struck me, Papa. That's what's wrong. You should have punished him for that."

Dain frowned at her. "And you, princess, are impertinent. The king punishes as he sees fit, and is not dictated to by others, least of all the princess royal."

The merriment died in her piquant face, and she stared up at him uncertainly as though finally realizing he was annoyed with her. "But Jonan was bad, Papa."

"So were you. Your cousin is not as quick-witted as you. He has not your status. He will never enjoy your advantages."

She nodded with satisfaction, her silver circlet gleaming on her brow. "I'm glad, Papa. He is such a fool."

"You must stop calling him names," Dain said sharply. "I am ashamed of you, insulting him to his face when he cannot answer back. You are cruel and mean when you treat him so, Tashalya. Your behavior disappoints me, and I am much displeased with you."

As her eyes filled with tears, her lip began to quiver. "I just wanted the master falconer to stop scolding. I wanted him to see that Arvi will do anything I want."

"Aye, and that's another thing," Dain said. "Using your falcon to fetch like a dog. She's a hunter, a wild creature born to sail the skies, not perform stupid tricks for your amusement."

"It wasn't stupid," Tashalya said very quietly. "If you knew all that Jonan keeps hidden in his pouch, you'd want to—"

"That's enough! I've told you often not to pry into secrets that don't concern you. Morde, child, 'tis ill done of you."

Sniffing fiercely, she held back her tears. He waited for her apology, but she stared back at him, proud and unyielding. Part of him had to admire her spirit; the rest of him despaired at ever being able to tame her.

Dain shifted his gaze to her protector. "Lord Matej, the princess is tired. She will return to camp."

Alarm flashed through her face. "No, Papa! Please!"

Ignoring her, Dain went on, "As for you, sirrah, when has it become your custom to stand aside while her highness is in need of you? How dare you let Jonan grapple with her highness, or even slap her?"

Matej's eyes widened. "Sire, they squabble as children do. Mayhap it's good for her highness to learn what a sharp tongue can provoke."

Astonishment intensified Dain's anger. "'Tis not a matter for you to judge, lord protector! Will you next let her break her neck in falling from a tree, in order that she might learn not to climb so high?"

"I intended no dereliction of duty, sire," Matej said hastily. "When he slapped her, I was caught by surprise, aye, but I would have intervened had your majesty not already been charging to her aid. As for Jonan, sire, he's a member of the royal household. Or am I to treat him differently now?"

Dain hesitated, caught by the dilemma Matej posed. Conscious of every man present watching and listening, particularly Prince Tustik, he curbed his temper. "Nay," he replied curtly. "But see that this doesn't happen again, or you'll be relieved of duty."

Matej bowed, but not before Dain glimpsed a flash of resentment in his eyes.

"Papa—"

Dain turned on his daughter. "As for you, Tashalya, you will stop teasing Jonan, and do not steal his property again. Is that clear?"

She stared up at him without repentance. "If I say yes, will I be allowed to stay here with you and not be sent back to camp?"

Lord Omas coughed suddenly behind his hand. Matej looked away. One of the courtiers chuckled, then hastily cleared his throat.

For once, however, Dain was not amused by her guile. "You—"

The sound of someone approaching interrupted him. Turning his head, Dain saw the twins coming through the trees, mounted on a gentle donkey and being led by a groom while their protector walked beside them.

Dain sighed. At only four years old, Mareitina and Ilymir were too young to go hunting, and so it had been arranged for their attendants to bring them forth to join their elder sister before midday, when the hunting was finished. He'd promised to take his children on a little expedition to visit the eldin runes. Or at least that had been the plan before Tashalya decided to misbehave. He frowned, for he hated having to punish her. Why, he thought in exasperation, couldn't she show some contrition? Then he could forgive her, and the day could continue as intended.

"Oh, good. They're here!" Tashalya cried. "Are we going to see the runes now?"

"Your brother and sister are. You are going back to camp."

Disbelief and rage warred in her face. "No! You promised!"

"And you promised to behave today."

"But you can't take them without me. That's not fair!"

"You should have thought of that before you picked on Jonan."

"Why do you take his side?" she yelled, striking the pommel of her saddle. "He's stupid! And he hates you. And I hate you, too! If I knew how to make a curse, I'd do it—"

From the fjord came a sudden roar, and a wind gusted through the trees with such force it whipped the branches violently and caused several of the horses to shy. Tashalya's pony reared up, breaking free of Matej's hold on its bridle, and tried to bolt.

Dain kicked his mount forward to block the pony's flight. Terrified, the pony reared again, and just as Tashalya's arms flew up and she toppled from the saddle, Dain leaned over and grabbed her. He pulled her up against his side and felt the violence of her temper. The wind buffeted them, swirling around Dain and the child, whipping dust and debris into his face, and making his horse neigh and prance in fear.

Tashalya was screaming in fury.

He shook her hard. "Stop it, Tashalya! Stop it right now!"

The wind only blew harder, circling in a funnel around them. Nearly blinded by the dust, his breath choked in his lungs, Dain used his mind forcefully to command her obedience.

Her screaming choked off in midcry. She stared at him in astonishment, and grew so pale he thought she might swoon.

The wind vanished as though it had never been, leaving only a hushed silence in the woods and a trail of broken limbs and fallen boughs in its wake. In the clearing, the courtiers slowly straightened up, righting their garments and soothing their nervous horses. Dain paid the others no heed. He did not take his gaze from Tashalya's for a moment, but inside his heart was pounding, and he knew despair as sharp as a knife's wound.

There was no denying what they'd all just witnessed. It had been her rage that had brought the storm. In truth, she *was* a *sorcerelle*—or would be once she was trained properly. Her magical abilities were growing so strong they could no longer be hidden. And he grieved for her, knowing she was going to become something remote and distant from her family, a creature they could neither understand nor govern nor live with. He would have to consult with Samderaudin, the court *sor-*

cerel, immediately. Perhaps she could be trained to control her gifts so that they developed no further.

Confusion and fear filled her eyes. She began to cry, and flung herself at his neck, hugging tight. "Papa! Oh, Papa!" she whimpered.

He held her small body close, cupping the back of her head, and closed his eyes against his emotions. "It's all right. Hush," he murmured, knowing he lied to her. "It's over."

"I'm sorry, Papa. I didn't mean to do it. I didn't mean any of it."

"I know," he replied, and wished to Thod he could undo what had happened. "I know, my sweet. Don't worry."

Sniffing, she drew away to rub the tears from her face. "I never cry," she said, her voice quivering. "I am a princess, and princesses mustn't cry."

And who taught you that, he wondered. "Cry all you need to, my sweet one," he murmured, and kissed her temple.

She gave him a tremulous little smile. "I'm sorry I said mean things to you, Papa," she whispered. "I really do love you."

"And I love you." The sight of her pale face, with shadows of exhaustion already forming beneath her eyes, worried him. "You had better go back to camp and rest for a while."

She jerked in his hold. "But I don't want to miss—"

"Hush, now. You need to take a nap. We'll do something later, just you and I."

That pleased her, as he knew it would. "Promise, Papa?"

"I promise."

Matej, looking wary indeed, led up her pony, and Dain handed her over to her protector's care.

The clearing remained silent. As Dain stared past his tear-streaked daughter at the solemn courtiers, his heart sank. There were too many witnesses this time. Word of what she'd done would spread like wildfire. The whole court would be awash with gossip by the time they returned to Grov in a few weeks.

Alexeika and I must discuss this without delay, he thought and felt a fresh stab of worry. The last time he'd mentioned his suspicions about their daughter's abilities, Alexeika had flown into a rage and refused to consider it. Now they had no choice but to face the truth and take action.

As Matej put his small charge on her pony and led her past the courtiers, most bowed to her in courtesy, but some did not. Normally she would have smiled and waved to them all in conceited good humor, but now she left their company in disgrace, a small wan figure who rode past her brother and sister without a word.

Dain bowed his head, aware that in the future she would receive less and less of the happy acclaim she'd always known. As news of this spread, she would be met increasingly with fear and possibly loathing. This bright summer day had turned to shadow for Tashalya, and never again would things be as they were.

Thod help her, he thought in anguish. *Thod help us all*.

Chapter Four

Openmouthed, the twins stared after their sister; then Ilymir tumbled off the donkey and came running across the clearing to Dain. "Tashie's in trouble!" he chanted gleefully, capering about and clapping his hands. "Tashie's in trouble!"

Ilymir, named for his maternal grandfather, was tall and straight for his four years, with fair skin, blue eyes, and hair streaked in colors of wheat and gold. Discounting Dain's frown, he gripped his father's stirrup. "I ride in front!" he cried, grinning and brandishing an imaginary sword. "I'm riding a darsteed an' my sword is Severgard!"

Dain, whose Mirengard would be passed to Ilymir one day when he succeeded to the throne, heard this declaration with a wince. Severgard belonged to Queen Alexeika. It had been her father's magicked weapon, and had been handed down generation after generation through the illustrious Volvn family. However illustrious it was, Severgard was the sword of a general and a prince, *not* a king. Even in play, Ilymir had no business preferring it to Mirengard.

Leaning down, Dain grasped his son's slender wrist and pulled the little boy up in front of his saddle. Ilymir snuggled happily against him, then drummed his heels hard on either side of the horse's neck so that Dain had to rein hard to keep the startled animal from shying.

"Let's gallop fast!" Ilymir shouted. "Let's fight a battle!"

"Not yet," Dain said, feeling as though he'd fought enough battles for one day. He tried to hang on to the squirming child and keep him from tumbling off. "And tell me why you intend to carry Severgard into war one day instead of my sword?"

Ilymir tipped back his head to grin at his father. His blue eyes were as wide and innocent as the sky. "Because Tashie said only the firstborn can have Mirengard. She's older, an' I'm littler, an' she gets first pick."

Feeling as though he'd been butted in the stomach, Dain dropped the conversation quickly. *Tashalya again*, he thought wryly. She was his favorite and, aye, he knew he'd spoiled her by giving her too much freedom from the start, but firstborn or not, she was female, and in Nether women did not rule. Shaken by Tashalya's behavior today, Dain told himself it was time to part Ilymir from his sisters and keep the boy more in his company as his heir and future successor. No matter what Dain's critics muttered about his children, Ilymir was clearly the most human of his siblings and all boy. That should be enough for the bigots and schemers who constantly grumbled against the eldin bloodline in the royal family. Dain realized he must teach Ilymir to be less easygoing under Tashalya's domination. She tended to fill his head with too much of her nonsense. Although it would be a battle, it was time she learned to take second place.

At that moment her attendants brought Mareitina to Dain. She smiled at her father in her gentle, dreamy way but did not speak. A shy little beauty with long fair curls that twisted and writhed constantly on her shoulders as though stirred by a breeze, she lived in the fantasy world of her imagination and seldom took interest in Tashalya's games. Ilymir, on the other hand, idolized Tashalya and was content to tag along at her heels as long as she'd permit it.

In truth, Dain was a little surprised that Mareitina had come along on this outing at all, for she was inclined to change her mind at the last minute and hang back, choosing to stay in camp playing games of her own invention with twigs and pebbles rather than go exploring with her father. But today she reached out her chubby arms to him with a beaming smile.

Smiling back, he lifted her onto his horse beside her brother. Ilymir, still issuing orders to his imaginary army and trying to kick the horse into going, snaked an arm absently about his sister's waist and kissed her ear so that she giggled.

When Dain dismissed his aides and courtiers, they bowed to him uneasily. Although he realized he should take the time to chat with them, thus turning their thoughts away from what they'd witnessed, he was too inwardly distressed to settle them now.

The hunting party broke up, its previous mood of high spirits and festivity dampened. Most of the courtiers headed back to camp, while Dain, his children, his protector, and his armed escort rode off through the trees toward a ravine a short distance away. Choked with rocks and spiky bushes, the ravine was narrow at its base with steep cliffs on either side. A shallow stream coursed through it, and birds flew up from the water at their approach.

Dismounting, Dain paused a moment to close his eyes and draw in a deep breath. There was peace here, a measure of serenity in this isolated spot, yet there was another element— old and eldin and indescribable—that he reached for to steady his churning emotions.

Leading his children by the hand, he took them slowly up the rocky trail to the cave he and Tashalya had found on a previous expedition. Ilymir peered inside the cave mouth, but surprisingly made no attempt to dart into the cool, dark interior. Mareitina climbed into Dain's arms and refused to stand on the ground.

"I want to go back, Papa," she whispered.

"Wait. Let's look first at the runes," Dain said, and showed them the markings etched into the rock.

He traced Ilymir's fingers over the runes, one by one, spelling out the meaning to the little boy. But although Tashalya had shared Dain's fascination with this place, Ilymir quickly lost interest, wanting instead to splash in the stream and throw pebbles at the small, dark brown birds flitting in the brush. Disappointment spread through Dain, but he reminded himself that few outings with young children went as planned.

Besides, this was as close to privacy and solitude as he was going to find, despite the twins and Omas and the Agya warriors waiting a short distance away. The Agyas had hobbled their horses and crouched on the ground, playing knucklebones. Omas was staring at the sky and whistling softly to himself.

Dain sighed, aware that for the time being he had a chance to think. He needed desperately to consider his multiplying problems.

Only his mind kept shying away from anything cohesive, and the children were a distraction.

Wandering away, Ilymir began picking berries—fortunately edible—and cramming them into his mouth until his face was smeared with purple juice.

Mareitina was gazing intently at the small crimson wildflowers blooming among the rocks. "Pretty," she said.

Sighing, Dain carried her a short distance down the trail away from the cave before he set her on her feet and let her pick a bouquet. Ilymir whooped and raced up and down the rocks.

"Papa," Mareitina said.

"Yes, precious?"

"If I make you a pie, will you not be sad?"

At that moment she reminded him of his sister Thiatereika, whom he'd loved with all his heart. Bending down, Dain kissed Mareitina tenderly and felt soothed by her chubby warmth. He told himself to stop worrying and just enjoy this time in the children's company.

Ilymir fell in the stream with a yell, but the water was shallow, hardly reaching to his knees. He came scrambling out, dripping wet and laughing in glee.

Mareitina laughed, too, and ran over to grab his hand. Together they jumped into the water, splashing and cavorting happily, ruining their clothes without a care beneath the hot sun. Half-tempted to join them, Dain watched in amusement and delight.

"Ahem," said a soft, dry voice.

Startled, Dain spun around and saw Prince Tustik riding up quietly. A thin-faced aristocrat of perhaps sixty years and a survivor of Muncel's reign of terror, the elderly prince knew everyone, remembered every detail with a memory that was astonishing, and could recite history, protocol, and the rules of diplomacy without hesitation. Although he served without seeking personal gain, and Dain had long considered him an invaluable adviser, he belonged—by right of birth—to the secret Kollegya as well as the official Privy Council. His arrival in the camp last night had been an unpleasant surprise. His presence here at the ravine now was equally unwelcome.

Annoyed by the intrusion, Dain started to order the man away, then held his tongue. It was perhaps better to get matters out in the open.

With a quiet word to Lord Omas, Tustik dismounted stiffly and climbed slowly up the rocky trail to join Dain. He bowed deeply, for, even here in the midst of nowhere, he kept to the strictest formalities.

"Forgive my intrusion, your majesty," he said in his quiet voice.

"Aye, *intrusion* is the perfect word," Dain replied coldly. "I've no need of courtiers just now, lord prince."

"Exactly." Tustik's eyes, dark and wise, smiled past Dain at the children. "I thought this might be a good place to talk in private."

Mareitina's squeal made Dain look around quickly, but Ilymir had scooped a double handful of water down her back, and she was laughing.

"The walls of a tent are thin, are they not?" Tustik continued, while Dain kept silent. "Out here, we have the advantages of isolation and very few listening ears."

"Last night you assured me nothing was wrong," Dain said warily. "Now I'd like the truth. What urgent matter has brought you all the way from Grov? What ultimatum or threat does the Kollegya present to me now? And why have you agreed to bring it?"

Tustik spread wide his thin hands. "You accuse me hastily,

sire. I do not represent either the Kollegya or the Privy Council today. Nor did I journey here on their business."

Dain stared at the old man very hard before finally nodding. "It seems I err. What is it you wish to discuss?"

"Jonan."

"Jonan?" he echoed in surprise. "Morde, I thought—never mind what I thought. Why him?"

"There's been a development in Grov. I've come to warn you so that your majesty has time to act. Now is the moment to eliminate that wretched boy, as I've urged before. The decision can no longer be put off."

Dain's bewilderment gave way to irritation. "I thought I had made my position quite clear. I will not discuss—"

"Hear what I have to say, sire. Please."

Something in the man's tone made Dain hesitate. "Very well."

"A nobleman named Count Soblinsk has come to court, applying for the post of Jonan's tutor."

Dain was so surprised he laughed aloud. "Nay, what jest is this? I dismissed the last tutor over a year ago. Pounding knowledge into Jonan's thick head is a waste of effort."

"Believe me, sire, I am not alarmed over something so trivial."

Dain sobered at once. "Continue."

"Your majesty does not recognize the name Soblinsk?"

"Nay. Should I?"

"He belonged to Muncel's court and received his title and lands through Muncel's charter. After the Battle of Grov, he renounced the usurper and pledged his fealty to your majesty in exchange for full pardon."

"He and so many others," Dain said, unimpressed. A few of the pardoned had proven to be sound and honorable men, but many remained scoundrels and ruffians. "What is he really after? Is he trying to keep his lands despite reclamation?"

"No, your majesty. He possesses a corner of Myrot, a useless swamp no one had ever held title to until Muncel awarded it to him."

Dain was thinking. "Useless or not, when a king charters you into a title you remain loyal to him."

"Exactly. Twice before, Soblinsk has sought permission to join your majesty's court. Both times he has been denied, and with just cause for he is not to be trusted. Now he has come again to Grov, petitioning for a post he insists has been left vacant too long. He seems extremely concerned about Jonan's welfare."

A finger of unease ran up Dain's spine. "I begin to understand."

Tustik nodded. "Yes, an old supporter of Muncel is seeking work in Jonan's pocket. Muncel's son is of age, or will be a month hence, and the traitors want him to rally around. It begins, sire. It begins."

Dain frowned. "You panic too easily, my lord. Deny the man's petition, and send him back to Myrot where he belongs."

"Forgive me, sire, but it can't be that simple."

"You mean the ploy is too obvious."

"Absurdly so. Soblinsk is a cunning blackguard and far from stupid. He's bound to know we would never agree to this request. I'm certain some other plot is afoot, but my spies have not yet discovered what it is. That's why I came here with such unseemly haste, to urge your majesty to end this problem once and for all."

"By dismissing Jonan from court?" Dain asked with a lift of his brows. "Morde, after today's behavior I am sorely tempted to kick his backside to the farthest corner of my realm. But if I put him in exile, how do I guard him so that no one gets to him? How do I give him a life of some freedom and decency? He is my kinsman, not a prisoner worthy of banishment."

"Your majesty is aware of the perfect solution. It is best done here, with little fuss and scant notice so far from civilization. No one need know about a quiet deed performed in the stillness of night. Or perhaps Jonan rides out hunting and his horse slips on one of these precipices. A tragedy, certainly, but then it is over, and one of your majesty's problems is solved."

Tustik's soft-voiced, emotionless description of murder chilled Dain to the marrow of his bones. Dain had killed many

men in battle and self-defense, and would not shirk to do it
again in the future, but this was unholy and wicked. Trying to
conceal his shock and revulsion, Dain stared into Tustik's
eyes, seeing a stranger before him, and wondered how far he
could trust any of the men he depended on for the protection
of his family.

Then he heard Lord Omas's laugh boom out over the soft
murmur of voices, and Dain's doubts vanished. He trusted
Omas and Miest, his personal protectors. He trusted the
Agyas, and both his aides. Chesil was General Matkevskiet's
son and Evo was a grandson of Count Romsalkin, both
staunch supporters. Dain even, Thod help him, trusted this
ruthless old man standing before him.

"The king's kind heart does him credit," Tustik said softly,
"but the boy is a stupid, worthless fool. For seven years your
majesty has sought to influence and develop him. Nothing has
been accomplished, nothing."

Dain threw up his hands. "You make your point, lord
prince. I cannot like the miserable wretch, kinsman or not, but
that's hardly his fault. He's not to blame for his ineptitude or
stupidity."

"No, he is not to blame," Tustik agreed. "He is to pitied,
and your majesty's kindness and the queen's compassion toward him have been commendable, but wasted."

"Oh, come! He's improved—"

"Sire, I fear his early childhood held too many horrors that
have damaged him beyond remedy. Were he sound of mind
and temper, I would applaud your majesty's leniency. He is
not to blame because he is hopeless with letters, an indifferent horseman, uninterested in sport, and easily bored. But
these defects give him no pursuits whatsoever, leaving him
without purpose or direction. Combine that with his impul-
siveness and hot temper, a foul, filthy temper he inherited
from his father, and your majesty has a problem growing
steadily worse."

"That's hardly grounds for—"

"By keeping him close by, you constantly tempt those in
this realm who would rather see Muncel's son on Nether's
throne than Tobeszijian's."

Dain set his hand on his dagger hilt. "They are traitors if they do!"

"Indeed, sire, they are. And were it not for Prince Ilymir, Jonan would be your majesty's heir. He's old enough now to understand that, and to resent it."

"Are you saying you think Jonan will turn against my family?"

"What will your majesty do," Tustik asked softly, "if it ever comes to a choice, say, between Jonan's welfare and Prince Ilymir's?"

The question plunged a dagger of ice between Dain's shoulder blades. He stiffened, glaring at the old man, his thoughts and emotions churning. He could not command himself to speak.

"Yes," Tustik said, watching him intently. "I am sorry to be so blunt, but your majesty must comprehend the full magnitude of this problem. I know you adopted Jonan to gain his loyalty, but Jonan is, unfortunately, a fool and easily led. When he reaches his majority, he'll no longer be legally under your majesty's guardianship, and he's as ripe for someone's plucking as a soft pear. Let him fall into the wrong hands, let his frustrations and inadequacies fester, and he'll bring this realm civil war."

The thought was alarming. Dain knew his resources were stretched too thin already. And if the threatened Grethori uprising happened while he was coping with insurrectionists . . .

"Sire—"

Lifting his hand to command the old man's silence, Dain turned away and went to stand by the edge of the stream.

"Watch me, Papa!" Ilymir shouted, and threw a stone upstream as hard as he could.

Dain smiled at him absently, his thoughts far away, his heart knotted with temptation. For, aye, there was a corrupted corner of him that agreed with Tustik's assessment and longed to take the easy solution. Murder in the wilds of the World's Rim. He had only to issue an order to the Agya captain, and it would be done. By Thod, he could do it himself by riding with Jonan into the forest on a simple pretext, ordering the boy to kneel at his feet, and breaking his neck.

Feeling sick, Dain pressed the heels of his hands against his eyes. Even now, after seven years in Nether, he could still be shocked by the casual cruelty of his subjects. Prince Tustik was a highly educated man of aristocratic birth and high station. He was civilized, beautifully mannered, and intelligent, yet he pressed for Jonan's execution with cold, precise logic, with no more emotion than if he intended to swat a fly.

Chattering, Ilymir and Mareitina climbed out of the water and shook themselves like puppies before they crouched on the ground and began happily smearing mud on each other. A corner of Dain's mind realized their nursemaid would have fits when she saw them, but he did not trouble to put an end to their play. Instead, he watched them, marveling at their tender innocence while he and Tustik discussed death over their heads.

What am I becoming, he asked himself in despair. *I keep secrets from my wife, and now I stand here contemplating the murder of my cousin. I have always believed myself too eldin, too gentle of heart to use the cruelty necessary to rule my subjects, and I've never been able to satisfy their thirst for blood. But, Thod help me, I fear I am changing. If I give way to them, if I become like them, then verily I am lost.*

Wearily he shoved his self-pity away, knowing he succumbed to it only because lack of sleep. Worry about Alexeika and now Tashalya, and concerns over the Grethori weighed on him heavily that day. Although he had brought back the Chalice of Eternal Life and restored it to its rightful place, he had not as yet succeeded in clearing the darkness entirely away from Nether. Perhaps it could not be done. If even a fine, worthy man like Tustik did not see the merit of mercy or clemency, if he could not understand that a son was not to blame for the sins of his father, then the Circle of kindness and brotherhood would remain forever broken.

And am I being an idealistic fool, Dain asked himself, *thrusting my own family into unnecessary danger because of stubbornness?*

The question troubled him deeply. He felt very disillusioned, and yet his conscience would not let him bend.

With a sigh he turned back to face Tustik. "When we return to Grov, you will assign a companion to Jonan, and let this fellow influence and guard the boy."

"Sire—"

Dain frowned. "Give him a small circle of suitable friends who won't make him a butt of ridicule. And see that he doesn't mix with the royal children without proper supervision."

"Sire, I fear such solutions have already been tried. You cannot buy an oaf friends. I implore your majesty to reconsider."

"He's not yet a traitor," Dain said angrily. "Do I judge him before he commits these crimes you fear?"

"'Tis not the boy I fear, your majesty, but the element he attracts."

"I attract enemies and danger, too," Dain said. "Jonan is not to blame for his father's supporters. I believe there is still good to be found in him."

Disappointment sagged in Tustik's eyes. For a moment he looked every one of his years. "I wish your majesty would accept the fact that nothing can be done for him. Nothing."

Fresh yells from the children caught Dain's attention. They were in the water again, and he took advantage of the interruption to order them out of the stream. While Ilymir twisted the hem of his tunic to wring water from it, Mareitina squatted beside him and began to make mud pies. With their wet, stringy hair, dirty faces, and dripping, filthy clothes, they looked like beggar children.

"I'm hungry," Ilymir proclaimed, apparently forgetting that he'd recently gorged on berries. "I'm really hungry! Like a beyar!" Throwing back his golden head, he growled ferociously.

Dain growled back, realistically enough to make Prince Tustik jump.

Ilymir yelped with delight. "We're beyars!" he shouted, dancing around his sister. "Beyars hungry enough to eat horses."

"Let's race back to camp and discover what's in the cooking pots," Dain suggested.

"Yes!" Ilymir shouted, with a whoop that echoed through the ravine. "Yes! Yes! Yes!"

Wincing at the noise, Tustik said, "Your majesty—"

"Perhaps," Dain said as a sudden thought occurred to him, "we could find Jonan a wife. That would occupy him and give him a purpose."

Tustik's brows rose in visible horror. "May Thod forbid such a course! Surely your majesty will not permit him to breed!"

"Damne, lord prince!" Dain swore in exasperation. "He's not a defective dog to be denied the most basic—"

A shout in the distance interrupted Dain. He broke off and turned, squinting against the bright sunshine as a horse and rider came up in a cloud of dust. Challenged by the Agyas, the rider dismounted and was allowed to stride up the trail to Dain.

Clad in chain mail and coated with road dust, he was a knight in the Netheran army, his surcoat carrying the badge of his sworn service. He saluted Dain briskly.

"Your majesty, I bring grave news from the southern border."

Dain wondered what problem assailed him now. "Speak," he said.

"We intercepted a Mandrian knight at one of the checkpoints. He was dying, and his message garbled. The commander speaks a little of that heathen tongue, and I carry a written text of what my commander was able to glean from the wretch."

A small parchment scroll, heavily sealed and tied with a cord was handed to Dain. He stared at it in dismay.

Tustik stepped closer. "Is Mandria at war? Was the man a courier?"

The knight shook his head. "Nay, my lord, he was no official courier. As for war in Mandria, we've heard no rumor at our checkpoint." Pulling a piece of cloth from the pouch slung over his shoulder, he handed it to Dain. "My commander bade me bring you the man's surcoat, sire. He said your majesty would understand what all this meant."

The torn, bloodied cloth spilled over Dain's hands. He held it aloft, but already he recognized it with alarm.

"Thirst green," he said, and looked up sharply. "The man's name? Have you that?"

"Nay, sire. He was a sentry-rank knight, but he gave not his name. I did not hear what he choked out to the commander in his dying breath, but he said little." The knight nodded at the parchment in Dain's hand. "It's there, your majesty, such as it is."

Dain dropped the bloodstained surcoat at his feet and stared at the little scroll with dread. What dire event had occurred at Thirst? A dwarf raid more savage than the usual . . . or even, Thod forbid, an attack of Nonkind perhaps? It had to be serious indeed for them to send word to him in such a disorganized way. Not by dispatch and courier, but a knight fleeing trouble to seek Thirst's lord and master. *Damne*, Dain thought, *this is strange*.

Clouds passed over the sun, and distant thunder rumbled behind the mountain peaks.

Suddenly he did not want to open the scroll. He had more than enough trouble to contend with already, and his critics in Nether believed his continued allegiance to this obscure Mandrian hold to be both foolish and unnecessary. But Dain had sworn an oath long ago to Lord Odfrey to guard and protect Thirst. He kept that oath still. *And one day soon, he vowed, Ilymir will be named Chevard of Thirst. In the fullness of time it will pass to Ilymir's son and so on, as long as my and my father's descendants rule this land.*

The thought pleased Dain and steadied him. No trouble, he knew, was ever vanquished by avoiding it.

Drawing a deep breath, Dain broke the seals and spread open the curl of parchment to read the bad news it contained.

Chapter Five

Alexeika bent to her paddling, sending the narrow skiff shooting forward across the fjord with deep, sure strokes of her oar. Overhead, the sun shone high and hot, casting a glare of spangles across the water. In the distance beyond Uthe Peak, dark storm clouds were massing, and now and then she heard the low, muted growl of thunder.

Time was running out. She frowned, pausing to glance back at the shore behind her, then tossed her long braid of hair out of her way and continued paddling. She wanted to reach her destination before the storm overtook her.

If only Lady Nadilya had not delayed her with endless questions and chatter . . . but Alexeika had finally managed to escape without her ladies-in-waiting or guards. This moment, while she was unencumbered, was her only chance to seek out the shrine she'd been told existed on the tallest of the rocky knolls dotting the center of the fjord.

"Rain coming," Sir Pyron said from behind her. "Best be turning back afore storm."

"Nonsense, sir," she replied, plying her oar steadily. "We're nearly there."

The breeze freshened, cooling her face but making it harder to paddle. She bent her back to the task, while her protector gripped the sides of the skiff with white-knuckled hands and muttered oaths beneath his breath.

Alexeika feared neither wind nor water. Much of her childhood had been spent on the banks of one fjord or another. She loved the mountains and these deep, narrow lakes between them. The purity of the air and the span of sky made her feel alive and close to the gods. And 'twas the mercy and favor of the gods that she sought now.

On the opposite shore, Uthe Peak towered high, its steep rocky slopes rising directly from the water. Snow capped its distant top, and tiny black dots showed her the circling flight of the eagles that lived in its rugged crags. A corner of her mind wondered briefly about how the hawking had gone this morning. Who, she thought with fond affection, had lost patience with the outing first? Tashalya or Faldain? They were so much alike, those two, both independent and stubborn.

Reaching the rocky little island, she trailed her oar expertly across the surface of the waves to slow her progress and slid the skiff into a berth between two rectangular stones. Iron rings—well rusted from age and exposure to the elements—were embedded in them.

Alexeika tossed Pyron a length of rope. "Make us fast."

While he obeyed, Alexeika scrambled out of the skiff and stood atop one of the boulders. A cliff rose steep above her, with a trail of sorts, fit for a goat, leading to its top. "Aye," she said with a smile. "We've found it. Hand me my rucksack if you please."

She held out her hands, waiting for her protector to toss it to her, but instead Sir Pyron, a stocky, sour-faced man with red hair faded to grizzle and a gruff, no-nonsense manner, held on to the rucksack while he climbed up the boulder to join her.

"Await here, majesty," he said. "I'll prowl this rock first and see all secure."

"Hurry."

Giving her a brusque nod, he started up the trail with

drawn sword in hand. The going looked steep and narrow, but he made short work of it and vanished out of sight at the top.

Alexeika curbed her impatience. She must be back at camp within the hour, for she'd ordered her attendants to let her lie quietly napping in her chamber without disturbance for that span of time. If all went as planned, she could make her offering and return before her absence was noticed. What she did here was her business alone; she wanted no gossip among her ladies about it, no questions.

While she waited on Pyron, she busied herself by unfastening the brooch at her shoulder and deftly untying her kirtle to step out of her long gown. Beneath it she wore a tunic and leggings, man-style. She folded her gown neatly and left it in the skiff, belted on her pair of daggers, which had been a gift from the king, then picked up her rucksack and advanced to the foot of the trail as Pyron came half-walking, half-sliding down, with a small cloud of dust and the rattle of dislodged pebbles in his wake.

"Well?" she asked.

He gave her a sketchy salute. "Naught on this rock save yon shrine, and it long abandoned by look of it."

She slung the rucksack strap over her shoulder. "I won't be long."

Pyron offered her his hand in assistance. "That's no easy trail up. Best have help."

"I can do it alone."

"Nay, it's—"

"Sir Pyron," she said sharply, "I need no help. Remain here, and guard the skiff."

He looked sour, but protested no more. Unsure whether to be amused or exasperated by his attempt to treat her like a helpless court lady, Alexeika started up the trail. *If he only knew the life I lived before I became queen*, she thought with a snort. She'd grown up among rebels fighting against the tyrant Muncel. Later, she'd stolen horses and survived imprisonment in Gant's wasteland. For her, the hardest part of being queen—aside from the necessity of curbing her tongue more than she liked—was the constant insistence of her attendants that she do nothing for herself. *Nay*, she thought, *I can climb a goat track as well as I can paddle a skiff, or swim, or even swing a sword.*

But Pyron was right; it *was* a steep and treacherous trail. The going proved to be tougher than she expected, with the ground inclined to crumble underfoot. Soon, she was puffing for air, her muscles burning from the struggle. Twice she slipped, but recovered and grimly kept going. Near the top, she had to drop to all fours. The coarse, low-growing scrub snagged at her wrists and ankles, leaving prickles in her clothing, but at last she stood panting at the top.

Gone soft from my easy life and too much childbearing, she thought to herself, and grinned in satisfaction at having reached her goal.

The view was magnificent. She could see the wooden structures of the village nestled along Uthe's flank. She could see the forest stretching to the south. She could see the royal camp sprawling along the eastern shore. Turning slowly about, she gazed at the vistas with delight, drinking in their beauty before shutting her eyes and tilting her face upward to the sun. In that moment, her worries fell away, and she was filled with a rush of happiness and pride.

"Call out if yer majesty requires aught!" Pyron yelled up to her.

His voice brought her back to her purpose. Sighing, she leaned over the edge of the cliff and gave him a brief wave before turning her attention to the altar.

Fashioned of crude stone slabs stacked in place, the altar stood as it had for centuries. Moss softened its north side, and the elements had pocked the stone. She circled it respectfully, seeking runes, and found only Riva's mark on it, which meant the information provided by the village wisewoman had been accurate.

"Good," she said aloud.

Kneeling, she withdrew from the rucksack a small bronze offering bowl and placed it on the center of the altar between two short sticks of peeled ash. Murmuring soft words of prayer to the goddess Riva, she sprinkled dried herbs about, then pricked her finger with the tip of her dagger and squeezed out three drops of blood into the bowl before dusting salt on top. She added a fourth drop of blood, while a tiny frisson of elation ran through her.

Bowing her head in supplication, she prayed, "Great goddess, hear my plea. I give thee thanks for thy blessing in granting the wish of my heart and allowing another child to quicken inside me. Help me, gracious goddess, to carry this child with strength and good health. Help me to nurture this child rightly."

She paused a moment, counting out the correct number of heartbeats before she could respectfully resume her prayer. "Great goddess, let this child grow up strong and good. And although it is thy divine choice as to whether we are granted a son or daughter, I ask for the honor of bearing my husband another son. This favor do I ask, but, gracious goddess, if it should be thy will to send us another daughter, then let me rejoice and be thankful. Let thy will stand above my own."

With her head still bowed, she added, "Watch over us, divine Riva. Help me to find a way to ease my husband's troubled heart in that matter which he hides from me. And if we please thee, may thy blessings continue. To Riva do I make this prayer."

Finished, Alexeika remained kneeling a while longer, gazing out at the view while she drew on the holiness and comfort offered by this ancient shrine. She would tell Faldain tonight, she decided. Although perhaps, depending on how today had gone with the children, he might be too weary to rejoice in the news of a fourth.

A smile curved her lips, and she tipped back her head with a sigh. Things were going well. Faldain had been a successful king these past seven years despite the abounding difficulties and occasional mistakes. *And I have been at his side*, she thought with pride and satisfaction.

It had been her suggestion that they come to the mountains for the summer. For the first time, the realm had been calm enough for Faldain to leave his seat of power and journey forth for a long absence from Grov. Thus, this year Alexeika had been spared the worry of the children catching sweating sickness, an annual pestilence that felled so many in Grov's sweltering humidity when the Velga River dropped low in its banks and ran sluggishly with filth.

Their leisurely king's progress had been successful, allowing remote, rural people the chance to see the royal family for the first time. And whatever had been troubling Faldain in Grov, ruining his sleep, diminishing his appetite, and wearing grooves of worry into his face, had faded away. She had seen him gradually relax, smile more readily, laugh with genuine feeling. She had loved watching him play with the children; he spoiled them and upset nursery discipline at times, but Alexeika did not mind. The children were plump and golden brown with health. And Alexeika had been able to abandon many of the mindless, numbing protocols and rituals forced on the queen. She knew she was not feminine or fashionable enough to satisfy the prissy standards of Grov's court, but here among the lakes and mountains she knew again her value and strength, as well as what was truly important.

Best of all, the event she had most hoped for, the objective she had most wanted to accomplish during this sojourn of rest and relaxation, had come about.

Smiling, she pressed her hand to her trim stomach and felt once more that deep surge of womanly pride. Already she had borne Faldain three stalwart children. This fourth would be blessed indeed, for he had been conceived on the shores of these shining waters, in happiness and contentment. Surely this child would always be special for that reason, and would know good deeds, loyal friends, and the protection of the gods all the days of his life.

As soon as the children were asleep tonight in their cots, as soon as their majesties had retired in private from attendants and protectors and all others, she would make the news a gift to him.

A shadow drifted across the sun, turning the air suddenly cool and unpleasant. The wind picked up, gusting through the scraggly firs behind her and stirring the pungent scent of their needles. Thunder rumbled closer, and beyond the peak she saw a brief flicker of lightning.

A sound from behind her made her whirl around, her heart

suddenly pounding and her hands on her dagger hilts, but it was only a limb snapping and falling to the ground.

Feeling foolish for her fears, she gulped in a deep breath and tried to calm herself. "Fool," she said aloud. "You still expect Nonkind to leap at you from every bush."

But despite her self-chiding words, her sense of unease increased. No longer did the place feel like a sanctuary. Its air of peacefulness had vanished with the sun, and she felt suddenly like an unwelcome intruder.

Quickly, she cleared the altar, sweeping the ash sticks and offering bowl into her rucksack. Too late did she realize her failure to properly clean the offering bowl according to ritual, but having made the mistake, she could not undo it. She wondered if the goddess would be offended and repudiate her prayers. Tears sprang to her eyes, and they upset her, too. Of all the changes and consequences of pregnancy, the foolishness of ready tears annoyed her the most.

"Alexeika."

Startled, she turned to see Faldain standing a short distance away, and so unexpected and sudden was his appearance that she could only stare. It was as though he had come to her by magic, or was this a vision? She'd heard no boat approach, not even the quietest splash of oars. She listened now, but heard no men talking below. Where, she wondered, had he sprung from? How long had he been standing there, watching her?

Clad in a simple burgundy tunic and leggings, his sword Mirengard strapped to his hip, his spurs jingling on his heels, his narrow circlet of gold glinting on his brow and holding back his thick black hair, he looked magnificent enough to make her breath catch in her throat. In her eyes, he outshone every other man alive. His blood was more eldin than human, yet he carried a human frame, one both tall and muscular with wide, powerful shoulders and arms that could wield a broadsword tirelessly. His dark hair was human as well, but he had eldin eyes, as pale a silvery gray as the rain that would start falling soon. Those eyes could pierce or soften, according to his mood. They saw much, and they saw her tears now.

In four long strides he reached her and gathered her close inside his powerful arms.

She clung to him, still feeling unaccountably cold and frightened, yet the clouds overhead parted, and the sun came out again, bathing them both in its golden warmth.

"Beloved," he said softly.

Her love for him swept through her like a tide, a force so strong she wanted to press herself into his body and become one with him. She wanted to be held in his arms like this forever, safe and steady, with his mighty heart beating beneath her cheek and his breath stirring through the top of her hair.

She had never loved another man like this. She never would. Sometimes the potency of her feelings for him frightened her. Faldain had only to come into her presence, and she found herself breathless and flushed, her pulse racing and thundering in her ears. Fine ladies were not supposed to care so obviously for their husbands; Alexeika did not try to be a fashionable lady. She was queen, married to the man she adored. If others chose to mock her for being stirred by Faldain's physical proximity, then she pitied them for their jealousy.

His lips sought hers, and she yielded to the power of his kiss, which sent her tingling all the way to her toes. When the kiss ended, she stood rosy and bewildered, her heart thudding for more.

He brushed away her tears. "What do you here, Alexeika?"

The question recalled her to her blunder. "I came to make an offering, but I have ruined it with a stupid mistake. Morde! I wanted everything to be perfect, and now it—"

"Hush," he whispered, kissing her again. "Surely Riva heard the prayer of an earnest heart and can forgive the error of a mortal."

She sniffed, wiping her eyes angrily. "I hope so."

"I wish you had waited for me to join your prayers here," he said quietly. "Tashalya will need both of us to be strong."

"Why? Oh, Faldain, what has she done now?"

"Don't you know?"

She shook her head. "I've been busy with packing and directing servants. I didn't expect you to return yet with the children."

"Tashalya was sent back to camp at midday. No one told you?" His eyes flashed. "The cowards!"

She waited, but he turned away, scowling so fiercely a qualm touched her. It was unlike Faldain to lose his temper, yet when he did he could simmer with anger for hours.

"Whatever it is, beloved," she said, "I would rather be told by you. Our daughter is—"

"She has to be given to Samderaudin," he broke in gruffly. "As soon as we return to Grov. I won't let Vaunit be the one to test her. We'll wait for Samderaudin."

Alexeika frowned in puzzlement; then abruptly she stiffened. "No! What are you saying?"

"It's always been a possibility with her, and now I'm sure." He took her cold hand in his and held it tightly. "She lost her temper with Jonan and me this morning, and conjured up a whirlwind."

Alexeika wanted to scream a denial, wanted to shout at him that he was mistaken, but instead she stood rigid, staring at him, knowing from the pain in his eyes that he did not lie. She said nothing at all. She felt too frozen to utter a sound.

"She wasn't hurt," he went on. "I was able to stop her in time, but we can't pretend now. The entire hunting party witnessed it. She must be evaluated and trained. She can't be allowed to continue as she is, uncontrolled, a danger to herself as well as others." He stopped, staring at the ground, then painfully raised his head to look at Alexeika. "Soon she'll figure out that she can hurt others with her powers, and I fear she will try."

New tears ran down Alexeika's cheeks. "You aren't going to give her to them."

"I must. For a time."

"Faldain, no! Not our child! She isn't like that. She's—"

"Alexeika, she's a *sorcerelle*! We can't deny it. Not after today."

"I have gifts," Alexeika said carefully. "You have gifts. Neither of us is . . . like that."

"I am hoping Samderaudin will find that her gifts are insufficient. If she can be trained to control them, to suppress them, then she can—"

Alexeika clutched his sleeve. "Please don't send her away. How can you? Your favorite!"

"The next time she's upset, the result could be more dangerous than a whirlwind," he said grimly. The anguish in his eyes mirrored Alexeika's. "While she's young, something can perhaps be done. If we wait until she's stronger, or until she hurts someone—"

"Who would she hurt?" Alexcika said scornfully. "Jonan?"

"Aye, possibly," Faldain replied. "Or . . . Ilymir."

"What?" Alexeika gasped. "She wouldn't! How can you think that? He adores her and follows her about like a puppy."

"And he is my heir," Faldain said harshly. "He's old enough now to appear in public with me, to ride at my side as Tashalya has been doing. I can no longer take her with me that way."

"Because you fear criticism?"

"Because Ilymir will rule after me, not Tashalya," he replied, ignoring her barb. "Because it is his right to be seen with me, while for her 'tis only a privilege. It's time for her to learn the difference."

"You will break her heart."

He nodded bleakly. "Aye, and I don't want to do it. Morde! If I could change—" Abruptly he broke off what he was about to say and began to pace back and forth.

She watched him, her heart wrenched, and did not know what to say that could comfort him. "I had hoped she would have a little more time, two more years perhaps, to remain your favorite."

"Aye, but her powers make that impossible. If I can get her trained, perhaps there's still a chance for her to live a normal life. Morde and damnation, what chance has she of growing up to marry? What prince of Mandria will accept a Netheran princess who wields magic?"

It was unlike him to swear so much, or lose heart like this. Alexeika went to his side to stop his fretful pacing. She touched his cheek with gentle fingers. "You look too far ahead and see too many worries," she said softly, trying to soothe him. "Let us deal with the present. She's very young. Sometimes gifts manifest themselves early, only to vanish. It could be so with her."

"Aye," he said, with a sigh. "Perhaps."

"Let us not fear the worst until we are told the worst," she said, trying to reassure herself as well as him. "And do not have her married as yet. There's time enough to be thinking of that."

He curled his hand around hers and kissed it. "As always, your good sense comes to my rescue. You are right. But I must still bring Ilymir forward, beginning now. I think I shall take him with me."

She frowned. "I don't understand."

"There's some trouble at Thirst. A messenger reached me only a short time ago with the news. I intend to ride there without delay."

"You must return to Grov," she said sharply. "You've been absent all summer. Whatever has happened at Thirst will keep a while."

"Will it keep until thaw? If I don't go now, I won't have time to make the trip before the long cold sets in."

"But what kind of trouble? And why can't Sir Bosquecel deal with it as he usually does? Why can't you send a delegate, Lord Thum perhaps? I am sure he would welcome a chance to visit his relatives, especially after having guarded your throne and interests in Grov all summer."

"Nay, I must see to matters myself," Faldain said grimly. "And I will take Ilymir. I intend to name him chevard of Thirst, and it's important that the men see him."

Astonishment filled her. "What folly is this? He's too young."

"He's not an infant."

"He's only four!"

"He can ride in front of my saddle. He'll have his protector, of course, and his nursemaid too—"

"Oh, a nursemaid on a forced march into Mandria. How long will it take you to get there? Three weeks of hard riding? Four? She can't do it. Ilymir can't do it."

"He can."

She shook her head stubbornly. "I am amazed that you could even consider it. And what, exactly, is this trouble you must go and investigate?"

"I'm not sure. The message was garbled and—"

"You're not sure?" she repeated angrily. "Anything could have befallen the hold. You know nothing of what you may find."

"Alexeika, he'll be in no danger."

"How can you promise that? Thirst could be in the midst of a war, or dwarf raids, or a Nonkind attack. A battleground is no place for him."

"I'll keep him from harm," Faldain said impatiently. "You know I'll protect him with my life."

"No."

"But—"

"No!" she shouted with such fury he took a step back from her. She glared at him, fuming. Ilymir would tire in the first hour of such a journey, and then he'd fret and cry and throw tantrums. The nursemaid could not ride like a warrior either. Alexeika wondered what Faldain could be thinking. But of course, she told herself, he wasn't thinking. He was distressed over Tashalya, even disappointed in her, and trying to turn Ilymir into an instant substitute for his spirited daughter. But Ilymir would never be like Tashalya, it was unfair to expect that of him.

"Now is not the time to show off your son to your men," she said as calmly as she could.

"Alexeika, if I thought there was danger awaiting us there, I would not take him. Whatever has befallen Thirst has already happened days, even weeks ago. By the time we arrive, it will be—"

"The boy is too young!" she broke in fiercely, wondering why Faldain could not understand something so obvious. "When he's ten or twelve, perhaps—"

"Will you coddle him and keep him a baby all his life? He's a well-made little boy, stalwart and brave." Frowning, Faldain stepped closer to her and tried to take her hands, but she snatched them away. He sighed. "I will not lose him in the forest. I will not forget to feed him. I will not let anything happen to him. This, I swear to you."

She looked into his gray eyes and believed his good intentions, but her mother's heart knew what was best for her son. "I cannot let him go," she whispered.

"Do you not trust me, Alexeika?"

"Of course I do. That has nothing to do with my refusal."

"I think it does." He frowned, watching her a moment. "I cannot explain it, except that a feeling has come to me that I should take him. That is all. I very much want him to go."

She hesitated, tempted to give in. Yet she could not. Sadly, silently, she shook her head. If Tashalya was Faldain's favorite, then Ilymir was hers. "I know what's best for him," she whispered. "Not this year."

Anger flashed in Faldain's eyes, a swift and cutting fury, then it vanished, and his gaze grew as hard and smooth as stone. He bowed to her formally. "Since you will not be swayed, I suppose I could exercise my kingly authority and take him without your leave."

Her mouth fell open.

"But I shall not," he said.

She sighed in relief. "Thank you."

"I want no courtesies," he snapped, scowling. "It seems I do live under my lady's thumb. I hadn't realized how much."

Disconcerted, she stared at him. Why was he so furious over so small a disagreement? They quarreled at times, of course, but not like this. She had never seen him look at her in this way. As though he no longer loved her, as though he almost despised her.

Panic swept her. Was it possible to lose his love? The very thought almost made her feel ill. Early in their courtship, she'd found it difficult at first to believe he truly cared for her, for he'd been so smitten with Lady Pheresa of Mandria when he and Alexeika had first met, and he was not the kind of person who gave his heart frivolously. Yet it seemed that somewhere along the quest to save Pheresa's life and gain his throne, he'd outgrown his youthful infatuation with the woman who'd subsequently become Mandria's queen. Often he'd explained to Alexeika that it was during their dangerous journey to Gant and back that he'd come to see her as the true maid for him. And when he held her in his arms, his ardor was unquestionable. Blissfully happy, she'd allowed herself to feel secure and safe. But now . . .

If she ever lost his heart, she knew she could not bear it. To live with him, to see him daily, and yet be denied his love . . . the horror of such a prospect nearly made her give in. Yet she was no weakling, no coward. She could not surrender her convictions just to make peace, for it would be a false peace. Their love had to stand beyond any other disagreement or trouble. They could not use it as a bargaining chip without cheapening and destroying all they meant to each other.

"Faldain, I'm sorry," she whispered. "I know you would never bring him to harm, but I—I just can't let him go right now. Surely you can understand a mother's instinct in these matters."

"I understand that you do not trust *my* instincts." His voice was curt and cold, the tone he used with tiresome courtiers. He had never used it on her before. It frightened her.

"Please," she said.

"Shall we return? I have much to do."

Alexeika frowned. Although it seemed she had won the argument, it felt like no victory, for clearly he intended to punish her with this cold petulance. *Let him sulk*, she thought angrily. *He knows he is wrong, but will not admit it.*

Tossing her head, she asked, "When do you depart?"

"We'll break camp at dawn," he replied grimly. "I've dispatched messages to the forces stationed at Bralstok. They'll join me at the border."

She frowned. "I knew there was something you weren't telling me! It *is* war, isn't it? Why else do you need extra troops plus the Agyas with us?"

"Nay, wife," he snapped. "I'm not taking the Agyas. You'll need them for protection."

"But—"

"We'll journey together as far as Tlesk; then I'll turn south and join my other forces. That way you'll have plenty of protection, and I'll see you well away from Grethori country."

"The camp can defend itself," she said crisply. "Why saddle yourself with unnecessary delays? We'll be half of tomorrow getting started, and we can make no time at all with the wagons. Clearly your majesty is eager to get to Thirst as quickly as possible."

Faldain said nothing. Looking up, she caught him staring out at the fjord with a mixture of worry and impatience on his face.

"The sooner you ride to Thirst and deal with what must be done, the sooner you can return to Grov," she said. "Take your Agyas and depart at dawn. I'll cope with all that has to be done here."

"Alexeika, forever practical and brave."

"Don't mock me!" she said furiously. "If you persist in seeing Thirst as more important than your other responsibilities, then who am I to stand in your way? Go there, and see to your hold. Leave now, this afternoon."

"I'll wait until dawn, and we'll break camp together."

Matching his coldness, she glared at him. "Why waste your time? Do you think I am incapable of guiding us back to Grov?"

His gaze narrowed. "Very well, since my lady is eager to see me go."

"Yes, go!" she shouted, stamping her foot. "Begone on this errand you find so compelling. Perhaps if you're quick enough you can be back in Grov within a few weeks of us."

"I hope so." He hesitated and seemed about to say something else, but then he compressed his mouth and turned away, striding to the edge of the cliff and making his way down the trail without her.

It took her a moment to realize that he was indeed going, without even a word of farewell.

Aghast, she hurried after him, nearly stumbling as she followed him down the steep trail. At the bottom, he turned to her and held out his hand in silence. She took it, out of breath and afraid, and gripped his fingers tightly.

Do not go, she thought frantically. *Do not listen to me. Do not believe all that I have said.* But she could not bring herself to speak.

His hand held hers as a stranger might; then he released

her fingers and stepped back with a curt bow. "Until Grov, my lady," he said and was gone.

She watched him borne away across the fjord while the skies grew darker and rain began to fall. Feeling blind and stiff, she eventually picked up her gown and put it on over her wet tunic and leggings, fastening the brooch with fingers that fumbled and trembled. As Sir Pyron untied the rope and climbed into the skiff behind her, she picked up her paddle so clumsily she nearly dropped it. Somehow, she turned them about and headed for shore through the cold, driving rain.

It seemed a very long way to shore, and her bewilderment would not leave her. How had everything gone wrong so quickly? She was sensible to keep Ilymir safe with her, no matter how much it angered Faldain, and yet their son wasn't really the issue between them. What had they really been fighting about? She did not know. She could not guess.

Suddenly determined that he should not leave this way, she paddled to shore as fast as she could through the slanting rain. She would share her good news by way of an apology, she decided, gathering her wet, cumbersome skirts and struggling up the muddy bank. He would not ride away without something good to cheer him.

But when she reached the royal tent, the king's burgundy-and-gold pennon had been struck, indicating his departure. Her flag flew in its stead, bedraggled in the downpour, and alone.

Chapter Six

Strangled with fury, Prince Jonan stepped back to allow a cluster of highborn ladies to precede him inside the palace. Most of them ignored him; a few shot him sideways glances and tittered behind their fingers. He stood as though frozen, his gaze focused beyond them, his big hands clenched at his sides and the collar of his tunic feeling a size too small. Twilight was falling across the terrace of the palace, driving the courtiers indoors. He edged back into the shadows, while more people passed him.

Archduke Vladno Krelinik, handsome, young, and resplendent in a sapphire blue tunic edged with bands of silver embroidery, appeared before Jonan. He produced a contemptuous little smile, teeth gleaming beneath a dark mustache. "Please, your highness," he said, making the tiniest sketch of a bow, "by rights you should precede me."

Fresh humiliation surged into Jonan's cheeks, setting them afire. He glared at the archduke, loathing him for what he'd said a few minutes ago in front of everyone, and resenting him for his mockery now. "No!" he said. "Go away and leave me be." His voice came out too forcefully and loud, causing other people to look in his direction.

Vladno's smile widened in deep satisfaction. Jonan realized that everything he did or said gave the archduke more opportunities to turn him into a fool, but he did not know how to extricate himself.

"I assure your highness that protocol dictates a person of your rank must go in before a person of mine," the archduke was saying smoothly. The men around him exchanged glances and smirked.

Jonan scowled, struggling to find the words he needed. "I understand protocol, Vladno," he said sullenly. "I d-don't want to go in yet."

"The queen has retired," Vladno said. "We're going to play live draughts, and I want your highness as one of my knights."

Someone laughed out loud, and Jonan's temples began to pound hard as though they might explode. The one previous time he'd joined the game, feeling thrilled by the invitation, he'd found himself hopelessly entangled as a playing piece, confused by Vladno's directions, and subjected to the unkind laughter of the courtiers as he blundered about. On that occasion, someone had even shouted, "'Tis as close to knighthood as your highness will ever come!"

"No, thank you," Jonan now said stiffly. "I do not care to play."

"Oh? It's not very difficult, providing you do as you're told. Of course, I realize that your highness cannot always do that. Such a pity."

Anger surged to the top of Jonan's head. Unable to stand his ground any longer, he whirled away and hurried down the terrace steps into the darkness. Vladno's laughter rang out heartily, joined by that of his friends. Jonan quickened his pace, stumbled on the bottom step, and nearly fell.

A palace guard in a cerise-blue cloak and cap grabbed his arm to steady him. Jonan jerked free and glanced over his shoulder. Yes, Vladno was still standing at the top of the steps, staring down at him. Obviously he'd seen the stumble, for he gave Jonan a jaunty wave and grinned.

Jonan turned and fled through a gap in the hedge. Twigs

caught the sleeves and hem of his tunic, snagging him until he managed to break free.

Behind him floated fresh laughter. "Thod, what a fool," sputtered Count Oselinov. "Thrashing in the shrubbery instead of taking the path."

"Their majesties need not waste good coin hiring fools and acrobats while we have such natural talent already in the palace," jeered Lord Pertok.

Vladno's rich laugh rang out at these sallies, and Jonan closed his ears to the rest. He plunged into the darkness beyond the torchlight lining the garden paths and ran through the night as fast as his long, clumsy legs would take him, ran heedless of flower beds and the artful undulation of the land until at last he tripped and pitched headlong into the dirt.

He lay there a long time, gripping grass in both hands, weeping in silent misery. He hated Vladno Krelinik, hated the whole court. They mocked him openly because the king was absent, but even when Faldain was in residence they found ways to torment Jonan. It had been the same since he was a young boy and released from the dungeons to live in the king's household. Someone had always found the means to hiss insults at him or corner him and torment him until he cried.

I'm too old to cry now, he thought, still sniveling. He sat up, aching all over, and tried to wipe the tears and snot from his face with his sleeve. His birthday had come and gone, celebrated grandly by the queen's order. Everyone had feasted, hailed him with toasts, and given him presents. It meant, he knew, that he was officially a man, ready for a man's life. But the boys who in past years had surrounded Jonan and taunted him for being "traitor-spawn" were now grown men, too, and they still tormented him with mockery and contempt. He knew, with a weariness reaching to the bottom of his soul, that the taunts, insults, and jeers would never stop. He would always be blamed for the evil actions his father had committed.

King Muncel had stripped many nobles of their estates and wealth. He'd executed those defiant to him and exiled others. His had been a reign of terror, blood-soaked and cruel, and Faldain had killed him in battle. Faldain could have ordered

Jonan's execution, although he was but ten years old at the time, but his cousin had been merciful. Sometimes, like tonight, Jonan almost wished Faldain had not spared him.

He could not go on living like this. No one understood how miserable he was, or how much he hated living at court. Or, perhaps, no one cared.

When he was younger, Jonan used to pray to Thod to grow up valiant and strong like Faldain, but Thod had not granted his prayers. He was nothing but a useless, clumsy fool, too stupid to be a scholar and unfit for a warrior's life. He half wished Faldain would send him away into exile. It sounded exciting and dramatic, like a story sung by minstrels. But another part of Jonan feared the idea, for he thought he might die of loneliness. Of course, he'd come to understand that it was possible to feel lonely in the midst of people as well. Especially when they were cruel and unkind. Sometimes he overheard the king's advisers talking about him. Jonan knew the Privy Council had asked the king to exile him, and the king had refused.

Faldain's kindness warmed Jonan's heart, for it seemed only Faldain and Alexeika cared anything at all about him. Yet Jonan was beginning to suspect that tolerance was not the same thing as genuine affection. What had he and Faldain in common save blood kinship, and that tie weaker than most? Jonan was well aware that he lived on Faldain's mercy. What if someday Faldain turned against him? What if Jonan's enemies fed their lies and whispers into the ear of the king and hardened his heart toward his cousin?

"One day he'll cast you back into the dungeons where you belong," the boys used to taunt Jonan. *"You'll live down there, rotting and festering until the beetles eat your flesh and the rats feast on your bones."*

It could still happen, Jonan thought with a sigh. If he ever offended Faldain and lost his cousin's patience, down he would go into the pit. He'd never forgotten how bleak and miserable it was in the cell he shared with his mother. She'd raged and paced incessantly, cursing Faldain and Muncel alike. No comfort had she offered Jonan, lying sick and coughing on his straw, his chest feeling as though a rock crushed it there in that damp, filthy hole. And eventually the guards had taken her out, lashing her wrists with ropes while she uttered terrible curses and said things so vile it made Jonan cry to hear her. They'd put a hood of black cloth over her head, and only then had she fallen silent. He'd known that they were going to kill her, and for a shameful, horrifying little moment he'd been glad. But when they led her out, fear had overcome him, and he'd thrown himself at the door, grasping the bars and calling out her name. She'd gone forth without a word of farewell to her only son. At that moment he understood that she loved no one but herself, and he'd meant nothing to her at all.

A few days later, he'd been released, washed, and taken before the king. Faldain had spoken kindly to him and promised him a place in his household forevermore.

Still, the king's promises aside, it was increasingly clear to Jonan that he had no real position here in the palace. He never would. When he was a child, he'd been grateful for the king's benevolence, but gratitude wore thin as a steady diet. Gratitude at the cost of belittling persecution from certain courtiers and grave disapproval from others was growing impossible to endure. He'd tried smoking tyneweed as an escape. It made him groggy, dreamy, and thirsty, did not really take away his troubles, and sometimes afflicted him with fearsome dreams. So he knew that tyneweed wasn't the answer for him either.

Perhaps he should simply run away, just get out and live on his own, casting off rank and privilege to become a simple wanderer. There were minstrel songs about that sort of thing, too, but he suspected he might get very hungry prowling about with no one to prepare his meals.

From the distance came the deep voices of boatmen lifted in song. Distracted momentarily from his troubled thoughts, Jonan scrambled to his feet and peered over the garden wall in hopes of catching a glimpse of them.

The stone wall reached only about waist high at this point, and from its base a stone cliff dropped straight and sheer into the Velga River far below. A full moon was rising into the sky, its soft light glittering on the silver ribbon of river winding along the foot of the cliffs. The old city sprawled across the valley, quiescent at this hour save for the cadenced tramping of city patrols and an occasional barking dog.

From inside the palace, the strains of lively zithren music heralded the start of dancing. For a moment the tune clashed with the singing of the boatmen. Jonan scowled, hunching his shoulders in annoyance. There was always something interfering with what he wanted to do. He leaned farther over the wall, bracing himself with his hands, and stared down at the barge floating by.

Aye, he liked the thought of running away. Perhaps he could join a guild of boatmen or merchant traders. He could travel hither and yon, seeing the world. There'd be no courtiers to sneer at him or resent him for things he'd had no part in. There'd be no sense of obligation or gratitude. There'd be no one to answer to.

Tipping back his head, he closed his eyes and inhaled deeply, drawing in scents of this fine, late-summer night. The air was fragrant from tiny white flowers unfurling their petals at dusk. They would go on perfuming the grounds each evening until the first frost killed them.

"Are you going to jump to your death?"

The voice, coming from nowhere, startled Jonan so much he nearly lost his balance. Shoving himself back from the low wall, his heart thudding against his ribs, he turned around and groped for the hilt of his dagger. "Who's there?" he asked, his voice weak with fright. "Show yourself!"

A maid stepped from the shadows beneath the nearby decorative trees and walked daintily into the moonlight with her gown hem held up off the grass. Jonan stared at her with alarm. He had no idea of who she was. Her face was a pale blur to him. He could hear the rustlings of her gown, and as she drew near the breeze drifted a whiff of her musky perfume to his nostrils.

Dismay swept him. He tried to slap some of the dirt from his tunic although if she'd been hiding there all this time, she'd undoubtedly seen him fall down and cry like a child. Angrily he drew his dagger.

She halted at once. "What kind of ruffian are you, to brandish your weapon at a defenseless woman? Truly I am no foe."

"If you laugh at me, I'll hit you," he said in a low, fierce voice.

"Hit me? But I've done nothing against you. I was only enjoying a peaceful stroll through this lovely garden when you tried to throw yourself over the wall." She tossed her head and partially turned away from him. "Go ahead and kill yourself, since you're so churlish. I care not!"

Jonan frowned at the dagger in his hand and slowly slid it back into its sheath. When he glanced back at her, she turned and started to walk away.

"Wait!" he called out.

Ignoring him, she kept walking. Impulsively he hurried after her and caught her by the shoulder.

With a gasp she whipped around, ducking out of his grasp and retreating a safe distance from him. "Who gave you leave to paw me? I'm no strumpet for your mauling!"

Shame flashed through him. Stepping back, he lifted both hands to placate her. "Please, no! I—I didn't mean to—that is, don't be angry. I mean you no harm."

"Then keep your distance."

Her arrogant tone reminded him of the way little Tashalya ordered him around. Meekly he backed up yet another step. "I beg your pardon," he said, finally recalling his courtly manners. "I only wanted—that is, I didn't mean—well, I just thought I'd tell you that I wasn't—"

"Yes?"

"I wasn't jumping!" he said, with a flush of new embarrassment. "I was listening."

"To what?"

"The boatmen's songs."

"What are those?"

"Come and listen."

She hesitated, staring at him.

Jonan extended his hand. "Come and listen. By the wall."

As he backed away from her, she came forward. They stood leaning against the low wall, staring at each other in the moonlight. "If you can close your ears to the zithrens inside the palace, you'll hear the singing down there on the river. Hush!" he said swiftly, as she started to speak. "Another barge is coming. Listen!"

In silence they gazed down. The harmonies drifted on the air, rising and falling as the men plied their poles to the rhythm of their singing.

When the music faded away, Jonan found himself staring at the girl and wondering who she was. Her pale hair was braided in a coronet around her head and allowed to fall onto her right shoulder in one loose, fat curl. According to court fashion her hair was supposed to be veiled. Instead, she wore some filmy scrap of cloth pinned to the back of her hair that fluttered behind her in the breeze but covered nothing. Petite, but well and generously curved, she came only to his shoulder. He wished he could see her face more clearly, but he dared not step closer. Her perfume seemed to cloud his mind, confusing him every time he inhaled it.

"Did you like it?" he asked finally.

"The singing? Yes. Peasant songs can be appealing on a night like this. What is your name?"

Surprised that she hadn't recognized him, he felt a rush of delight and relief. She was talking to him because she *wished* to, not because of who he was. In his excitement, he stepped closer to her, but then remembered to keep his distance.

"I—I'd rather know yours," he answered.

She laughed, but there was only amusement instead of jeering mockery in the sound. "What gallantry! I was warned to beware of you fine courtiers and your polished flirtations. Are all the lords of the court as forward as you?"

Her admiration made his chest swell. Although clearly she was new to court, the idea of her thinking him polished and sophisticated made Jonan feel strangely grown-up.

"'Tis not flirting to seek a sweet lady's name," he said. "Please, will you not give it?"

"I dare not," she replied. "My father would be furious if he knew I'd slipped out and was strolling the gardens alone without my handmaid Bethina, much less talking to a courtier."

"What is your father's name?" Jonan asked.

She laughed and shook a finger at him. "You are sly and devious, trying to trick me."

"Nay! How are we to be introduced if you won't tell me who you are?"

"We can't be introduced," she replied. "Father must be accepted at court before I can be presented to her majesty. He says it could take weeks to get an audience."

"We have but recently returned to Grov," Jonan said in puzzlement. "Did he ride in our company?"

"Oh, no. He dared not seek the king's audience so forwardly." She sighed. "We have been waiting here most of the summer in terrible heat and misery, and still the king is gone, so we must wait longer."

"I'm sorry my—I'm sorry the king is away," Jonan said, realizing he'd nearly given himself away. "What does your father do?"

"Oh, he's very important. At least he is in Myrot. Oh, dear! I shouldn't have told you that."

"I know nothing about Myrot," Jonan said. "Is it far away?"

"Yes. I was so excited when my father brought me here with him. I've never traveled anywhere before."

"Has your father much land that he tills?"

"Of course he doesn't till it!" she said sharply. "He has serfs to do the work."

"Then he must be a count."

"Yes, Soblinsk," she said, and clapped her hands over her mouth.

Feeling rather clever, Jonan began to chuckle. "Count Soblinsk. And now I know who you are. Or almost. Please tell me your name."

"You are full of trickery, and you've learned enough. But please keep my secret, and do not betray me when officially we meet."

"When will that be?"

"I don't know. I told you. Perhaps the king means to hold Father's past against him always, although his majesty has given favor to other men who were much more—well, I am not supposed to talk of such matters." She sighed. "I get tired of being cooped up all day with my companion. Bethina's old and already asleep for the evening, but it's too early to sleep. I love it out here. Don't you?"

"The gardens are pretty at night," Jonan agreed. "I think you are probably pretty, too, if I could see you better."

Her head snapped up, like a startled doe's. "Well, you can't. You mustn't. If Father finds out I slipped out or that I've been talking to you like this, he'll punish me."

"Oh, no," Jonan said involuntarily. "I don't want you to get into trouble."

"Jonan!" Prince Tustik's voice called out across the garden. "Jonan, come indoors!"

Irritation swept Jonan. Why couldn't the old lizard leave him be? It seemed of late that everywhere he turned, there stood Prince Tustik, watching him with fierce black eyes. Now his identity was revealed, and this wonderful girl would laugh at him unkindly like all the others.

She was staring at him. "Are you Jonan?" she asked softly. "Prince Jonan?"

He was tempted to lie, but what good would it do? "Aye. I am."

She sank to a deep curtsy before him. "Oh, your highness! What an honor! I had no idea. I beg your most gracious pardon for having shouted at you. Please forgive me if I have offended you in any way."

Astounded, Jonan could only stare at her. "What?"

She remained in obeisance at his feet. He could not help but notice that she'd given him the deep curtsy reserved for the king, but her error was charming. No one had ever shown him such respect before.

"Please rise," he said, "You have no need to beg my pardon."

"But I—"

"Please." He extended his hand, and, after a moment's hesitation, she put hers within his grasp. How slender and delicate her fingers felt. He found his heart beating absurdly fast, and his breathing was all tangled up.

She rose to her feet and stood gazing up at him with a smile on her face. Somehow the careful distance she'd been keeping between them had vanished. He could see her eyes now, shining in the starlight.

"'Tis the king you curtsy to like that," he told her gently. "Not someone like me."

"But *you* are the rightful—"

"No," he said firmly, cutting her off. "I'm not. It's forbidden for you to say such things."

"I'm sorry. I was always told—"

"My cousin is king. He's a very good king, and he treats me well. When you are presented to him one day, you'll see for yourself."

"I suppose so," she said. "I'd better go back now before Father finds out I'm gone."

"May I escort you?" Jonan asked.

She hesitated before giving him a shy little nod. It made him want to sing.

Instead, he tucked her hand inside the crook of his arm and carefully began to stroll along one of the paths with her. She had not yet said, but he supposed she was staying in the guest pavilion, a separate facility standing on the grounds a little apart from the main palace. Many visitors from other lands resided there while waiting to be received by the king.

He helped her avoid the guards patrolling the grounds, and eventually they found themselves before a dark window on the north side of the pavilion. The lights shining from some of the palace windows did not reach that far, and the moonlight overhead was blocked by a tree's spreading canopy. The darkness folded around them as he wished he could fold his arms around her. Such notions alarmed him, yet they were exhilarating, too.

She started to reach for the window latch, but Jonan gripped her hand tighter to make her wait.

"Will I see you again?" he whispered.

"I do not know. I cannot say, your highness."

"Promise!"

"But I—"

"Promise, or I won't let you go in."

She giggled, then muffled the sound behind her hand. "All

right. Tomorrow night, if I can get away. At the wall, where we met this eve."

He bowed over her hand, wanting to kiss her dainty fingertips but not quite daring to. "And you'll tell me your given name?"

"I can't without formal introduction, your highness. You tease me too much."

"Please?"

"No."

But he heard pleasure in her refusal, a little trill in her voice that encouraged him to forget his terrible shyness a little. "And if I command you to tell me?" he whispered.

She pulled her hand away, and, reluctantly, he let her go. Pushing open the window, she started to step inside, then abruptly turned back and leaned close to his ear. "Sofina," she whispered, her breath warm on his skin. "Lady Sofina Soblinsk. Good night, my prince."

And she was gone.

He stood there a long while, awash in confusion and delight. It seemed amazing that an evening that had begun so ill could end so pleasantly. He smiled to himself as he slipped stealthily away from the pavilion and headed across the grounds toward the palace.

He thought, although it was too soon to be sure as yet, but he thought he'd made a friend. It was a thrilling notion that spread a curious feeling of warmth and security through his heart. A real friend, someone who liked him for himself, someone who did not jest at his expense, someone who did not mock him. Well, tomorrow night if she met him as she'd promised, he'd know for certain. *Lady Sofina*, he thought with a little smile. He couldn't wait to talk to her again.

It felt strange and different to have something to look forward to. *Please, Thod, let her friendship be real*, he prayed. *Let it not be just another trick Vladno is playing on me.* He warned himself to be cautious, to not dare to believe too much just yet.

But all the same, as he slipped into his quarters, he found himself humming beneath his breath. No longer did he want to run away, for he was happy.

Chapter Seven

Smothering a yawn, Alexeika left the brightly painted chamber where at last her children lay sleeping, snug in their wooden beds. It had been a long day of small, domestic crises and queenly duties, and tonight the children—wildly excited about the garden party planned for tomorrow—would not settle down. Ilymir didn't want a bath. Tashalya, who'd been suffering bad dreams, was afraid to go to sleep but, instead of admitting it, threw a tantrum that caused all the draperies and bedclothes to billow violently and sent one of the junior nursemaids running out, screaming. Mareitina wanted to be told a story. Alexeika believed she would almost rather fight a hurlhound than try to cope with such imps as hers. But at last they grew quiet, and as she stroked their hair and told them stories about their grandfather the general, their eyes grew heavy and their breathing soft.

Straightening her aching back, she tucked a strand of loosened hair behind her ear. How sweet and innocent they looked under the glow of lamplight. Her heart melted with tenderness as she watched them for a few minutes.

She could not help but marvel at the miracle of Ilymir, her

boy-child. Still young enough to shower her with kisses and bring her flowers—although sometimes without their blossoms attached—his cheeks were starting to lose their baby roundness. His hair shone like spun gold on the pillow. He smelled of wild grass, soap, and little boy. She touched her lips ever so gently to his brow and turned to Mareitina. Her youngest child's bed was leafed out where sprouts had grown from the wood posts and panels. Even in sleep, Mareitina twitched and hummed softly beneath her breath. Her golden curls stirred gently as though a breeze blew through them.

"My eldin child," Alexeika whispered, and brushed her fingertip lightly over the pointed tip of her daughter's ear. Mareitina mumbled in her sleep and turned over.

The nursemaid reached out to smooth the covers, and Alexeika went to Tashalya, sleeping with arms and legs sprawled everywhere. Her elder daughter was nearly too big for the bed painted a charming shade of yellow, with roses carved into the panels. Soon Tashalya would be old enough to have her own chamber separate from the others. Alexeika gazed down at her, this willful and most difficult of her children, and wondered where Tashalya's little spirit would walk tonight in her sleep. *Please guard her slumber, gentle Riva*, Alexeika prayed silently, *and let her not wake this wing of the palace with her screams and night fears*. Tashalya was proving to be as poor a sleeper as her father. Alexeika desperately longed for a night of sound, unbroken sleep, and smothered another yawn.

"They are well, majesty," the nursemaid whispered, anxious to please. "See? They are all fast asleep now."

Alexeika smiled, yet something made her linger. As she gazed around the chamber, nothing looked amiss or out of place. Toys were tidied in the cupboard. The tall window had been shut, and the salt crystals sprinkled across the sill glittered in the moonlight.

She did not want to leave them. Why she could not say, but she was suddenly certain that she should spend tonight in their company. Turning around, she opened her mouth to give the necessary instructions, only to find Sir Pyron right behind her. She hadn't heard his approach at all, and she flinched.

"Pardon, majesty," he said in a hoarse whisper, "but it's time you were going."

Thus reminded that yet another meeting awaited her, one she'd completely forgotten about, she frowned in annoyance. "Thod blight all meetings!" she blurted out before she could hold her tongue. "I'll not be told what I—but, nay, sir, you are right." She sighed. "I must attend it."

Nodding acknowledgment to the protector on duty, speaking a courteous word to the nursemaids curtsying to her, she stepped out into the passageway and headed for her apartments.

She hoped the meeting would bring her news of Faldain. Nothing, since they parted in anger that day, had she heard from him, and the continued silence distressed her more than she wanted to admit. It was unlike Faldain to hold a grudge, especially after she had conquered her pride and sent a written apology by messenger to him. Although he disliked writing, for the Netheran language had proven difficult for him to master—and his lacking in what should have been his native language embarrassed him greatly—it was his custom to include private notes to her in his dispatches whenever they were parted. She loved receiving his missives, so carefully penned in schoolboy letters. Well aware of how hard he must have labored over them, she saved them all in a small chest of fragrant, carved wood. But this time, there'd been nothing. That he could be so cold and unyielding over so trivial an issue hurt her deeply; she'd not believed him capable of such behavior. She felt as though she was being punished, and that was unfair, for she'd only done what she felt to be right. She did not understand why he would not forgive her, he with a heart so generous he had pardoned more men than he should have at court.

A little spark of resentment rekindled inside her. She wished she *had* let him take Ilymir. It would have served him right to cope with a small boy inclined to grow more excited than was good for him. She wished she could see him coaxing Ilymir to eat at a campfire in the middle of nowhere, when the child currently refused to eat meat or any green-colored vegetables. And if the separate items on his trencher touched each other, he would not eat any of it. *Aye, husband*, Alexeika thought grimly, *next time I shall let you have a taste of managing your son. It will do you good.*

She quickened her step along the crimson carpet lining the passageway. Two of her ladies-in-waiting followed her, their gowns rustling softly. Sir Pyron, who'd paused to murmur something to the guards on duty at the nursery door, caught up with Alexeika.

She glanced at him with a lift of her brows. "A problem, sir?"

"Nay. Just giving yon men reminder that patrol guard roster changes at dawn tomorrow. For the month to come, it's auxiliaries on duty."

Fresh annoyance pricked Alexeika. She'd protested against the auxiliary troops to no avail. Last year, Faldain had yielded to the pressure of the Privy Council and agreed to utilize some of the so-called civilized Grethori tribes for guard and patrol duty. Although all had gone smoothly thus far, she could not cast aside her low opinion of the tribesmen, for she would never forget how she'd been treated as a captive. She did not trust them and never would. Worse, it was one thing to employ those painted savages to supplement dwindling numbers of the army in the farthest provinces, but to allow them within the very grounds of the palace—to trust them so far—the very notion made her teeth grind together.

"'Tis madness," she said, quickening her pace. "The very height of folly. Pyron, must we have them within the palace walls while the king is away?"

Her protector shot her a look beneath rust-colored brows and grunted. "Am I to send for the guard captain?"

She knew what that meant. Protests and questions and delays. Life here in the palace moved according to strict routines. Change was regarded with suspicion and doubt. She knew very well that the guard captain was related to Archduke Fyliks Minshilev, one of her strongest critics and, she suspected, a member of the powerful Kollegya. The guard captain might come and listen to her demands to keep the roster free of Grethori guards, but he would take no action. As a queen consort without true sovereignty, her will alone was not enough to command him on a matter as important as palace security.

As these thoughts flashed through her mind, she glared at the impassive Pyron, and said quite distinctly, "Thod damne your impudence, sir."

"No doubt he will one day," her protector answered with a grin.

Clustered outside her door were beautifully dressed men and women waiting officially to bid her good slumber. In reality they were there to slip her private petitions penned on elegant pieces of parchment. The requests ranged from the most trivial matters to rather urgent pleas. It was an archaic custom; she was expected to select the worthier petitions and ask the king to lay them before the Chalice of Eternal Life at the next service.

Alexeika kept her features expressionless as she walked past the supplicants.

"Majesty . . . blessed queen . . . gracious lady . . ."

As they murmured, they held out the tiny curls of parchment. Alexeika never slackened her pace. One of her pages collected the petitions while lackeys opened her door for her. In she swept past her guards on duty, to find her receiving chamber well lit with oil lamps. More ladies awaited her, but so did Lord Thum and Prince Tustik.

Both men turned and bowed to her. Alexeika smiled at them to mask her weariness. For now, after her long day of inconsequential duties appropriate for the queen, she must meet with these two men closest to the king in order to govern a little behind the scenes. Few of her officious courtiers knew that in Faldain's absence it was Alexeika making some of the decisions. She had Thum to thank for that.

The day that Faldain had left and she'd tried unsuccessfully to catch up with him before his departure, she'd entered her private chamber in the tent dejectedly, only to find an Agya warrior kneeling there on the carpet with a box, tied, corded, and heavily sealed, in his hands. Dismissing the man, she'd opened the box and found Faldain's royal seal inside it. Angry with her or not, he'd entrusted her with the entire kingdom. She could write any order and affix the seal beneath it to make it law. The very magnitude of possessing the seal awed and terrified her at the same time. Faldain could not have honored her more with that gesture of implicit trust. Although she'd betrayed him once, long ago, in keeping the Ring of Solder hidden from him, she would never betray him again, and well he knew it.

For a long time that night she'd held the box, weeping for the man she loved so much, and now she guarded the seal with her life. At present it was locked away in a secret vault in her bedchamber, and she believed not even Thum and Tustik knew she had it.

Greeting the men, she seated herself and allowed an attendant to place a small footstool beneath her feet. Although late, the evening remained warm, and her slippers were pinching so tightly she longed to kick them off. The page brought the petitions to her, but she ordered them sent to Priest Dazkin and dismissed him.

The absurd little dog her children had given her last Aelintide came frisking up to paw at her skirts. One of her ladies handed the animal to Alexeika. He licked her face, then settled himself importantly on her lap, shivering happily as she caressed his floppy ears.

"I regret the hour has grown so late," she said to her visitors, while her ladies-in-waiting curtsied to her and departed. A servant brought wine. Thum accepted a cup with pleasure, but Tustik looked pinched of expression as though he'd grown impatient at being kept waiting. She forced herself to smile at him. "The children took longer than expected."

"Perhaps children's needs are smaller than the realm's at this time," the old man muttered, but then seemed to collect himself and bowed to her with a frown of apology. "Forgive me, majesty. It is so many years since my children were young that I have perhaps—er—lost the patience I should have."

Raising her brows, she made no answer.

Thum gave her his gentle smile. "We shall try to be brief."

"Thank you, Lord Thum," she replied formally, but her smile met his with the warmth of old friendship. "The days grow ever longer, it seems."

"Yet not enough gets done," Tustik said testily. "Let us begin, your majesty—"

He was interrupted by the arrival of Sir Pyron's relief. With a quick bow, her protector relinquished her safety to an equally grizzled and battle-scarred warrior named Sir Wulim. Tall and broad-shouldered, with a nose flattened from too many breaks and iron gray hair that curled around his ears, Wulim bowed to the queen and took a position quietly near the fire.

She spared him no more than a glance before returning her attention to Tustik. Clearly he had news of some import. "Do you bring me news of the king?" she asked eagerly. "Has a courier come from him this day? Is he safely arrived at Thirst?"

The prince sighed and glanced at Thum. The younger man's hazel eyes met hers with nothing beyond their usual gravity. Still tall and thin, Thum had kept his boyish freckles, but his red hair and neatly trimmed beard had darkened over the years to auburn. He wore a long tunic of rich forest green and the fine gold chain of his office. In one hand he held a scroll. The other rested casually on his belt.

"No news of the king today, majesty," he replied, his Mandrian accent crisp. "I confess, it does worry me a little, for 'tis unlike him not to relay frequent word. Since he left Bralstok for upper Mandria, however, I'm sure he's been busy."

"Or he's fallen into a trap," she said.

"He's too wily to be caught," Thum assured her. "No better warrior lives."

"Aye," she agreed. "What then, my lord?"

Thum held up the scroll. "News of some import."

"Good or bad?"

"Troubling. We intercepted a Mandrian dispatch that proves what I've suspected. Klad's raids into lowland Mandria have provoked war at last."

"Morde!" she said in annoyance. "Skirmishes only, or declared war?"

He pointed grimly at the Mandrian royal seal at the bottom of the document. "Declared by Queen Pheresa herself. This is merely an announcement, sent by dispatch to all her lowland holds. Specific orders are to follow. I don't know whether my men can intercept any of those."

Speculation whirled through Alexeika's head, but she forced herself to concentrate. "What does this mean for Nether? Can we be drawn into this conflict?"

"Not unless Pheresa calls on us for aid." Thum's mouth puckered wryly. "Somehow I doubt she'll do so."

Alexeika nodded her understanding. There was no need for Thum to refer more openly to the last time Pheresa had called on Nether for help. In the third year of Faldain's reign, a time when he was sorely beset by a Grethori uprising and a failed coup within the palace, Pheresa had insisted that he give her Netheran troops to wage civil war on her husband's forces. Fortunately, Faldain had been too wise to commit Nether to what could have become a bloody civil war in Mandria. Much to Alexeika's relief, he'd resisted the beautiful queen's lures and enticements and come home swiftly where he belonged. But Pheresa had not forgiven what she considered a breach of their treaty. In the years since, she'd been decidedly prickly.

"How many Kladite chieftains have united to wage this war?" Alexeika asked.

"As usual your majesty grasps the essential question," Thum said. "That information is something we are trying to discover, and quickly."

"Do any of these chieftains control our trade routes?" Alexeika put in. "Will our trade be jeopardized?"

"It depends on how far the conflict spreads. If Mandria sends an army into Klad, we know we're likely to be cut off from Kan Tang."

She drew in a sharp breath. "No! We need Tang. He is our best supplier of horses."

"Netheran herds are being rebuilt, your majesty," Tustik said in assurance. "Improvements in breeding stock mean that we need not remain as dependent on Klad animals as we were previously."

"Of course," she said impatiently. "But we are not yet where I want us to be. The army remains in critical need of good horseflesh, and thus far demand continues to exceed supply." Frowning, she turned her attention back to Thum. "What will war mean to our timber business?"

"I will be meeting with the guildsmen tomorrow," Thum replied. "We've had trouble enough convincing the Kladites to build settlements. This could well collapse the market."

"That leaves Saelutia to buy our timber," she said worriedly. "A ready market, but with less profit to it. Damne! How am I to replenish our treasury when our trade suffers this way?"

"We still have our fur markets in upland Mandria and Nold."

"Aye, of course, Lord Thum, but that could be jeopardized, too, when Mandria's gold is spent on weapons instead of luxuries." She drummed her fingers on the arm of her chair. "We need five more good years, and I think our economy will be strong enough to withstand such problems. Nether has such vast resources . . . it's absurd for us to be importing anything. What about the food and wool we receive from Mandria?"

"Again," Thum said, "as long as the conflict does not spread into upland Mandria, we should see few problems. Unless trade is suspended by royal edict."

Alexeika caught on immediately. "You mean, unless Mandria learns we are trading with Klad."

Thum nodded. "By treaty we are allies with Mandria, not with Klad."

"By treaty, your majesty," Tustik said, "we should suspend all trade with Klad immediately to indicate our support and good wishes toward Mandria."

Alexeika thought of the stalwart Kladite horses in the army stables. Tireless, spirited, fleet of foot . . . they were excellent replacements for the spindly nags used previously. Some of Nether's best horse bloodlines had died out during the bad years. Determined to compensate for that loss, Alexeika knew that a strong army needed strong horses just as much as a strong kingdom needed a strong army. She frowned at Tustik. "Supportive of our ally or not, we can't afford to cut off our supply of horses."

"But, your majesty—"

She held up her hand. "I do understand our obligations toward Queen Pheresa," she said. "But Nether must take care of its needs first. We will continue to trade with Klad as long as possible."

"We do not want to offend Mandria at this time."

"We never risk offending Mandria," Alexeika said with a quick shrug. "Faldain is forever giving Pheresa conciliations when he should be stronger. But what Mandria does not know need not offend her."

Tustik cleared his throat. "Er, perhaps, majesty, with the king presently *in* Mandria, we should tread as lightly as possible."

"Of course," Alexeika agreed. "But she's a warmonger, this queen. First she sought a civil war, then war with the sea raiders. Now she goes against Klad."

"Her father was a marechal of the realm. No doubt it's in her blood."

"*My* father was also a great general," Alexeika said with a quick flare of temper. "You do not see me sending armies into battle at the least provocation."

Thum's face had grown stiff during her remarks. Now he said coldly, "Queen Pheresa is a woman ruling alone. For that reason, her realm is a target for any aggressor barbarian who thinks her weak. Would your majesty have her give way to her enemies?"

"I see your allegiance remains in the south," Alexeika retorted.

A tide of red surged up Thum's neck. "I serve Nether. The king does not doubt my loyalty, your majesty. Why should you?"

A glance at Prince Tustik's horrified face cooled Alexeika's temper. Realizing she'd allowed her jealousy against Pheresa to offend Thum, her husband's best friend and ablest ally, she lifted her hands swiftly in appeal.

"Nay, my lord," she said, with a sigh. "I doubt you not at all, nor will I ever. Faldain has no better friend than you. Forgive me for my rash tongue."

The wrath subsided from his countenance, but his hazel eyes were not fully appeased. "The queen is gracious to give me an apology. It is, of course, accepted."

Alexeika nodded and leaned back in her chair, but inside she was raging at her own stupidity. Would she never learn to govern her temper? Pheresa was a weakness, and she'd exposed that vulnerability to both these men. Aye, she trusted them because Faldain did, but more importantly, did they trust *her*? They granted her great honor by consulting with her this way in secret, but she must perform her duties more ably than this if she was to keep them on her side. The swiftest way to lose their respect was by acting like a fool. And since she had plenty of enemies already at court, she could ill afford to lose the best allies she had.

Her head ached, and she felt desperately tired. The baby, she thought, wishing she could rub her pounding temples. Already it was starting to pull down her strength, quicker than her other pregnancies had done. *Please, little one*, she thought. *I need all my energy until your father comes home*.

Meanwhile, the silence was growing uncomfortably long in the room. Alexeika sighed, aware that she must further rectify her mistake without delay. Her father had taught her long ago to be open in admitting error, to apologize with honesty, and never to let pride keep her from righting a wrong. Her apology had been a quick one, but it was not sufficient.

Shooing the little dog off her lap, she gazed up at Thum. "Alas, my lord, you know too well that I dislike Pheresa for reasons that are womanly and foolish, and such personal feelings have no place in this discussion. I understand that Mandria is our most important ally, and friendship between our two realms must continue. I know also where your loyalty lies. I was wrong to question it, even in jest."

This time, she saw the fierce anger fade from his eyes. He bowed.

With a sense of having averted disaster, she said quickly, "If we do not suspend trade with Klad, how else can we make goodwill toward Mandria? Should we offer Pheresa armed assistance? Our defenses are stretched thin at present. And it is surely unwise to put ourselves in an indefensible position by pouring gold into the coffers of one side while offering troops to the other."

"Quite so," Thum agreed hastily, his brows high.

"Sending armed forces into Mandria is not advisable," Tustik murmured.

Thum nodded. "I believe the king fears there will be trouble with the Grethori tribes by spring. We can ill afford to spare the men."

"If we sent our Grethori auxiliaries to her, we would be well rid of them while keeping them from the temptation of joining an uprising," Alexeika said.

The men exchanged glances, and Thum's mouth twitched as though he held back an involuntary smile. "'Tis something to consider," he said.

"But a radical move," Tustik pointed out. "We must not violate the king's strict policy against supplying forces to other sovereigns."

Thum looked thoughtful. "Perhaps we should offer Queen Pheresa information. It will prove useful to her, thus maneuvering her into a position of gratitude, yet it does not commit us to expend men or arms on her behalf."

Alexeika liked the idea. "Good! But if we supply information, will that not reveal our network of spies?"

Thum shrugged. "Mandria knows we spy on them, just as they spy on us. We'll simply be confirming that we have better resources than they do."

"And perhaps, majesty," Tustik said smoothly, "it will do Mandria no harm to learn that we are regaining our former supremacy among the kingdoms in this regard, as in so many others."

Alexeika nodded. "Very well. It seems we are in consensus."

"Lord Thum plots with unsurpassed mastery," the old adviser said. "I further recommend that we inform King Faldain of these developments immediately. If all Mandria is swept into these hostilities, he doesn't want to be caught unawares."

"Yes," she agreed. "Let it be done at once."

"Good," Tustik said. "Now, despite the late hour, there is still one other matter to be presented to your majesty."

"Yes?"

"The king and I discussed Jonan's future before his

majesty's departure for Thirst Hold," Tustik said. "There is trouble brewing around the boy now that he is grown."

"He will always tempt rebellion," she said calmly. "What of it?"

"It has begun."

That startled her. "Tell me what you know," she said quietly.

"A Count Soblinsk is petitioning for permission to become Jonan's companion. He was a noted supporter of Muncel."

She drew in her breath with a hiss. "You know my position on past traitors."

"Indeed I do, majesty."

"What did the king say to this?"

"His majesty's mind was much distracted at the time, and he did not take the problem seriously."

She frowned. She had grown up watching this land wage civil war, war that had scarred her early life and caused her father's death. She thought about how treason could fester and spread, unseen and unsuspected, until it erupted in violence. Were it up to her, she would banish Jonan to the most remote corner of the World's Rim, never to be heard from again.

But she did not say that. "Faldain feels that Jonan must continue to be treated as a member of this family."

Tustik was nodding. "Of course, but your majesty and I both know that the king has a soft heart. When it comes to crushing rebellion, sometimes a ruthless hand is needed."

"Go on."

"Another troubling development has occurred tonight," Tustik said. "Although Soblinsk has not yet succeeded in personally approaching the prince, his daughter has."

"Did she, by Thod!" Thum exclaimed. "How came that about?"

But it was Alexeika who answered. "Jonan lost his temper after dinner and ran out into the gardens to pout. Was it then? I do not recall seeing him in the gallery the rest of the evening."

"Yes, your majesty." Tustik sighed with palpable annoyance. "Her name is Lady Sofina."

"'Tis a pretty name," Thum said. "Do her looks match it?"

Tustik ignored his question. "I regret such a development greatly, your majesty. I have hired a protector for the boy, but the fellow has not yet assumed his duties. Tonight, Jonan slipped through my fingers, and the meeting was accomplished. By those who observed him escorting her to the merchants' pavilion, he seemed quite taken with the lady. I believe they are planning another assignation."

"Jonan in love?" Alexeika said with a smile. "Hmm."

But Thum frowned and whistled softly beneath his breath.

"Is she comely?" Alexeika asked. "Is she very young?"

"I am informed that she is," Tustik replied.

"Jonan is hopelessly shy with maidens," she said. "No doubt it will come to nothing."

"Such a course is far too dangerous," Tustik said in icy disapproval. "It puts Jonan too much in the influence of a suspected traitor, for if the lady gains Jonan's heart, will not her father likewise gain his trust?"

"What do you suggest?"

"Removal of father and daughter from the palace grounds. If they must hang about, let them hire a house in the city. It was a grave oversight on the part of the chamberlain to give them accommodations at all."

Alexeika held up her hand. "Very well. Issue the order tomorrow, but do it with courtesy. Say they must make room for the trade delegation from Saelutia that is expected to arrive shortly."

Tustik's dark eyes glimmered with satisfaction. He gave her a low bow of respect. "Your majesty is very prudent, I regret I was not able to prevent this unfortunate acquaintanceship, but I vow I'll see it ended without delay."

There was a hint of vindictiveness in his voice as he spoke. Alexeika noticed it and felt a momentary qualm. Was Tustik simply worried about fomenting plots, she wondered, or did he hate Jonan so much he imagined trouble where none was brewing? For her part, she felt sorry for the unfortunate boy. Although evidently the maiden was most unsuitable, for had she any morals at all she would not have been wandering the gardens after dark to pounce on Jonan like a vixlet after its prey, poor Jonan would never understand why he could not be friends with her.

She sighed aloud. "We are forcing Jonan to hate us by treating him this way. If he grows confused about where his loyalties should lie, 'twill be small wonder."

Tustik met her eyes without remorse or apology, and in that moment she realized this was exactly his plan. She sat forward with a sharp exclamation. "My lord prince! You—"

The old adviser held up his frail hand. There was a slight tremor of palsy in it, but his eyes were rock steady. "Majesty, some things are best left unsaid. I see that we understand each other. Let that be enough."

She frowned, more shocked by his ruthlessness than she wanted to admit. "We will not be silent, lord prince. We will discuss this now."

"The sooner Jonan is goaded into making a serious mistake," Tustik said implacably, "the sooner the king will agree to the most advisable course regarding his cousin's future."

He was as cold-blooded as a snake, Alexeika thought. She forced all expression from her face to give nothing away, but inside she was determined to warn Faldain of Tustik's intentions as soon as she had the chance. And not by messenger, she told herself sharply. In person. She did not doubt Tustik's loyalty to the crown for a moment, but he was trying to manipulate Faldain, and she would not stand for that.

"I wonder, my lord prince," she forced herself to say smoothly, "why you do not allow Soblinsk and his daughter to remain and ensnare Jonan all the quicker?"

A brief, mirthless smile stretched Tustik's lips. "Nay, your majesty. That would be contrary to the king's direct orders."

"And isn't provoking Jonan to unwise actions also contrary to Faldain's wishes?"

"I am not responsible for Jonan's behavior," Tustik replied austerely. "That young man will either choose to be docile to what is best for him, or he will not. 'Tis his decision to make." He bowed. "If I may wish your majesty a good night?"

She forced herself to thank him for his counsel, but although Tustik departed, Thum lingered a moment, toying with his gold chain and frowning thoughtfully.

"Damne, what a ruthless old demon Tustik is," he said. "Dain won't like this."

She sighed. "Clearly Prince Tustik doesn't intend for the king to know."

"Bah! Tustik is bound to know your majesty will tell him. Or should I send the warning in my next dispatch?"

A chill passed through Alexeika. She shook her head swiftly. "Perhaps that's what he expects you to do. Perhaps he's laid a trap for you as well. Or me. I think we should both take care."

"As you wish."

"I don't understand him," she went on. "Why did he show his hand this way?"

"Why shouldn't he? He's nothing to fear."

"I suppose not," she said with resentment. "After all, he belongs to the Kollegya, does he not?"

Thum's smile grew faint. "Ah, so your majesty knows about that secret body."

"Of course." Her eyes flashed at Thum. "I'm not a fool."

"No one, my lady, has ever supposed that you are."

She frowned. "Whatever comes, Faldain must be warned about Tustik's methods. He needs to know what manner of man advises him."

"Dain has never been easily fooled," Thum said with a grin, and for a moment he was once again the leggy boy she'd first met tagging at Faldain's heels. "His grace is able to read men's natures very well."

"Aye, but he gives them too many second chances," she said in frustration. "That is what worries me!"

"I think it is the king's safety that worries you," Thum said softly. "Do not fret about him. He is well able to cope with whatever has befallen Thirst. Now, I bid the king's lady good slumber, and take my leave."

She called her servants and readied herself for bed, but once lying down she found herself wide-awake in the darkness, prey to many worries.

Come back quickly, my love, she thought, all too aware of the emptiness of her bed. She missed Faldain with an ache that grew fiercer with every passing day. Where was he? Why did he not send word? What was keeping him from returning as quickly as he'd promised?

The longer he stayed away, the more mischief and intrigues that would be done in his absence. The court was obviously growing restless and uneasy. There could only be more trouble to come. And it was up to her to somehow thwart it all until Faldain returned.

Chapter Eight

Tho chapel bell of Thirst Hold was ringing the end of mass. People slowly filed out, chattering Dain, who had not attended the service, stood beneath the gnarled old rowan tree in the tiny churchyard, reading the grave inscription of Queen Pheresa's unnamed infant buried there. She had a son now, he'd been told, a stalwart little lad the knights of Thirst were eager to toast and talk about. Dain was glad Pheresa had finally found her way, securing her throne despite her enemies and forging her own destiny, but he wished more than ever that he'd brought Ilymir with him. 'Twas his son the men of Thirst should be boasting of, not hers.

"Your grace?"

Turning, he saw Sir Bosquecel slowly limping up to him. The hold commander had been lamed in an accident four years past when Pheresa used Thirst for a refuge in her tragic winter of exile, and on this damp autumn day he moved more stiffly than usual. An efficient man dedicated to his duty, Bosquecel had been the first to befriend and champion Dain long ago when he was but a lowly foster there. Since then, Bosquecel's loyalty had been steadfast. He had served ably all these years, but he was growing old. His hair was mostly gray now, and there were deep lines carved into his face. He suffered a deep, rasping cough that he made light of, but which Sir Aflein, master-at-arms, said had bothered him constantly since the spring.

I'll have to find a replacement for him soon, Dain thought, and wondered how this proud man would accept pensioning.

"Word has come from Lunt," Sir Bosquecel said with a smile. "They're willing to sell us building stone from their quarry providing we can cart it."

"Good. When the first frost firms the road, you can set to the job."

"Aye. 'Tis a queer lowlander idea, setting little dams across the marsh, but if your grace thinks it will work—"

"It's brilliant," Dain broke in. Sir Bosquecel had also developed the habit of repeating phrases and conversations, as though he'd forgotten how many times matters had already been discussed. "A pity you didn't start building during high summer, when the water is low. But if the task is done now, draining the higher marshlands during the winter months, by next thaw the serfs should find the ground ready for farming and fertile indeed."

"Better than our worn-out fields," Sir Bosquecel agreed, coughing. "Morde a day, our harvest looks paltry indeed. We'll have a lean winter this year, that's sure."

He'd been repeating that observation at least once a day. Dain sighed. "When supplies run low, you have my permission to hunt stag, and you can always buy food from Lunt or even Busaire. I'll be sending a strongbox of gold to supplement the treasury for such emergencies."

"Your grace is kind indeed," Sir Bosquecel said with gratitude. "Now about the—"

"I'm leaving Thirst on the morrow," Dain interrupted.

"So soon?" the commander asked in obvious dismay. "But, your grace, we haven't—"

"I must return. I've tarried here longer than intended," Dain said firmly. "Don't tell me yet another crisis has arisen since yesterday."

"No, your grace. It's just that you're seldom with us, and we—I fear we would seek to keep you with us always."

Dain smiled and headed out of the churchyard, shortening his stride so that Sir Bosquecel could keep pace with him. Peat smoke lay fragrant on the air, and a trick of the breeze shifted the scent of marshland to Dain's nostrils. He inhaled with pleasure, thinking of other autumn afternoons there and in Nold when he was growing up.

Chesil came hurrying to him, his crimson clothes and blue sash in vivid contrast to the green tunics and hauberks worn by Thirst men. "Sire, your horse is ready, and the huntsman awaits your majesty's pleasure."

Dain nodded, and Sir Bosquecel smiled. "One last coursing of stag?"

"Aye," Dain said, pulling on his gloves. "Into the Dark Forest, and before you fuss, I can remember my way about."

"I hope so," Sir Bosquecel said, squinting with worry. "You're not a foster anymore, running about half-wild. The clans have been quiet lately, but if they—"

Dain clamped his hand briefly on the man's shoulder to silence him. In truth he'd welcome an encounter with a band of dwarves if only to inquire after those he'd known as a child, and he intended this last afternoon's ride to be a visit to Thia's resting place rather than an actual hunt for game. But none of that did Sir Bosquecel need to know.

A few minutes later, with a mingling of Thirst men and Agyas gathered around him, the dogs prancing excitedly with lolling tongues and wagging tails, he set forth wrapped in a burgundy cloak, waving to the serfs who cheered him.

His visit to Thirst had been a curiosity, for despite the seeming urgency of the message that had sent him galloping southward, it seemed there was no disaster, no emergency. Sir Bosquecel denied having sent a man to Nether or issuing any other request for help. Thirst had been hit with several raids lately, and the bridge had almost been destroyed in one such skirmish, but that was not out of the ordinary and certainly did not warrant the king's presence.

But once he arrived, Dain found himself mired in endless appeals and small problems. The growing season had been a poor one, and the harvest now being gathered was pitiable enough to worry them all. The bridge, which guarded the major trade route between Mandria and Nold and was Thirst's chief responsibility, suffered rot in its timbers and needed rebuilding. Some of the hold's walls were cracking, and Sulein's old turret was crumbling along the foundation so dangerously that Dain had ordered the structure pulled down. He wanted the hall enlarged, for its warren of cramped passageways and small rooms were woefully inadequate to house an entire royal party when Dain paid official visits.

There had been runaway serfs to punish, marriages to approve, the accounting to go over, and the knights—many of them newly hired—to inspect. Countless details, piled up since his last visit, seemed more disorganized than usual, and Sir Bosquecel's failing health was a matter of great concern to Dain. He'd talked to the physician, who looked very young and far from wise. He'd met the priest, who seemed less fanatically rooted in the precepts of the Reformed Church than many of his predecessors, but acted wary and defensive as though he believed Dain might cast him out. He'd even talked with an informal gathering of the upland chevards, most of whom were worried about the war with Klad and what part they'd be called on to play in it.

And so the days had slipped by while Dain set aside his kingly responsibilities to deal with the simple problems of a chevard in a remote hold. He enjoyed himself, although he missed his family, yet knew he must return to Grov without further delay.

By nightfall, the preparations for his departure were finished. His men were sharing a round of cider in the guardhouse, and the uproarious laughter and jesting could be heard as far as the hall itself. Sitting at his desk in his wardroom, the dogs stretched out by the hearth and a fire sending forth light and warmth, Dain summoned Sir Aflein.

Chesil admitted the master-at-arms, who looked nervous and ill at ease as he entered under Lord Omas's watchful eye. Sandy-haired and stocky of build, the man was perhaps three or four years older than Dain, quiet of manner, and alert. He sported a short brown beard, and his green eyes were intelligent. Dain had taken the trouble of checking the rosters before summoning him, and knew that Sir Aflein had sworn his oath of service last year. He was the younger son of a landless knight in service at Busaire Hold west of Lunt. An uplander bred and born, he looked strong and steady. These past three weeks Dain had observed him going about his duties and liked what he saw.

Sir Aflein's gaze darted about the small wardroom, which looked much as it had from Lord Odfrey's day, with its large wooden chest, map cases, and desk cluttered with papers, accounting books, and inkpots. The small window was firmly shuttered against the night, and a pitch-soaked torch hanging from a wall sconce smoked and flickered with soft, hissing pops.

The man seemed a bit disappointed, and Dain understood that he'd probably been expecting to see more pomp and riches on display. "Sir Aflein," he said in greeting, "be seated."

Looking startled by so great an honor, the master-of-arms cautiously seated himself in the king's presence but perched himself on the edge of his chair as though ready to jump up at any moment. It pleased Dain to see that the man did not fidget, and although his nervousness in the intimate presence of his liege lord and master was understandable, his green eyes were unflinching without quite meeting Dain's gaze in full. No doubt Sir Aflein believed it dangerous to meet the eyes of an eld, but Dain did not hold that old superstition against him.

"I leave on the morrow," Dain announced, breaking the silence. "I'm putting you in charge of Thirst."

Sir Aflein's nostrils flared in surprise. "But Sir Bosquecel—"

"The man's ill," Dain said sharply. "By all the signs, this is going to be a harsh winter. Whatever ails the commander is likely to grow worse, and if so, he won't be able to carry out his duties as he should."

Sir Aflein sprang to his feet. "You won't relieve him, your grace! Not him! He's the best commander that ever served, and after all he's done for you, why, you can't just throw him aside."

"I can do whatever I please," Dain said coldly and stared at Sir Aflein until the man wrestled himself back under control.

"Forgive me, your grace, for offending you. But I beg you, don't—"

"I do not intend to reward Sir Bosquecel's many years of superb service with base coin," Dain said in a tone that caused Sir Aflein to lose color. "I think I am better informed than you as to the quality of the man's service over time. He served Lord Odfrey as well as he has served me. I owe him a great deal, and I do not forget my debts. I have no intention of relieving Sir Bosquecel from his command. But neither do I expect a sick man to carry out the difficult task of seeing this hold through a winter when it hasn't enough food to last. And by all accounts there could be serious trouble if Kladite forces cross the border. You will take over, Sir Aflein."

The knight started to speak, but Dain rose to his feet with a look that silenced the man.

"You will officially keep your present duties, but it will be up to you to carry the burden of responsibility for this hold while calling no attention to yourself. You will make sure that Sir Bosquecel gets adequate rest and is not challenged beyond his present abilities. If he regains his health, well and good, and you will gradually relinquish true command back to him. If he worsens, you will assume complete control, and I will expect you to send me a private report immediately. Is that clear?"

Sir Aflein looked stunned. "Aye, your grace."

Dain nodded. "I am placing total reliance on you. I think you are the man for the task. I have no doubt you will fulfill my expectations."

"Your grace, I—"

"It won't be easy, especially if Sir Bosquecel's orders are contradictory to yours, or less than wise. But I expect you to meet those challenges capably. The safety of the hold comes before anything else. Are we agreed?"

"Aye! And . . . thank you."

"Don't thank me yet," Dain said ruefully, relaxing his stern demeanor. "I've saddled you with a brutal job, especially if Sir Bosquecel misunderstands your purpose."

Sir Aflein thought that over and frowned. "Then he isn't to know?"

"No."

"That's best, isn't it? Kinder. For him, I mean."

Dain nodded, still watching him.

Sir Aflein sighed and lifted his gaze fully to Dain's for the first time. "I'll do my best, your grace. He'll not know; that, I swear on my honor. Thirst will stand against the Kladites if they come, and it won't starve."

"I have relied on Sir Bosquecel for years as I have relied on no other man," Dain replied. "I see I have chosen another as dependable."

Sir Aflein flushed slightly and saluted, then strode out with his shoulders erect and new fire in his eyes. Dain watched him go, before pulling the gold circlet from his brow with a sigh.

"You've got a loyal man there for life," Lord Omas rumbled.

"I hope so."

"Aye, you know it, sire," Omas said with a twinkle. "You've a clever way with men of his rank. He'll never forget this chance you've given him."

A tap on the door preceded Chesil. "Vaunit wishes to see you, sire."

Without waiting for Dain's permission, the *sorcerel* glided in past Chesil. Of the court *sorcerels* under Samderaudin's dominion, Vaunit was the most active, the most approachable, and the youngest. Nevertheless, silver threads glinted in his shoulder-length hair, and his skin was worn and leathery from age. He was as dark-skinned as a Saelutian, but like all his kind the many years of casting magic had altered his appearance until it was impossible to ascertain his origins. His ears were large and pointed, with tufts of gray hair growing from the tips, and his fingers were unusually long, with thick dark nails like talons. His heavily lidded eyes, hued reptilian yellow and as cold, held the ability to read men's thoughts. Like all his kind, Vaunit answered only what he wished to and often spoke in riddles, but if the mood struck him, he could be more forthcoming than most.

It seemed such a mood was on him now. "Send these minions out," he said gruffly. "Faldain must listen to what I say."

Chesil scowled in umbrage, and Omas planted his big feet, but Dain was sufficiently surprised by the *sorcerel's* agitation to send both aide and protector out of the wardroom without question.

He nodded at the roll of vellum clutched in Vaunit's hand. "Have you been starcasting for Thirst? What do the portents—"

"Listen." Vaunit unrolled the heavy vellum, which was marked with drawings and diagrams in multihued inks. The chart itself shimmered at the edges, and some of the circles and radiating lines seemed to shift and move slightly if Dain looked at them from the corner of his eye. The entire chart smelled of magic, and he found himself leaning back from it uneasily.

Vaunit tapped the vellum. "The portents are greatly unsettled. Here and here and also here. Thrice have I cast the stars for Faldain, and all readings are different."

Dain frowned. "Then the casting is false. Samderaudin says—"

"Bah! I have cast true!" Vaunit said with ire. "This color shows the initial lines. This color shows the second reading. And this color shows the third. All different. All true. None favorable. I strongly advise Faldain to return to Nether without delay."

"We leave on the morrow," Dain said with a touch of exasperation. "You know that."

"Hurry is advisable. Through Dark Forest. Fastest way."

Worry began to spread through Dain. It was unlike Vaunit to be so clear and forthright. Such a strong warning from the *sorcerel* was disturbing.

"What's happened?" he asked, suddenly thinking of Alexeika and the children. "The queen—"

"Look to your throne," Vaunit said, his yellow eyes boring into Dain's. "All is at risk, especially the life of Faldain. All is danger, converging at every turn."

Dain's eyes widened. He curbed an impulse to order his departure then and there. It was dark, and in this land night was no time to be abroad. Furthermore, he had made it a rule never to act solely on the counsel of the *sorcerels*, for to take that path was to risk plunging into a different kind of trouble. He had to think independently, and use his wits.

"This danger," he said, "does it beset me now, or is it yet to come?"

Vaunit let the chart roll up with a snap. "Three castings," he repeated. "Three sets of unfavorable portents. What does the number three signify?"

For a moment Dain felt himself to be a boy again, struggling through one of Sulcin's lessons. He frowned. "The three worlds?"

"Excellent. Nether is ruled by a clever king."

"You're wasting time."

"And you do not wish to listen." Vaunit spread wide his hands, and the chart levitated into the air and unrolled itself to float in front of Dain. "The first world is shown here. See the many lines of danger? Many here and here, signifying the actions of several enemies."

"Aye, that's nothing new," Dain said, with a grimace.

"The second world crosses the first. See?" Vaunit's finger traced a long yellow line across the chart. "Is not good for it to cross this way."

Despite his doubts, Dain glanced down at the Ring of Solder on his finger. The second world was a place of nowhere, neither physical nor spiritual, but a sort of crossing point between the two. He'd entered it as a very young child, riding with his father, who'd hidden the Chalice of Eternal Life to save it. Dain had entered the second world again while a prisoner of the Believers who'd taken him to Gant. But the next time he'd gone of his own volition, using the Ring's special powers to find the Chalice and return it to its rightful place. By the laws of magic, he could use the Ring only once more in his lifetime. To violate that rule would see him trapped in the misty second world forever, as his father had been trapped. Dain shivered.

"Are you saying my enemies are traveling through the second world in order to reach me?" he asked.

"Some, yes. A very strong enemy."

Gant, he thought grimly, and nodded. "And the third world?"

Tall and grim, his silver hair flowing over his shoulders, his face cast in shadow as he stood with his back to the fire, Vaunit stared at Dain for a long time. "You know the significance of this portent?" he asked instead of directly answering Dain's question.

"It means death."

"Yes."

"Whose? Mine?"

Vaunit turned away. The chart rolled up and floated over to his hand.

Dain felt very cold. "You've forecast my death."

"All men die. Even kings."

Dain felt as though his mind had separated itself from his body. He seemed to have no control of himself and could not turn away or stop himself from asking more questions. "When?" he asked.

"The casting is very unsettled," Vaunit replied obliquely. "Never have I seen such a chart before. To understand it is difficult. All can change in an instant because Faldain does not—"

"When, Vaunit? You know, or you wouldn't have burst in here with this warning. Why won't you tell me?"

"How many times can a mortal die?"

Impatient with the riddle, Dain frowned. "Once."

"Then why does the chart show many deaths?" Vaunit shook his head. "How can I say when among them? Which death do I choose in warning? Perhaps you will cheat death as you have before. Perhaps you will not. Either way, it will be soon, and you are destined to see the third world."

Dain felt as though the wind had been punched from his body. He sat down abruptly, glad that Vaunit had insisted on telling him this privately. He did not want Omas, Chesil, and the others fussing over him. Although he faced the possibility of death every time he rode onto a battlefield, that was far different than having a *sorcerel* predict it like this.

Soon, he thought, shivering again despite the warmth of the fire. A bit desperately he looked up. "Will I see Alexeika and my family first?"

"Who can know whether I am right or wrong? I will consult Samderaudin about this matter when we return. In some things he has greater knowledge than I."

Had Dain been less upset, he might have felt stunned to hear such an admission. The *sorcerels* were not noted for modesty, and they could be jealous of each other and fiercely competitive. But just then he was thinking of Alexeika and their stupid quarrel. He missed her fiercely, and suddenly all he wanted was to hold her and make amends.

Coming to Thirst had been unnecessary, due to some misunderstanding as yet unexplained. "Was I tricked into coming here?" he asked slowly, feeling a chill drain through his body. "Was this a ruse to get me away from Grov?"

"Yes," Vaunit replied. "Faldain will seize any excuse to come to Thirst, even a false one. Faldain should hurry back to Nether. If Faldain wishes, use the Ring."

The temptation seized him, raw and hot, but Dain closed his fist and refused to look at the Ring. "No," he said grimly, holding down his fears by sheer willpower. "What are you up to, Vaunit? You know the Ring is to be used on behalf of the Chalice and nothing else."

"So you think, Faldain," Vaunit replied grimly. "But a day is coming when such principles will be tested."

"What are you trying to tell me?" Dain demanded. "Damne! Can't you speak clearly for once?"

"I have said all I know." The *sorcerel* glided over to the door and although he did not set a hand on it, the stout wooden panel swung open for him. His yellow eyes met Dain's. "It begins now. Your enemies have found you. Tarry not, for you are far from where you belong."

PART II

Chapter Nine

Dain was met at the Netheran border by a contingent of four hundred knights under the command of Count Pemikalievy. Looking stern behind a bushy, iron gray mustache, his nose missing from an old battle wound and replaced by one of leather, Pemikalievy wore a gray surcoat with black insignia. His cloak was heavy, dark gray wool. That afternoon, beneath overcast skies, Pemikalievy seemed almost to materialize from clouds and rain. His army waited silently at the edge of the forest bordering the road. Bristling with arms, they rode under Nether's green-and-white pennon.

Dain reined up alertly and nodded for Pemikalievy to approach. He knew the man's pragmatic reputation. The count was a battle-hardened veteran, one of the few good men who'd switched his allegiance from Muncel to Faldain and given his new king no cause to regret it.

The count saluted him briskly. "Majesty."

"What trouble do you come to report?" Dain asked without wasting time on courtesies. "Has Gant attacked our eastern border? Or have the Grethori tribes gone on a rampage?"

Pemikalievy blinked, and he nodded with respect. "It's

trouble with the Grethori. Your majesty is better informed than I thought, and I've ridden ahead of the first courier."

"Where did they strike?" Dain asked with a sigh, thinking of how he would now have to ride west for war. "How long ago?"

"A week past. They attacked the palace."

The men around the king cried out with surprised oaths. Dain sat in his saddle as though pole-axed. He could not speak, could not breathe. It was not possible. Runtha's palace was well fortified, and far from Grethori territory. But then his wits began to turn, and he thought of the auxiliaries, used first for troops and later for palace guards. Alexeika's furious arguments against them was why first the Privy Council and then the Kollegya had begun to criticize her degree of influence. To keep peace, Dain had sided with the Kollegya instead of his wife. And now, he tasted bitter regret for having been a fool.

There were questions he had to ask, things he had to know. In a faraway corner of his mind rose a fear so terrible, so dire he dared not consider it. He could not bear to utter the questions racing in his mind.

Pemikalievy met his gaze with sympathy. "I'm sorry I must bring your majesty such terrible news."

"The auxiliaries," Dain whispered.

"Aye. They killed their officers and turned on the palace—"

"I sent an order weeks ago for the auxiliaries to be stationed away from palace duty. Who ignored my order?"

"Sire, I know not."

The men exchanged looks, and Lord Omas began to swear softly beneath his breath.

"The attack came in the afternoon," Pemikalievy continued, "while the royal family was in the garden. There were no defenders save the protectors and a few courtiers who tried to intervene."

Dain's head was buzzing. He felt both cold and hot. Pemikalievy's voice seemed to fade in and out of his hearing. "Alexeika," he whispered.

"The queen lives," Pemikalievy said swiftly. "She was injured, but she lives, sire."

Dain found himself able to breathe again. "Verily?"

"Aye. She will recover."

Relief swept Dain with such intensity he shut his eyes.

"Wine for the king," Chesil ordered. "Laure! Fetch your master's cup."

They fussed over him, but Dain pushed away the proffered wine impatiently. "Thod be thanked," he said. "If she is well, all else can be borne."

Pemikalievy looked grave. "I would not say the queen is well."

"Alive, though!" Dain said fiercely. "She is alive. She is not lost to me."

Vaunit, his yellow eyes narrowed and intent, rode up. Kolas—captain of the Agya forces—blocked the *sorcerel's* path, but a look from Vaunit made the Agya back away. Halting beside Dain, Vaunit said nothing, but an unseen force surrounded Dain as though Vaunit had cast some sort of magical net to protect him. It was like being draped with a cobweb, and the touch of it sent new fear thudding through Dain's head: *Not the children. Not the children.*

"Lord Pemikalievy," he said hoarsely, "what else have you to tell me?"

"The queen is a valiant woman. She fought like a warrior in the defense of her young. But even she could not prevail." Pemikalievy hesitated then lifted his chin. "Princess Tashalya has been abducted and carried off by these villains. Prince Ilymir is—is—dead."

Vaguely, Dain was aware of voices around him, voices raised in anger and distress. He felt nothing, and did not know whether that was because he'd been shocked beyond emotion or whether Vaunit's spell was shielding him in some way. There was the overwhelming need to scream out his grief and strike blindly with his sword, but he did neither of those things. There was nothing he could do save somehow hold himself together while his men stared at him with grief and worry.

"Give him wine," a voice kept saying, but Dain brushed the jeweled cup away.

My son and heir, he thought. A mental image of Ilymir's grinning little face and merry blue eyes filled his mind, and with it came such agony he groaned aloud. As for Tashalya . . .

He realized that he could not cope with so much horrible news all at once, could not face the blackness yawning inside him or the hurt that was as raw as a sword cut. Seeking action, he thrust it all back and concentrated on Pemikalievy's scarred face.

"Count," he said, "do you and this force of men ride in pursuit of my daughter's abductors?"

"Nay, your majesty. I am here for your protection."

Dain looked around a little wildly. "We must find Tashalya!"

It was Chesil's hand that gripped his arm, Chesil's tilted eyes that gazed into his. "Sire," he said firmly, "first we must ride to Grov."

"Nay!" Dain said. "She's not there. They will sell her. 'Tis their way, Thod damne their eyes!"

"Sire," Chesil told him, "you must go first to the queen. She has need of you now, *neya*?"

The Agya's words reached through the panic that had momentarily gripped Dain. Tears stung his eyes, for he did not think he could endure returning to the palace or gazing upon his dead son's face. Mutely, he shook his head.

"The queen needs you, sire. Go to her, and let us then see what has to be done."

Dain thought of his beautiful wife, whom he loved, and suddenly he knew Chesil was right. He should go to her, certify for himself that she would recover. The idea that a barbarian—one sworn to service—would dare strike her down swept him with burning rage, and at that moment he longed for combat for the sheer relief of plunging his sword into Grethori vitals.

Alexeika . . . poor, sorrowing mother . . . how could she endure something like this alone? His fierce warrior maid was

not as strong as she pretended to be, and he knew she needed
him. As he needed her.

Grimly, he gathered his reins and pointed his face north.
"Let us ride!"

Several days later, the midday sun was slanting into Alexeika's chambers when Lady Nadilya came tiptoeing in to
whisper the news. "The king has returned, my lady. He is
within the palace now!"

Alexeika sat up with a wince, pressing her hand to her
painful ribs, and tried to rub the crust of dried tears from her
eyes. Faintly in the distance she could hear the fanfare of
trumpets. Her heart soared for a moment, before she remembered all that weighted it down. She wanted Faldain desperately. She wished he could come to her immediately, but she
knew it would not happen. The moment he arrived, he would
be set upon by officials, courtiers, officers, and others, all with
questions and reports.

"Did you see him?" she asked. "Was he well?"

"I did not see him, my lady, but I am told he looks grieved
and pale. His temper is fearsome. Already he has shouted at
some knave with such force a lamp exploded." Lady Nadilya
wrung her plump hands. "Will he blame us for what's happened? Will he—"

"Be silent!" Alexeika snapped, vexed past bearing by her
attendant's stupidity. "Order the servants to bring water and
bathe me. I want the green robe, and my hair must be
brushed."

Her preparations began, slow and gentle ones to spare her
unnecessary pain. After a few moments she stopped giving instructions, for the effort made her head ache. Her side hurt,
too, and she was forced to lie down and rest. And as her maidservant brushed her hair with slow, gentle strokes, humming
softly to soothe her, Alexeika felt the grief she could sometimes hold at bay come welling up to overtake her anew. They
had bathed her face in cool, scented water, and she did not
want to greet Faldain with her eyes puffy and swollen, but she
could not stop her tears.

When he came in at last, scattering her women before him like brightly hued leaves, Alexeika was still weeping. She looked up, and he seemed to fill her vision. At first he was a blur, then she blinked her tears fiercely back. He looked terrible, paler than she'd ever seen him, with dark smudges beneath his eyes. He was thin and obviously tired, and the anguish in his gray eyes rent her heart anew.

Wordlessly, she held out her arms. With a soft moan, he dropped to one knee beside her bed and gathered her close. Her grasp tightened on his muscle and sinew, feeling the hardness of his body, the rough scratch of his clothing. She held him, oblivious to the pain it caused her wounded side, and drew in his presence as her lungs drew in air.

"Oh, Faldain, beloved," she whispered brokenly. "I can't believe you're home at last."

He said something too muffled for her to understand. A shudder passed through his frame, and she realized he was crying.

She clutched the back of his head, his black hair soft against her cheek.

"I went to his tomb," Faldain was saying brokenly. "It is so little, Alexeika. So little!"

She thought of the funeral, and how the drums had beat outside all day. The procession had gone forth without her, for she was too ill to attend, but she'd watched from her window until her head began to pound and she felt too dizzy to stand. They had buried her son without her. He'd gone alone, little Ilymir who was afraid to sleep in the dark. Now he was in the dark forever.

Tears streamed down her face. "I wish I had let you take him with you," she whispered. "Thod forgive me, but if he'd gone with you, he'd have been safe."

"Hush. Don't say that." Faldain drew back from her and wiped his face. He met her eyes and shook his head. "Don't say it."

She had to, however. "Please forgive me. I was wrong that day. I tried to catch up with you. I tried to write to you. I—"

His fingers touched her cheek. "Don't think about it now. We can't undo what happened."

Such gentle words gave her no comfort. "Was it bad at Thirst?" she asked, seeking distraction of any kind. "What happened there?"

"Naught of importance."

Faldain looked away from her, a muscle working in his jaw. She took notice of how tense he was and how fatigue had worn his face. Her hand burrowed out from the covers and sought his, curling her palm against his, their fingers entwined. He dropped his head and drew in a deep breath.

"Alexcika," he said slowly, still not looking at her, "what happened here was my fault."

"Nay!" she exclaimed in surprise. "How can you say so? What mean you?"

"I listened to fools instead of good sense. I heeded the Privy Council's wishes instead of your sound advice." When his gaze met hers, his eyes were so bleak with self-blame they frightened her. "Agreeing to let those savages serve here! Morde, but what stupidity possessed me?"

"It was a mistake," she said softly, fighting the urge to agree with him. "You had reasons for your decision. How could you know—"

"How could I fail to know, when I think of what Grethori are? My order to send them away was ignored, and by Thod I'll see this treason repaid!" He released her hand and gathered himself as though to rise, but she reached out and took hold of his sleeve.

"Who betrayed us?" she asked urgently. "Are you saying a Netheran commander turned them against us?"

Anger surged into his face until he looked dangerous and violent. She knew what he was capable of in battle, and she saw in him the determination to hunt down every man responsible for this attack.

"How many protectors live?" he asked grimly.

Her head was aching again. "I know not. They tell me nothing. Even little Mareitina is not brought to me. I am a prisoner here."

"Not a prisoner," he said, gentling his tone to one more soothing. He pushed a lock of her chestnut hair back from her brow. His touch gently skimmed her bruise, but it was enough to made her flinch. "I'm sorry," he said, and kissed her cheek. "You are hurt, and I come here making you feel worse instead of better."

She tried to smile, wishing he would stay. "I am stronger every day," she assured him. "It's just that my head aches so."

"You took a sword cut to your side."

"It's not deep, just infernally painful across my ribs," she said. "I need to be up. There's Tashalya to find. Oh, Faldain, they took her. They took my little girl!"

"I'll get her back," he said, pressing her down. "I swear to you that I'll find her."

"How?" she asked fretfully. "The trail is cold."

"I can track my daughter," he said with a confidence that caught her attention.

"How? By sensing her presence?" She gripped his hand fiercely. "Is she alive? Is she unharmed?"

"She's alive," he answered. "Dwell on that comfort. I'll go after her as soon as I question the—"

"Never mind questions," Alexeika said. "Find her and bring her back now. Think of what the Grethori are capable of. They're worse than monsters. They'll—"

"Hush," he said, trying to soothe her. "Don't dwell on it. I'll—"

"But I *have* to think about it. I was their captive once. They are so cruel. They might do anything!"

"I know, but I must reason this through. I was tricked into going to Thirst, for they would not have dared this perfidy had I been here. The auxiliaries were put on duty two weeks early. Who changed the roster? And why is Lord Matej alive with less injury than my queen? What kind of protector is he, to let my children come to such harm? I sense Gant's hand behind this. And I'll get to the bottom of it!"

"I don't care about conspiracies now," she cried fretfully. "I want my daughter back. I want my son."

And she began to cry again, despite her intentions to be strong.

"You're tired," Faldain said, standing up.

She didn't want him to go. "Promise me you'll bid me farewell before you ride after Tashalya."

"I promise." He sighed. "I must go and see Mareitina now."

"Bring her to me. I long to see her, but no one tells me the truth. Is she hurt, too?"

He frowned, looking as though he could not bear much more. "I will tell you all I know when I come back. Now rest, beloved. Rest and get stronger."

She shut her eyes because she could not bear to watch him walk away. Through the pounding in her head she heard him murmuring to someone, perhaps the physician. Then all was quiet and still around her. She would have given everything she owned to hear the children come running in to her, yelling, laughing, all of them talking at once. She would have given anything, even her life, for that.

Chapter Ten

The dungeons consisted of a twisting maze of underground chambers and passages. Pitch-soaked torches did little to drive back the gloom. Damp permeated the stone walls, listening on the floor, and in the darkest corners patches of white, furry mold grew thick on the ceiling timbers. Striding past a chamber equipped with all manner of devices for torture, Dain spared no glance for the rows of tongs and pincers, the wooden boots that could be tightened gradually to crush all the bones in a victim's foot, the iron bands with tiny spikes inside, the hood made of leather that was dampened thoroughly and stretched in a tight fit over the head so that it tightened as it dried until the victim smothered or died of a cracked skull.

Surrounded by an entourage of armed guards, his protector, and aides, the king passed cells where condemned wretches thrust their hands through the bars. He ignored their cries for mercy. He did not hesitate or slacken his pace in the darkest, narrowest passages. He did not hold a corner of his cloak to his nostrils against the stink of misery, mildew, and filth that permeated this place. Dressed for battle in breastplate and mail, his sword belted at his side, he wore a face of stone. His gray eyes glittered with a fury that warned all to keep their place. His heart was flame, and his entrails felt as though they'd been skewered. All his senses were heightened, and he thought and acted more quickly than usual, yet he felt also a sense of detachment, as though a stranger had possessed his form.

Less than an hour before, he had visited the nursery, empty now save for one lone child. Mareitina, the survivor, lay curled up in a tiny knot on her bed, her thumb in her mouth, her blue eyes staring sightlessly. She did not stir when he knelt beside her and spoke. She seemed unaware of anything around her. But when he gently touched her shoulder, she shuddered and screamed with such terror he hastily backed away from her, his heart thudding and his anguish stronger than ever.

The chief nursemaid, tears streaking her face, came running. "She can't be touched, sire. None of us can handle her."

"Do something!" Dain commanded.

The woman only stared at him while Mareitina went on screaming, flailing and fending off invisible enemies with her small hands. Furious at the nursemaid's inaction, Dain scooped Mareitina into his arms, grappling with her as she fought against him like something demented. Her wails went on and on, shrill and heartrending, despite his efforts to rock and soothe her.

"It's no good, sire," the nursemaid said, wringing her hands. "Put her down, and let her cry it out. She'll quiet in time if she's left be."

Fury scorched him before he wrenched his emotions under control. He glared at the woman, but did not trust himself to speak. Mareitina went on struggling, and he held her pinned so that she could not harm herself while he paced back and forth across the room with her. He talked to her in a soft, soothing voice, using his mind, too, in an effort to calm her. But she seemed unable to hear him. And at last when her struggles grew weaker, he realized it was because she was exhausted, not comforted. Her body remained rigid and tense.

Tears streamed down her cheeks, and she continued to keen a mindless sound of fear and grief.

Sorrow swelled his heart, but he forced himself to remain calm. After a moment, he touched his mind to hers in the eld way.

Her thoughts were chaotic with terror, like a wild forest creature driven to panic. He could not reach her. Not knowing what else to do, Dain summoned up his small amount of magic and began to sing an eldin spellsong. He sang of the woods, of leaves turning red and gold beneath the bite of frost, of acorns falling and little mice scurrying to collect the nuts in their dens, of a stream rushing and babbling over round stones, with fish darting here and there like streaks of silver. He sang to her of moss, and bark, and twig. He sang to her of the sweet, minty taste of calmel berries. He sang to her of pebbles, smooth and brown or flecked with quartz and mica that glittered in the sunlight. He sang to her of the birds, the little brown-streaked fintas with their saucy upturned tails, hopping here and there among the late-summer flowers in search of insects.

And eventually Mareitina lay quiet in his arms, her head pressed against his shoulder. Now and then a shudder passed through her small frame, and she whimpered. He smoothed her golden curls back from her hot face, painfully aware that her hair did not stir and move as usual but hung in a lifeless tangle. Twins were unlike other children; she and Ilymir had shared a special bond and companionship now torn violently asunder. Worse, his gentle, unworldly Mareitina, a child so tender that she could not bear to witness the anger of others, had been exposed to brutal violence. How could he begin to undo what she'd suffered?

When he finally felt her relax and heard the shift in her breathing, he stopped singing and let the quiet steal over them. Her thumb found its way back into her mouth, but she was calm now. When she fell asleep, he slipped her back into bed and drew the covers over her shoulders.

For several minutes he watched over her slumber, his emotions churning until he felt raw inside. Why, he wondered, hadn't the Grethori stolen her, too? Why hadn't they taken all three children? Why take one, kill one, and leave one? It made no sense to him, for this was not their customary practice. In the back of his mind lay the conviction that the answer to his question was the answer to a larger puzzle.

Meanwhile, he summoned up a little prayer of thanksgiving that her life had been spared, even as he remained aware that her gentle soul had been so traumatized she might never escape the shell she'd withdrawn into. Tonight, he told himself, he would have to attend official rites and prayers and see whether carrying Mareitina into the presence of the Chalice would restore her sanity. If not, then he would send for healers from the eld folk to do what they could for her.

"She'll do now, sire," the nursemaid whispered. "When she sleeps, it's for hours at a time."

Dain left the chamber, beckoning for the woman to follow, and when they were out in the passageway he turned on her. "You're dismissed from your post," he said harshly.

The woman's plump face turned white, but Dain was unmoved. He glared at her. "How many days," he demanded, "have you let her scream herself into exhaustion like this?"

"But, sire, she'll let no one touch her. Everything we've tried only makes her worse."

"I'm not interested in your excuses. Be thankful I do not punish you for such cruelty."

Pressing her apron to her face, the woman backed away from him, sobbing, and Dain gave orders for the entire nursery staff to be changed.

Now, in the dungeons, he had more violent matters to deal with, and he made his way into the deepest levels with a quick, impatient stride. He would be meeting with his advisers soon, and he had Samderaudin yet to consult, but there was time for this encounter. He'd made sure of that.

The page running ahead of him shouted, "The king!"

The passageway opened into a round chamber crowded with several guards watching a pair of torturers lift Lord Matej onto the rack. Everyone paused as Dain entered the room. The guards saluted, and Matej began to struggle.

"Sire!" he called out weakly. "I beg your majesty to have mercy!"

Dain stared at him without expression and refused to answer. The torturers finished strapping Matej down on the wooden platform with swift efficiency despite his squirming kicks and struggles. In the torchlight, the planks of the rack were streaked with old stains. *Before this day is through*, Dain thought grimly, *there will be new ones*. Matej, stripped to the waist, his feet bare, had obviously just been flogged. A yellowish green bruise marred one side of his face; according to the report, that blow to his head was the only injury he'd sustained in the assault.

Assured and cocky no longer, he pleaded with Dain again. "Please, sire. I did my best to save the little princess. Please have mercy on me!"

"You live," Dain said in a harsh voice that made several of the men glance at him sharply, "and the princess royal is gone. You live, and my son lies dead. What mercy do you deserve?"

Matej's eyes glistened in the torchlight. "Please!" he whispered. "I fought them. I swear to your majesty. I was outnumbered and knocked down. By the time I regained my feet, still dazed, the princess was gone. Gartik was fighting at least four of the Grethori at once. I saw the prince already slain at his feet. What could we do? It was over."

Dain turned to the sergeant at arms. "Where is my son's protector? Why isn't he being questioned?"

"We've talked to Sir Gartik, sire," the sergeant answered, keeping his gaze correctly on a point past Dain's shoulder. "He lies in the infirmary with a sword cut to his shoulder. His account is much the same."

"Bring him here," Dain ordered.

Again the men exchanged swift glances, as one of the guards saluted and hurried to do Dain's bidding.

"He is wounded, sire," the sergeant said hesitantly. "Will your majesty not wish him to be healed before he is—"

"There is no time," Dain cut in. "Treason has infected the palace."

"Aye, those murdering Grethori savages—"

"More treason than that!" Dain shouted, and two of the torches went out with a pop. The men stared at him in fear as he strode over to the rack and glared down at Matej. "I walked

the gardens where the attack occurred. I sensed Nonkind evil
lingering on the site. I sense it here."

The man stared up at him, mute and pale, trembling visibly. There was guilt stamped on his soul, and Dain knew it.

"Sire," the sergeant said in a low voice at Dain's shoulder,
"no Nonkind were sighted. I was with the force that went after
the savages. 'Twas Grethori and naught else. We caught up
with them, and those at the rear did fight like demons, but
they were men, sire. They bled and died, and we caught only
four alive while the others escaped."

Annoyed by his interruption, Dain turned his gaze on the
man with such coldness that the sergeant blanched. "I've had
that report," Dain said. "I'll deal with those prisoners later."
He looked once more at Matej. "I know Gantese perfidy when
I find it. You, Lord Matej, are either a Believer—"

"No! I swear I'm not!"

"—Or you were bribed into standing aside while this evil
was done."

"I fought, sire," the man babbled. "I fought! I swear it!"

Dain gave a curt nod to one of the torturers. The man
turned the wooden crank, and Matej cried out in fear; then, as
the platform under him spread apart and he was stretched, he
screamed in pain.

Tears and sweat glazed his face. He stared up at Dain be-
seechingly. "I was sworn to protect her. I did my best!"

"Confess the truth!" Dain shouted. "Who corrupted you?
Who gave you money?"

The man shook his head frantically. "I fought, sire. All
those who witnessed the attack will tell you I tried."

"Had you *fought*," Dain said with contempt, "you would
now lie dead, or Princess Tashalya would be safely in the
nursery. Come, Matej, give up your craven lies. You are unharmed while my queen lies wounded, my son is dead and
buried, and my daughter suffers in the hands of wretches who
will torture and ill use her in unspeakable ways!" He bent
lower over the man, so enraged it was all he could do not to
reach out and throttle him. "You took Gantese gold. And you
did not defend her. Admit it!"

"No!" Matej cried. "No! I swear I—"

The torturer turned the crank again, and his voice rose in a scream.

"Sire," the sergeant said, "the other prisoner is here."

Dain swung around to see two guards half-escorting, half-supporting Sir Gartik. A wiry man with pale hair and skin, Gartik's shoulder was heavily bandaged, and he looked feverish, but his eyes were alert enough as they darted from face to face. When he saw Matej shivering and moaning on the rack, he swallowed hard before he met Dain's gaze.

Whatever he read there made him sink to his knees before the guards could stop him. He bowed his head. "Have pity, sire."

But Dain, so well known for his tender heart and forgiving ways, remained unmoved. "The king has no pity today," he replied. "How much were you paid by the Gantese agent?"

Gartik's head jerked up, and he stammered out a denial, but not before Dain had seen the guilt that flashed in his eyes.

Dain set his jaw. "Now we find the betrayer. How much were you paid, Gartik?"

"No, sire! I took no bribe. I—"

"How much were you paid?"

"Nothing! I swear it!"

Dain glanced at the torturers, and they gripped Gartik by his arms, hoisted him on his feet, and shackled him into a stout wooden chair. Half-fainting, the man stared with bulging eyes as a wooden boot was fitted onto his foot and the screws tightened. He was breathing hoarsely, panting like a runner, and when the first shudder of pain shook his body, Dain stepped forward.

"You will never walk again, Gartik. Were you paid sufficient compensation for that?"

Gartik's eyes were darting desperately from face to face. He held out an imploring hand to Dain. "Great king, you're a merciful man, a just and kind man. Have pity, for Thod's sake. I loved the prince. I would have done anything to save him, but they gave us no chance. They were on us without warning. Too many for us to fend off. They were at him before I could—"

"How much were you paid, Gartik?" Dain asked. "Who was the agent who approached you?"

"No, sire! No! Have pity!"

Dain turned to the torturer, and said calmly, "When you have crushed this foot, seal the wound with pitch and start on his other foot."

"Aye, majesty," the man said with relish. "And then his hands?"

"If necessary."

Gartik began screaming. "No! No! No! Forty dreits of gold. That's what I was paid. Forty dreits! All I had to do was let us be taken by surprise. That's all I was told. I swear! I didn't know they meant to kill the boy. Ransom, they said. Ransom. I'm telling the truth, in Thod's name. Great king, have pity. I didn't *know*."

An angry murmur swept through the guards present. Gartik went on rambling and pleading, sobbing until he was incoherent. A part of Dain felt sickened by how he'd broken this man; the rest of him did not care.

"Great Thod," Omas breathed. "A Gantese plot. How—"

"Sire, I had no part of this fool's treason," Matej yelled from the rack. "I swear it!"

"You knave!" Gartik said furiously. "I gave you ten pieces of—"

"Shut up, you filthy dog! I never took it! He tried to bribe me, sire, but I withstood him. I'm loyal to the king."

Dain felt a wave of disgust engulf him. Abruptly he spun on his heel and strode out. In the passageway out of sight of the occupants of the chamber, however, he paused as though he stumbled into an invisible barrier. For a moment he had to shut his eyes, bracing himself with one hand pressed to the stone wall.

"Sire?" Omas said worriedly. "Time you took a rest. You haven't sat down since we arrived. You need to eat and—"

"How could they do it?" Dain whispered, forcing open his eyes. The stupidity and greed he'd just witnessed, with its tragic consequences, sickened him. "How could they?"

"Why does any man commit treason while those around

them keep their honor?" Omas replied. "Some are weak fools. Others believe in causes."

It hurt like a knife thrust. Dain fought against doubling over. "My son will never inherit my throne," he said bleakly. "Is that the cause you mean?"

Omas's broad, hearty face creased with compassion. "I fear it must be, sire," he said softly. "It is bad enough, the fighting of man against man. But to turn against the little ones . . . ah, morde. What can anyone say to that?"

From behind them in the chamber arose another scream from Matej. Dain straightened himself and did not glance back until the sergeant came striding out to join him.

"The interrogations will continue, sire," the man said grimly.

"Indeed they will," Dain snapped. "I want every piece of information those men know."

"It will be done."

"If it takes too long, get a *sorcerel* down here to finish the task."

The sergeant's eyes widened. "But—"

"Gantese traitors in the palace . . . I want all the servants questioned, especially the nursery staff. I want the guards investigated as well."

"Sire!" the sergeant said in shock. "It wasn't us that—"

"The duty roster was changed two weeks early," Dain broke in furiously. "Who decided that?"

"I—I couldn't say, sire."

"Who disobeyed my direct order to move the auxiliaries off palace duty entirely?"

"I don't know, sire."

"All commanding officers will report to me. The entire palace is to be searched. And every officer on duty that day will give a full accounting. Now get to it."

Not waiting for the man's response, Dain strode out.

By nightfall, much of the plot had been uncovered. The king's order, sent by dispatch, had not reached the palace. The courier, missing for weeks and considered a deserter, was now believed dead. Two officers and ten guardsmen had confessed to taking bribes. The investigation continued, but Dain—

weary to his bones as well as heartsick—had learned enough
to confirm his suspicions.

He sat in his council room, scowling, while thoughts
wearily chased through his brain. His advisers and two of his
generals clustered before him, richly clad and serious of mien.
The hour grew late, and lamps burned soft light about the
room, the flickering illumination making the faces and figures
painted on the wall panels appear to dance and shift. Thum
hovered near Dain's chair, his freckled face worn with sorrow.
He had married the previous year, taking as his bride a shy,
rather plain-faced maiden with soft eyes and a sweet disposi-
tion. As yet they had no children. Now minister of state, holding one of the most powerful offices in Nether beneath the
king's authority, Thum's steady advice and wily strategics had
steered Dain through many hazards since he took the throne.
Dain was thankful to have him there.

Taking no part in the discussion raging between Tustik and
Unshalin, Thum's hazel eyes watched Dain rather than the
meeting. "How fare you, old friend?" he asked quietly, while
the debate crisscrossed the room. "How fares the queen?"

"She's poorly," Dain replied, rubbing his gritty eyes. They
burned with fatigue, for he could neither rest nor sleep. Time
had become his enemy. It kept trickling away, washing
Tashalya farther and farther out on a tide of danger, while he
delayed here. Yet he must deal with certain matters before he
rushed off in pursuit. Or so argued his mind, while his heart
thundered to be gone. "I looked in on my lady before this
meeting, but she was asleep."

"And the Princess Mareitina?"

Dain shrugged. "No longer hysterical, but I can't reach her.
I've asked the priests if it's advisable to take her into the presence of the Chalice, but—"

"Your majesty!" Count Unshalin called out pompously.
"Despite all the reports, it seems fantastic that Gant is behind
this plot. The Chalice protects us from—"

"The Chalice discourages the presence of Nonkind, but it
guards us not from the evil of weak and greedy men willing
to commit treason for gold," Dain said.

"But the Grethori are not allied with Gant—"

"Perhaps," Dain broke in, thinking of the information he'd gleaned from Vlink the spy several weeks ago. "Perhaps not. Let us cut to the crux of the matter. A plot has been laid against me. It was not by chance that I was lured away to Thirst Hold. And it was not until I was absent from Grov, but my family here, that the Grethori took action. It was not by chance that my son—the heir to Nether's throne—was slain, or that my firstborn was abducted."

Unshalin gripped his heavy chain with both hands and bowed. "Sire, we grieve over these events, but Princess Tashalya is only a girl-child."

Dain jerked to his feet, and silence fell over the room. "Never say that in my presence again," Dain said coldly while Unshalin changed color. "She is firstborn! The eld folk understand the potency of that. So do the Grethori savages. So do the Gantese. In the wrong hands, she can be turned into leverage against me. She must be recovered."

"Sire," Tustik said, coming forward, his voice precise and measured, "we all know that the princess royal is your favorite child and that you—"

"I will get her back," Dain said harshly.

"Three companies of troops were sent in pursuit, your majesty," Tustik said. "They failed to find any trace."

"There are other ways to hunt," Dain replied. "I will ride at dawn. Meanwhile, the palace is to be purged of spies, agents, and secret Believers. When I return, I expect to find every guilty man and woman held accountable."

The advisers exchanged looks, and some of them shook their heads doubtfully. Tustik spread out his thin hands. "If your majesty is correct in thinking this enemy waited until your absence to strike, what might next happen when your majesty departs again?"

"What if this is a trap for your majesty?" Minshilev asked. Short and stocky, he cocked his head at a belligerent angle as though to negate the worry shining in his eyes. "And Princess Tashalya is the bait?"

Unshalin nodded. "The man makes a valid point, sire. Besides, autumn is coming on. Your majesty could be trapped in snowfall, your return hindered. And then what would happen?"

Dain could see at least another hour of pointless discussion and argument. He frowned. "Thank you, my lords," he said, forcing himself to utter courtesies instead of swearing at them. "I shall depart at dawn with an army. Lord Thum will continue his duties in my absence, and I rely on each of you to carry on with matters of state as necessary. That is all."

They stared at him, looking shocked, stunned, or horrified. None of them, however, dared argue with him. Dain glanced at Thum, aware of his friend's grave concerns but unwilling to discuss them. He set his hand briefly on Thum's shoulder and gripped it hard.

"May Thod preserve you," Thum whispered.

Meeting his eyes, Dain nodded before leaving the council room in silence.

His path back to the queen's apartments took him through the Gallery of Glass, where his richly dressed courtiers thronged. At Dain's appearance, they rushed forward to greet him with bows and deep curtsies. Brow furrowed, his mind occupied with all that remained to do, Dain strode through their midst without pause or acknowledgment. Overhead, the hanging globes of bard crystal swayed gently in the breeze flowing in through the open windows. They sighed and sang soft melodies as Dain walked beneath them.

This long chamber, a marvel of mirrored walls, tall windows, and the countless globes and prisms of bard crystal, had been restored at enormous cost. Bard crystal, known to some as king's glass, had been imported from Saelutia, Mandria, and even Nold in order to collect enough. Dain remembered the first time he entered the room, when its magnificence lay in ruins, the mirrors shattered and fly-specked, the globes stolen, the floor scarred and gouged, and the furniture gone. Even now, with all his present worries, as he strode past the place where Gavril had struck him down with the evil sword Tanengard, memory rose up vividly enough to make Dain falter.

He recovered quickly, but at his side Omas shot him a look of concern. Ignoring it, Dain continued through the gallery, his stride faster than ever. Protocol demanded that he respond to the highest-ranked nobles paying him obeisance, but Dain had no time for courtesy. Except . . .

Catching sight of Lady Devenya Osolesk, he halted before her. The lady's pallor and reddened eyes were in sorry contrast to her gŏwn of cream-colored velvet trimmed at the sleeves and hem with pale islean fur. With trained grace, she curtsied deeply to him.

"My lady," Dain said to her while all looked on, "the king is informed that your husband and brother were among those who came to defense of the royal family."

Her mouth trembled, but she managed to look up and meet his eyes without tears. "My brother will recover from his wounds, sire," she whispered.

"That is good. The king grieves with you over the death of Lord Osolesk. He was a fine man. His valor will not be forgotten."

A tiny smile came and went on her pale lips, but she lifted her head with pride and seemed heartened by his kindness. Nodding to her, Dain walked on.

He saw Archduke Vladno Krelinik bowing a bit stiffly, one arm held in a sling. Vladno had also tried to defend the family. Dain spoke to him briefly, thanking him for his courage. "In these dark days, it is good to know the loyalty of true friends," he said.

Vladno inclined his head. For once the young archduke's customary smirk was absent. "I am your majesty's man to the death," he replied.

There were others to be noted and thanked, but as Dain glimpsed Jonan skulking at the rear of the assembly, he left them with a nod and beckoned to his cousin with a snap of his fingers.

Murmurs spread through the courtiers as Jonan turned bright red and came stumbling up. He bowed with a jerk. "I'm—I'm sorry about Tashalya and Ilymir, sire," he mumbled. "It's awful."

Dain ignored his clumsy attempt at condolence. He stared at Jonan very hard, and several phrases from past conversations clicked together in his mind. "You'll ride with me on the morrow," he announced.

People stared in surprise. Vladno's mouth fell open. Jonan stared at Dain in unconcealed dismay. "But—but, sire, I don't—I can't be of help."

Dain's stern expression never lightened. He knew the boy was too hapless to be of use in a fight. No doubt he'd have to be kept at the rear of the company and guarded lest harm come to him. But Dain had no intention of leaving the boy behind. Gantese plots were rife within the palace; no doubt insurrectionists were equally hard at work. Tustik's warnings about Jonan and palace coups were suddenly very clear.

"You are my kinsman," Dain said to him loudly enough to be overheard. "I want you at my side. No argument, boy! Be ready to ride at dawn."

Jonan's mouth hung open, but Dain strode on without giving him a chance to protest.

As he left the gallery, the buzz of countless conversations rose behind him. Someone came hurrying after the king, calling out, but Omas fended him off with a growl, and Dain never looked around to see if it was Jonan or someone else.

"Now, sire, you'll go to your chambers and rest," the protector said firmly.

Thinking of the queen and the dispatches he needed to write, Dain flogged his aching brain to decide which task should be done next. *The queen first*, he thought, *then the dispatches*. Then he would sleep.

"You need to eat," Omas was saying. "And if you'll forgive me, sire, you're reeling on your feet. You'll be unfit to ride tomorrow if you don't give yourself—"

"Samderaudin," Dain said to Evo, as though he'd heard nothing Omas said. "Have him waiting in my chambers. Privately. I'll see him as soon as I leave the queen."

"Yes, your majesty," the aide said.

Dain glanced at Omas. "What's the hour?"

"Late," the protector said grimly, glaring at him.

Dain nodded. "Time you were relieved. I want you fresh tomorrow."

"Sire—"

Dain held up his hand. "I know." He met Omas's brown eyes, and for a moment they were not king and protector but instead friends. He sighed. "I'll rest when I have Tashalya safely home."

Chapter Eleven

Dain entered the queen's apartments unannounced and unnoticed to find a grim-faced Alexeika busily stuffing articles of clothing in a pair of saddlebags. Severgard was lying on the bed beside her pair of daggers and her old suit of chain mail. Still attired in her bedgown with a pale green robe worn over it, Alexeika had braided and pinned up her shining lengths of dark chestnut hair, exposing the bruise on her temple.

Her ladies-in-waiting were not in evidence. Her maidservant stood in the doorway wringing her hands, as Alexeika moved back and forth. "Oh, my sweet lady," the woman was moaning. "Mercy of Riva, what shall become of us?"

"I don't care," Alexeika said curtly. "I'm not leaving her in the hands of those vile—"

"I promised I'd get her back," Dain interrupted. "And I shall."

Gasping, the servant ducked out of his way. Alexeika spun around so fast she staggered and had to catch herself. In two strides he had her in his arms, gathering her close.

With a sigh she melted against him. "Oh, Faldain," she said in relief. "I was told you'd gone—"

"I've been questioning the children's protectors," he said. "And making sure the Privy Council understands that Thum continues to bear authority in my absence. It was a Gantese plot, beloved. The protectors took bribes."

She looked up at him swiftly, her blue-gray eyes ablaze. "What?"

"Aye. It took torture to wring the confession from them, but I'm sure."

"But the Grethori have nothing to do with Gant," she said, frowning. "I don't understand."

He explained, but soon realized she wasn't paying attention. She stood gazing at nothing, various expressions crossing her oval face.

"It doesn't matter now," he said, gripping her shoulder. He realized how much he'd missed her, how much he needed her. He tried to gather her closer, but she shrugged away from him and began to pace slowly back and forth across her chamber. She was holding her side as though it pained her, but she wore that determined, driven expression that he recognized all too well.

"I ride at dawn," he said. "Alexeika—"

"Good." She shot him a glance and nodded at her belongings. "I'll be ready."

"You aren't going."

"I am!"

"You're wounded," he reminded her gently, trying not to upset her more by arguing with her. "And your head aches. I can see that it does."

She scowled. "It's better. I'll be able to ride. Faldain, I must go after her! She'll be so frightened."

"I know. But Mareitina needs you, too."

Alexeika's eyes widened. As he'd intended, she pounced on the distraction. "You saw her? How is she? What do the physicians say? Why won't the fools let me see her?"

"She needs treatment that they can't give her," he replied, and saw fresh hurt fill her eyes. He wanted to take it away and undo all that had happened. The fact that he couldn't made him feel helpless and inadequate. He knew it was absurd, but he felt as though he'd failed her and the children alike. "She's too shocked to know who is with her or where she is. If she's touched, she becomes hysterical."

Alexeika began to cry. "Poor little one."

"I was able to calm her, but that's all. I think we should try the healing powers of the Chalice first, but if that doesn't avail, I have also sent word to Nilainder, asking for a healer."

She lifted her hands to her mouth. He went to her, but before he could touch her, she glared at him.

"The Grethori will pay for this, for all they've done," she said. "I will see them slaughtered for it. I swear this, Faldain."

He curled his fingers around hers. "I've already taken that oath. You have no need to swear it, too."

"You won't do what I intend to do to them," she said furiously. "You'll find them. You may even rescue our little girl. But you won't hurt them as I want them hurt. You won't—"

"Would you have me compete with you in boasting of what I intend?" he cut in. "Am I to prove that I am as bloodthirsty as you?"

"It's why I must go," she said firmly, twisting her hand from his. "I must see this done."

"You're not well enough," he said. "Mareitina needs your care. And I need you here, guarding my throne."

"You have Thum to do that."

"We thought ourselves secure. I thought the worst was behind us. I was wrong. I've grown complacent, Alexeika, dependent on the Chalice to guard us. I've been tricked, and I find my palace riddled with spies and traitors. Thum is only one man, and Mandrian."

Her eyes widened. "You doubt him?"

"Never. But I need you here."

"I'm a woman!" she shouted in frustration. "I can't do anything. I have no authority."

"You have the seal, which I entrusted to your care. Give it to me now."

She stared at him, her eyes hot and unreadable for a moment, then she went to do his bidding, producing it from a secret place he did not see. He opened the box she held out to him and took the heavy seal from its velvet lining.

"I'll prepare a secret document of authority for your use,

should it become necessary. I would to Thod I could name you my successor should anything happen, but—"

"No," she said, looking stunned. Color surged into her face, then ebbed away. "No."

"I will give you the authority to choose my heir," he told her grimly. "If not, Jonan will succeed me, and I can't permit that to happen. Swear to me you will fight him, and fight all who support him. Swear to me, Alexeika!"

"I—I—how can I?" she blurted out. "The law forbids a woman to—"

"I would to Thod there was time to rescind such a law," Dain said.

"Neither the Kollegya nor the Privy Council will allow me any say."

"Make them heed you. You must hold the realm, Alexeika. Only you are strong enough to do it. And see it goes to the proper hands."

"Whose?"

"Thum will advise you."

She was staring at him as though she'd never seen him before. Emotions flashed in her face, and abruptly she turned and threw the wooden box across the room. It smashed against the wall and broke.

"I can't stand this!" she cried out. "You—you're preparing for your death."

"'Tis a contingency," he said quietly. "Only that. I don't intend to die, beloved, but without Ilymir I cannot leave Grov without some kind of plan in place."

She rushed to him with a wordless cry and held him close. "This is a nightmare. I keep hoping I'll awake and find it a bad dream. But it goes on and on. I don't want to lose you, too!"

He held her, breathing in the scent of her hair, and kissed her long and hard, with all his longing and need. To stay with her, to spend the night wrapped in her silken embrace . . . he wanted it more than anything. Even to stand here, holding her this way, brought an aching war between his desire for her and the need to accomplish all that must be done before his departure.

"You aren't going to lose me," he said gruffly. "And we

aren't going to lose Tashalya. I'm going now to talk with Samderaudin and ask him to part the veils of seeing. If he can tell me where she's been taken, I'll be on them before they have a chance."

Her hands tightened on his shoulders. "Be careful," she said passionately. "Promise me that you'll be careful."

He took her hands and kissed her palms. "I promise."

"You've given me the hardest job," she whispered. "Staying behind and waiting."

"I trust Thum more than any man in this kingdom," Dain said solemnly. "And I trust you above Thum."

She stared at him mutely.

He kissed her hard and long. "Now," he said, forcing himself to release her. "I must go."

She clung to his arm. "I have something more to tell you, something I meant to say at the fjord, our last night there." Her eyes lifted and held his. "I am with child again."

He was stunned. It seemed impossible, like a tiny ray of hope in the darkness. "Alexeika!"

"It will come in the spring." Tears shimmered in her eyes. "I wanted it to be a surprise, a gift."

"It *is*!"

"But there's never been the right opportunity to tell you. And now you are going once more, and everything is so—this baby can't replace Ilymir. I don't want him to!"

He kissed her hand, loving her more than he ever had before. "Don't say that. Don't think that. This baby is hope for us. We'll never ask it to take Ilymir's place. Never! But we can go on. We have to. For this little one's sake, and for Mareitina."

"And for Tashalya," she whispered.

A lump choked his throat. He swallowed and nodded emphatically. "I won't come back without her," he said.

She stared up at him with trust and hope, and he kissed her once more before he pushed himself away and left.

Samderaudin was not waiting in Dain's quarters when he arrived. Dain stared at the tray of food that had grown cold beneath its covers and quelled a childish urge to fling it on the floor. "Where is he?" he demanded of a wide-eyed Evo. "Was my command not sent to him?"

The boy, thin and fair-haired, stared at him in alarm. "Aye, your majesty."

"Then why in Thod's name isn't he here?" Dain shouted.

The lamps flickered and almost went out. Evo gulped, mumbling something inaudible, and Dain nearly shouted at him again before realizing what he was doing. He stopped himself, frowning at the boy so ferociously that his young aide turned pale.

I cannot go on this way, Dain told himself. He was nearly out of control, so close to the edge of exploding that if he did not stop himself soon, he might do or say something unforgivable. Evo did not deserve his wrath, and he felt ashamed of himself for treating Evo, and his other attendants, so harshly.

For the first time since he'd heard the news at the border crossing, he simply stopped. A huge wave of fatigue rolled over him, making him sway. *Omas was right*, he thought numbly. *I've been driving myself too hard.*

"I'm sorry, sire," Evo was stammering. "I'll go and see if I can urge the *sorcerel* to attend your majesty more promptly."

"Stop." Dain gave him a vague wave and dropped heavily into a chair. "You can't herd Samderaudin. He'll come if he intends to obey me. Otherwise, he won't. Laure!"

The squire materialized, looking Dain over with a slight frown, and set to work pulling off his boots. He took away armor and sword, and Dain tugged the circlet from his brow with a sigh, tossing it onto the desk next to his food tray.

"Shall I serve you?" Evo asked nervously.

Dain nodded, and the boy removed the covers and set bowls of food before him. Dain hardly glanced at his dinner. His head was buzzing, and he felt wrung out from all the emotions he'd gone through.

A cup was pressed into his hand. "Here, sire. Your favorite wine."

He didn't want it. Suddenly all he desired was to fall into bed and sleep for a year. But he couldn't do that. He still had dispatches to write and the document of authority to prepare for Alexeika. He could send for a clerk and dictate the dispatches and orders, but the other paper had to be secret. He would have to compose and write it himself, and that would take him a long time.

Wearily, he sighed.

"Drink it, sire," Evo urged him worriedly. "Please."

"Leave his majesty be, boy," Laure said in a sharp voice. "He's tired and doesn't need your nagging."

Lord Miest came on duty, pausing in the doorway to exchange a brief, inaudible conversation with Omas. His gaze slid over the untouched food and the cup held slackly in Dain's fingers, and he sighed.

With an effort, Dain roused himself and looked up at the protector. "We leave at dawn," he said. "You'll come, too. It will be a hard ride for you after no sleep, but I'll need you."

"Of course, sire," Miest said. He bowed to Dain and took up a stance over by the fire, alert and silent. Unlike Omas, he never protested or argued or exceeded his place. He was simply there, dependable and quiet, ready anytime he was needed.

A good man, but not a friend. Dain had sworn long ago when he lost Sir Polquin and Sir Terent in his defense, that he would never again befriend a protector. But he could not help liking Omas, and now he told himself the giant was right. He needed to care for himself if he intended to accomplish his objective of rescuing Tashalya.

Lifting the cup, he swallowed its contents quickly, then picked at his food. It was tasteless and cold. He liked it not, but he ate it anyway. Just as he finished, Samderaudin arrived.

The *sorcerel* glided into the room with no visible motion of his feet. His tilted, pale yellow eyes were intent, and his face was as smooth and unlined as a sheet of parchment, the skin rigid as though the years had stretched it taut. The moment he entered the room, the air seemed to charge from his presence, like the atmosphere before a lightning storm. His clothing smelled of herbs and magic. He was ancient, potent, the keeper of innumerable secrets.

Laure and Evo retreated from him warily. Miest stood

taller, with his hand resting casually on his sword hilt although Samderaudin could crush him with a word.

Rising, Dain faced the *sorcerel*. "Have you done as I requested?"

"The veils will not be parted," Samderaudin replied.

It took Dain a few seconds to comprehend his meaning. Even then, Dain stared at him hard, not quite willing to believe what he'd just heard. "Are you saying you cannot find her?"

"Darkness surrounds the princess."

"But she lives?" Dain asked sharply.

Samderaudin's pale yellow eyes shimmered in the lamplight. "That, I sense strongly. So do you."

Dain nodded, for on some deep, inward level he had a link with Tashalya. They had always been bonded this way, since the moment of her birth, when he'd held her and gazed deep into her blue eyes.

"You, Faldain, can find her better than I."

"I need your help," Dain said in protest. "I must find her quickly before the savages harm her."

"If to harm her they intend, already it is done. You," Samderaudin said, his voice humming and resonating through the chamber, "have time to do all that will be accomplished. Take heed, and do not rush into what you do not understand."

Dain was in no mood to be advised to wait. "I leave at dawn," he said through his teeth. "Will you accompany me?"

"Is that your order?"

Warned by the note in Samderaudin's voice, Dain said nothing.

"Wise," Samderaudin said softly. His eyes gleamed. "Very wise. You are swept with anger tonight. You want to wage war and shed blood. You are not thinking. You come to perilous times."

"Is that a prophecy?" Dain snapped. "Vaunit has already foretold my death. Will you do the same?"

Samderaudin steepled his fingers together, and tiny sparks flew between his talons. "Look carefully before you act," he replied obliquely, parting his hands to draw flaming symbols in the air. "Nothing is as it seems."

Frowning, Dain wrinkled his nostrils against the smoke of Samderaudin's little magic display. "Who, then?" he asked. "Where?"

The *sorcerel* went on drawing in flames and did not answer.

Dain's frown deepened. He was too tired to deal with riddles. If Samderaudin would not, or could not, give him the help he asked for, he did not intend to waste time trying to guess the *sorcerel's* meaning.

"That is your choice," Samderaudin said, as though Dain had spoken his thoughts aloud. "But beware the desire for battle. That path holds great danger. There is more at stake than a missing child."

Dain struggled to keep his temper under control, aware that Samderaudin was deliberately trying to provoke him. "The missing child," he said with forced patience, "is my daughter. My firstborn. I know what that means to the Grethori. They can create magic from that, some spell, I know not what."

Samderaudin stopped drawing symbols of fire and turned to face Dain. "This is true."

"But if they sell her to an enemy—"

Samderaudin lifted his bony hands with a smile. "Now Faldain is thinking. Now you understand."

"Who paid them?" Dain asked hoarsely, clenching his fists. "Who incited them to commit this foul deed?"

"Torture all who have been captured, and the complete truth will still not be found."

"But—"

"Darkness surrounds Tashalya. Know that, and pay heed. Those who have taken her want something from you. Give it not, and they will discard her. Then you can have your daughter back."

Such cold-blooded advice made Dain scowl. "The Grethori do not ransom prisoners. I dare not wait."

"Then you are lost, and your enemy is victor."

The pronouncement made Dain shiver, but he tried to hide his alarm. Desperately he sought a way to gain Samderaudin's help. "She has the ability to become a *sorcerelle*," he said at last. "Had all this not happened, I intended to consult with you about her training."

Samderaudin narrowed his eyes. "You want her trained to avoid her gifts, to let them wither inside her, unused!"

"Aye!" Dain retorted, glaring right back. "That's true!"

"It is too late for that."

"All right," Dain said raggedly, "if it must be, I'll accept it. I'll let you train her fully. But help me find her. Help me get her back!"

A map of Nether materialized out of thin air and shimmered before Dain. He heard Evo cry out in startlement, but he did not flinch. Instead, he leaned forward eagerly, peering at the misty landmarks that came and went in little flickers.

Focus your mind, Samderaudin said into his thoughts. *Seek her. Close your eyes and seek her.*

Dain obeyed, shutting his eyes and forcing himself to calm some of his inner turmoil. The task was nearly impossible, for he held such forces of sorrow, grief, rage, and worry inside him that he felt he might explode if he bottled it much more tightly. But at last, by small degrees, he forced it down, compressing his emotions into a smaller and smaller bundle, while he spread his senses forth.

Tashalya! he called.

When she was very, very young, he'd taught her to listen for the touch of his mind to hers, and to answer if ever she felt him call to her this way.

Now, battling down a fresh surge of worry, he focused himself and called again: *Tashalya!*

Vaguely he felt an unfamiliar force wrap itself around him, augmenting his call, increasing his power in a way he'd never experienced before. It was Samderaudin, he realized, helping him.

He called a third time: *Tashalya!*

And from far away, he sensed a tiny spark in answer. *Papa!* she called back. *Oh, Papa, come!*

And then it was gone, that tiny voice, as though he'd only imagined it.

"Swiftly," Samderaudin growled in his ear. "Point to the map. Swiftly!"

Dain stabbed his forefinger through the air and opened his eyes. He was pointing at the Kransval Mountains, a rugged range partway across the realm. *Not the World's Rim*, he thought in relief. *Not that far away.*

The Kransvals stood as a gateway to the northern steppes, vast grassy plains that offered golden grazing in summer to the herds of danselk that migrated across them. In winter, the steppes were a harsh, forbidding place of violent winds and gusting blizzards.

It's autumn now, he thought, and felt fresh urgency knot his entrails.

"Ah," Samderaudin said in satisfaction. With a wave of his hand, the map vanished in a tiny puff of smoke. "The king has found his own answer."

"Yes," Dain said. He swallowed hard, feeling relief and urgency crossing him in waves. He knew now where to go. He could ride northwest with all speed, cutting through the valleys to save time up into the foothills of those mountains. "Thank you, Samderaudin."

The *sorcerel's* yellow eyes bored into his. "Cannot wait?" he asked softly. "Will not wait? Why not use Solder's Ring and get her fast?"

Vaunit had tempted him thus, too. Dain stared down at the Ring on his finger, carved with the ancient runes, the great milky stone pale in its setting. The quick answer. The perfect solution. He could be there in less than a breath.

Angrily, he shoved the temptation aside and glared at the *sorcerel*. "It's not to be used for personal gain!" he said fiercely. "Only to serve the Chalice. You and Vaunit know that!"

Samderaudin's eyes glittered at Dain strangely. "Not even for this will Faldain be corrupted," he whispered as though to himself. "Not yet. Interesting."

Dain's brows drew together in alarm. He had to struggle not to step back from the *sorcerel*. "I will not repeat my father's mistakes."

"Is it worthwhile to be the perfect one? In not making Tobeszijian's mistakes, what mistakes has Faldain made instead?"

There was no answer Dain could give without admitting things he didn't want to say. He felt suddenly hot and confused; the air seemed too stuffy.

"It is decided," Samderaudin said, and Dain felt released by some invisible force, as though he could breathe again. "Perilous times have you chosen. The risks could be less if you use the Ring."

"No," Dain said. The constant fascination of the *sorcerels* with the Ring of Solder worried him. He'd long suspected that they coveted the Ring's power. "I'll ride there, with my men."

"Then beware of what is to come, for the price is costly."

Dain's mouth went dry. "Then you agree with Vaunit's prophecy."

"There is no error in what the portents say." Samderaudin's eyes bored into his. "Beware, Faldain. You have betrayed fate often, but this time it may betray you."

Chapter Twelve

Jonan had never been more miserable in his life. For the past fifteen days, he'd been jounced in a saddle in all types of weather and terrain. After the first brutal day, he was so sore he could barely walk, and the following morning he yelped when he climbed into the saddle. The men laughed at him, and Faldain had sent him a look of such impatience that Jonan, burning with shame, had tried to hide his misery. But the discomfort only grew worse, until he whimpered and moaned and pleaded for permission to turn back. The king had flatly refused, and the torture continued.

The wind and dust made him cough, and at night he wheezed and suffered. At the very least he'd expected the king to order tents pitched at their nightly campsites, with cots and chairs and other amenities. But, nay, they slept on the hard ground like common troops, rolled in blankets with not even a pillow for comfort. When they ate, the cold rations were usually dreadful, hard cakes of meal and lard, smoked meat with the consistency and taste of string, and canteen water to wash it down. Jonan's stomach, always delicate, rebelled against such fare. He often rode queasy, gritting his teeth and using all his willpower not to be sick.

There was no chance to get clean. He felt as though his teeth were permanently coated with dust, and his eyes stung and watered. If they did not ride fogged with dust, then they were subjected to the violence of autumn storms. Lashing winds and cracks of lightning made him flinch while torrential downpours soaked him to the skin and turned the footing into boggy mud.

And through it all, the king rode in full armor, his face grim and his manner curt. Jonan feared this bleak mood of his cousin's, and he witnessed the care of the men and officers in not provoking Faldain's temper.

Twice, they encountered road bandits, fearsome brutes who burst from the trees in ambush with yells and flashing weapons. Both occasions had caught Jonan entirely by surprise, and although the battles were swift and easily won by the knights, Jonan found himself trembling for hours afterward, starting at the least sound, and unable to feel secure. He had no gift at handling weapons, and he wished with all his heart that he'd not ventured into the wilderness. Not that Faldain had given him a choice.

I hope we don't find Tashalya, Jonan thought resentfully. *I hope she has been sold into slavery and is gone forever. The little she-cat got what she deserved.*

Of course he dared not voice his opinion aloud, especially not in the vicinity of Faldain. His cousin's worry and strain were so evident that Jonan couldn't help but feel sorry for him. He blamed Tashalya for causing her father such trouble and grief. *And me*, he thought. *If it weren't for her, I wouldn't be out here risking my life.*

The whole attempt to rescue her seemed futile to him, anyway. They were too far behind. They'd never find her, although according to rumor the king was following some magical trail Samderaudin had given him. Jonan feared that Faldain would never give up, and they might ride hither and yon for months, perhaps years, in search of the brat. It was an impossible quest, and Jonan daydreamed of himself, suddenly

endowed with manly courage, standing up to Faldain and
counseling him to give up his quest.

"You must accept the fact that she's lost forever," Jonan
imagined himself saying. "You've done all that a father can.
Now it's time to turn back."

He pretended that Faldain, grown haggard and thin, would
look at him with agreement and praise his good sense. And
the men would cheer Jonan's name in relief and gratitude as
they all turned back toward Grov.

"Here, yer highness!" shouted his protector, jolting Jonan
from his daydream. "Watch yerself and don't slap me in the
face with these branches."

Blinking, Jonan stared at his protector's irate face and realized he'd been letting the brush they were pushing through
swing freely behind him. "Back off a bit, Sir Basil. You ride too
close."

The protector scowled. "That's Bansil, not Basil!"

"Oh, yes." Jonan felt the tips of his ears grow hot, and he
swiftly faced forward, kicking his horse faster through the
low-growing pine boughs. The pungent smell of the needles
made him sneeze, and he could overhear the protector muttering and grumbling beneath his breath.

Jonan hated the surly fellow who'd been assigned to him.
Why couldn't he keep a civil tongue in his head? And what
did it matter if he couldn't remember Bansil's name?

"Hsst! Yer highness, hold up!" Sir Bansil whispered.
"Din't ye see the signal?"

"What signal?"

"Quiet!" Gesturing vehemently, the protector stared past
Jonan toward the front of the column.

The thick trees hid most of the men ahead of Jonan, and he
couldn't see whatever Bansil was watching for. Shivering in
the shade, Jonan wished they could have stopped out in the
open sunshine. His throat felt scratchy and sore, and he suffered from a steady ache above his eyebrows. By nightfall he
probably would be ill, and they did not even have a physician
in attendance.

"We're to close ranks," Sir Bansil said in a low voice.
"Quietly now."

Frowning, Jonan urged his horse forward. As he ducked out from the pine grove into the open, he found himself staring openmouthed at the mountain rising above him. It looked steep and forbidding, with more mountains stacked behind it. Snow glistened on the summits, and he shivered with a sinking heart.

"Merciful Thod, I don't want to go *there*," he said.

An officer in the garish Agya colors of crimson and blue was waiting for him, gesturing impatiently. "You, highness," he said with haste, not even bothering to bow in respect, "will go to the front, near the king. We can guard both of you better if you are together, *neya*?"

Nervousness claimed Jonan. He frowned, hunching his shoulders beneath his cloak. "Is there danger?"

The Agya's dark face frowned. "*Aychi!* Of course there is danger. Grethori signs are everywhere. Quickly, come!"

Jonan's mouth went dry. By the time he tried to protest, it was too late. Sir Bansil and the Agya were on either side of him, and his horse was trotting with theirs past the knights toward the head of the column, where Faldain's pennon flew in the cold wind. The king was standing in his stirrups, his lean, chiseled face intent as he studied the trail ahead.

The sight of the narrow track winding steeply up the mountain slope made Jonan's heart quail. "Sire," he said, his voice squeaking, "we can't ride through all these mountains before dark. Why don't we camp here now, rest, and then set out—"

Faldain turned. "Oh, it's you, Jonan," he said absently. With a deftness that Jonan envied, he loosened his sword in its scabbard before unstrapping his helmet from his saddle and ramming it over his head. With the visor up, he stared at Jonan with fierce gray eyes.

"Now, boy, make sure you don't forget your instructions."

Observing the men also preparing themselves for battle, Jonan was all too aware that he, like the squires, wore no armor and carried nothing besides a dagger for defense. His heart began to thud, and he felt dizzy.

"Sire," he said unsteadily, "are we about to fight?"

"If Thod is with us," Faldain replied grimly. But then he

sent Jonan a quick smile. "Nay, lad, 'tis unlikely today, but every knight knows not to ride into enemy territory unprepared. According to the scouts, there's been a band of Grethori camped recently in the saddle between this peak and the next. We're less than a day's ride behind them now. Very close! So we must go swiftly, and I think we should keep as quiet as we can. Sound can echo very far in the mountains, and I ask you to remember not to talk. Jonan! Are you paying heed?"

Jonan looked up. "I—uh, yes, sire."

"Stay close to me at all times. But if there should be any trouble, I want you to fall back and join the squires. Sir Bansil will protect you, but you are responsible for getting yourself out of the thick of battle. Is that clear? None of the men can bother with your safety."

The king's eyes were as clear and pale as rain. *He's not afraid*, Jonan thought in amazement, and prayed that his own sense of panic did not show. "But if your majesty knows we're about to ride into battle, why don't you leave the squires and—and me behind?"

Lord Omas's laugh rumbled behind his thick mustache, and exasperation crossed Faldain's face.

"Have I not said we won't catch them today?" the king asked. "Tomorrow, perhaps, if fortune smiles on us."

"Then why all this bother?" Jonan frowned. "I don't—"

Faldain turned away and began issuing a series of orders to his officers.

Jonan felt as though he might cry. "Please," he whispered. "I want to go b—"

But no one was listening. The king spurred his horse forward, and before he realized it Jonan found himself swept along up the mountain. The trail wound steeply, and soon the column narrowed to two men abreast. Numb with fear, Jonan was grateful that Sir Bansil chose to ride on the outer edge of the trail between him and the canyon falling away on the other side.

Gradually his heart stopped thumping so hard, and he realized that while the men around him were very alert, they exhibited no fear. Neither were they gripping their weapons. Jonan's sense of acute panic faded.

Besides, he had other problems. The higher up the mountain they rode, the worse he felt. His throat hurt more and more. There wasn't enough air to breathe, and his chest felt as though it had been filled with rocks. Worriedly, he thought of the empty vial in his saddlebags. He'd used up his medicine days ago, for breathing so much dust on the journey had made his lungs hurt, and he used the potion to help him sleep. Now, he realized, he was riding into very real danger far different from bandits or Grethori. No one present understood how bad this thin air was for his chest.

Wheezing and starting to feel light-headed, he struggled to fill his lungs and was afraid he would die soon.

By the time the trail widened and leveled off in a notch on the side of the mountain, Jonan had had more than enough. Patches of snow lay in thin drifts beneath the bushes. A cloud drifted over them, wrapping them in gray mist so that they were forced to halt until it drifted on and the sun came out again. The air struck him like knives of ice, and his fingers had turned blue. He leaned over in the saddle, wheezing desperately, and began to cry.

"Here! What's the matter?" Sir Bansil asked him in a hoarse whisper. He gripped Jonan's shoulder and shook him. "Straighten up and look sharp lest the king see this."

But Jonan, terrified and struggling, hunched himself in a knot and wept on the neck of his horse.

The king turned his horse around and joined them. "What ails the boy?" he asked softly.

"Naught but a soured temper and a yellow back," Sir Bansil muttered.

Faldain gripped Jonan by his hair, pulling him upright. "Have you no inkling of what's at stake here? Did I not ask you to keep quiet? Did you not give me your word, Jonan?"

Staring at his cousin through tear-filled eyes, Jonan couldn't summon enough breath to explain. He sobbed harder and began coughing.

Faldain handed him a waterskin with a frown, and Jonan

gulped the cold water, spilling half of it down the front of his tunic.

"Ah, Thod's teeth," Lord Omas said in disgust, "he's so lily-livered he's crying like a babe."

"No—no—I just need—" Jonan wheezed to drag in air, but choked on his tears and the water, and went into another spasm of coughing.

"He's ill," Faldain said.

"Nay, majesty," Sir Bansil said. "Just scared out of his wits, more like. I've seen him do this before, work himself into a state when there's something he don't want to do."

"Send him down," Faldain said. "I'd no idea he was this afraid."

Shame filled Jonan. "Not a coward!" he gasped out. "Can't breathe!"

"Sick or scared," Faldain said curtly, "we've no more time to waste. Can you pull yourself together and not slow us down, or are you going to collapse again?"

His impatience and lack of sympathy made Jonan seethe, but already Faldain was shaking his head.

"This will not do," the king said. "Wait here until the entire company has passed you, then ride down and camp by the stream we crossed earlier. I can ill spare the men to guard you, but it has to be done."

"But I—"

"You'll stay there," Faldain said sternly. "I know not how many days it will be till I am able to return for you."

The chance to get off this awful mountain was too good to miss. Jonan wheezed in relief and nodded meekly.

"Chesil," the king said, "I put you in charge of Prince Jonan's safety."

The aide's bronzed face creased in dismay. "*Aychi!* I am sworn to the king's service, not this coward's."

"Chesil Matkevskiet!" Faldain said in annoyance. "Do you dare protest my order?"

Chesil bowed. "Nay, sire. Forgive me." But as he spoke, he shot Jonan a look of resentment.

"Lord Miest will go as well," Faldain ordered. He glanced

around and beckoned. "Pemikalievy, pull out a dozen men to go with his highness."

"Sire!"

Casting Jonan a look of scorching contempt, Pemikalievy made his selection.

"Thank you, sire!" Jonan called out.

Faldain flicked him a harsh glance and moved his horse onward. The knights chosen to escort Jonan down the mountain stayed beside him, while the rest of the company rode by with sidelong smirks. Even the squires, riding at the rear, cast Jonan looks of contempt.

Chesil, sitting rigidly next to Jonan, waited until the others had gone out of sight before he shot Jonan a glare and spat eloquently.

Heat surged into Jonan's face. He sputtered, but the rest of his escort was glaring at him, too.

"You should b-be glad to go back down," Jonan managed to gasp out. "You should thank me."

It was the wrong thing to say. Chesil's dark eyes narrowed. Swift as a striking snake, he gripped the front of Jonan's tunic and yanked him partway out of his saddle.

"Never say that to me again, *neya*?" he said in a soft, furious voice.

Swallowing hard, Jonan stared at him helplessly, and, after a long moment, Chesil released him.

Jonan smoothed the wrinkles in his tunic with a shaking hand. "You—you forget I am the king's cousin," he said raggedly, trying to sweep them all a look of hauteur and failing. "You must treat me with courtesy."

"Shut up," Chesil said, and kicked his horse forward. "Let us go."

Furious, Jonan found himself with nothing else to say. He began to cry again and wiped his face on his sleeve, smearing snot and tears together, while he concentrated on breathing. When Sir Bansil yanked the reins from his hands and began to lead his horse as though Jonan were a baby, his humiliation was complete. If they ever got home, everyone in the realm would know that he was not only the son of the most despised sovereign Nether had ever had, but that he was a coward and a failure as well. After coming all this way and enduring the most wretched physical hardships, he was being sent back in disgrace. And for something he couldn't help.

Chesil was a brute, Jonan thought miserably. Giving himself airs because he was the king's favorite aide. Everyone knew that Agyas were practically savages themselves, and hardly better than the Grethori. He glared at the back of Chesil's head, watching the young man's barbarous hair beads swing, and wished he dared say what he was thinking aloud.

As for Faldain, Jonan fumed, he hadn't even tried to understand. He'd been deliberately cruel, dragging Jonan on this brutal journey and subjecting him to hardship and suffering. Now he'd encouraged the men to despise Jonan.

As Jonan was led down the trail, choking and crying, he realized that he hated Faldain more than any of the others, more than Chesil Matkevskiet, Tashalya, or Prince Tustik, who'd forbidden him to see Lady Sofina again.

I hope you fail, he thought viciously. *Handsome, perfect, warrior king. You, Faldain, have everything, and I have nothing. I hope you never find your beastly daughter. I hope you suffer for that the rest of your life.*

Leaning forward as his horse lunged and scrambled over a broken gap in the trail, Dain glanced uneasily at the trees surrounding him. They grew thick and dark, with a ridge of boulders rising behind them that he did not like. This looked like a place for ambush, and he rode with his hand on his sword hilt.

Ahead, however, the trees thinned. Realizing that they were nearly above the tree line and eager to get back into the open, Dain held back the temptation to spur his horse. Lathered and nervous, the animal picked its way along the precipitous trail, pebbles shifting under its hooves.

Although Dain knew it was best not to look down, he spared a glance to his left and saw the specks of Jonan's sorry little band winding its way along the switchbacks far, far below.

Dain tightened his mouth in exasperation. Although he'd

kept Jonan out of the hands of court intriguers, he should have left the boy behind at one of the villages they'd passed. This journey had certainly failed to make a man of the wretch. Morde, how could Jonan have been given every advantage and still turn out to be such a craven coward? He was glad he'd let the boy turn back, although it annoyed him to lose the men, and he already regretted Chesil's absence. Evo tried hard, but lacked Chesil's efficiency. As for Jonan, well, it was a pity the boy had displayed his cowardice so openly before the men. Sighing, Dain reminded himself that bravery could not be forced into an individual, and he'd been wrong to try. Now he'd have to worry about the boy's safety here in Grethori territory, when surely he already had enough to occupy his mind.

Riding out into the open, Dain squinted against the sun. The wind was bitterly cold, robbing him of breath for a moment. Wheeling his horse to a halt, he gazed about. The ground was level in the clearing, but a short distance before him yawned a chasm that plunged to infinity. To his right rose the rest of the mountain, with the trail snaking up through rocks and snow to the summit. Above, the sky arced blue and bright, streaked with clouds that seemed to snag on the jagged mountain peaks as they drifted overhead.

Omas came up beside him, turning to watch the rest of the column straggling up the narrow trail. "Strung out too much," he muttered. "This is Thod-forsaken country. I like it not."

Dain pointed north. "Somewhere, beyond these mountains, lie the steppes. I have never seen them."

"Agya lands." Omas grunted, digging his forefinger inside the rim of his helmet to scratch. "Naught but danselk herds and giant beyars in that region. Not worth the journey."

"Maybe." Dain turned his gaze to squint at the eagles soaring amidst the peaks and canyons. He thought of Baz and home. He thought of grief and vengeance and the relentless force in his chest that kept driving him forward in the search for Tashalya. And the closer he came to where his senses had told him she would be, the fainter his link with her became. He was losing her, he thought, battling down a surge of worry.

All day, despite the Grethori tracks they'd found, he'd felt like she was no longer reachable.

But he must not lose heart now, he told himself. He was close. He had to be.

At that moment, boulders on the cliff above the trail came crashing down, accompanied by Grethori war cries. Several squires and a few knights at the rear of the column went plunging to their deaths. The alarm was sounded, and with a swift glance at how many men remained on the trail, Dain yelled at them to hurry.

No more than half the column had gained the clearing thus far. The rest still on the trail were in terrible danger. Shouting in fear and anger, they tried to save themselves, but that broken place in the trail had to be crossed one rider at a time. Bottlenecked and crowded from behind, the men swore and flogged their panicking horses.

More boulders went crashing onto the trail, and more men went plummeting to their deaths. Hearing the screams, Dain slammed down his visor and steeled his heart. He could do nothing for them save attack in retaliation.

As a battleground, the clearing was too small for proper maneuvering, and the sheer drop on one side made it dangerous indeed. He looked around, swiftly evaluating the odds, and pointed at the trees with his sword.

"Pemikalievy, rally the men! Attack their flank now!"

As the commander bawled orders, Dain rose in his stirrups and brandished Mirengard over his head. "For Nether!" he shouted.

And the men roared back their cry: "Faldain! Faldain!"

Dain led the charge into the forest, but Grethori were already rushing forth to meet them. Running on foot or mounted on stubby ponies with shaggy manes, the tribesmen had painted their faces in garish colors and braided their long hair and mustaches with the finger bones of slain enemies. Shrieking dementedly, they burst forth from cover, waving swords, clubs, and war axes. Above the din rose the shrill scree of their pipes, a noise so discordant and horrible that it hurt the ears. Having fought Grethori before, Dain knew their vicious tricks and lack of honor. He also knew how to kill them, and his heart blazed with the desire for vengeance.

Grimly, Dain met the first charge, and guided his horse straight at a man on foot. The savage leaped to one side, reaching out as though he intended to yank Dain from his saddle, but Dain's warhorse swerved and knocked the man down, trampling him, while Dain turned and met the sword of another foe.

Mirengard shattered this one's weapon, and one of the flying splinters of metal impaled the Grethori's eye. Screaming, he fell back against another comrade rushing to attack Dain with a war club, and Dain killed again.

More mounted Grethori came charging forth from the trees, galloping into the fray. Their weapons glinted in the sunlight.

"They mean to drive us back over the edge, sire!" Omas shouted.

Dain glanced over his shoulder and saw that his protector was right. With Grethori streaming at them from one side, a chasm behind them, a goat track on their right and a worse trail going straight up on their left, they were in a damnable position. He knew it. His men knew it.

Aware that if his knights lost heart now, they would be defeated, Dain spurred his horse into rearing. Lifting his sword high so that sunshine flashed down the blade, Dain yelled his war cry, and his men shouted in answer.

That's when he glimpsed the Grethori chieftain, a burly man with long dingy hair separated in plaits, a face painted yellow and green, and a pair of scimitars held Agya style in his hands. Savage exhilaration rose in Dain. That was the one he wanted. If he could defeat their chieftain, the Grethori would flee. Seldom would they fight without a leader.

Dain galloped straight at the man, mowing down those who got in his way. Omas rode at his left flank and another knight stuck to his right.

Shrieking curses in his own language, the chieftain kicked his shaggy mount forward to meet Dain. They clashed together, swords flashing violently, and when neither succeeded in killing the other in that first strike, Dain cursed, and the chieftain howled in anger.

Dain spurred his horse into rearing again. The warhorse, responsive to his signals, lunged and struck with deadly forefeet shod with spiked iron. The chieftain's pony staggered to its knees, nearly tossing its rider, and Dain swung a mighty blow at the chieftain's head. Somehow the Grethori managed to parry what should have been a fatal blow. While one scimitar fended off Mirengard, the man's other blade slashed viciously at Dain's torso but bounced harmlessly off his breastplate. The chieftain was yelling something shrill and impossible to understand. Dain roared a curse at him and smote him hard, sending him reeling in the saddle. Another blow from Dain toppled him, and the chieftain fell.

That's done them, Dain thought in fierce satisfaction. He knew how fearlessly these men could fight, but without their leader they would turn and run. And he intended to chase them through these mountains and to the very gates of perdition if he had to.

Only, it seemed he'd guessed wrong about the identity of their chieftain, for the Grethori did not flee. Instead, the shriek of the pipes grew louder and more frantic. Omas was shouting something, but Dain couldn't hear what he said. He fended off an attack from a screaming youth painted with stripes of vermilion, and then a ball of fire exploded near him.

A pine tree went up in a whoosh of flames, and the blast nearly rocked Dain from his saddle. His horse reared in fear, scrambling backward, and as Dain struggled to control the maddened animal he furiously wondered what *sorcerel* fire was doing there. But there was no time to think, for two more Grethori were coming at him. He hurled his dagger at one, and although it was an awkward throw with his left hand, he managed to cut the Grethori enough to deflect his attack. The other came on, screaming as he swung his sword. It was an old-fashioned broadsword, heavy and crudely made, and the man was clearly ill trained in how to use it.

Dain feinted and reversed his swing, slashing up with Mirengard and catching the man in the ribs. Bleeding from his side, the Grethori stumbled back, nearly dropping his sword, and Dain pressed him hard. But as he leaned down and swung, he noticed that Mirengard's blade was glowing very white.

At that instant he smelled the magic, a terrible smell, like burned blood, and another ball of fire exploded from nowhere. It erupted right under the nose of Dain's horse. Screaming, the animal reared up and fell back. Toppling from the saddle, Dain kicked his feet clear of the stirrups, and, when he hit the ground, he rolled desperately to keep the horse from landing on top of him and crushing him to death.

Just as he scrambled to his feet, something heavy walloped him in the head, and the reverberation through his helmet shook him so badly he dropped to one knee. Sweat was streaming into his eyes, stinging them, but he glimpsed movement in front of him and heaved himself up just as Omas sprang between him and his foe.

Roaring Netheran oaths, Omas slew the man, and Dain whirled to stand back to back with his protector just as a tribesman on horseback charged him from that direction. Dain swung Mirengard to meet his enemy's sword, blocked the blow that could have cleaved him in half, and slashed across the Grethori's side.

As the man fell from his saddle, screaming, something heavy rammed into Dain from the opposite direction. He staggered, nearly losing his footing, felt the pony gallop past him as a blade sliced the air scant inches from his visor, and fought to keep his balance on the blood-soaked, trampled ground.

Behind him, Omas shouted, and Dain whirled in time to meet another attack. This Grethori came running at him on foot. The man was taller than most of his kind, and bulged with muscle. His neck was like a bull's. His red hair swung long and unbound in a filthy tangle, and sewn to his jerkin were the tiny skulls of human infants. *This*, Dain realized, his arms on fire and his breathing ragged, must be the true chieftain. The man also wore the leggings issued to auxiliary troops, and with a jolt of fury Dain recognized him as one of the traitors. Ilymir's face danced before Dain's vision, as did Tashalya's. Dain saw his wife, lying injured and grieving, her indomitable spirit nearly broken, and rage burst in him, car-

rying him forward into a run even as Omas shouted at him to
come back.

Laughing like a madman, clearly taunting Dain, the chieftain planted his feet in the swordsman's stance taught to him
by a Netheran master-at-arms and swung his weapon to meet
Dain's with a degree of skill the rest of his men obviously
lacked.

Steel raked steel as the two blades slid together and locked
at the guards. Dain strained against his enemy, but the man
possessed enormous strength. In fact, the more effort Dain expended, the stronger his opponent seemed to become. Mirengard was glowing more brightly than ever and began to
vibrate with a force that shook Dain's wrists. He heard the
sword humming with a song he'd never heard from the eldin-
forged blade before. Then in surprise he realized it was not
Mirengard's war song he heard, but the Grethori sword's. Astonished that this barbarian had somehow acquired a magicked weapon, Dain held on grimly, hearing something
elusively familiar in the sound and wondering what in Thod's
name he faced.

He stamped hard on the Grethori's instep, causing the man
to roar with pain and stagger. Swiftly Dain tried to disengage
his sword, but Mirengard's blade seemed stuck to the other
weapon. He could not budge it, despite a mighty heave of his
shoulders.

The Grethori's eyes danced with mirth and contempt. He
spat at Dain and uttered what was clearly an insult.

"Sire!" Omas shouted. "Behind you!"

Sensing someone charging him from behind, Dain tried
once more to break his weapon free, but the swords were
humming together with such intensity the sound hurt his head.
Mirengard vibrated harder than before, and he heard the songs
of the two blades shift and blend as though somehow the
weapons were trying to become one.

Impossible, he thought, but there was no time for puzzles,
no time to think of a way out. Desperately, Dain twisted in an
effort to face what was coming. He was strong enough as he
turned to force the chieftain to shift his feet, but he still could
not separate the swords. Horrified, for never had he encoun-

tered anything able to seize magicked steel thus, Dain found
himself trapped between the chieftain and the warrior rushing
at him with a bloodcurdling yell. Omas lunged to intervene
but was struck down from behind. The huge protector staggered and fell to his knees, and the enemy closed in on Dain
from all sides. His only hope, Dain realized, was to drop
Mirengard and retreat.

But his hand was stuck to the hilt and would not release it.
Astonished, Dain struggled to loosen his grip without avail.

The oncoming Grethori, urged on by the chieftain, smote
Dain in the head, clubbing his helmet with an impact that rang
like a gong. The world went black. Dain felt himself falling
forever, his body boneless and out of control. A vague, dim
portion of him felt his wrist twisted painfully before Mirengard was wrenched from his hand. Then he hit the ground
with a jolt that snapped his teeth together. Another blow
struck his chest, and it seemed as though his breastplate split,
for there came afterward a pain so terrible it robbed him of
breath.

Enraged, he struggled against the darkness, refusing to accept this as the finish Vaunit had foretold. He would *not* die
here in the wilderness at the hands of these barbaric savages.
He was king of Nether. He led the best warriors in the world.
He'd fought tougher foes than these and come out the victor. It
couldn't end this way, not in failure, not in defeat.

Yet he couldn't see, couldn't hear for the terrible blackness
that held him. Dimly he understood that he was teetering on
the edge of unconsciousness and if he did not fight his way
back, he would be lost forever. He struggled to open his eyes,
struggled to sit up, but just as he managed both, ruthless
blows hammered his chest and head. Agony came, exploding
the blackness into white, and he was gone.

Chapter Thirteen

Deep in a mountain cave far from the site of the battle, Tulvak Sahm leaned over a red-hot cauldron of boiling water and conjured forth a vision within the steam. At first there were only misty shapes; then the vision sharpened and clarified. The shapes became the faces and forms of men fighting a battle. Sounds filled the air—the grunts of warriors landing blows, the screams of the dead and dying, the frantic neighing of horses, and the violent clash of weaponry. Netherans fighting Grethori. Tulvak Sahm leaned forward intently to watch. It seemed the ambush was proceeding exactly as planned.

The *sorcerel* watched as the two balls of spellfire he had given to the savages were released with great effectiveness. Pleased, Tulvak Sahm leaned closer until he could feel the caldron's steamy heat. He had taught the *sheda* well, it seemed. The Grethori might be savages, but they were far from fools.

When the hated king of Nether toppled from his saddle and was surrounded by his enemies, Tulvak Sahm chortled and rubbed his hands together. When the hated king of

Nether was struck down from behind, Tulvak Sahm cheered. And when the hated king of Nether was battered with axe and club and lay dead on the ground, Tulvak Sahm threw up his hands and called out praises to Ashnod.

At that moment a rush of joy filled Tulvak Sahm's body. Sparkling light arced from his fingertips and showered around him, filling his lair with a pale red radiance while shadowy wraiths flowed forth from the darkest corners like moths drawn to a flame. Ignoring the wraiths that swirled around and through him, Tulvak Sahm exulted in his moment of triumph. For seven long years, he'd watched and waited, biding his time for the perfect moment to strike revenge, and now all had gone exactly as he'd intended. King Faldain's few, pathetic years of rule were over. This upstart, this half-eldin sovereign whose very existence was an abomination in the nostrils of Ashnod, would no longer hinder Gant's great plan to annex the realm of Nether. And when news of the pretender's demise spread across the land, truly all Believers would rejoice.

Smirking to himself, Tulvak Sahm rubbed his hands together. The air reeked of the magic he was expending, and he inhaled deeply. Ah, yes, it was good indeed to watch the death of an enemy, especially one as hated as Faldain. Thanks to him, Tulvak Sahm had lost his place as King Muncel's most influential adviser and court *sorcerel*. In the aftermath of the Battle of Grov, Tulvak Sahm had been forced to flee for his life.

Worse, he was denied refuge in Gant. So displeased was Ashnod with Faldain for having defiled the Chamber of Fire with atrocious god-steel before daring to escape . . . so displeased was Ashnod with Faldain for returning the Chalice of Eternal Life to Nether, driving out Nonkind and persecuting Believers in a purge that ran the length and breadth of the kingdom . . . so displeased was Ashnod with Faldain for having sought to restore the alliance between humans and eldin that the dark god repudiated Tulvak Sahm completely. He, greatest of all *sorcerels*, had been punished by the Chief Believer, banished to the second world in disgrace, and held there for agonizing months by the power of *magemons* before he finally managed to escape.

The injustice of it all still burned in Tulvak Sahm's heart. He knew exactly where the blame should lie. Faldain—infidel that he was—had dared step into the magical realm without guidance, had dared make a god-steel sword his own when such weapons were not designed for a mere man to wield, had slipped through the second world as though accustomed to walk such dangerous paths, had commanded visions and soul-merged with the wraith of Tobeszijian, had brought forth the Chalice as though he knew what it really was, and had even wrought a spell that rejuvenated the foul Tree of Life. All this a mortal had done, showing other men that the guidance of *sorcerels* was unnecessary. Truly Faldain was an arrogant blasphemer, daring what no other man dared, unworthy of all he meddled in with such ignorance and blind luck. His doom today was far less than he deserved.

Watching the victorious Grethori looting and mutilating Netheran bodies, Tulvak Sahm smiled at the vision through swirls of steam. *Now*, he thought, *all will change*.

He spoke a brief word, and the vision ended. The bubbling water boiled over the side of the caldron with a hiss, putting out the fire. The small, black-winged shapeshifter spell-chained to its perch flapped its wings and hissed. Tulvak Sahm turned his brooding eyes toward the rear of his cave, where a pale child bound hand and foot stared at him in anguish.

"Enjoyed that, did you, princess?" he asked in his guttural voice. "Watched all, did you? Your father is dead. Did you see him struck down? Did you see him die?"

She was young and tender, obviously afraid of him, but defiance still flashed in her pale blue eyes. "He *isn't* dead!" she shouted. "He isn't! You can't kill him. He's the bravest, strongest warrior in all the land."

Tulvak Sahm stared at her avidly, his mind awash with the future stretching before him. For years Tulvak Sahm had resisted many temptations to strike Faldain down. Nursing his hatred, he had forced himself to wait while Faldain prospered, while Faldain married and sired children, while Faldain forged change and reform across the realm, tearing down much that Muncel had accomplished. Not until a few weeks past, when the time was at last perfect and all the auspices converged in perfect alignment, did Tulvak Sahm unleash his revenge.

The first part of his plan—masterminding the attack on the royal family during Faldain's absence—had succeeded perfectly. Faldain had raced hither and yon like a puppet pulled on strings, with no inkling of the fate that awaited him. *Arrogant fool*, Tulvak Sahm thought. *Your Chalice did not protect you from me!*

But Faldain's death was not all he wanted. As he'd waited through the long years, a larger revenge, one infinitely more cruel, had taken shape in his thoughts. It required exceptional patience, but Tulvak Sahm counted that no cost as he turned his attention to the second part of his plan. This firstborn daughter of Faldain possessed magical powers of special strength and complexity. From afar, from the moment of her birth, Tulvak Sahm had sensed her abilities, and the prospect of molding her into an extraordinary *sorcerelle* such as the world had never seen before filled him with excitement and anticipation.

Already, although she did not realize it, Tashalya's lessons had begun. The first lesson had been a punishment for unleashing her temper against him. The second had been to watch her father die.

Gliding closer to her, Tulvak Sahm stared down into her white face. Poor little child, he thought, how mortal she was, how foolish. She thought she defied him by making faces and spitting insults. She did not realize that he had already delved into her mind and absorbed her knowledge. Thanks to her, he had been able to devise the magic spell that caught Faldain's magicked sword and brought about his defeat in today's battle.

Just thinking about the pretender's bewilderment there in his final moments when he struggled against the spell like a fly caught in a spider's web was so delicious, so perfect that Tulvak Sahm tipped back his head in delight. He already anticipated the day, years hence, when Tashalya would be grown and completely his creature. He would tell her then of her role in her father's demise, and if she shrugged indifferently, he would know his training had succeeded, and if she grew enraged and turned against him, he would enjoy smashing her like an insect. Either way, he would carry forth his revenge against Faldain through this generation and the next.

Tomorrow he would begin Tashalya's real lessons, after she'd had time to grieve for her father and exchange defiance for vulnerability.

When the time was right, he would deliver her—and Nether—to Ashnod. The prosperity he'd known in Muncel's court would return to him tenfold; his importance would once more exceed the blighted Sumderaudin and other treasonous *sorcerels* who served Faldain. And all would know Tulvak Sahm to be the most powerful enchanter of the first world. Perhaps he would even please Ashnod enough to be transformed into Chief Believer.

Filled with plans and ambition, Tulvak Sahm cast his gaze avidly over the child. "You still do not believe what you have seen, princess, but I will make you believe."

"He isn't dead!" she shouted. "I won't believe you. I won't!"

"Did you not see him die?"

She stared at him with enormous eyes. Her chin quivered, and she jerked at her bonds as though she wanted to attack him. "It's a trick. A false vision. I make them for Ilymir and Mareitina at night when the servants are asleep and don't know we're playing. You want to make me be sad, but I won't be. I won't! And when Papa comes for me, he'll kill you dead. He has a magicked sword, and he'll—"

"But your father is dead," Tulvak Sahm said. "He is dead because I wished it."

"You aren't stronger than Papa! You aren't!"

Fire shot from his fingertips in a long line of flame that missed her head by the slightest margin. She screamed and flinched away as far as her bonds would permit. Tulvak Sahm lowered his hand, ending the flames, and the air smelled of ash and smoke. The child was panting with fear, her mouth open, her heart thudding visibly beneath the bodice of her gown.

"Now do you believe me?" Tulvak Sahm asked quietly, his gaze mesmerizing hers. "Do you, Tashalya?"

Tears shimmered in her eyes. Her mouth trembled.

"He will never come for you," Tulvak Sahm said relentlessly. "Never. You belong to me now. You will be mine forever."

She flinched at his words but, defiantly, still said nothing. He laughed at her, baring his fangs, and she began to cry with harsh sobs that racked her small frame.

"Papa!" she whimpered, curling up. "Oh, Papa!"

Jonan and his escort had nearly reached the bottom of the mountain when Chesil's head snapped up. "*Aychi!*" he cried. "Listen!"

Sir Bansil and the other men paused and fell silent.

Jonan listened, too, but he heard nothing. "It's just the wind," he said, shivering and clutching his cloak tighter. "Let us go."

"That's a man's scream," Chesil whispered, his expression intent. "And a war cry." His dark gaze snapped past Jonan to the other men. "They've met an ambush. I feared it would be so!"

"And us down here," Sir Bansil said. He tossed Jonan's reins to him without warning. Jonan grabbed and missed, having to lunge again to catch them while his horse pranced and slung its head.

"Bansil, you dog!" Jonan said angrily, coughing.

Ignoring him, the men drew their weapons and turned around to head up the trail.

"Wait!" Jonan called desperately. "You can't go back. If there's fighting—"

"Fighting! *Aychi*, I want some of it. Come, men! Let's away!" Shouting, Chesil spurred his horse forward.

All the knights followed him, except Sir Bansil, who stared after them with longing, his hand white-knuckled on his sword hilt.

Jonan watched him in alarm, certain the protector also intended to desert him. "Sir Basil! I—I mean, Sir Bansil, we must go to the stream as the king ordered us. It will be safe there away from the fighting—"

"Ah, morde!" Sir Bansil swore, glaring at him. "Yer far enough from the fighting now, ye craven fool."

Jonan stared at him, openmouthed. "How—how dare you speak to me like that!"

"That's our king up there, and in trouble. And me strapped here to a great baby." Sir Bansil tightened his mouth and spat "Ah, damne, I'm going."

He kicked his horse up the trail without a glance back, leaving Jonan behind.

Openmouthed, Jonan stared after him in disbelief. "Deserter!" he shouted. "Knave! If Faldain's hit an ambush, the rest of you will die in it as well!"

None of the men looked back or gave any sign of hearing him. Jonan's horse fidgeted and nickered. He wrenched its head around and kicked it hard, intending to ride to the stream and make camp as he'd been instructed. After all, the king had told him to stay out of any battles. He wasn't a knight. He wasn't allowed to wear armor or carry a sword. He was supposed to stay with the squires. *And what is shameful about that?* Jonan asked himself. *I am following orders as is proper.*

Furthermore, he was a prince of the realm, and he deserved to be treated with more respect. When next he saw Sir Bansil, Chesil, or even Lord Miest, he would urge the king to punish them for their behavior today.

Still, as he rode into the forest where afternoon shadows crossed the ground, Jonan forgot his resentment. He was alone, terribly alone, he thought uneasily. If anything happened to Sir Bansil, who would see to his personal safety?

A burst of movement in a bush made him rein up sharply, but it was only a bird flying away. Swallowing hard, Jonan couldn't help but recall gruesome campfire stories about Grethori tribesmen. They didn't follow the rules of combat. If they caught the squires, they would probably slaughter them up there on the mountain. And he realized fearfully that if they found him down here, they would kill him, too.

Maybe he should keep going and head back to Grov. He was sure he remembered the way. At least he thought he could manage to retrace most of the route. Aye, then he'd be the only one with sense enough to return whole and alive, while these fools perished for Tashalya.

Only . . . there would be no praise, not if he was the only man to return. The people at court would despise him even more than they did now. They would brand him coward and deserter, and no one would believe or care that the king had ordered him to leave the battle. They would simply judge, the way they always did, and they would blame him for it all.

Even the queen, who was kind and beautiful, would not understand. She had strict views of honor, and there was none in being a coward.

Jonan pulled his cloak tighter around him, shivering and feeling confused. What was he to do? What if no one came down the mountain for him? Who was to prepare his meal tonight? Where was his bedroll? Who would build the fire? He could freeze without warmth and sustenance, and he had neither strikebox nor food pouch with him. What in Thod's name was he to do?

Above all things, he knew he did not want to die alone. Despite his fear, he understood that he should rejoin his companions.

Slowly, terrified to go but more afraid to stay, he turned his horse around and started cautiously up the trail.

It took him a very long time to make his way to the battleground. Shadows were lengthening; the air was brutally cold; indigo smudged the distant mountains, and the sunset's reflection glowed across the snowy summit above him. His lungs hurt, and he wheezed and panted as he held his horse to a cautious walk. If he ascended slowly, it was easier to breathe, and after he cut a strip from his cloak and tied it over his nose and mouth, he felt much better.

The sounds of fighting had long ago ceased. But as he came close to the area, he heard a wailing cry of grief that echoed through the canyons and off the crags. Startled, he reined up and sat there quaking with his dagger in hand.

Men were talking; he heard Netheran being spoken but nothing else. That meant the Grethori must be gone. After a few minutes his thudding heart slowed, and he eased his horse warily up the trail.

When he reached the trampled clearing, he saw it strewn with corpses, scattered weapons, pieces of armor, and even articles of clothing. Most of the bodies had been stripped. Many were mutilated. Chesil, his crimson tunic dark against the shadows, was running from body to body in a frantic search, with Lord Miest at his heels. Sir Bansil was closing the sightless eyes of a dead man. Some of the other men were helping the survivors. The air smelled foul.

Realizing it was blood and death he smelled, Jonan was nearly sick. Somehow he managed to control himself, and dismounted onto shaky legs.

"Well," Sir Bansil said, standing up with a look of amazement. "Look at who's come."

The other men stared at Jonan. Half-embarrassed, half-defiant, he stared back, still clutching his dagger in his hand and wheezing for air behind his cloth mask. He expected them to laugh, but they didn't. After a moment of quiet, they went back to their self-assigned tasks, leaving him to stumble over to Sir Bansil's side.

His protector said nothing, but knelt to roll over a headless corpse. Smeared with gore, the body had been stripped of its chain mail and boots, and two of its fingers had been cut off. Sir Bansil seemed to be looking for something; after a moment Jonan realized it must be the dead man's head he searched for. Abruptly, Jonan turned away, ripping his mask off in time to be violently sick. By the time he straightened, shivering and wretched, he found that Sir Bansil had moved on without him.

Staggering along in Sir Bansil's wake, Jonan realized that had Faldain not sent him down the mountain, he and his few companions would be dead right now. A feeling of gratitude toward his cousin surged through him, and he looked around somewhat blindly.

Where is Faldain, he wondered. *Why is he not striding about, issuing orders?*

"Lord Omas!" Chesil cried out.

Everyone looked up, and Jonan hurried forward with the others to where Chesil was bending over the king's protector. Miest grimly lifted Omas's limp body, supporting it while Chesil pulled off his helmet. Blood trickled across Omas's white face, soaking his thick mustache. More blood stained his hauberk.

"He lives," Miest said hoarsely, pressing his fingers to Omas's throat. "Aye, he lives."

He and Chesil exchanged somber glances, and the rest of the men remained silent.

"Sir Bansil, help him," Miest said, gently easing Omas to the ground. "I must find the king."

Chesil resumed his search, only to halt a few feet away. He stared intently at something lying on the ground, and Jonan hurried to his side. There in the dirt lay Mirengard. The famous sword, with its engraved blade, its hilt jewels glittering in the rays of the setting sun, the very emblem of the king's power and might, had been tossed down the way a child discards an unwanted toy.

Looking aghast, Chesil sank to his knees beside it. "Woe!" he cried out. "Great woe to us!"

Jonan stared at the sword. He knew it was magical and special. Only the king was permitted to hold it. Never before had he been so close to it, and he found himself transfixed by its beauty. Without thinking, he bent down to pick it up.

"Don't touch it!" Miest said sharply, and Jonan flinched back. The protector strode up, still wiping Omas's blood from his hands. "No one but the king has the right to Mirengard."

Jonan scowled at Miest, for he could see no harm in merely touching the beautiful object. It wasn't as though he intended to keep the sword or brandish it about. Besides, the blade should be cleaned. "It shouldn't be left in the dirt," he protested.

"True, but just your highness leave it be," Miest said. "You've no business handling a weapon that dangerous."

Stung by the criticism, Jonan glowered at him.

"But where is the king?" Chesil asked. "Think you he's been captured, *neya*?"

"Thod forbid," Miest said.

"Thod permit!" Chesil retorted. "I know not how such a valiant warrior could be overcome, but the alternative is—"

He broke off, his jaw working.

"Over there," Miest said, pointing.

Jonan saw yet another body, lying apart from the others very close to the precipice. Chesil stared, took a step forward, then stopped. Miest strode past him, moving fast, and with a muttered oath Chesil hurried to catch up. Jonan followed them more slowly, not eager to gaze on another atrocity, yet unable to stay back.

Lying facedown, this body was tall and powerfully built. It had been stripped of armor and clothing. Sword cuts glistened on its back where the blood was drying.

Miest's face looked frozen. He knelt stiffly and rolled the body over. The scalp was missing, and the face had been so mutilated it was unrecognizable. All the man's fingers were missing, as were his toes. Near the bloody head lay a helmet, badly dented.

His face contorting with anguish, Chesil picked it up. "'Tis the king's."

"Thod help us," Miest said, and bowed his head.

Sir Bansil came running. The other men followed, forming a circle around the corpse. At first none of them would speak. No one seemed to know what to do.

"Is it really him?" Sir Bansil whispered, breaking the silence at last. "Can't be, can it?"

"None of the others have been this butchered," someone said in a gruff voice.

With his head still bowed, Miest said nothing but instead simply placed his hand on the dead man's chest and wept.

One by one the others knelt, some uttering prayers, others groaning aloud. Feeling numb with disbelief, Jonan sank down with them. He could not take his gaze from the corpse or its bloody, disfigured face. How could the king be dead, he wondered. 'Twas impossible.

Faldain had always been greater than anyone else Jonan

knew—stronger, more clever, able to discern a man's secret intentions, quick to stop a foe, yet equally willing to forgive a transgression. From childhood, Jonan had dreamed of growing up to be just like his cousin, only not all dreams came true. He'd gradually come to understand that he would never be brave like Faldain. He would never be handsome like Faldain. He would never be strong and valiant and heroic like Faldain. For some time now, he'd felt like such a miserable failure, and yet . . .

Today, Faldain lies dead, Jonan thought, dry-eyed, while around him the men wept, *but I am alive. I am not courageous, but I did not perish. Is that not a sign of some element of greatness in me?*

Reeling from such thoughts, Jonan stared at his cousin's body. It seemed impossible that Faldain had come to such an end. It was too quick, too brutal, too final. Faldain had fought so many wars and won so many battles. Everyone, Jonan included, believed him invincible. But he wasn't. Despite his gifts, his eldin magic, and his strength, he was just a man, like any other, and therefore mortal. He was also, Jonan told himself, something of a fool. Had he not insisted on pursuing a futile quest to bring back a child surely already doomed, none of this tragedy need have happened.

Miest took off his cloak and solemnly spread it over the king's body. "Let Thod take our king's spirit to the third world," he said. "Let Thod have mercy on Faldain, our prince and king."

The others, Jonan included, kissed their Circles and repeated the prayer. The wind blew and gusted, buffeting them with its bitter coldness.

"It is over," Miest said hoarsely.

Jonan barely heard him. Both Faldain and Ilymir were dead. A sudden rush of excitement stirred him. *That means I am the king*, he thought. *By law and right, I am the king*.

But who, he wondered in a daze, would follow him? Not these men, surely, who a short time ago had treated him with such contempt. He longed to see them turn to him in respect and awe, bowing to him as was proper, but he did not believe it would happen. They had abandoned him once already that day. He trusted none of them.

Chesil dropped the king's helmet and bowed his forehead to the ground beside the body. "Vengeance for my king do I swear," he said fiercely, his voice muffled against the dirt before he sprang up. "To my last breath, I will hunt down these dogs and make them pay!"

The men jumped to their feet, drawing their swords and shouting agreement. Chesil ran a short distance up the trail and looked back, beckoning. "Let us go after them—"

"Stop!" Jonan shouted, his voice shrill with disbelief. "Are you mad? It's nearly dark. We're outnumbered."

Chesil glared at him and spat. "Coward. If you are afraid, stay here and quake. I know what I owe my king!"

"You owe him respect," Jonan said angrily. "We have to take him back. We have to go now."

Miest frowned at the blaze of coral and lavender streaking the sky. "We can't track them in the dark. Too easy for the murdering devils to lie in wait for us."

"Aye," Sir Bansil said reluctantly. "There's not enough of us left to do 'em any harm. And what about the wounded?"

Chesil strode back to them, his face knotted with fury, his beaded hair braids swinging along his jawline. "Will you let this villainy go unavenged? Aychi! To think that I have served with such dishonorable—"

"Watch yer tongue," Sir Bansil broke in sharply. "I'll take no Agya insults from ye."

"We need an army," Jonan said, trying to distract the two men from coming to blows. "With the whole army, thousands of the best knights in Nether, we could drive the Grethori from these mountains forever."

"That takes time. We must act now!" Chesil shouted.

"And do what, lad?" Miest asked sadly. "Aye, I know your blood is up. We all feel the grief and shock right now. But the prince here is right. Running ourselves into the next trap won't help the king, or the realm. Best we get a huge fighting force together, aye, and sorcerels, too. And then we crush these savages once and for all."

"But it will take weeks to assemble the full army," Sir Bansil said thoughtfully.

"Winter will be on us by then," another man chimed in.

Chesil looked at them one by one, his eyes aflame with contempt and frustration. "Too late! I say we cannot wait, *neya?*"

"We'll do this right," Miest said grimly, giving him a look. "We'll make it count."

Chesil spat. "Waiting. Counting. That is not the Agya way."

"Well, it be the Netheran way," Sir Bansil replied fiercely. "Come thaw, we'll rout these dogs, aye, and their villages and womenfolk, too. We'll run them out of Nether for all time. By Thod, we will!"

The men nodded and muttered agreement.

"But now it's time to go home," Jonan said.

"Aye," Miest agreed. "The prince is right."

Jonan's chest swelled. He was delighted to find Miest on his side. It made him feel important.

"And what about Princess Tashalya?" Chesil asked. "Do we abandon her? Do you think the king would be pleased to see us turn tail and ride home in defeat, without her?"

Jonan's sense of satisfaction collapsed. Alarmed that Chesil might yet persuade the men to agree to his foolish course of action, he said quickly, "She's likely dead, or sold into slavery by now."

"Is that a reason to give up?" Chesil retorted.

"How can we find her without the king's guidance?" Jonan glanced urgently at the faces of the other men. "He was the only one who knew where to go. Where, in all this"—Jonan flung his arm at the mountain range stretching before them—"do we search? We need a *sorcerel* with us to track her, and how can we get one if we don't go back to Grov? The king should have brought one with him, but he didn't. And now we can't go on."

Silence fell over the little company, and even Chesil said nothing. Jonan squared his shoulders, amazed at himself because he'd actually managed to speak eloquently without stammering in confusion. *I'm not always a fool*, he thought. *Perhaps they will start to realize it.*

Miest finally cleared his throat. "Let's see to our dead. There's much to be done yet, and I think it would be wise if we were quit of this mountain before dark."

"How do we get them home?" a man asked. "The Grethori have stolen their horses. And we've no preserving spell."

"We'll haul them off this blighted mountain," Miest said grimly. "And bury them below."

"And the king?" Sir Bansil asked. "Do we bury him, too?"

"We must take him to Grov," Jonan broke in, unable to remain quiet. "With full honors and a state funeral."

The men exchanged glances, and with a wordless sound Chesil turned away. Jonan frowned, unsure of what he'd said to upset them.

"Isn't that proper?" he asked in puzzlement. "The queen—"

"Aye, the queen," Miest said with a sigh. "The poor queen."

Something was wrong, but Jonan still did not understand what it was. No one spoke. They stood about as though lost, and even Chesil seemed to have no spirit left in him.

Miest fetched Mirengard, holding it in a fold of his surcoat, and reverently knelt beside Faldain's body. "Bansil," he said.

Sir Bansil lifted the cloak swathing the body, while Lord Miest gently laid the naked sword atop its master and folded Faldain's bloodied hands over the hilt. The blade glowed pale white, and Jonan stumbled back in fright.

"What is that?" he blurted out. "What does it mean?"

"Mirengard will preserve the king," Miest said. Respectfully, he bowed to the corpse and backed away. Jonan saw tears streaking his face. Turning his back on the others, Miest stood gazing out into the distance, his shoulders and back rigid as though he were coming to a decision.

Jonan watched him, feeling breathless with anticipation. *Lord Miest is on my side*, he thought rapidly. *He will proclaim me king now, and make them bow to me. Now is the* moment. *I never dreamed this could happen, but it's here. I must be ready.*

He stood taller, holding his head high.

Miest's gaze swept past him to look at the others. "Let's quit this blighted place," he said gruffly. "We've the dead, and the living, to see to before we take our beloved lord and master home."

Chapter Fourteen

It was customary to begin preparations for Aelintide by furnishing the palace against winter drafts. On a grim gray afternoon when sleet was pelting outside and the tile stoves radiated warmth in the restored sections of the palace, the servants were doing exactly that by carrying forth carpets and hangings from storage. As they shifted furniture and unrolled wool carpets across the wooden floors, musty odors filled the air, for many of the rugs were old and stained from multiple winters of hard use. They should have been aired outside during the summer, but apparently the task had not been done. Alexeika wished she could afford to throw them out and acquire new ones, but she refused to spend the money.

Besides the carpets, there were the tapestries to be hung up, and many of the old hangings were tattered from rot or stank of woodsmoke and mildew. She had hired women to ply their needles repairing hangings, embroideries, tapestries, chair coverings, and linens, but the task was an enormous one—never finished—and on a day like this, rather daunting.

To get away from the dust stirred up by all the activity, Alexeika went on an inspection of the ruined and empty west wing. The Privy Council had met that morning, but Alexeika had scant hope of discovering what they had discussed. Lord Thum, who should have presided over the meeting, had departed for Thirst Hold a week before to thwart Queen Pheresa's levy of men, gold, and supplies in support of her war against Klad. Thirst could ill spare any of what was demanded, yet failure to comply could be held as violation of the hold's original charter. If the queen had grounds to declare the hold in rebellion, she could legally lay forth a claim to the deed and force Thirst back into her ownership. Remarking that the Queen of Mandria had grown wily and enjoyed advisers who were far too able, Thum had set off, grumbling about the weather, and promising to return to Grov as soon as possible. Until he returned, Alexeika was without her most reliable source of information within Nether's government, and it made her uneasy.

Strolling about the deserted part of the palace with the chief architect, Alexeika tucked her hands in a fur muff to keep them warm and examined what had once been known as the Gallery of Gold. The architect was a short, balding man in robes trimmed in vixlet fur, and he seemed oblivious to the icy air that made their breath visible as he chattered excitedly about archaic moldings, support beams, and the exorbitant cost of importing artisans from Saelutia to restore and gild what could again be a magnificent chamber.

"Truly, your majesty, it would rival the Gallery of Glass, and in fact, according to the historical records, this gallery was the official room of state prior to—"

A page came running up, breathless and white of face. "Your majesty!" he called out. "Your majesty! The king is at the city gates."

The oppressive days of waiting fell from her shoulders. Something inside her leaped, and with only the briefest courtesy she abandoned the architect in midsentence, gathering up her skirts and hurrying back to the central part of the palace.

People were clustering at the tall windows overlooking the city, chattering excitedly. The bells were ringing across Grov, and the honor guard came clattering across the central courtyard to line up their mounts at attention. Hastening along,

Alexeika considered her gown and hair, wondering whether she had time to change her attire, and decided not.

"Your majesty!" Lady Nadilya called out, hurrying to catch up with her. Eyes shining, she curtsied. "This is joyous news indeed!"

By then Lady Emila and Lady Buni also joined them with excited chatter. Lady Emila took Alexeika's muff and gloves, handing them in turn to a servant. Lady Buni was carrying the queen's pomander and sweet box, fashionable accessories that Alexeika usually forgot about or mislaid. Smiling, Buni placed them in Alexeika's hands, while Nadilya brushed a cobweb from Alexeika's hem, and Emila adjusted the veil of gossamer-thin silk covering Alexeika's hair.

During these hurried preparations, Alexeika found her heart thudding absurdly fast. *He is home,* she thought, happy for the first time since the attack. *I have so much to tell him. The baby kicked this morning. The price of fur is up, and our treasury grows fat because of it. But, oh Riva, first I want to be held in his strong arms and know that he is home and safe.*

She turned to her page. "Inform the nursery to make ready. I want a tray of fig comfits dusted with sugar and waiting in Princess Tashalya's new bedchamber. Order water heated for her bath and instruct the nursemaids to lay out her prettiest clothes in welcome. Oh, yes, and remind the servants that Princess Mareitina is not to be disturbed. I do not want her and Tashalya to meet until I am present. We must take no risks by shocking Mareitina too suddenly. Can you remember all that I've said? Well, hurry!"

The page streaked away, and Alexeika stepped away from her ladies' busy hands to head for the Gallery of Glass. The tall doors were opened for her, and a page on duty by the doors called out, "Her royal majesty, Queen Alexeika!"

The long room was filled with courtiers, and the mirrors reflected them so that twice as many people appeared to be standing about. A buzz of anticipation rose through the crowd. Alexeika walked through their midst with her head held high and her eyes shining. She could barely keep herself from flinging dignity aside and skipping like a young girl.

Smiling, Prince Tustik advanced to meet her. "We all share your majesty's joy at the king's homecoming."

"Thank you. How long?" she asked.

"The message came a few minutes ago from one of the sentries at the gates. He said horsemen are approaching under the king's banner."

"And the princess royal?" she asked eagerly. "Is she with them? Was she seen with his majesty?"

"That, I do not know."

She walked on through the bowing courtiers, smiling back at them, too excited to contain herself. These long, bleak days of mourning and waiting had been hard, but now the ordeal was nearly over. She could not wait to see her loved ones.

From the courtyard outside came shouts and the sound of trumpets, but the fanfare was a brief one. Wishing she could run outside to greet Faldain home, Alexeika forced herself to sit quietly in her chair beside the throne and wait. Then the door at the opposite end of the gallery boomed open, causing the chatter to die away. Alexeika craned to look, hoping to see Faldain striding in with Tashalya perched on his shoulder.

Let them both be safe, she prayed, clutching her hands together. *Let them both be unharmed*.

Three men entered, each bedraggled and muddy, and none of them was the king. As she saw Chesil Matkevskiet, Lord Miest, and Jonan, Alexeika's happy anticipation slowly collapsed, and puzzlement took its place.

Faldain had not returned, she realized in dismay. He had sent this unlikely trio of messengers in his stead. Why? What had gone amiss? Fearing it meant that Tashalya had not yet been found, Alexeika gripped the carved arms of her chair more tightly and fought back useless conjectures.

Lady Nadilya edged closer to her as though to provide comfort, but Alexeika was sitting ramrod straight in her chair, her gaze never leaving the men who approached her through the staring crowd.

The fact that they had not changed their muddy attire before appearing in her presence could only mean bad news. She saw how pale and weary Lord Miest looked. Drawn, his skin yellowed and unhealthy, Chesil seemed to have lost

weight. Jonan showed a ghastly pallor, his eyes shifting fever-
ishly from side to side as odd changes of expression darted
across his features. All of them looked to be near the end of
their endurance.

Partway to her, Chesil halted and caught at Jonan's arm, so
that only Miest reached the queen. Resting his hand on his
sword hilt, so fierce and begrimed did he look that Sir
Wulim—on duty as her protector—stepped into Miest's path
with his dagger drawn.

"Unhand your weapon or surrender it," he growled.

Halting, Miest wavered a moment before he blinked
dazedly and dropped his hand from his weapon. He stared
over Wulim's shoulder at Alexeika with a look that sent fire
and ice through her brain.

Tashalya is dead, she thought; then in desperation she assured herself that Faldain would not send tragic news to her
by messenger. He would tell her himself . . . unless harm had
befallen him, too. Why else would one of the king's protectors be anywhere other than at his side?

"Lord Miest is welcome," she forced herself to say aloud.
Her voice sounded strangely calm despite the thudding of her
heart. Suddenly her limbs felt so heavy she could barely
beckon him forward. "Let him pass, Sir Wulim."

Miest dropped to one knee before her. "I bring bad tid-
ings," he said hoarsely, his voice thick with emotion. "The
king is dead."

Someone screamed, and voices broke out in horrified babble. Alexeika rose to her feet, her throat constricted by disbelief. The roaring in her ears distorted sounds, and she prayed
she'd heard amiss. But as she stared down at Miest, the naked
grief in his face told her it was true.

"Dead," she forced out through stiff lips. "Faldain is
dead?"

"Aye, majesty. We've brought his poor body home."

The man went on talking, but Alexeika heard nothing else
that he said. The roaring around her grew louder. She felt terribly cold and strange. An immense weight seemed to press
her down.

Then there was nothing at all.

PART III

Chapter Fifteen

This was not grief. This was a wound so mortal it could not be survived. Alexeika came floating up through layers of darkness and confusion. At the sound of weeping, she opened her eyes.

Lady Nadilya sat beside her bed, sobbing quietly into her hands.

Tears, Alexeika thought bleakly, served no purpose. They would not bring him back.

A rush of pain went through her heart, and she sat up. At once, there was a flurry around her. Gentle hands tried to press her back. Voices tried to soothe her. She pushed them all away and left her bed. Unsteadily, her limbs feeling stiff and awkward, she walked over to the window and stared out unseeingly at the garden where Faldain had married her. The memory of that day had remained vivid, every color and detail clear in her mind. She could hear Faldain's voice, strong and sure, as he pledged his vows. She remembered standing beside him in a gown of dark green velvet finer than anything she'd ever worn, swathed in a veil of sheer silk gauze said to have belonged to Queen Nereisse. Staring through it had turned everything misty and unreal. When the vows were over, and the priest had drawn a Circle around them, Faldain lifted her veil, his handsome face so serious and intent he was almost frowning.

She remembered feeling a tiny spurt of fear that already he regretted his decision to wed her, but then his lips took possession of hers, and she'd known a moment of fire and thunder that drove away all doubt.

Now, standing in the icy draft coming in around the window, listening to the weeping and worried murmurs behind her, Alexeika began to tremble. She pressed her fingers against her lips, trying to remain strong.

He could not be gone, she told herself. It could not be true. Thod was not so cruel as this, to tear the very heart from her. Yet even as the protests rose inside her, she castigated herself for such blasphemous thoughts. 'Twas not Thod who deserved her blame, but whoever had struck Faldain down.

And still she could not believe it. Would not believe it. She told herself that if Faldain was truly dead, she had to cope with it. There were things to be done. Decisions to be made.

Only, she could not make them. She could not deal with any of it. She had not the strength. Once, she'd been tough and valiant, able to stand up for herself and dependent on no one. But having been joined to Faldain, heart and soul, and knowing the security and warmth of his love in return, she could not imagine going back to lonely solitude. How could it be done? How could she bear it? Had she not already sufficient heartbreak and sorrow?

"Your majesty."

She turned around to face the people crowded into her chamber. For a moment, as she looked from countenance to countenance, she recognized none of them. Then she blinked, and their names and faces came back to her.

"My sweet lady," Nadilya said softly, taking her icy hand. "Come and sit down. You must rest. I will unbraid your hair and brush it, then you will sleep."

Alexeika stared at her as though she were mad. "Why should I sleep?" she asked harshly. "I want to see him."

"No, no!" Nadilya cried out in dismay. "It's too soon. The

king is not as yet prepared to lie in state. You can't look on him yet."

Alexeika shot her a look of scorn. "Don't be such a fool," she said, and walked out.

Sir Pyron, who'd come on duty while she lay in her swoon, hurried after her, limping and swearing under his breath. Before she reached the carved wooden staircase at the end of the passageway, he caught up with her. "Majesty, wait! Wait afore ye rush into more grief."

Alexeika halted angrily. "I must see him!"

"Aye, but not till he's made ready."

"I'm no shrinking court miss, sir! I've seen death before."

"Not like this." Sir Pyron spoke more gently than usual. His eyes were troubled. "Let yon *sorcerels* work a spell to make him look proper. Right now, he's no fit sight for anyone."

Holding herself rigidly erect, she gripped the newel post that was carved into the form of a serpent. "I know what the Grethori do," she said. "I have fought them. I have been their prisoner. I know what to expect."

"Aye, but the body be more than a fortnight rotted, even with all they tried preserving it. And his sword's magic ain't done much of what it should."

She closed her eyes against the horror of what he was telling her.

"And since yer breeding, then—"

Her head snapped up. She stared at him, wide-eyed. "Why say you such a thing?"

"True, ain't it?"

Reluctantly, she nodded. There was very little that could be concealed from a protector. "But you'll say nothing of it," she ordered him fiercely. "'Tis a secret for now, and news that's for the king to announce, no one else!"

Sir Pyron nodded at her midsection. "Could be the next king right there. Needs good care and no more shocks."

"I'll determine that."

"Aye, but yer not yerself right now. Not up to this kind of misery."

She stared at Sir Pyron, her mind awash with too many

thoughts that she could not deal with just then. Only one thing remained clear to her. "I must see him. I *will* see him."

Sir Pyron grimaced, and she thought he was going to defy her. Instead, he loosed a great sigh and inclined his head. "As ye wish."

The king's apartments included a narrow, windowless study crammed with maps and scroll cases kept in order by a clerk, a sitting room where Faldain received his children each night before their bedtime, a bathing room, a dressing room, a small, square bedchamber furnished with little besides a tile stove and bed cabinet that he slept in during the winter, and a spacious chamber of state made grand by its tall windows, tapestries, throne, regal bed adorned with Faldain's coat of arms embroidered in gold on the hangings, and two enormous stoves tiled in green and white that stood at opposite ends of the room. On certain occasions the king was obliged to sleep in the bed of state and breakfast there before a group of courtiers chosen for the honor of watching him eat and dress. He and Alexeika had spent their wedding night there. Each of her children had been born in that bed, before solemn witnesses, while a pale Faldain paced up and down like a caged lyng.

She expected to see him in the bed, lying arranged beneath a pall of linen embroidered with the royal crest and a flag of Nether's green-and-white silk suspended over him. Instead, she found his body on an ordinary wooden table that looked as though it had been carried up from the kitchens. A plain white cloth lay draped over the body, which a cluster of men in gray robes was busy cleaning. The wooden floor was littered with pails of filthy water, baskets of rags, and crocks of lime. A tiny kettle of what looked like molten wax hung suspended over a brazier of red-hot coals, and one of the men was busy stirring it with a narrow wooden paddle.

The stench of death and decay robbed her of breath. She halted in her tracks and pressed a fold of her sleeve over her nose and mouth. Nausea rose in her throat, but she mastered it somehow and forced herself forward.

The members of the Privy Council stood watching on the opposite side of the room, many of them standing near the windows with pomanders at their nostrils. They looked grim, repulsed, and afraid.

When Lady Emila loosed a choking moan, Alexeika sent her ladies back out into the passageway and resolutely advanced into the chamber. Samderaudin came into sight, bowed to her, and glided away without a word. A trio of priests stood apart from everyone else, their Circles glittering from long chains. They clutched icons and worship elements while they muttered prayers.

At her entry, soft-voiced conversations ceased, and everyone turned to stare.

She longed to scream at all of them to get out. Was it her tears they wanted to watch? Was it her grief and despair they wanted to feed on? Could she not, in this most terrible moment, have just a few moments of privacy with her beloved husband?

But she held back her anger, knowing she had no justification to drive them away. Faldain was their king, and he belonged to them, even in death.

A wave of dizziness passed over her, rendering her clammy and cold. She fought it off and walked forward. Her footsteps echoed hollowly on the bare wooden floor. Someone had rolled the carpets and stacked them in a corner out of the way. There were wet puddles where water had splashed, filthy stains that would have to be cleaned up before the courtiers were allowed in to stand vigil.

Her eyes filled with the tears she hadn't intended to shed. Each time Faldain rode away to war, she'd known this might happen, and yet there could be no true preparation for it. She remembered the day she'd watched her father die in battle and how she'd seen little Ilymir slain before her. Each time, she'd thought she could never endure anything more horrible.

How wrong she'd been. This was the worst. Her body seemed no longer hers. It moved of its own volition, for she did not command it. Her heart raced so fast she could barely breathe. *I cannot do this*, she thought frantically. *I cannot see him like this. I have not the strength to see him dead.*

Yet something drove her forward and kept her walking with her back held straight and her chin high. She knew it was necessary to gaze on Faldain's face, before the death mask was sealed in place and he was closed away forever in a tomb. She had to touch him and feel the cold emptiness of his flesh, or she would never be able to believe what had happened. Some part of her would be forever listening for the sound of his return, forever running to the window to look out in hopes of seeing him ride home. No matter how much she shrank from the task, she had to face the truth.

With tears spilling unheeded down her cheeks, she stopped beside the body and waited until one of the men in gray lifted the cloth and folded it back to reveal her beloved's face.

Only there was no face to see. Only gruesome, terrible gashes and wounds where the Grethori had hacked at him. Even his scalp was missing. Behind her, she heard gasps and moans from the onlookers, but she uttered no sound. She stared, frozen in place, unable to move or even blink. The room was spinning a little, but she would not let herself faint a second time. Her heart was thudding hard like a funeral drum.

For this was not Faldain's body.

She stared, hardly daring to let herself believe the evidence of her own eyes. And inside her, as the hard twisted knot of her emotions and fears uncoiled with joy and relief, she knew astonishment that Faldain's men and attendants could be so mistaken.

But am I seeing the invention of my own hopes? she asked herself. *Am I deceiving myself?* She was determined to be sure.

"Fold back more of the shroud," she commanded.

The man complied, baring the corpse to its waist. As Sir Pyron had warned her, it was in poor condition, yet this was not her husband's frame, not his musculature. Those were not his ears. His blood was pale, courtesy of his eldin heritage, not clotted black like this. His old scars were not to be found. Mirengard still lay atop the body, held beneath swollen, fingerless hands. Of course it had not worked its magic, for this corpse was not its master's.

For a moment her heart sang; then she reached out and pulled Mirengard off the body.

A roar of protests surrounded her. Even the priests hurried forward.

"Your majesty, what are you doing?" Prince Tustik demanded, aghast. "The sword is needed to preserve him until the embalming is finished."

Mirengard's hilt was burning her palm. She could feel its magic repudiating her grasp so violently it was all she could do not to fling the sword across the room. And a sharp stab of joy pierced her, making her hang on despite the perspiration beading her temples. This was her proof, the last test she needed to be absolutely sure. If Faldain were dead, the sword would not fight her like this. Its magic, attuned to him, hummed and throbbed against her palms, hurting her while she rejoiced.

"Let it go, majesty," Sir Pyron said worriedly. "Take no harm from it. Let it drop!"

The sword was like something alive in her grip, trying to twist itself free, its magic scorching her flesh. By sheer willpower, she managed to carry it across the room and lay it on Faldain's throne.

An attendant hurried forward as though to move it, and she flung out her throbbing hand. "Leave it be!" she commanded.

"But, your majesty," Tustik said, frowning in consternation as he joined her. "The sword can't be left there. Such a positioning symbolizes the king's return and will be misconstrued."

"It will stay," she said fiercely, her gaze stabbing from one face to the next. "The king *will* return, and only his hand can move Mirengard from the throne."

"Dear lady, I fear your reason is affected—"

"That is not the king!" she cried, pointing at the corpse. "Faldain lives!"

Hope sparked in Tustik's dark eyes, then vanished. He shook his head. "Alas, I fear he does not."

"Think you I don't know my husband? Look at the bloodstains. Look at the wounds. Would a man who is three-quarters eldin be bloodied so dark?"

"Aye, that's true!" Sir Pyron said.

Tustik shot a glance at the others. "Could a mistake have

been made? Bring Lord Miest and Chesil Matkevskiet here at once."

Shortly thereafter, both men came in. They averted their gaze from the body.

Alexeika regarded them with scant patience. "You have not brought home the king."

Shock ran through their faces. Miest frowned, but Chesil's bronzed face lit up. Holding his thumb and fingers in a circle, he lifted them to his lips and forehead in a salute.

"Ah, majesty, how this gladdens my heart," he said in a ringing voice. "However regrettable the mistake, I rejoice to know the truth. Verily Thod has been merciful."

But Miest was frowning and shaking his head. "Your majesty, I'm sorry. We've made no mistake. Despite the terrible disfigurements, that is the king."

"You've brought home a human body, not an eldin. Did you not think to look at his ears? They are not pointed like the king's."

Miest's bewilderment seemed to grow. "In Thod's name, how is it possible? I have served his majesty for five years as protector. I would recognize him."

She looked around in exasperation. "Samderaudin! Is Lord Miest enspelled?"

"Clearly," the *sorcerel* replied.

"Undo it!" she commanded, but Miest looked alarmed and began to back away.

"Best to let it wear off naturally," Samderaudin said. "Best to leave him be."

"Was I enspelled, too?" Chesil demanded. "Was that why I could not note a detail so obvious? Were we all fooled? *Aychi!* What evil has been wrought?"

Alexeika glanced about at the onlookers. Why did so many of them stand like sheep, with stupid, disbelieving looks on their faces? Did they want Faldain to be dead? Aye, she suspected they did. And she hated them for it.

"Perhaps the Grethori bobbed his majesty's ears," Unshalin said.

It was an unconscionable thing to say, but even Alexeika was too shocked to utter a reproof.

Strolling forward with his hands hooked importantly on his gold chain of office, his fat gut projecting ahead of him, the count scowled. "They mutilate their fallen enemies. That is the most likely explanation."

Alexeika sought to keep her temper. "The king was badly wounded by a magicked sword before the Battle of Grov and carries the scar on his left shoulder. Why, then, is there no such scar on *this* body?"

A soft murmur ran around the room. She saw Tustik speak to another member of the Privy Council, who hurried away.

"I remember no scar," Miest was saying awkwardly. "We found his majesty's helmet and—"

"There, my good man," Unshalin said, patting his shoulder. "Do not distress yourself."

"We were fools to be turned back," Chesil said, lifting a clenched fist. "I knew we should ride after them. We could have caught up easily. We weren't that far behind."

"His highness gave orders for us to deal properly with our dead," Miest said angrily. "And he was right."

"Who?" Alexeika demanded. "Who issued the order that kept you from riding to the king's rescue?"

A tide of red slowly rose up Miest's face. "Why, Prince Jonan, of course. If the king is dead, is he not our new sovereign?"

The room erupted in argument. Alexeika stood rigid, so angry she could not for a moment speak. "Jonan!" she spat out at last. "Are you mad? Or a traitor? Or both?"

Looking alarmed, Tustik lifted his hands placatingly. "Now, your majesty—"

She wished she wore her daggers. She would have gutted Miest where he stood. "The king taken prisoner, and you did nothing!" she accused him furiously. "You let Jonan pronounce our sovereign dead and gave him honor for it! 'Tis treason that's been done, and nothing less."

"No, your majesty!" Miest said, looking horrified. "I swear—"

"Liar! Betrayer!" She beckoned to the guards standing at the door. "Arrest this man and hold him for questioning. Hold all the knights who were party to this deception. Bringing home a false corpse and calling it the king's body. You knave, I'll see your head on the gate for this!"

As the guards came forward, Miest drew his weapon and rushed at her, shouting something incoherent. Sir Pyron seized her arm and pulled her out of harm's way barely in time. Chesil hurled one of his daggers, and the weapon thudded home in Miest's chest and quivered there.

As he staggered, looking surprised, his sword fell from his hand and clattered on the floor. An expression of despair flickered across his face, and his eyes sought Alexeika's in appeal. "What have I done?" he whispered, and collapsed.

When one of the guards rolled him over, he was dead.

"Touch not this body," Samderaudin said into the hush, and the guard backed away. "The spell that clouded his wits can spread by touch to others." He walked up and stood staring down at Miest's body with his yellow eyes glittering. "A strange little spell, weak and easily countered, yet most effective." He sniffed the air like a dog. "*Sheda* magic, I think."

"Get him out of here," Alexeika ordered. "And take away this other body as well." She turned away, hugging herself as she tired to hold down her fury and loathing. She'd encountered a Grethori *sheda* long ago when held as their prisoner, and the old crone had nearly destroyed her before she managed to escape. Since then, she'd vowed to never let the savages gain control over her life again. And now they had her daughter and her husband in their clutches.

Not until the gray men had departed with their tools and both corpses did she turn to face the members of the Privy Council. "There must be war declared on all Grethori tribes," she said. "The army must be mustered and sent into the mountains with orders to sack their villages. Destroy their warriors and scatter the women and children far from our borders. And the king and princess royal must be rescued at once."

"Let me see to it, majesty!" Chesil volunteered eagerly. "I will hunt down these evil dogs to the ends of the world and beyond. This I swear, *neya*?"

She found a smile for him, pleased that his loyalty remained unquestioned. "First, you will report to the captain of the guard and answer all questions necessary. And, yes, you may guide the army into the mountains."

Bowing to her, Chesil hurried out. Through the open doors at the end of the chamber, she saw a guard fall into step beside him in the passageway.

Alexeika glanced around. "Let the chamber of state be cleaned at once and restored to its customary order. And you," she said to the nearest guard, "see that no one touches the king's sword or moves it from the throne."

Looking startled, the man saluted with alacrity. "Your majesty's will is done."

Nodding, Alexeika started for the door, but Prince Tustik blocked her path.

"Ah, yes," she said, meeting his gaze. "There is the matter of Jonan to discuss. Will it please you to join me in perhaps an hour's time, lord prince?"

Tustik bowed, but Unshalin blustered forward. "Why not have this discussion now?" he said loudly. "And why should the queen meet alone with Prince Tustik when this matter is rightly for the Privy Council to ponder?"

"Ponder all you like," Alexeika snapped, "but the queen may talk to whom she pleases *when* she pleases."

His small eyes flickered with resentment, but he bowed in apology. "Your majesty—"

"I'm going to say prayers for the safety of my husband and daughter," she said, far from pleased at being obliged to explain herself. She nodded to Tustik. "And then I shall receive whatever advice the Privy Council sees fit to send me through Prince Tustik. I hope that is now clear?"

Tustik raised his brows in silence, but Unshalin turned a dark shade of red. "That is the king's prerogative," he said arrogantly, "not the queen's. The Privy Council is not answerable to your majesty."

"Legally, no," she replied, curbing her temper. "But as a matter of courtesy, especially in these circumstances, I expected better of you, Count Unshalin."

He frowned at the rebuke, and she supposed he would seek retaliation in some petty way for having been bested in this confrontation. At the moment she did not care. He thought himself powerful enough to speak to her as he chose, but she was no common noblewoman, no ordinary lady, and he'd erred hugely by forgetting that. He'd underestimated her, she realized; perhaps they all did. If so, they were fools.

She stared at him in regal silence, mentally picking the best places to stab him, and as the silence stretched out, he finally huffed to himself and stepped aside.

"In an hour," she said to Tustik, and swept out, with her head high and her skirts rustling furiously.

Chapter Sixteen

Twilight cast inky shadows across Alexeika's sitting room. While she paced up and down its confines with her brow knotted in distress, her mind awhirl with conjecture and strategies, the servants moved about on silent feet to fill the tile stove with wood, light the lamps hanging suspended from wall brackets on short black chains, and set out a tray of wine and goblets. Unable to bear their presence any longer, she dismissed them all and sent even her protector to stand outside the door.

Back and forth she paced like a caged lyng, her mind awash with fury at the Grethori and fear for Faldain. The ambush had obviously been a trap, and Tashalya's abduction had been the bait.

But why should the Grethori devise so elaborate a ruse to take Nether's king? Trap him to kill him; aye, Alexeika could understand that. But take him hostage? Was he to be ransomed for all—and likely more—lying in Nether's treasury? Gladly would she pay any price, were the matter that simple.

She believed there was more to this, however, much more. Some enemy's hand was at work, moving Faldain here and there about his realm like a piece in a game of draughts. Well, Alexeika told herself, the game had to stop. It was time to find the enemy and make him pay dearly.

As for Faldain . . . where was he? A prisoner of the Grethori? Or had he been sold into Gantese hands? Either way, he had to be in terrible danger.

Panic clutched her heart, and she came to a breathless halt by the window, pressing her hot cheek against the ice-cold glass. *Don't give way to emotions*, she told herself fiercely. *Stay strong. He depends on you.*

Yet tears welled up in her eyes. She pressed her hand against the bodice of her gown, where the Ring of Solder hung concealed on a thin gold chain around her neck. Faldain had given it to her before he departed, placing the very power of his kingdom in her keeping despite her protests. Thinking of the one previous time when the Ring had been in her possession—on that occasion without Faldain's knowledge—she squirmed with remembered shame. Faldain had forgiven her for her transgression, which another man might have considered treason, but it had been very hard for her to forgive herself.

His trust and love were utterly hers, his kingdom in her hands to guard and protect. It infuriated her that at this moment, when Faldain's court should be concerned with sending him aid, it was scrambling instead for the chance to choose his successor. The ungrateful dogs, how dare they forget all that Faldain had done for them? She longed to burst into the Privy Council and confront its members. There was a time when she would not have been willing to wait like this. But she'd gained a bit of wisdom in her years as queen. She knew she must bide her time, moving behind the scenes as long as possible. *Morde*, she thought impatiently. Waiting was very hard, especially when she kept thinking of Faldain hurt or imprisoned somewhere, in desperate need of help.

My love, she thought in anguish, *where are you?*

A soft tapping on the door scattered her thoughts. She pulled herself together and turned as a page entered.

"Prince Tustik, your majesty," he said.

She lifted her chin, standing straight and composed despite

the fire in her cheeks and the thudding of her heart. "The prince is granted my permission to enter," she said.

Advancing over the threshold, Tustik bowed low to her. She noticed with fresh ire that he had taken the time to change his garments. Elegant in gray velvet trimmed with fur, he wore a matching cap adorned with black soutache, and a gold chain studded with sapphires glittered across his chest. His dark eyes, set in that thin aristocratic face, met hers like basalt.

She gave him no chance to waste time with courtesies. "You have kept the queen waiting," she said sharply. "Perhaps you misunderstood my command that you attend me in an hour."

"Perhaps the queen was unwise to exert her will so openly," he replied. "The queen has the privilege to command, but not the right."

The rebuke stung, but Alexeika did not back down. "The queen is not without resources. It is time that the Privy Council—as well as the Kollegya—understood that."

"And does the queen intend to seize the throne for herself?"

Infuriated, she took a step forward before she could control herself. "Such a remark is unworthy of you, lord prince, and an insult to me."

"I beg the queen's pardon," he replied with a bow. "Shall we begin anew?"

But she could not bear the intricate dance of political talk. She had not the patience, not now when Faldain's throne was at stake. "Has there been a palace coup?" she asked.

Tustik raised his white brows. "'Tis not a coup to choose a successor to a dead sovereign."

Just in time she stopped herself from attacking that. He was baiting her, she realized, perhaps testing her, although Thod knew why. She wanted to scream at him; instead, she frowned and met his gaze with hers on fire. "Faldain is *not* dead."

"Does your majesty know this for certain?"

"You were present, lord prince, when I proved that corpse was not the king's."

Tustik nodded. "Yes, I was, your majesty. But you have not proven his majesty to be alive."

She brushed this detail aside. "Of course, but why the ruse?"

"Ruse, your majesty?"

"Yes! This elaborate trick to convince his men to bring that body home. Why do all that if he were not alive and held hostage?"

Tustik stared at the wall for a long moment before he replied. "For the sake of the realm, majesty, it might be best if the king were pronounced dead. Better that than to tell the people he is a hostage. Especially when we know not the actual facts."

"Why lie to the people?" she countered, her voice sharp to mask her fear. "Why say he is dead if he is not? Doing so would declare the throne to be empty, and the people would then demand a successor. I'll agree to nothing so foolish."

"I do not believe the Privy Council has asked for your majesty's agreement," Tustik said dryly.

She shot him a look of alarm. "Has the Council gone mad? If it does this, then its members commit treason."

"That accusation is perhaps a trifle hasty."

"Is it? Why do you toy with me, Prince Tustik? What are you trying to accomplish by alarming me in this way?"

His serious expression softened slightly, and he gave her an elegant little salute of one swordsman to another. "Well done, majesty. You have not betrayed your strategy in how you intend to hold the throne for the king. Already rumors are flying across Grov of his demise. The merchants' pavilion is in an uproar."

"A pox on the merchants' pavilion," she said. "Lock them in and let them send forth no couriers to spread this lie."

He shook his head. "Your majesty might as well try to hold water in your fingers. A funeral and a period of mourning would hold the realm paralyzed until the long cold sets in. That would give us time."

"For what?" she demanded. "To muster the army and send it into the mountains? And what if the king is liberated, only to find a usurper on his throne? He'll turn against all those responsible."

A very faint smile curled the corners of Tustik's mouth. "Would not such a usurper, such a pretender, be considered a traitor?" he asked softly. "Of *course* King Faldain would retaliate against his enemy."

She gasped in understanding. "You would do all this just to see Jonan arrested for treason?"

Tustik did not reply, but she did not like what she read in his gaze.

"And if the king were not found?" she forced herself to ask. "If the king did not return?"

"It is a risk," Tustik admitted. "No decision has been made as yet to take it. But as a strategy it should be considered."

"No!" she said vehemently. "I refuse it absolutely."

"Your majesty knows I deplore the idea of Jonan's very existence," Tustik said in exasperation. "But whatever our opinions, we must deal with the realities of this situation. The king is absent, and we have no idea if he'll return. Jonan is his majesty's heir."

She thought of the unborn child growing in her womb and turned her back to the man. Should she announce the pregnancy? Once her condition was officially known, she would be obliged to withdraw into seclusion. She dared not let herself be shut away, isolated from news and information, kept apart from political events, ignorant of everything happening in the palace and the realm beyond the confines of her quarters. She would be able to do nothing unless she kept her pregnancy hidden as long as possible.

Well, she told herself, she still had the document of authority written by Faldain, along with the royal seal and the Ring of Solder. Tustik had come here hinting to learn if she possessed any such emblems of power, but could she trust him on this matter? Succession was too important, too fraught with pitfalls for her to make a misstep now.

Going to her small writing table, she pulled out the document Faldain had signed, and handed it to Tustik. "Jonan will never sit on Faldain's throne."

"I see." He read it over twice and handed it back. "Your

majesty, I would to Thod above that we could be discussing the reign of Prince Ilymir with yourself as regent, but that is not the situation."

She realized he was trying to buy himself time to think, but that he deliberately mentioned her son to distract her with grief made her furious. She stared at him hard, refusing to reply, and his gaze dropped first.

"Gant is agitating our eastern border," he said. "Word of the trouble came just a short time ago. If those fiends start a new war, we cannot afford to be without a king. Faldain's absence could not have come at a worse time."

She drew in a sharp breath. "He was right!"

"Majesty?"

"Faldain was right. He said all along that Gant was behind the Grethori attack on us. No one believed the connection, but he must be right. And if the Chief Believer has been behind our troubles of late, manipulating us like puppets, and luring Faldain into a trap, then—"

She broke off, too upset to continue.

"And now the realm is threatened," Tustik said in soft agreement. "Our border garrisons must stay on full alert. It is vital that we send additional troops east to strengthen the forces already stationed there."

She did not need to have the problem explained to her. She understood all too well. "Which means we cannot spare the number of men necessary to drive the Grethori forth from their hideouts."

"Precisely. And with the weather already turning—"

"But we can't wait until thaw," she said in protest. "Faldain's life may be in the greatest peril. We can't abandon him, or Tashalya." Clenching her hands together, she paced back and forth. "We'll divide our forces, sending forth knights with *sorcerels* to the east and the Agya army west in search of the king."

"No *sorcerel* will ride with an army if the king is not present," Tustik said flatly. "That is the custom."

" 'Tis a stupid one!" she burst out.

"Nevertheless."

She wanted to yell at him about the countless old-fashioned, witless customs that held Nether trapped in a backward past, so imprisoned by its traditions that it couldn't change, couldn't grow, couldn't advance. Somehow she held her tongue, knowing that Tustik needed no such lecture. He was educated and well traveled. He had lived in Mandria as an exile for a time before Faldain was crowned; he had witnessed that kingdom's advances and wealth. Nether, so much larger, so rich with untapped resources, remained impoverished and backward, its people fearful of change.

Sighing, she said, "And of course without the king, the Agyas won't take orders either."

"That is *their* custom. Sometimes, as your majesty knows, they won't even obey their sovereign."

"Aye, they wouldn't serve Muncel," she said. "But they revere Faldain! Surely they will ride to his aid."

"Indeed. But Faldain favors the Agyas too much already in the opinions of some. It is best to keep them integrated within the main army."

"Best for whom?" she demanded impatiently. "Advisers and ministers, members of one council or another? What good are these stupid political maneuvers when the king's life is at stake?"

"Majesty—"

"Yes, yes, I know!" She grimaced and forced herself to modulate her tone. "I know."

"Even if General Matkevskict is willing to send forth his men to search the mountains at this time of year, we need Agyas in the east as well. They are our best fighters, and we cannot afford to face Nonkind armies without them."

She nodded, painfully aware of how hard Faldain had worked to persuade his separate armies to merge into a strong fighting force for the betterment of the realm. And now, it seemed, he might have to pay for that strategy with his life.

"Majesty," Tustik said, "please reconsider allowing Jonan to be named king."

She lifted the document. "His majesty gave me this to prevent Jonan's succession. Now you, the very last person I expected, plead on Jonan's behalf."

"Indeed," Tustik said bitterly. "The irony has not escaped

me. I abhor that foolish boy and the line he springs from. His mother was a foul-mouthed harridan, a bloodthirsty bitch. His father sold his soul to Ashnod. Blasphemers and murderers, the pair of them. My wife and children perished for their amusement, killed as entertainment for the court."

"I know," she said with sympathy, thinking of the mother she'd never known because Queen Neaglis had ordered her execution. "I am sorry."

He nodded, lost in the past, his face twisted with a depth of passion it seldom showed. "I was hauled out of the dungeons to watch my family die. If I could reach into Beyond, majesty, and strike at Muncel's twisted soul, I would do it. And to put his son, *his* seed, on the throne where kings such as Solder, Runtha, Tobeszijian, and Faldain have sat . . . no, majesty, I feel this injustice to my very core. But I will always put the good of the realm first, and if that means temporarily upholding Jonan's claim, then I'll do it."

"And I will use every means available to prevent it," she said with equal determination. "To my last breath, I will oppose this plan."

"You'll need more than that document to fight succession by right of blood."

I have it, she thought, but said nothing about her unborn child.

"Does your majesty have possession of the royal seal?"

"I do."

"Will your majesty surrender it?"

"Never."

He nodded. "I expected no other answer, but it had to be asked."

"Who is next in line after Jonan?"

Pursing his lips, Tustik raised his brows. "Vladno Krelinik."

She thought of the archduke, who was handsome, idle, and a mischief-maker. But although spoiled, Vladno was a valiant man at heart. He had risked his life on the day of the attack to defend her and her children; she owed him an enormous debt of gratitude for that. Unlike Jonan, Vladno would be an acceptable successor to Faldain.

"Put the throne in his hands, however temporarily, and he will never willingly surrender it," Tustik said. "Nor does he deserve to be manipulated and ruined in a political ploy. He is no traitor, nor of traitor's blood."

"Agreed."

"Jonan, however, can be easily sacrificed when the time comes. Meanwhile, we need a monarch."

"Put a crown on Jonan's head and still he would not be a king," she said in disgust. "No, lord prince. I will not change my mind. I find this plan devious, even despicable. I will not support it."

Tustik's expression grew cold indeed. "Just how far will your majesty go in opposition?"

"As far as is necessary," she replied flatly. "I am committed, with all that lies at my disposal, to preserving the throne for Faldain's return."

"Your majesty realizes, of course, that the Privy Council and Kollegya are already critical of the amount of power you have seized. This year, pressure was brought to bear on the king regarding the amount of influence he allows you to exercise."

There it was, the steel revealed at last within the velvet. She felt as though she'd taken a hit, and inside she was thinking, *so this is what has troubled Faldain for so many months. This is what he would not confide in me.* Anger flashed through her at the idea of the Kollegya meddling in what should lie between a man and wife, and she guessed that the Kollegya had met that night instead of the Council.

Contemptuously, she said, "There are too many fools in this court worrying about trifles instead of what is important. I have the king's ear, aye! By his choice rather than my request. If I am ambitious, 'tis for Nether, both realm and people. If I am more outspoken than most women, blame my father and my upbringing, for why should a person of intelligence and ability—whether male or female—be constrained from exercising both? Does the Kollegya fear I want the throne for myself?"

Tustik nodded.

In one sense it was almost a compliment for these men to

so fear her abilities, but their doubt and mistrust equally infuriated her. "What I seek to do is for his sake, not my own," she said vehemently. "I preserve the throne for him. It is his, as long as he lives. He charged me with guarding it, and I will do that, no matter what the cost."

"But has your majesty considered the cost?" Tustik asked urgently. "Even the king dares not openly defy the Kollegya. For you to—"

"The king is above these men. They have no true power over him," she replied, using bravado to mask a quivering dart of alarm. "His will counts above theirs."

Tustik was shaking his head. "Forgive me, but that is a naive view of the situation. Faldain has learned better."

She thought of the lines of strain carved in her beloved's handsome face, thought of his fatigue and the worry that often filled his eyes. 'Twas not the hard work of ruling that had worn him so, but the petty, self-serving, vicious machinations of men who met in secret to oppose Faldain's good intentions and make his life a misery. She despised them for what they'd done to her man. Despised them for what they were trying to do now.

"Faldain is no puppet," she said angrily, "but Jonan will be. That's what this is about, is it not? All the talk about potential war and disaster is just an excuse."

"Your majesty—"

"And *you*," she said with scorn, "constantly claiming to loathe and despise Jonan, yet you are the one who runs first to call him king."

Tustik's thin nostrils flared, and his mouth clamped so tightly a ring of white surrounded it, but he controlled himself. "This is what comes of sharing too much information with your majesty," he muttered. "If *this* is what you think of me, perhaps it would be best if I withdrew my assistance entirely."

"Now you threaten me," she retorted. "I see you have exchanged your concern and loyalty for pettiness."

"Your majesty clearly does not trust my judgment or advice, although I must warn you that even the queen's loyalty might be called into question over this."

Disbelief widened Alexeika's eyes. "The Kollegya would not dare accuse *me* of treason!"

"Your majesty has admitted possession of the royal seal. Your majesty is determined to thwart the legal naming of a successor to the throne, no doubt in your favor. Your majesty's personal ambitions will be exposed for what they are . . . an intention to rule Nether in defiance of custom, tradition, and law."

"Get out. Thod damn you, get out!"

He met her wild, furious gaze with one like ice. In silence, he bowed to her and departed. As the door closed behind him, her emotions overwhelmed her. Seizing the nearest object to hand, a delicate box made of parchment-thin wood inlays, she hurled it at the door and shattered the trinket into splinters.

But giving physical vent to her fury brought her no relief, for she realized that she'd just lost her one ally in the Kollegya. Her temper, her wretched, uncontrollable temper, had cost her dearly that night. But she did not care. Tustik had no right to threaten her, to threaten the queen, whatever his intentions. He was playing a dangerous game, one that could easily end in disaster. She refused to be a part of it, for her responsibility lay with the charge Faldain had given her. And even if she must stand alone against his enemies, she would do it.

Chapter Seventeen

Hobbling on her crippled feet, and leaning on her wooden staff decorated with tiny, tinkling bells and the polished skulls of infants, the *sheda* of the Wind Tribe made her way through snowy twilight across camp. Flanked by *mamsas* who carried large leather pouches, she passed the looms, cooking fires, and drying poles. She passed tents where curious faces peered out, only to withdraw abruptly in respect. She skirted the round, flat-topped stone of Adauri, with its sacred circle of *ini* stones, and thus reached a tent in the center of camp, guarded by warriors armed with spears.

Here, she paused a moment to catch her wheezing breath. Overhead, a full winter's moon was rising through tattered snow clouds to shine cold and white. The *sheda* closed her eyes a moment to feel the moon's power pulling through her. Ah, yes, at last it was time.

She stepped forward, and one of the *mamsas* opened the tent flap for her to enter the warmth and light inside. Two women, painted according to the spells of strength and watchfulness and armed with daggers and magic bones, stood over the prisoner.

They raised their vermilion-painted palms to the *sheda* in respect and effaced themselves to one side. The *sheda* shuffled closer to the pile of furs serving as bedding for the prisoner and peered at the famous King Faldain. Although young, already he was of legend. A fierce and wily warrior, he possessed the courage and strength she needed. It had taken much to capture him, much bargaining for the spell, much planning for the deed, much lying, and much risk. All the *sheda's* skill and magic had gone into the deception necessary to gain Tulvak Sahm's spellfire. In exchange for that knowledge, she had committed her tribesmen to killing the pale-eyes who pursued them into these mountains. Faldain of Nether was to die. So had Tulvak Sahm ordered and decreed. But it did not suit the *sheda's* purpose for Faldain to die, not yet, and so she had wrought a spell of great slyness, fooling both the pale-eyes and the dangerous *sorcerel*. Had Tulvak Sahm stayed close by to see his wishes carried out, she could not have succeeded, but in him was much arrogance and self-importance. He thought her lower than the worms that crawled in the dirt, and he did not believe she would dare defy him. Now, the great king was hers, and Tulvak Sahm's plans for revenge did not matter one speck against what the *sheda* intended.

Faldain lay on his back, naked save for the beyar hide thrown across his loins. He had been brought to camp four days earlier, wounded and unconscious. Thus far, he had not roused. The axe cut to his chest was not deep and would not kill him. The head wound was more serious, and at first she'd been angry with the men for damaging him too much. She feared he might die, but his heart was strong, his body strong. Whether his wits were crushed forever did not matter, as long as his body lived.

It was time to begin. The *sheda* lifted her hands, and in silence the *mamsas* assisted her, helping her first to kneel on the ground before taking her staff and laying it reverently on the ground within her reach. They handed her the magic pouches and added sticks to the fire until it blazed hot and bright within its circle of polished small *ini* stones. Without being told, the guardians went to stand by the tent flap, to prevent anyone from entering as the magic began.

Gathering her powers, the *sheda* began a low chant while the *mamsas* bowed their heads. The *sheda* withdrew a bronze bowl from one pouch. Stained dark from blood and fire, this bowl held the resonance of so many spells cast over the years that it had almost taken on a power of its own. She balanced it on her fingertips, feeling the tingle of contact between its metal surface and her flesh. When she coughed across the top of the bowl, a swirl of mist filled its concavity. She inhaled deeply, drawing the power spell into her lungs. She would need all her strength to work the spell. There could be no mistakes.

Setting the bowl on a piece of woven cloth, she laid her sacrificial knife beside it. The *mamsas* began a different chant, one now running counterpoint to hers. The fire blazed higher, casting forth a puff of black smoke that hovered in the air and stank. On the furs, Faldain stirred and moaned. The *sheda's* eyes turned in his direction, but she did not lose the rhythm of her chant. The spell had begun, and she could not afford to let it falter. After a moment, he lay quiet again. She saw sweat glistening on his shoulders, but her old bones felt none of the intense heat filling the tent.

One of the *mamsas* opened the second pouch, and from it the *sheda* took the skull of a woman from a pale-eyes settlement, abducted and killed last month for this purpose. She held it up, chanting more loudly, and felt heat ignite between her palms and the curve of bone. Carefully, she laid the skull on the ground, tilting it on its side, then pulled out more of the woman's bones from the pouch, part of the spine, a scattering of ribs, the arms and legs, one hand, and one foot. Holding each piece aloft and chanting over it until she felt the magic heat pass from her flesh into the bones, she arranged the skeleton until it resembled a body lying on its side. Last of all, she brought forth the vital part, the pelvic bones and hip cradle, which she passed through the fire.

The flames blazed higher in hues of orange, white, and blue, and dimly in the farthest recesses of her mind, the *sheda* heard the victim's screams as she was killed. She smiled grimly to herself, thinking of another young woman, one of great beauty, even for a pale-eyes. Untouched, with a spirit of wind and fire, the maiden had stood out from all the others captured with her. Defiant and strong, her courage shining flame in her eyes, she had been chosen to bear the dragon-child that would deliver the tribes of Grethori from their oppressors. Accordingly, this maiden had been prepared and the magic laid in place. She had filled the eyes of the *sheda's* youngest son Holoc, driving him mad with lust, and the *sheda* had wrought her most potent spell over both in preparation for the joining to take place on the stone of Adauri.

But there had been no union, no planting of Holoc's seed into a fertile womb. The maiden had escaped. With the cunning of a woman, the strength of a man, and the guile of a demon, she had shook off the bonds of her spell, resisting the lust that should have burned in her blood until she was writhing in readiness for her destiny. She had fled the camp and vanished, and the spell madness had been so entwined around Holoc that even the *sheda* could not free him in time. Off he'd gone in pursuit, and the demon maid had killed him.

How the *sheda* had raged for months afterward. Holoc had been the last issue of her womb. She had no other sons to follow him. Her grand scheme for the deliverance of her people lay in ruins. All that had been foretold and shown to her from the hour she became a *sheda* was wrecked because she chose too strong a demon to mate with her son.

Then had come word that the demon maid was wed to King Faldain. As she chanted, the *sheda's* gaze traveled to his unconscious face again with involuntary admiration. This king of legend, this mighty warrior had dared unite with a man-woman demon, and he'd tamed her, something Holoc— even with the *sheda's* spells—had been unable to do. Which meant that Holoc was unworthy to sire the dragon-child, and the gods had stopped the *sheda* from making a terrible mistake. When Tulvak Sahm recently approached the elders with his bargain for the king's death, the *sheda* had realized the gods were handing her the proper means of bringing the deliverer into this world. Faldain would sire the dragon-child and pave the way for the downfall of the pale-eyes.

Smiling, she forced herself to concentrate on the spell. With the female skeleton assembled before her, she slid her

hand into the first pouch and drew out a small, covered basket. Inside it lay the locks of dark chestnut hair cut from the
head of the demon maiden, and some of her droppings shriv-
eled and hardened from time. Shaking these objects into the
bronze bowl, the *sheda* abruptly changed her chant to one
more forceful. Raising her hands, she conjured forth a pale,
ghostly image that slowly rose from the bowl into the air.
Swirling like mist, it gradually became a face and form, and
there, turning about in the heated air, was the demon maiden's
visage. She still looked rebellious and fierce. The *sheda* added
more strands of her hair to the bowl and wove a spell of
beauty into the image that enhanced the large, blue-gray eyes
and oval perfection of face. The lashes grew dark and long.
That shining, thick mane of hair seemed almost real.

Lowering her hands, the *sheda* carefully drew the image
away from the bowl and cast it over the skeleton. Although
her voice shook and quavered from the strain, and she felt
momentary palsy in her hands, she drew on sheer determination and fitted the image in place.

For a few moments, it shimmered there atop the skeleton,
a ghost fading in and out among the bones. Alarm clutched
the *sheda's* heart. She gestured swiftly, and one of the *mamsas* led a guardian to her. As the young woman knelt in compliance, the *sheda* gripped her wrist and cut it swiftly with the
sacrificial knife. She captured the spurt of blood in the bowl,
chanting loudly to cover the sound of the guardian's moans.
The girl tried to pull away, but the *sheda* held her with a
strength born of magic, squeezing to hurry the spurting flow
of blood.

When she had enough, she released the girl, who slumped
fainting and pale to the ground, and poured the fresh, fragrant
blood over the skeleton. Of life and beauty and desirability,
she chanted, willing her creation to come into being.

The ghostly image grew stronger. Under the force of
magic, flesh covered the bones. The face that formed over the
skull duplicated that of the demon maiden Faldain had mated.
The body lying on the ground, naked and lushly curved,
looked like hers as well. Luxuriant dark tresses spilled over
her shoulders. The eyes, rimmed with dark lashes, opened,

and the rosy lips parted. Wordlessly, the *glimmage* sat up, gazing around with empty eyes, and stretched.

The chanting fell silent. Panting for breath, her old heart thumping from exertion, the *sheda* felt the exhaustion knotting her body with pain, but she was too triumphant to care. She had brought a *glimmage* to life. There was no more difficult spell to cast in women's magic, but she had done it. Gathering herself, knowing that despite her terrible fatigue her task was not finished, she finished draining the blood from the guardian dying beside her and gave it to the *glimmage* to drink.

The creature lapped it like a cat, and a rosy hue tinted its cheeks. It raised its lifeless eyes to the *sheda's* face and stared. Empty, compliant, obedient, in some dim way it recognized its mistress-creator and waited to do her bidding.

Exhilarated, the *sheda* caressed that shining head of hair and wiped a smear of blood from the creature's mouth before turning her gaze on Faldain. She hobbled over to him and rested her fingers on his throat, feeling the steady beat of his pulse. Chiseled of feature, his broad shoulders thick with muscle and sinew, he carried the exotic look of his mixed blood. She let her fingertips dance over his skin, and knew a sudden wish to be young and lithe again so it could be she who danced with him in the spell, she that took the power of his body, she that bore the dragon-child. With her blood throbbing, she loathed her span of years and ancient body, so gnarled and twisted like the trees that grew on cliffs. She curled her wizened palm around the angle of his jaw and let desire flame to life inside her, a desire so hot and fevered it shook her and made her gasp.

"*Sheda*?" one of the *mamsas* asked in concern.

"Quiet." Still breathing hard, she turned and cut her own wrist over the bowl, expertly draining the proper amount of blood without weakening herself. While one of the *mamsas* bound up the cut, she gave her blood to the *glimmage* and watched while the creature lapped it up greedily.

"Now are we bound together," the *sheda* said in satisfaction, casting her eyes avidly at Faldain. "I will feel what my creature feels. I will be a part of what is to come. The child will still be *my* child, half-mortal and half-magical, and I will train him with magic into a fearsome leader. And all the tribes will be one vast horde, destroying our enemies forever."

"Do we begin?"

She nodded at the *mamsa* who'd asked the question. "Prepare the spells of desire. Make them potent."

Nodding, one *mamsa* moved the *glimmage* closer to the fire, which burned normally now, and the other began to mix bright colors of paint in mollusk shells. Using fine brushes made from horsehair, they knelt by the *glimmage* and began to paint her breasts and belly with scrolling patterns of vine and flower while they chanted the accompanying spell.

The air grew fragrant and heavy with desire until it almost shimmered. Wheezing a little in her excitement, the *sheda* leaned over Faldain and cut a lock of his black hair. She tucked it away inside her private amulet bag, trembling a little, for the action made her feel like a young girl keeping secrets. It was only training, she told herself, and wise training indeed always to keep some small part of the enemy, but in her heart she knew she wanted more than that.

Forbidden, she thought. *Since my younger days I have yearned for all that is taboo.*

To distract herself from such unsettling thoughts, she forced herself to concentrate on the spell she now had to cast over him.

"When you wake, valiant warrior," she whispered, cackling a little in her glee, "it will be your wife you want, as the desert craves the kiss of rain. Her breasts will pillow your head. Her thighs will be like silk. Her fragrance will make your senses swim. Her heat will draw you like a moth to flame. To her will you join, and with her will you make the life that is to come."

Faldain moaned, shifting his head to one side. She caressed his brow before she finished stirring her potion of spices and secret ingredients. Lifting his head slightly, she held the liquid to his lips, and he drank thirstily, his eyes dragging open for a moment before he fell asleep once more.

Pleased, the *sheda* retreated from him and sat down near the tent flap to rest. The air smelled of spells, lust, and the mystery known only between a man and woman. Outside, she could hear the guards muttering restlessly, and she smiled to herself at the weakness of men. They were obviously stirred by the tracings of magic escaping the tent, but none of them would dare to enter. Meanwhile, the *mamsas* went on painting the *glimmage* until she was beautiful, fragrant, and adorned.

"Put the creature on the furs," the *sheda* commanded. "No! Under the beyar hide beside him."

She watched critically while the *glimmage* was settled in place next to Faldain, and at last nodded in satisfaction. The *mamsas* assisted her to her feet and handed her staff to her. While one gathered up the bowl and knife, replacing them in one of the pouches, the other dragged out the body of the dead girl. The surviving guardian ducked outside, only to be seized by one of the warriors.

"Finished in there, Tuka?" he asked with a laugh. "Want to share anything with me?"

A *mamsa* spoke a curt reprimand, and the warrior released the girl swiftly. The men straightened themselves and looked away from the emerging *sheda* with respect and fear.

The night air cut like a sword edge through the *sheda's* robe. She stared up at the moon, sending forth her prayer to the gods for success, and cast a sharp look at the men. "Guard our prisoner well," she commanded. "He is strong and wily. See that he doesn't escape."

"The *sheda's* will is ours," they replied in unison.

She shot each of them a harsh look. "Let no one enter. Let no one interfere."

Chuntok swaggered up, appearing suddenly from the shadows to loom over the *sheda* in the moonlight. Still smug at having vanquished the king of the pale-eyes, Chuntok had achieved a tremendous coup, gaining enormous respect from the other men. No doubt he planned to boast of his conquest for years to come, but at present the *sheda* was not pleased to see him.

"He is awake now?" Chuntok asked.

"No."

"When? Why do you not make him stir?"

Angered by his interference, she eyed him fiercely. "Keep

your place. When the time comes, I will give him to you, as we agreed."

Chuntok looked sullen. "He is my prisoner. I caught him—"

"With my spell," she broke in sharply. "Do not let your pride swell too large, chieftain."

"I want his finger bones," Chuntok said. "They are mine by right."

"When I give him to you," the *sheda* said, "you can take all his finger bones for your braids. You can impale his head on your tent pole. You can drag his body around the camp three times in victory. But you will wait to kill him until my purpose is finished."

"How long?" he rasped out. "How long?"

"When my purpose is finished." She met his gaze, holding it and exerting her will until he frowned and looked down in sudden respect. "You will not be cheated of your spoils, Chuntok. But keep away from him until I permit his death."

The chieftain muttered in his beard, but moved aside. The *sheda* limped past him, her staff bells tinkling softly with her passage, but she was not satisfied that he would obey her. He was not one of her sons, and although tribal custom decreed that he must defer to her will, she knew he wanted a matriarch of his own family to become *sheda*. Although he was strong and a good hunter, Chuntok was a fool, and the *sheda* had no intention of letting him foil her carefully laid plans.

As soon as she was out of his earshot, she halted and beckoned to one of the *mamsas*.

"Yes, old one?"

"Gather Vinlin and Mola," the *sheda* commanded softly. "Cloak yourselves and stay on watch. If Chuntok disobeys me—"

"He would surely not dare, old one!"

The *sheda* snorted. "He surely might. Watch him. If he tries to interfere, block him from the tent and call to me. I'll unleash spellfire on him."

"But he is chieftain!"

"And my word is law," the *sheda* said grimly. "I work the will of the gods. Remember that. If necessary, I will teach the whole camp a lesson."

The *mamsa* lifted her palms hurriedly. "The *sheda's* will is my will." And she hastened away.

Slowly the *sheda* continued back to her tent. In the cold darkness she lay down and wrapped herself in a beyar hide. Her body ached from exertion and the cold, but she paid that no heed. Her thoughts and spirit were attuned elsewhere, as she waited.

Chapter Eighteen

Jonan's head was spinning from the sweetness of Sofina's perfume. Her rosy lips were soft and warm beneath his, so pliant that he felt himself going mad. A fire raged in him, both sweet and fierce. He couldn't breathe, yet this wasn't the usual constriction in his throat and chest. This was fabulous, like a dream. The softness of her curves pressed against his body excited him until his arms tightened.

She squeaked. "Gently, my love! Don't crush me."

Recalled partially to his senses, Jonan pulled back. They were sitting side by side on a bench in the abandoned part of the palace. The air was icy cold, and a small lamp on the floor cast the only light. They had been meeting there in secret every evening since Jonan's return. At first they dared talk briefly before Sofina grew frightened that her father would notice her absence. But two nights ago, she'd let him hold her hand, and this evening he'd suddenly turned to her while she was chatting, pulled her into his arms, and kissed her.

He was clumsy and unpracticed, but Sofina did not repudiate him. Instead, she sighed, melting into his embrace, and now his head and body were throbbing, and he found himself panting for air as though he'd run down to the river and back without stopping.

"Did I hurt you?" he asked. "I—I didn't mean to."

She giggled, her golden brown eyes twinkling in the lamplight. Her lips, a little swollen from his ardor, parted slightly. He reached out and gently rubbed his thumb across them. She moaned a little, and that primitive, pleasured sound made him want to possess her, body and soul.

Instead, he shifted restlessly on the hard bench, not daring to give way to his desires, and sat on his hands.

"You're trembling," she said in wonder. "Dearest Jonan, have you never kissed a girl before?"

He found himself mesmerized by the rise and fall of her bodice, of how generously her curves filled the velvet, of how the lamplight was glowing on her blond hair. What would it be like to see her, all of her, he wondered wildly. To see her hair unbound and falling free, to see her pale flesh shining white and—

"Jonan?" she asked, and laughingly caressed his cheek. "Why do you look at me that way? Why did you stop?"

His heart was so full he could not find the words he wanted to say. Mutely he captured her hand and pressed his lips to it.

"Oh, Jonan," she whispered, leaning closer, "how special you make me feel."

The slam of a door made them spring apart. Footsteps, quick and angry, strode across the wooden floor, echoing hollowly through the cavernous gallery.

"Sofina!" called out the man approaching, still indistinct in the shadows. "You wicked piece, did you think I wouldn't find you?"

"It's Father!" she whispered, and gripped Jonan's arm. "He's so strict. I know he'll punish me."

A surge of protectiveness rose in Jonan. "If there is blame, it will fall on me, not you," he said to her quickly. "Fear not."

"Have you no sense?" her father was saying as he stepped into the dim circle of lamplight. He was a stocky man with heavy shoulders. His beard was cut close to a sharp point and grew black and thick as though to compensate for his bald head. His eyes were dark, deep-set, and angry above a hooked nose. "Have you no pride, no sense of decency? Slipping off with court swains. Where is your modesty? I've warned you that once you ruin your reputation, I can't afford a dowry large enough to make a suitor overlook it."

She began to cry, and Jonan couldn't bear it.

"Count Soblinsk," he said, "the blame is mine. Do not scold her—"

"I'll do as I please with my daughter, you insolent young pup," Soblinsk replied. Standing with his feet braced apart, he tilted back his head and glared up at Jonan, towering above him. "Have the goodness to step aside before I order my servants to whip you for—"

"Father!" Sofina cried out in anguish, coming out from behind Jonan. "Take care what you say. This is Prince Jonan."

Soblinsk's mouth snapped shut. His black eyes shifted from Jonan to his daughter and back again. Color surged into his face, and he bowed deeply. "Your majesty," he said in a voice altered to profound respect, "I beg your pardon. Had I known I was addressing the king, never would I have dared utter such discourtesy. Please forgive me for the insult I have paid you."

Despite the man's mistake, Jonan couldn't help but be flattered. However, Count Unshalin had talked to him man to man a few days ago, warning him to take care and not consider himself king until he was proclaimed so officially.

"Er," he said awkwardly, trying to untangle his tongue. "Of course. That is, I'm not the king, and you haven't insulted me. But—but you shouldn't scold Lady Sofina. She's done nothing wrong. I persuaded her to meet me here. I can't talk to people, you see. Not well. Not when they're in groups, so we came here to be private. To talk. And—and that's all."

"I see," Soblinsk said.

The neck of Jonan's tunic felt a size too small. He knew his explanation was one no father would accept, especially a man with a daughter as beautiful as Sofina. But if he tried to say more, he feared he would only make things worse. For the truth was that they hadn't been talking at all, and he'd lied to this man, and Sofina had let him kiss her, which wasn't modest or proper at all but was in fact marvelous. His heart boomed in his chest, and he felt caught between anxiety and the ecstatic knowledge that Sofina must love him as much as he loved her.

"I served your majesty's father," Soblinsk said, breaking the silence at last. "And King Muncel was gracious enough to reward me with a title and estate. For the past seven and a half years I have awaited the opportunity to serve you, as well. And now . . . well, permit me to offer myself in obedience to whatever your majesty desires. To the last, I am your man."

And he bowed again.

Jonan could hardly believe his luck. "You are not angry, Lord Soblinsk?"

"I would not dare to presume," Soblinsk replied, and smiled.

Relieved, Jonan grinned back and shot a glance at Sofina. She was patting her veil nervously as though she feared it had slipped and was revealing too much of her hair. She would not meet his gaze, not boldly right in front of her father.

"If I may have permission to explain," she said in a soft, breathy voice, her eyes still lowered. "Father, when his highness asked me to talk with him privately, I did not wish to offend by refusing."

"Certainly not," Soblinsk said heartily. "I quite understand. It is one thing to flirt and gossip with courtiers, but another to obey the summons of our king."

"I am not the king!" Jonan said in alarm, glancing over his shoulder although surely this abandoned part of the palace had no spies. "I beg you, Lord Soblinsk, do not call me that."

"But you are nothing less. Rumors abound, but we all know the facts. King Faldain lies dead, whether the Privy Council acknowledges it or not. They seek to keep your majesty from your rightful inheritance, but I assure you that there are many who are loyal to your majesty and ready to support your claim. Just say the word, and we'll storm the palace, if need be."

Alarmed, Jonan lifted his hands. "No, no, Lord Soblinsk. I beg you, no such talk. Please! If the queen says my cousin lives, I believe her."

"The queen did not see that terrible battlefield," Soblinsk replied gravely, his dark eyes holding Jonan's mesmerized. "You did. I would rather believe what your majesty witnessed than a grieving widow's hope."

A tiny spark of confidence lifted Jonan's chin. *Morde*, he thought, *I was there, all right. What if she's wrong? We were all so certain until we came back. She must be wrong. Still, Count Unshalin must think it likely I'll be crowned, or he would not have talked to me the way he did. And now this man, a friend of my father's, has offered me his support. How many others are there? Why have I never met them before?*

"How long will your majesty wait before asserting your claim?" Soblinsk asked.

Such a blunt question rendered Jonan nervous again. "I—uh, I don't know."

"Does your majesty have allies?" Soblinsk asked softly. "Advisers?"

"Oh, yes. Prince Tustik gives me advice all the time. And just the other day, Count Unshalin was kind enough to speak to me."

"Hmm," Soblinsk grunted.

"Is that not sufficient?" Jonan asked, feeling unaccountably anxious. "They are influential men in my cousin's court. Since I have no importance, I do not expect—"

"Your majesty, I must protest this modesty! Of course you are important. Your father was king of Nether! Your bloodline is a noble and honorable one, stretching back through generations of proud tradition. Not important? Who has dared teach you to think so ill of yourself?"

Jonan had the impression that if he said a name, Soblinsk would seek out that person and run him through on the spot. "Morde," he said in awe. "Would you champion me?"

"In an instant, sire. The way you are treated, the insults

and gibes, oh, yes, I know of them. I would see you repay the persecution you have suffered all these years."

Jonan liked him very much. Shyly, he said, "I really would like to be king, I think. Only it seems to take a lot of work. Cousin Faldain is always very busy. He has to make many decisions and understand how things come about. I'm not clever like that, you see."

"Oh, but, sire," Soblinsk said kindly, "you don't have to rule the way your cousin did. That's what councils and ministers of state are for. To serve their king and deal with such matters for him."

"But my cousin—"

"King Faldain was a foreigner in his own realm," Soblinsk said. "He wasn't raised according to Netheran customs and cannot be considered a proper model for your majesty to emulate. But King Muncel—"

"My father was cruel and wicked!" Jonan said rather shrilly. "He did bad things, and he had people killed. I don't want to be like him. He always frightened me."

Silence fell over the room. Soblinsk's mouth was crimped in a tight, angry line. Jonan didn't want to annoy this man, but he knew he had to say what he did. He remembered his father's vile temper, how his shouting could be heard across the palace grounds or down the stairs. He remembered how the servants—and many of the courtiers—used to cringe when his father walked past them. Nearly everyone at court was afraid. Didn't Count Soblinsk recall how it was? But Jonan dared say no more.

"I see that these years in Faldain's household have marked you," Soblinsk said with a heavy sigh. "King Muncel was not a handsome man and not as physically strong as Faldain. Well, fine looks and strapping muscles are not everything. And, aye, he had a ferocious temper."

Jonan nodded fervently.

"But you see, he was trying very hard to keep Nether from starving. The crops were bad. The livestock died. There was famine and pestilence. All those things troubled your father greatly. How could he not lash out in exasperation from time to time?"

"But the Chalice was gone," Jonan hastened to say. "Of course the land was cursed without it."

"That's right. And who took the Chalice away from us?"

Jonan frowned. The way Soblinsk put things was so different than the way Faldain and others talked about the past. Confusion swam through his mind, and he struggled in an effort to keep things straight.

"Your majesty," Soblinsk said quietly, "who took the Chalice away?"

"Tobeszijian."

"That's right. Faldain's father."

"But Faldain brought it back!"

"Well," Soblinsk said in a reasonable tone of voice, "of course he did. But why did he wait so many years to do so? Nether suffered much during that time. Many perished needlessly, you know."

"I—I hadn't thought of it like that," Jonan said.

"Ah, well, it is something to consider. And to this day, your cousin keeps the Chalice hidden so that none but a very few can see it. Did you know that the Helspirin Cathedral was built specifically to honor the Chalice?"

Jonan shook his head.

"You've been there?"

"Of course!"

"Then you recall all those high, narrow windows at the end of the sanctum?"

Jonan smiled. "The sunlight streams in during morning service. It's very pretty. But usually the royal family attends chapel here."

Soblinsk grunted. "Nonreformed service?"

"Yes."

"Would your parents have wanted you to disregard Writ and the sacred precepts of Tomias?"

In Jonan's memory, neither of his parents had been very devout. And he rather liked nonreformed chapel, with the old priests in their blue robes and green surplices. They kept service brief and simple. He felt comforted and happy afterward. In contrast, the mass at the cathedral could be very long, especially if the archbishop thundered forth a sermon on Writ, and there were many complicated rituals to follow at the proper time. He frowned at Soblinsk but dared say nothing.

"Those windows in the sanctum were designed so that the light of the Chalice could shine out, especially at night. Then all the people, whether of high estate or low, could see it if they walked past the cathedral. Everyone could experience its blessing, and feel reassured of its benevolence. The Chalice should be available for all to worship, not just a chosen few."

"That would be good," Jonan said eagerly. "That would be pretty. I've seen the Chalice once, just once. It's never in the chapel."

"No, your cousin keeps it shut away. I suppose he fears it would be stolen were more people given access to it."

"No one would dare!" Jonan said indignantly. "It's sacred!"

"Tobeszijian dared. Like a common bandit, he rode into the cathedral on a darsteed, defiling that holy place with a demonic creature, and wrested the Chalice from the very hands of a cardinal. The Chalice has never been returned to its rightful place, not even by Faldain, who has kept it for himself. Surely your majesty agrees that it is not right to keep it hidden in the darkness in a secret vault."

"Uh—"

"Have church officials not protested this, pleading for the Chalice to be returned to Helspirin, and has not your cousin always refused?"

"I don't know," Jonan whispered, feeling troubled. Faldain always did what was right . . . or at least Jonan had thought so until now. He frowned. "I do not think you should criticize the king. It isn't respectful, and Faldain is a good king. He has been kind to me."

"Of course," Soblinsk agreed with a friendly smile that cleared the frown knotting Jonan's brow. "I was merely chatting about past times and raising questions. Perhaps I am boring your majesty?"

"Oh, no!" Jonan said. "But I wish you would call me highness instead."

"Must I? Very well. I will obey the wishes of my sovereign and master," Soblinsk said with a bow. He looked past Jonan and held out his hand to Sofina. "Come, daughter. The hour grows late, and since I have failed once more to gain audience with the queen, thanks to Prince Tustik, we must return to our quarters and finish our packing."

"Oh, no!" Sofina said in distress. "Oh, Father, must we?"

"I'm afraid we must," Soblinsk said. "Come. Tomorrow sees our departure from court."

She went to her father, casting Jonan a quick, shy glance from beneath her lashes. He thought he saw tears sparkling in her eyes, and the sight of them nearly undid him.

"Why are you going?" he asked. "I wish you would not."

"Unfortunately, your highness, we must," Soblinsk said with a shrug. "My petitions to be received officially have all been denied. And although I've used every art of persuasion I know in order to tarry here as long as possible, this latest order to depart is one I cannot ignore."

Anger swelled in Jonan. "Who gave this command?"

"Ah, well, does it matter?" Soblinsk asked. "Your highness understands the protocol here. If I am not permitted a place at court, I cannot linger indefinitely. Our quarters in the merchants' pavilion are hardly suitable to our station and certainly not appropriate for my daughter. I have tried to wait until I could see the king."

"Yes, I'm sure he would receive you," Jonan said.

"But, alas, he has vanished and may be dead. In his absence, the officials here are unforgiving about my past loyalties and choose to ignore the fact that the king himself pardoned me." Soblinsk shrugged. "We must go. There are delegates soon to arrive, and our quarters are needed."

"But this is monstrous unjust," Jonan said.

"Sofina, make your good-byes to his highness."

She curtsied deeply to Jonan. "I have enjoyed our friendship, your highness," she said softly, lifting her tear-drenched eyes to his. " 'Tis hard to say good-bye."

The thought of her going away wrenched Jonan. She was his only friend, and he loved her.

"Can you not take accommodations in Grov?" he asked

desperately. "Winter is coming on. 'Tis not the season to travel. And—and Aelintide is only two days hence. Can you not stay for the celebrations?"

"Alas, no," Soblinsk replied. "As for staying in Grov, I wish my purse were fat enough, but the innkeepers are robbers. I am not a wealthy man, your highness. I hoped in coming here to advance my fortune, but it is not to be."

"I wish you could stay."

Soblinsk shrugged. "There is nothing that can be done unless . . ."

"Yes?" Jonan asked eagerly. "What?"

"Unless your highness granted us permission to join the court. Then we could be quartered here in the palace."

Sofina clapped her hands in excitement. "Oh, Jonan! Could you do that for us?"

He felt a tide of heat and confusion rising from his collar. Dismay swept him, for he knew what Prince Tustik would say if he even dared approach the old lizard with such a request. "I—I think not," he stammered. "I'm sorry. I—"

Disappointment drove away her smile. She sent him a look that made him feel as low as a worm.

Desperately, he turned to the count. "I haven't any influence, you see. I have no standing, no authority. I just couldn't."

"It seems to me that a king has the authority to do anything he pleases," Soblinsk said softly. "Ah, well, even the heir to the throne should be able to invite his friends if he chooses. But I see that my daughter has presumed too much on your highness's favor. We have erred, and we beg your pardon for it. Come, Sofina. We must go."

Taking Sofina's hand, he wheeled about and strode away so quickly she had to trot to keep up. Listening to the rapid clack of her heeled slippers over the scuffed wooden floors, Jonan hated himself for being such a stupid, useless fool. They were going away, and he knew he would never see her again. Come the Aelintide feast, she wouldn't be here for him to talk to. Nor would he be able to give her the gift he had wrapped and concealed in his rooms.

"Wait!" he called out, hurrying after them. "I'll try," he

said. "I can ask, but Prince Tustik does not think much of me."

"Prince Tustik must defer to your highness, not the reverse," Soblinsk said, while Sofina smiled radiantly at Jonan. "You outrank the man. Especially now."

Jonan thought that over. He intended to obey Count Unshalin's advice and not think about being king yet, but he was *almost* king. He was the heir, the next in line because little Ilymir had died and Faldain had no other sons. The idea of it pleased him greatly, and he squared his shoulders.

"Yes, Lord Soblinsk. It's only right that my wishes should be considered, and if I ask—"

"Perhaps it would be better," Soblinsk murmured, "if your highness simply issued a command to the chamberlain."

Jonan felt a qualm. "Do you think he would pay heed to me?"

"He must." Soblinsk smiled at him in encouragement. "Your highness need only be firm about your desires. Otherwise, we must go."

Jonan swallowed hard, but another glance at Sofina gave him courage. "If I do this favor for you, Count Soblinsk, will you do one for me?"

Soblinsk's dark brows lifted. He seemed a bit surprised, but inclined his head courteously. "Of course."

"I want permission to see your daughter."

The man began to frown, and Jonan hurried on before he could lose his courage. "I understand that you are very strict. I do not want you to punish her for meeting me like this. And I want to go on seeing her. She is my friend. I like to talk to her."

Sofina giggled behind her hand.

She's thinking of what we've been doing besides talking, Jonan thought, and hot, guilty pleasure flashed through him.

"I see." Soblinsk's dark eyes were not as fierce as Jonan had expected. "Does this mean your highness has a special interest in my daughter?"

Jonan swallowed hard and fought the urge to squirm beneath Soblinsk's dark gaze. "Well, I—I—yes."

The count bowed to him. "Then my daughter and I are

honored indeed. It is one thing for her to flirt idly with young swains of no consequence, and another for her to find favor with the future—possibly present—king of Nether. If I am given a place at court, your highness may indeed extend—ahem—friendship to my daughter."

Exhilaration flew through Jonan. He exchanged a delighted look with Sofina and reached for her hand, but Soblinsk did not relinquish his hold on his daughter.

"Till the morrow, your highness," he said. "I leave you to fulfill your end of our bargain."

Chapter Nineteen

The lamplight was burning low, some of the lamps sputtering faintly as they ran out of oil. Kneeling on a cushion, her hands gripped together with such tension they ached, Alexeika watched intently while the *sorcerelle* spoke quiet, incomprehensible words that sent shivers up her spine. Her spirit seemed to thrum with the power that was being summoned here, and her own limited gifts—erratic and never completely under her command—stirred within her, prickling her skin, until she felt wild and restless. It was all she could do not to jump up and pace about, but she forced herself to remain still. A gray mist swirled in the center of the room, while Alexeika's protector and ladies-in-waiting looked on in anxious silence.

The *sorcerelle*, her body slender, straight, and elongated so that it hardly seemed a feminine shape at all, her eyes slanted and the hue of silver, her skin as black as charred wood, her hair hidden entirely beneath a headdress of gray silk, lifted her hands high and spread them wide. Between them appeared a mist that swirled thin at first, then thickened until it was cloud white. It hovered there perhaps waist high above the floor, and Alexeika held her breath.

Faldain, she thought anxiously, trying hard to govern her own desire to part the veils of seeing, *where are you?*

The *sorcerelle* turned her gaze on Alexeika and frowned. "Cease!" she commanded sharply.

There was a stir from Alexeika's entourage, but no one dared speak. Alexeika accepted the rebuke by bowing her head in silence and trying hard to still her chaotic thoughts. She had been warned before this session commenced that if she allowed her natural powers to interfere, the *sorcerelle* would not answer for the consequences. It was hard for Alexeika to sit back and let anyone else perform a task she wanted done and could tackle herself, but she'd persuaded herself to rely on the *sorcerelle*, whose powers and ability far exceeded Alexeika's limited gifts.

The cloud remained there, white and thick. After a moment of tense silence, while Alexeika's body trembled with the effort she was expending to hold herself blank, the *sorcerelle* spoke a word that cracked in the air. The cloud parted in twain, and Alexeika leaned forward with a gasp of anticipation.

There, between the two halves of mist, should be her beloved's face. She wanted to see him so terribly.

A shape, nebulous at best, shifted in the mist only to vanish. Faldain did not appear at all.

The *sorcerelle* waved her hands, and the cloud dissipated. A sigh of disappointment ran through the room. Alexeika felt stunned with disbelief.

"No," she whispered.

Lady Nadilya appeared at her shoulder. "Your majesty, I'm sorry. Let me help you up."

Alexeika ignored her to glare at the *sorcerelle*. "What was that? Could you not part the veils? Why did you not find him?"

The *sorcerelle* tucked her hands into her wide sleeves and turned to face Alexeika. Her dark face held no expression at all.

When she made no reply, Alexeika shot to her feet. "No!"

she said harshly. "I won't believe him dead. You must try again."

"Not now," the *sorcerelle* replied. Her silver eyes shifted away from Alexeika's. "There is no more seeing to be done tonight."

Tilting back her head to meet the tall *sorcerelle's* gaze, Alexeika searched for some spark of compassion, some hint that she could draw hope from. "Did you sense nothing?" she whispered. "Not even a part of him, some element of his spirit?"

"Twice have I parted the veils," the *sorcerelle* said coldly. "The child I do not see. The king I do not see. They are dead . . . or hidden by strong magic."

"Which? At least tell me that! I must know."

The *sorcerelle* bowed to her without reply and glided from the room.

Acute disappointment washed over Alexeika. She closed her eyes a moment, and when she opened them she found herself sitting in a chair, with Lady Emila hovering over her and Lady Nadilya ineffectually patting her hand. Lady Buni, who belonged to the Reformed Church and gravely disapproved of proceedings such as these, stood apart from the others and stared coldly.

Alexeika wished they would leave her in peace. She did not want criticism, sympathy, or comfort. She wanted to find her loved ones.

Tears were running down Lady Emila's face. "I'm so sorry," she whispered, her large eyes brimming with pity. "Your majesty loved the king so. And now this proves there is no hope—"

Jerking her hand from Nadilya's clasp, Alexeika sat erect and glared at Emila. "It proves nothing! If you spread a rumor that the *sorcerelle* has pronounced his majesty dead, I shall dismiss you from court in disgrace."

Lady Emila turned white. Her eyes bulged in alarm. "Majesty, I—"

"You have my leave to go," Alexeika said curtly. She glanced at the rest of the ladies. "All of you."

They exchanged worried glances. Lady Nadilya said,

"But, your majesty, the hour grows late. May we not first help prepare you for retiring?"

"No." Alexeika knew that if she endured one more minute of their pity, she would lose the last ragged shreds of her temper and self-control. "Leave. I want none of you."

They curtsied to her, one by one, and filed out, murmuring and shaking their heads. "That is what comes of these evil rituals," Lady Buni said in a loud whisper. "More heartbreak, when she would be better served offering her prayers properly to Tomias in church."

Alexeika's little dog darted in through the open door, weaving in and out through people's legs before running to paw at Alexeika's skirts. When she ignored it, the silly beast danced on its hind legs and whined to get her attention. She laughed, despite her heartbreak, then suddenly scooped the dog into her arms and buried her face against its fur, while it whined and wiggled in delight. *What am I to do now*, she wondered. *I should have had the veils parted in private, but I wanted witnesses to see Faldain alive.*

Instead, there had been nothing to see. Fresh rumors would fly through the palace, despite her effort to silence Emila, and the empty seeing would be claimed as proof that Faldain was dead. Thinking of the pressure to come, the insistence of the Privy Council that a successor be named immediately, Alexeika fought to keep her courage.

If the Council forces my hand, I shall announce my pregnancy, she decided grimly. *I have no other choice.*

"Your majesty," a shrill young voice said.

Horrified that the page had been admitted when her emotions were so naked and exposed, she looked up with a frown. Checking the reprimand that rose to her lips, she reluctantly nodded permission to the child to speak.

He bowed low. "Your majesty, I am bidden to report that Lord Omas has regained consciousness."

Her misery dropped away, momentarily forgotten, for this was good news indeed. She stood up, spilling the dog from her lap so that it yelped indignantly. "Inform the physicians that the queen will come at once."

Bowing, the page hurried away. Alexeika summoned her

servants. "Prepare me for the outdoors," she commanded. "Sir Pyron, notify the guards that I shall need escort."

The infirmary was part of the sprawling palace complex. At one time it could be reached through a wing of the palace, but because of neglect and structural damage over the years, that way was no longer accessible. Wrapped in a fur cloak and accompanied by an entourage that included two ladies-in-waiting, her page, her protector, and several guards, Alexeika trudged across icy pavement, following a trail of straw that had been laid down for her safe footing, and went up the stone steps into a vestibule where the chief physician and his assistants waited.

There were courtesies to be observed, despite her impatience, but at last she was ushered down a gloomy passageway paneled with wood and smelling strongly of camphor. She walked past an open doorway and glimpsed a large room filled with cots. Some were occupied; others were empty. The servants and common guards were brought there whenever they suffered injury or mishap. Officers and those of higher station were usually tended in their quarters, although the infirmary contained a handful of small, private chambers.

She was taken to one of these now, but the physician hesitated before the closed door.

"Your majesty asked us to send word as soon as Lord Omas was conscious, but I must warn you that he is very weak and unlikely to be coherent. Lengthy questioning will have to wait until later. I have told General Matkevskiet this already, and sent him away."

"Matkevskiet!" she said in surprise.

"Yes, he came to collect his son, who did not want to leave until he could talk to Lord Omas."

She frowned in sympathy. "Poor Chesil. The Agyas believe it is dishonorable to survive a defeat. 'Twas not his fault that the king ordered him to turn back and thus saved his life." She hesitated a moment, her hands clenched inside the folds of her cloak. "Was the general able to learn anything from Lord Omas of what transpired?"

"I permitted no questions, as I have explained. Lord

Omas's extraordinary strength is all that enabled him to survive the journey home. He needs rest, not interrogation. I urge
your majesty to make allowances for these circumstances."

"Of course, but I must know what he witnessed. I must
know what happened!"

Refusal knotted the physician's face, but the appeal in her
eyes made him unbend. "Only a few moments," he said, tug-
ging at his beard. "And as soon as he tires, your majesty will
please withdraw."

She nodded, impatience beating inside her, and accompanied only by the physician and Sir Pyron, she entered the sick-
room. It was hardly larger than a cubicle. The walls, ceiling,
and floor were all constructed of unpainted wood battered and
scuffed from hard use. A lamp hung suspended from the ceiling by a chain and hook. Candles burned on a small table con-
taining a basin, bandages, mortar and pestle, and a narrow
tray of potion bottles.

Omas, that cheerful giant of a man who had been Faldain's
protector, shadow, and loyal friend, was lying on a tall, narrow bed that looked too small for his frame. One of his arms
was bandaged, as was his side. She noticed that the little finger on his left hand was missing, and felt sick at the thought
of some Grethori savage hacking it off for a prize. His face
looked gaunt and feverish beneath his thick brown mustache.
His brown eyes, usually a-twinkle, had sunk listlessly into
their sockets. They stared at her without recognition until she
gently took his large, callused hand and spoke his name.

"How fare you, dear Omas?" she asked quietly.

He blinked and tried to lift his head. "Majesty—"

"Hush," she broke in, concerned by how feeble his voice
sounded. "Lie still, or the physician will not let me talk to
you."

Omas subsided with a faint moan and lay there a moment,
breathing audibly. His fingers curled weakly around her hand,
and he tried to smile. "'Tis good to see the queen," he whispered. "Good to be home."

She held back the prickle of tears, knowing she must act
cheerful for his sake. She smiled at him, trying to formulate
her questions so as not to distress him. "'Tis good to see *you*

home once more," she replied. "Not many survived that cowardly ambush."

He frowned. "How many?"

"Oh—" Dismayed at having put herself in such a corner, she glanced at the physician, who was scowling in disapproval, but she knew Omas would not be soothed by evasion. "Pemikalievy," she said softly. "Kolas and another Agya. You."

"They say the king is—"

Her fingers tightened on his. "Taken prisoner," she told him.

"I saw the pallet . . . his body . . . he—"

"Hush," she said, trying to calm him while the physician began to fuss among his bottles, pouring a mixture of foul-smelling liquids into a small cup. "The body carried home in state was *not* Faldain's. I have seen it, and I know."

Something terrible and bleak in his brown eyes cleared away. He brightened. "Good news."

"Yes, very good news," she agreed.

But then his smile faded. "Prisoner of—of those damned dogs."

"Did you see what happened?" she asked, pushing a strand of his matted hair back from his brow.

He closed his eyes, but when the physician tried to put the cup to his lips, he scowled and jerked his head away, causing it to spill. "Get back," he growled at the physician, and looked at Alexeika. "Caught us on the trail. The king fought like two men. Splendid. He went for the chief . . . best strategy."

She nodded. She, too, had fought a Grethori chieftain.

"I slipped . . . enemy got between us. Spellfire spooked the king's horse. He came off but rallied." Omas paused a moment as though collecting his strength. "Spellfire. Odd. Never needed a *sorcerel* before to fight Grethori."

Her thoughts whirled over this information. Chesil had not mentioned it in his report, but of course Chesil had not been present during the initial attack. Of the four survivors brought home, only Omas had been close to the king during the fighting. She frowned. "The Grethori do not possess such magic. Were Believers present?"

"Saw none." His eyes drifted shut.

"Your majesty," the physician said in warning, but she held up an imperious hand to silence him.

"Omas," she said, and the protector's eyes slowly dragged open. "What happened to the king? After he was unhorsed?"

"Saw him fighting. Tried to join him. Took a sword through my ribs." Omas sighed with failure in his eyes. "Couldn't . . . couldn't . . ."

He slept.

Gently, she placed his hand at his side and smoothed the blankets over him. Emerging into the passageway, she exchanged a grim look with Sir Pyron before turning to the physician.

"Will he recover?" she asked.

"He has amazing strength," the physician replied, pulling at his beard. "Of the four, he has the best chance."

She nodded, pulling on her gloves. "Make sure he has the best possible care. Tell him the queen will visit again."

The physician bowed, and she hurried out into the cold night. Despite the late hour she intended to send for Prince Tustik. Omas's account proved the connection between the renegade Grethori auxiliaries and Gant. The Grethori would be dealt with—never, as long as she lived, would she forget the revenge she intended them to pay—but it was Gant that deserved the largest reckoning.

And so shall they have it, she thought grimly.

Until then, Gant had remained cowed from its defeat at the Battle of Grov. She knew Faldain had worried about when Gant would strike back. He'd tried to watch the borders, but none of them had expected this kind of cowardly, sneaky attack through assassination and trickery. But if the Gantese wanted war, Alexeika thought grimly, they would have war. Nether was strong enough, its army rebuilt and well trained. The Chief Believer would wish he'd never dared start this, for, by Thod, she meant to see it finished.

When she reached her apartments, however, a page was waiting in her sitting room with a message that drove all thoughts of war temporarily from her head.

He bowed. "I bring your majesty compliments of Priest Dazkin. He bade me tell you the eldin have come."

It took her a moment to understand. Until then, there'd been no reply to the message Faldain had sent on Mareitina's behalf. She'd almost given up. But if the eldin had sent a healer as requested, then perhaps poor Mareitina might be cured. Alexeika clutched that hope with painful desperation, and felt certain that at last their luck was turning.

"Eldin?" Lady Nadilya asked in curiosity. "What brings them here? Do they want permission for another pilgrimage? You, boy, go and tell them to wait for a proper audience and to make their request through the chamberlain. The hour is too late for the queen to receive such creatures. She is tired—"

"You and Lady Emila have my permission to retire," Alexeika broke in, dismissing them.

Looking both bewildered and curious, they curtsied and went out. Sir Wulim tapped on the door, ready to relieve Sir Pyron of duty, but Alexeika frowned.

"Sir Pyron, I want you for this. Sir Wulim may serve tomorrow."

As a puzzled Sir Wulim retreated, Alexeika turned to the waiting page with a smile. Aye, she was tired, but that did not matter. Eagerly, she gestured to him. "Run and tell Priest Dazkin that I shall bring the princess at once," she said.

Darkness, pressing close. A gleam of candlelight flickering ahead like a small beacon. Endless steps spiraling down from warmth to chilly to icy cold. Mareitina's weight, heavy with slumber, in her arms. Panting from worry and haste. And above all, the urgent need for silence and stealth. Make no sound. Rouse not the curiosity of the guards or spies. Evade the courtiers slinking along quiet passageways for their own private assignations. Slip into the bowels of the palace and hurry, hurry down a passageway smelling of damp and soil. Don't pause. Don't think. Just hurry.

Wrapped in a cloak against the cold, for this most ancient portion of the palace was unheated, Alexeika carried her child through the gloomy Hall of Kings with Sir Pyron at her heels.

A nod to the guard on duty saw the trapdoor opened for her, and she descended old steps of stone worn from the tread of countless feet down into the small dark cave where the first Circle had been drawn. She halted at the very foot of the steps, flustered from the quick taking of Mareitina from her bed and the rapid trip from that end of the palace to this. All the way, she'd been gripped by the illogical fear that if she did not hurry, the eldin might take offense and depart. They were mysterious folk, attuned to their own ways and aloof from most humankind.

She blew a wayward strand of hair from her eyes and wished with all her heart that Faldain were there to deal with these strangers. Some were gentle and friendly; some were not.

Sir Pyron, who had gone down the steps ahead of her, cast a swift glance around before he stepped aside for her to proceed. Alexeika fended off her nervousness as Priest Dazkin hurried forward to meet her. There were very few of priests of the old religion living, much less trained in the proper service of the Chalice. Many of Dazkin's order had been defrocked; a few like him had managed to flee; the rest had perished in the purges ordered by Cardinal Pernal of the Reformed Church. Dazkin's surplice of dark green silk, embroidered with circles, hung crookedly over his blue robes as though he'd dressed hurriedly. The hour, Alexeika realized indifferently, must be growing very late. When he greeted her, making the sign of the Circle over her and her child, Alexeika's gaze shifted past him to the two cowled figures standing silent and watchful near the altar.

The chamber was a small place, with crudely hewn walls and a dirt floor. Stone benches stood in rows within the outline of a large circle formed by white stones. In the center of the circle stood the crude stone altar—very old—beneath an archway made of ash wood. Behind the altar burbled a living spring of water pure and cold. Basins of salt stood at either end of the altar, and on it were arranged the reliquaries and Element candles, small offering bowls of polished bronze, runestones, the bell of Nota, an incense burner, and knives of ritual. A fragrant-leafed vine grew from the dirt floor, green and flourishing despite the lack of sunlight. Its boughs entwined around the altar, and once, on the day Faldain was crowned, the sacred vine had bloomed, sending a sweet perfume up through the wooden floor into the Hall of Kings. Next to the altar, standing beside a small cauldron, stood a pillar of painted wood that supported a paneatha with old, gilded icons of the gods dangling from its branches.

Behind the altar, beyond the spring at the far wall, beyond the small hearth supporting the Perpetual Fire, rose a tall, polished obsidian pillar. Atop that column of dark stone, its base surrounded by thin, peeled wands of white ash, the Chalice of Eternal Life cast its pale nimbus of light over all. Said to have been entrusted to Solder First by the gods, the Chalice was the holiest of holies, its benevolent power revered by the people who worshiped it and coveted by those who sought to use its power for gain. Its soft radiance never grew brighter, never dimmed. It looked so beautiful and cast such a special, gentle light that its true power was sometimes underestimated. But the Chalice contained a potent force of unlimited magic. It could heal, and it could maim. It could restore life to a dying land, and it could rain destruction from the heavens were it channeled for evil.

Although she revered it and had seen the miracles it could perform, Alexeika was thankful not to have the responsibility of caring for it or guarding its safety. The king was the ordained guardian of the Chalice. Despite the priests who tended this place, the ultimate safekeeping of this sacred vessel rested, by the will of the gods, in the hands of Nether's sovereign. Faldain's father had died trying to protect it. Faldain had nearly been killed in restoring it to its rightful place.

Alexeika walked partway to the altar and paused, as was courteous. Both eldin stood with their backs to the Chalice, cast in silhouette against its radiance. That they could stand there, so close to the Chalice without discomfort or fear, was a testament to their innate honesty and worth.

Yet once she stopped, she could not force herself to continue. Her lungs seemed incapable of drawing complete breaths. Hope and relief and worry tangled inside her until she hardly knew what she felt anymore. But she did understand that she needed to remain calm if she was to succeed in persuading the eldin to help her. They had come; that was surely an indication of their good intentions, but with the eld folk it was best to take nothing for granted.

Right after Faldain left in pursuit of Tashalya's abductors, Alexeika had brought Mareitina to the chamber in hopes of restoring the child's mind and spirit. She had knelt before the altar while the priests prayed over her little girl, to no avail. She had held Mareitina in her arms while Dazkin filled the Chalice with water from the spring and held it gently to the child's lips. Mareitina stared into space and would not drink. Even when the priest dribbled a little of the purified water into her mouth, Mareitina did not swallow. Although since then Mareitina had suffered no more hysterics and nightmares, she remained lost somehow, withdrawn into a shadowy world inside herself. The Chalice had not healed her broken mind. Nothing reached her.

Now, with her anxiety and hope surging higher than ever, Alexeika closed her eyes. *Please,* she prayed with all her heart, *have mercy on my child and let her be well again.*

One of the eldin advanced toward Alexeika, and as he drew near he pushed back his hood to let the soft, holy light shine across his face.

He was slender and no taller than Alexeika. Despite a youthful, almost boyish face, he had hair that was entirely white. It waved and curled in constant motion about his pointed ears. The sight of it sent a prick of remembrance through Alexeika; her hand cupped the back of Mareitina's head, feeling the child's thick hair lying as lank and lifeless as it had been since the attack.

"Your grace," the eld said to her in a soft, musical voice that spoke Netheran with odd inflections. "The summons of the king has reached us, and we have come."

"You are the eld healer?" Alexeika asked.

"I am Nilainder. I serve as a guardian to the Tree of Life. This"—he turned and gestured at the other figure still standing apart—"is Healer Vontaximir. May I take the child?"

Alexeika handed over her daughter. Holding Mareitina tenderly, Nilainder carried her to the healer. In silence, her heart thudding with hope, Alexeika watched while Vontaximir lightly ran his fingertips across Mareitina's face and arms. She awakened with a tiny whimper, but when Vontaximir grasped her hand, the child fell back asleep. Although no words were uttered aloud between the two eldin, they stared intently at each other for a moment before Nilainder placed the child in the healer's arms and inclined his head. Then he returned to Alexeika.

"This is a special child," he said in his soft, fluting voice. "A child of the sky and soil, forest and waters. She has been seriously damaged. The loss of her twin makes her incapable of coping with all that has happened."

"Please," Alexeika whispered, "can the healer cure her?"

Although Vontaximir said nothing, Nilainder turned his head as though listening. He bowed before facing Alexeika again. "I am bidden to utter a rebuke for what has been done to this child."

"The Grethori savages are to blame," Alexeika said harshly, her anger as sharp as ever. She doubted time would ever dull what she felt against them. "They did this to her. They slew her brother right before her. She saw everything."

Mareitina flinched in her sleep and snuggled closer to the healer.

"Are they solely to blame?" Nilainder said quietly.

Startled, Alexeika frowned at him. "What mean you?"

"What of the violence here, your grace? Violence in hearts and minds, so many men-minds pushing and contending. There is war to come. What of the weapons, carrying blood and ghosts of blood, stained over and over with battles and strife? This is no place for such a child. She does not belong here in this palace of dead stone."

"This is her home," Alexeika said sharply. "She was born here. Where—"

"Your grace pretends not to understand," Nilainder broke in. "But between us there should be no pretense. Let us consider what is best for the child."

Fear began to entwine about Alexeika's heart. Staring at him, she shook her head. "No. Oh, please."

"She needs respite and rest, peace and tranquillity. Most of all, she needs safety from all that is wrong and harsh. Will you give her this?"

"I know she's not like other children," Alexeika said. "We have always tried to protect her. The king understands her needs best, for his mother was pure eldin."

Nilainder bowed. "Nereisse, princess of our folk, queen of men. We honor her memory."

"Yes. Mareitina has always been more easily frightened, and her brother shielded her from many things. Now—" Alexeika's voice broke. She swallowed quickly, trying to contain her emotions. "She used to live in an imaginary world of her own invention, and now she will not leave it. I cannot reach her. We've tried everything."

"You think in the man way," Nilainder said gently. "Your heart is fierce, and your will strong. Put aside the rage and grief inside you. Listen to your small amount of eldin heritage, for it will whisper that there is truth in what I say. Do not dwell on the past. We are concerned only with the present."

Alexeika drew in a sharp breath, ready to argue, then forced herself to nod. "What must I do?"

"Give her to us."

"For a time, until she is better—"

"Give her to us. She belongs among eld folk, for she is eld and cannot thrive here."

Tears welled up in Alexeika's eyes, blurring Nilainder's face. "Not forever!" she gasped. "No! I didn't send for you to take her permanently. I want you to heal her, nothing more."

"We offer healing, your grace."

She stared at him, feeling cornered, and angry about it. "You mean this is the only way?"

He nodded.

"But I can't! She is my daughter, my baby. She's all that remains—"

"Mareitina cannot substitute for what your grace has lost. She can never be her sister Tashalya. Nor can she be her brother. Ilymir shielded her and protected her against the battery of her senses in this man-place. The breaking of their bond has left her exposed and vulnerable to what she cannot endure."

"What she witnessed . . . the shock of it . . ."

"No, your grace. Seeing the brutality no doubt shocked her, but it is not what has driven her inward. She needs to be with her kind, safe from all that would harm her. We can protect her as your grace cannot."

Alexeika's knees felt weak. She had to stiffen them lest they buckle beneath her. Trembling, she stared at this eld in horror at what he was asking her to do.

"How long?" she asked.

Nilainder did not answer.

"Not forever!" Alexeika said in protest. "When the king bade me send to you for help, he did not—we did not expect you to take her from us entirely. She is a princess of the royal house. Where would she live? Who would attend to her? How would she—"

"She will be raised among eldin royalty, among those who are kin to King Faldain. She will know no need, lack, or want."

"But she will not have us!" Alexeika cried. "She will not have her mother or father."

"Even Queen Nereisse was permitted to return to her own kind each year to renew her battered spirits and regain her strength," Nilainder said. "We of the eld folk have our own ways. We live within the cycle of nature. To disregard it is to imperil us. No doubt it is King Faldain's custom to withdraw into the forest at times to nurture himself."

Alexeika thought of Faldain's eagerness to seize any excuse to ride to Thirst, so close to the Dark Forest where he'd been raised. She thought of his hunting sessions, when he rode for hours but brought home no game. He went not into the woods to kill, she realized, but to commune with what Nilainder was talking about. Being Faldain, he hadn't explained or made a fuss. He simply found a way to see to his needs when he had to.

Staring at her daughter's sleeping face, Alexeika did not want to give her up, and yet she *did* understand what Nilainder meant. Mareitina was so very different from her siblings, so defenseless and innocent. Alexeika had sometimes watched her daughter at play and wondered what was to become of her when she grew older. *And what will Faldain say,* she asked herself, *when he comes home and learns I have given our little girl away?*

She drew in a sharp breath. "Is there nothing that can be done for her here?"

"Nothing."

"I'll try the Chalice again. The priests say in time she might—"

"Your grace," Nilainder said, "a mother's love is strong, always strong enough to do that which is necessary. You love your child, and you will give her to us in order to save her life and sanity."

Refusing to acknowledge the truth of his words, Alexeika stepped forward as though half-intending to wrest Mareitina from Vontaximir's arms, but Nilainder did not move out of her way. She looked into his eyes, and felt her resistance crumble. "But she is the last one," she said in a whisper.

"Not true."

Alexeika's hand moved involuntarily to her stomach. "A moment ago you said that Mareitina cannot substitute for Tashalya or even Ilymir," she said in anguish. "Neither can a new baby take her place. What in Thod's name are you asking from me?"

Nilainder said nothing.

She looked at Vontaximir in appeal, but the healer's face could not be seen beneath the shadow of his hood. He held Mareitina without moving, and she understood that nothing she could do or say would alter his decision.

"Is there no other way?" she asked. "Must I lose her to save her?"

"Have you ever had her?" Nilainder asked.

Alexeika closed her eyes against the burning tears that filled them. She knew her protests were only wasting time.

After a moment she forced herself to meet Nilainder's gaze. Here, in this holy place, she knew she could not lie to him or to herself.

When she stepped forward again, Nilainder moved aside.

In silence she walked up to Vontaximir and looked at her sleeping daughter. She smoothed back Mareitina's tangled blond hair and gently kissed her brow. Mareitina sighed in her sleep, but did not awaken. Alexeika stared at her through a blur of tears, trying to imprint the sweet face on her memory. No more adorable smiles and hugs. No more stealing glimpses of Mareitina standing in the garden with wild birds alighting on her outstretched arms in the dappled sunshine. No more tenderly proffered gifts of grass heads or picked flowers or pebbles warmed by the clutch of Mareitina's hand. No more piles of twigs artfully arranged in the middle of Mareitina's bed, much to the nursemaid's disgust.

A gentle, special, marvelous child, yet a difficult child, mysterious and often impossible to understand, a child as foreign and strange as the healer who now held her in his arms. None of them, save Faldain perhaps, had understood her. He'd often said that she was the most like his sister Thiatereika, and whenever he mentioned his sister—which was rare—Alexeika always heard a wistful note in his voice that betrayed how much he still missed her. And now, to lose Mareitina, too, after so much loss, such terrible loss.

She took her daughter's small hand and held it between hers, grieving quietly.

"With us, she will live," Vontaximir said, startling her. His voice sounded like leaves rustling. She had never heard such a voice before, and she could barely distinguish his words. "With you, she will die. A true mother makes the right choice."

Alexeika sighed. "I cannot bear to see her suffer more." She looked into the shadow of Vontaximir's face. "Please, someday, let us see her again. If she wants to come back, let her."

Nilainder came up beside her. "It is not our way to hold any creature captive. Mareitina will be safe."

She felt tears rising in her with scalding force, but she choked them back. It seemed cruel, impossible, that she was doing this. *All my loved ones are gone*, she thought. *I've lost them all, perhaps forever*.

She knew she should not think that way. Faldain would return. Tashalya would return. There was a new child to prepare for. But all the same, as the two eldin bowed to her and trod silently up the steps into the shadows with her little girl, she stood bereft and alone under the light of the Chalice and felt the bitter ache of sorrow.

Chapter Twenty

Dain roused slowly, drifting through layers of confusion. *Funeral drums*, he thought with irritation. *Why must they beat so loud?*

After a while he realized the drum was his skull, and tiny demons were pounding on it. He hurt all over, and he was too hot. Why had the servants built the fire so hot? His sense of irritation grew sharper, and he wanted to escape the throbbing agony in his head. Rolling over, he felt someone lying beside him. Soft, silken arms slid around his waist.

"Alexeika," he murmured.

Cracking open his eyes, he glimpsed her lovely face. It did not seem quite right that she should be there. Had she been away? He tried to remember, but doing so made his head throb worse until he groaned aloud from it.

Home, he thought. Perhaps he'd been away instead of her, away doing something important. Aye, only he had the feeling the task was unfinished. Despite his efforts, he could not recall what it was. Everything inside his head seemed slippery and elusive.

"Alexeika," he said again.

She drew him closer in her arms, her body curving against his in the familiar way. Gladness and relief swept through his confusion, and all he cared about was that he was with her where he belonged.

Lurking in the gloomy Hall of Kings, Jonan wondered how much longer the queen was going to say her prayers. He'd been trudging to his quarters, his mind teeming with thoughts of Sofina and all that her father had said, when he'd glimpsed the queen moving along a passageway she seldom used. She was cloaked as though to go outside, and without her usual entourage except for her protector. And she was carrying something bulky beneath her cloak, which seemed so odd that Jonan's curiosity was piqued. On impulse, thinking he might perhaps be able to make his request on Soblinsk's behalf, Jonan followed her as far as the Hall of Kings.

The guards on duty there permitted him to enter, and Jonan had hurried in just as the queen descended the narrow old stairs through a trapdoor and vanished from sight. Another palace guard, glowering fiercely beneath his fur cap, drawn sword in hand, stood at the top of the steps.

"Private prayers," he growled. "Bide here, yer highness."

Jonan had no choice but to wait. He'd been there only once before, and never had he been privileged to enter the actual holy of holies where the Chalice was kept. He did not much think he wanted to. Magic frightened him, especially because of what it had done to his father, and he avoided it as much as possible.

The Hall of Kings was cold, for its only source of heat was a vast hearth where no fire was kindled. He could feel the icy draft blowing from its chimney. Shivering, he wished he'd worn his cloak as he wandered around the gloomy old chamber. In the torchlight, he stared at the ancient weapons arranged on the walls and stood for a while before Solder's throne. It was a crudely made chair of wood blackened by age and grime. Above it hung an old triangular sword reputed to be Solder's weapon. The blade was made of black iron, and its edge was jagged in places. The hilt was wrapped with leather so old it was cracked and nearly rotting away.

If I am crowned king I will sit on this ugly old throne and I will have to hold that sword, swearing oaths that date back to the coronation of the First, Jonan thought. A ripple of excitement passed through him.

Turning away, he paced down the length of the narrow Hall. Odd to think that the original court used to meet in this derelict place. The wooden floor sagged from age, and on the walls huge tapestries depicted kings, saints, and battles from the dim mists of time in faded, dusty colors. Some of them were tattered, and they smelled of mildew. When Jonan began to wheeze he retreated hastily.

I will have them torn down and thrown away, he thought. He did not understand why Faldain and Alexeika kept such nasty old relics in every nook and cranny of the palace.

He was daydreaming of the future when Sir Pyron came up the steps into the Hall. The protector glanced around, saw Jonan, and glared at him.

Although protectors were permitted more impertinence than most, Jonan still felt stung. Straightening his shoulders, he strode forward just as the queen emerged through the trapdoor. Whatever she'd carried before had been left behind. Jonan wondered what it was.

The guard saluted her crisply and moved over to the wall near the paneatha. Jonan did not see what the man did, but with a rumble and scrape, a portion of the wooden floor slid closed, concealing the secret stair once more.

"Cousin Alexeika!" Jonan said eagerly. "Your majesty, may I talk to you?"

She walked toward him with Sir Pyron on her heels. Jonan saw that she'd been crying. Her eyes were red and puffy, and her face looked so white and stricken that it had lost its usual beauty. Astonished, he stared at her and nearly forgot what he was about to say. Sympathy for her filled him, and instead of blurting out his request, he hurried up to take her hand.

"Were your prayers of any comfort?" he asked, wishing he could ease her burden of grief and worry. "If I can do aught for you, please—"

"Not now, Jonan," she said wearily, drawing her hand from his. She cast him a look of impatience from eyes that were flat and bleak. "You have no business wandering about the palace at this time of night, spying on folk and skulking in the shadows."

"I wasn't—"

"In Thod's name, for once keep yourself out of trouble and leave me in peace."

Sir Pyron pushed him out of the queen's way, and she walked on. Hurt by her rebuff, Jonan stood there listening to the sound of her fading footsteps. He could not believe what had just happened. Never before had he received an unkind word from the queen. Whenever their paths crossed, she always acknowledged him with courtesy. So many times she'd included him on outings with the children, letting him share their lessons and treats alike. Whenever he'd gone to her with his troubles, she'd listened. He'd adored her all his life, and now it was as though a curtain had been pulled aside, and her true opinion of him was revealed.

She didn't really care about him or even like him. She was exactly like everyone else at court, only she'd hidden it until then behind a hypocritical façade.

Had she struck him, it could not have shocked him more. Waiting about to offer her solace had been a complete waste of time, and he would never try to comfort her again. She deserved no pity from him.

Hurrying along the passageway, his resentment boiling hotter with every step, Jonan threw aside the last of his doubts and old loyalties. He'd been a little worried about some of the statements Soblinsk had made; now he told himself the count was right about everything.

Jonan didn't even want Faldain to return anymore. *I am the rightful king*, he thought. *They should all be bowing to me, even her. I am first in consequence, and it's time everyone in the palace treated me with respect.*

On the morrow, he decided, he would go before the Privy Council and assert his rights. Faldain was dead, and the queen had no right to obstruct a legal succession. Jonan told himself that he would make Sofina his queen and her father his chief adviser, for he had learned tonight who his real friends were. Henceforth there would be no more hiding in the background, trying to avoid the slights and humiliations flung his way. He'd wear a crown with authority over everyone, and not one courtier or servant in this palace would ever again dare sneer at him.

When I am king, he promised himself fiercely, *I shall make all of them pay. However much they feared my father, they will learn to fear me all the more.*

In the dead of night, Alexeika awakened with a jolt. "Faldain," she said aloud, and the sound of her voice pulled her upright in the darkness.

She'd been dreaming about him, and she drew up her knees and hugged them, missing him with an ache more intense than ever. So much had happened in the past few hours. Her heart and spirit were sore from the emotions wrung from them, yet she found herself unable to return to sleep. Instead, her mind traced over and over what the *sorcerelle* had said. Concealed by magic or dead.

Dreadful news, either way, and yet she did not understand the strange, recent reticence from the court *sorcerels*. Samderaudin, who had been one of the few individuals to support Faldain back before most of his subjects even knew he was still alive, much less returning to claim his throne, had of late expended nominal effort on Faldain's behalf. It was as though the *sorcerel* did not want Faldain found.

Impatient and restless, Alexeika pushed herself out of bed and prowled about her chamber. She had never felt so trapped or helpless, and she hated it. There must be something she could do.

Pushing open her window, she leaned out into the cold night. Above her, stars twinkled in a dark sky. The air was dense and heavy with cold, burning her lungs with every breath. She welcomed the cold, for her mind felt like it was on fire.

There'd been fresh snowfall during the night, and a fluffy mound of it had drifted across her windowsill. She plunged her hands into its cold dampness and remembered a past occasion when she'd parted the veils and summoned Faldain to her in spirit. That had been their first meeting, in a way. She'd never forgotten it, or the priest Uzfan's anger afterward.

She frowned, focusing her eyes on the snow cupped in her hands. And without further hesitation, she reached inward for the old, seldom-controlled gift, using her love to power her summons.

"Faldain!" she called, closing her eyes and concentrating with all her might. "Faldain, come to me!"

The force of her need, worry, and longing jolted her entire body and nearly made her cry out. Her eyes flew open, and there before her swirled a tiny cloud of mist. Elation nearly scattered her control, but she held on and found her focus again. Dimly she glimpsed figures moving in the vision. She squinted, leaning forward in an effort to see, but something inside her hurt from the effort. Fearful of bringing inadvertent harm to her unborn child, she clutched her stomach and nearly released the vision.

In that instant the mist cleared. She saw Faldain lying asleep, firelight flickering across his face. His face was drawn with exhaustion; his hand rested possessively on the dark hair of a woman sleeping draped across him. Both were naked; both were clearly spent from passion.

Shocked and unable to believe it, Alexeika blinked, and the vision vanished. With a jerk, she shut the window and hugged herself in the darkness, breathing raggedly as though she'd run a long distance. How could this be, she wondered. All this time she'd been going out of her mind with worry, and he was sporting with some wench.

No! cried a corner of her mind. Faldain would never betray her. He simply would not do anything that cheap and tawdry, and yet she'd seen him. The vision was clear.

She found herself wishing it had remained murky and therefore open to question. But there could be no doubt at all.

Of course the *sorcerels* knew. She understood suddenly why they'd formed this conspiracy of silence, claiming their visions were dark and showed nothing. Had it not been for their lies, she might have disbelieved what she'd conjured forth tonight.

Was this the first adultery he'd committed, she wondered, or one instance among many? She felt a stab of grief so acute she doubled over with a gasp. Somehow she staggered back to bed and collapsed there, aching and shivering. His honor had always seemed absolute, unassailable. She'd respected him so much for it, had never doubted him at all during the years of their marriage.

Yet he was a man, very much a man. He had journeyed far from her, and this had been a long parting. But was he so ruled by his lustful appetites that he could not keep himself chaste until he returned to her bed? She could not even imagine giving herself to anyone but him. Never had she dreamed that he would not do the same.

Alexeika's old insecurities came flooding back. Lying there huddled beneath her covers, unable to grow warm again, she knew the special, infinitely precious, bond between her and Faldain had broken.

She did not cry. She could not. All her tears had been burned away by shock. Instead, she felt empty and betrayed and alone.

And in her heart, she hated him.

Chapter Twenty-One

A narrow beam of sunlight came in through a small hole in the tent cloth, stabbing its way down onto Dain's face. He awakened by degrees, becoming aware of the groaning shift and sway of the tent around him as wind gusted against it. The weight on his chest turned out to be Alexeika's head. She was sleeping half across him, her dark hair fanned out. Smiling in contentment, Dain lifted one of her tresses to his nostrils.

It smelled vaguely of horsehair, not the usual fragrant herbs that she preferred. He frowned slightly and turned his head.

Pain spiked through his temple with such a vengeance that his eyes teared. He shut them, sinking lower in an effort to make the throbbing agony go away. Although he tried hard to make no sound, a faint moan escaped his lips.

She stirred drowsily, her hands sweeping across his naked body in ways that brought him pleasure. But not enough to dim his headache this time. He caught her by the shoulders and drew her up to cradle her head on his shoulder.

"Enough, beloved," he mumbled, squinting against that dazzling little beam of sunlight. It was shining right in his eyes, and between that and the tears from his headache, he saw her beautiful face through a blur.

She smiled at him and let her fingers wander provocatively before she began to toy with his pendant of bard crystal. The touch of her fingers made the crystal emit soft, but discordant notes that he'd never heard from it before. After a moment he caught her hand and brought it to his lips. She snuggled closer, and from outside he heard some men talking softly, laughing together.

Not understanding what they said, Dain frowned in vague puzzlement. The wind gusted against the tent, shifting it against its ropes, and he shivered from cold.

Summer is over, he thought. *We'll have to break camp soon.*

Alexeika went back to fingering the crystal. As she rubbed it, a terrible, off-key note made him wince. Thinking it had been cracked, he pulled it a second time from her grasp and tried to look at it. But his head seemed too heavy to lift, and the effort made the interior of the tent spin slowly around him. Closing his eyes for a moment, he grew increasingly uneasy. Something seemed wrong, but he could not determine what.

Bits of memory dribbled through his mind, but they didn't make much sense. He'd been hunting, aye, hunting hard. For what? Beyars? He could smell that animal's strong, rank odor close by. His hand closed on the rough fur of a pelt. Aye, he thought, hunting. And trouble of some kind. Had he been thrown from his horse? He thought so. That must be why his body felt so sore and stiff. Well, they would break camp soon and go back to Grov. There'd be less time to hunt then, and perhaps that was a good thing.

Only . . . he squinted up at the tent pole looming over him. Why was there a tear in his tent? Why was his tent so small? What was that peculiar smell pervading the place? If the sun was up, where was Laure, who should be fussing about, bringing food and ordering the servants to build up the fire? Why was he lying on the ground in this nest of furs instead of in his camp bed? Why hadn't Alexeika said a word to him all night? Why stayed she so silent now? He could tell by the sound of her breathing that she was wide-awake.

But when he dared shift his head enough to look at her, she lay there with her eyes shut, pretending to sleep.

Smiling crookedly, he bent his head to kiss her.

Her lips parted beneath his, and he tasted something rotten, like dead flesh. The foulness of it drove him back with a gasp. He sat up on one elbow, gasping and spitting.

"What—"

She sat up, too, staring through him in a vacant way that made him frown.

"Alexeika?"

She appeared not to hear him. Her blue-gray eyes bored through him as though she knew not who he was. In silence she reached out for him, but he gripped her wrists and forced her hands away.

Inside him, fear was building, the heart-pounding, frantic kind. She smiled at him with an emptiness that made him twist her around so that he could examine the back of her neck. There was no hole there where a soultaker usually attacked its victim.

Relieved, he let his hands slacken, and he sank down with a sigh. "Sorry," he mumbled, wincing as new pain speared his skull. "Nightmares again. I thought you'd become Nonkind."

She should have laughed, but she didn't. She should have answered him and soothed his absurd fears, but she didn't. The sunshine poured over her, and in its bright, clear light he thought he could see her skull beneath her face.

Worried that he was losing his wits, he blinked hard to clear his vision. At that moment she tilted her head, and some trick of the sunlight made her eyes vanish. In their place were only empty sockets. Only it wasn't the light or a hallucination. She bent closer to him, caressing his jaw tenderly, and her eyes were still gone.

Horrified, he gripped her arm, and her flesh sloughed off in his grasp. With a yell, he shoved her away and tried to scramble to his feet. But his legs were weak and unsteady. They nearly gave under his weight, and his feet were tangled in the furs. Smelly, dirty furs, he noticed with sudden clarity, blinking around him. And this was not his royal tent, but some crudely fashioned edifice he'd never seen before. And, more importantly, this was not his wife, this creature getting slowly to her feet. Her eyes had reappeared, and her face looked like Alexeika's again; enough to make him doubt his sanity, until he saw the naked bone gleaming beneath the tattered flesh of her arm where he'd gripped her too hard.

For the first time, too, he noticed the smeared paint all over her naked body. A garish red, it almost looked like human blood, but it was not. The tent stank of animal hides, decayed flesh, and burned magic.

He sucked in his breath and this time succeeded in gaining his feet. His legs remained weak, however, and he staggered sideways, gripping the tent pole to keep his balance. It was nearly cold enough for him to see his breath, and he looked around desperately for his clothes, his armor, and his sword. They were not in evidence. He grabbed up one of the thinner pelts and twisted it about his loins for a garment.

She came at him with unexpected speed, and flung her arms around him. Her strength was not human. He struggled a moment, with his arms pinned to his side, before he was able to free himself. Immediately, she latched herself on to his side, her hands stroking him obscenely. A memory of the night's passion flamed through him suddenly.

In fury, he turned on her and struck her hard across the face. She went reeling back without a sound, her mouth grotesquely open, and sprawled on the ground. The blow should have hurt her, but she seemed to register no pain. At once she came crawling toward him, lurching to her feet, her hands grasping for him. Again he shoved her back.

"Get off me, obscenity!" he snarled. "Go back to the darkness that spawned you!"

Her eyes, so exactly like Alexeika's, stared at him without life, and it was like seeing his wife dead, yet undead. The idea that he had lain with Nonkind so horrified him that all he could think to do was run.

But as he reached down for the tent flap, she came after him from behind and clung to his back. With fury and revulsion boiling up inside him, he turned on her with a terrible oath and struck her as he'd never struck a woman in his life. Suddenly all he wanted to do was destroy this creature whose very existence defiled all that he loved and cherished in his wife.

Every blow, every rake of his fingers tore more of her flesh away. It was a strange magic that had fashioned her, for she seemed to be coming apart, piece by piece, under his assault. Sickened, he stopped.

Then came yelling from outside, and a pair of Grethori men rushed inside. They took in the situation at a glance and leaped on him, grabbing his arms and holding him despite his fierce struggles to heave them off.

Raging at whatever kind of Grethori magic had been used on him, he renewed his efforts to break free until he managed to knock one of his captors flying.

"Unhand me, you knaves!" he roared, and turned on the other one.

A fist crashed into the side of his face, and his head rang. Grayness danced around him, and although he struggled to hang on to consciousness, he felt his knees buckle. Semiconscious, he was dragged outside into bright, cold sunshine that hurt his sensitive eyes. More Grethori warriors came running up to surround him on all sides where he sprawled in the dirt. He could hear their incomprehensible chatter fading in and out of his hearing and gritted his teeth in an effort to stay awake. He now remembered fighting them—aye, 'twas a battle, not a hunt—and remembered something going wrong with Mirengard before everything fell into yawning blackness.

One of the men kicked him in the ribs, and he curled up, gasping and sputtering. *Stay awake or perish*, he thought groggily. At least the pain in his ribs helped clear his head. He fought his way to his knees and swayed there while the men formed a hostile circle around him.

Outnumbered, he thought, blinking hard to keep his vision from blurring again. A scraggly row of garish tents formed a camp in what looked to be a narrow canyon. The rock walls rose steep and high on either side, looking difficult, if not impossible, to climb. To the rear of the tent where he'd spent the night, he glimpsed ponies milling restlessly about in a rope pen. A shallow stream trickled through the camp, spangled with reflected sunlight. Downstream, he saw a few Grethori women washing and pounding clothing with stones while others were tying possessions into bundles and stacking them as though in readiness for departure. An old woman in a vermilion-and-black-striped garment chased a gang of scrawny children and dogs away from a cooking pot, scolding and swatting them with a long wooden spoon. Next to the largest tent, two girls were disassembling a wooden loom with the swiftness of long practice. Perhaps it was the chieftain's tent, Dain thought, for the two ponies tethered next to it gave it a look of prosperity. The trophy pole by the tent flap was hung with skulls and tattered scalps that fluttered in the cold wind.

The sight of them brought him a confused recollection of knights plummeting off the trail to their death, men fighting and screaming and dying around him. *My men*, he thought bleakly, and wondered how many had perished in the ambush. But why was he here? The Grethori did not take male prisoners.

Glimpsing a movement from the corner of his eye, Dain dodged just in time to avoid being clubbed. A howl of anger rose, and his attacker swung again. Ducking, Dain launched himself in a low tackle at the warrior's legs and knocked him staggering off-balance. Spitting curses, the man kicked Dain in the jaw, and although it was a glancing blow, Dain's head felt as though it had been split asunder. He collapsed, unable to cope with the pain, and, with shouts, the others pummeled and kicked him until he lay curled up in the dust, breathless and hurting.

A shout backed the men away from him. The chieftain strode up, taller than the rest of his warriors, his red hair glinting in the sunlight, his face scored with cruelty. Dain recognized him as the man who'd defeated him through magic trickery and glanced swiftly at the man's belt for Mirengard. The chieftain did not wear the famous sword of Nether's kings. No doubt its magic had caused him to throw it away. Squelching bitter regret, Dain told himself it was better that the sword had been hurled into a chasm than defiled by becoming war loot.

The chieftain wore the remnants of an auxiliary uniform, and as Dain frowned at him in dawning comprehension, he threw a mocking salute before marching back and forth with exaggerated movements. "Hail to pale-eyes king," he said in guttural Netheran and thumped his chest. "I am greatest warrior. I claim victory!"

Aching for a weapon, Dain lurched to his feet. "Where is Princess Tashalya?"

Eyes sparkling, the chieftain reached inside his jerkin and produced a small circlet of silver that glinted in the light. With a jerk of his heart, Dain took an involuntary step forward, but rough hands shoved him back. His mouth was suddenly so dry he had to swallow twice before he could speak.

"Where is she?" he demanded hoarsely. "In Thod's name, let me see her!"

The chieftain laughed low in his throat and pulled out a second small circlet, which he held aloft with the first. Trophies of Ilymir and Tashalya, Dain realized. A slow chill sank through his body, and he felt blank and empty. Finally, he forced himself to meet the chieftain's gleaming eyes.

"I am Chuntok!" the man said gleefully. "Greatest warrior of all tribes! I have defeated pale-eyes king in battle. I have taken the scalps of his men. Soon I will take his life, and I will wear the bones of his fingers to mark my honor. I will eat his blood and join his strength to mine."

He pointed at the other end of camp. "Down there, you will hang on the pole while I take my trophies. Then will my men hack off whatever bits of you they want and leave what is left for the vultures. But first, pale-eyes king, you will know one thing more."

Dain sprang at him, but the men shoved him back. Panting, Dain fought off a bout of dizziness and glared at Chuntok. "Where is my daughter? At least let me see her before you kill me."

Chuntok smiled scornfully and cast a look round at his men. "Behold the soft ways of pale-eyes king," he said in contempt. "Hear his pleas for useless girl-child, sold and gone."

"Sold!" Dain choked out. "You—"

"He is coward and weakling. He is dung," Chuntok said, and met Dain's gaze intently. "He does not even offer challenge to warrior who killed his son."

Bawling out a wordless cry, Dain turned on the man nearest to his right, using elbow and fist with brutal force. The Grethori staggered and fell to one knee, but even as the others sprang at Dain, he'd seized the dazed warrior's dagger and launched himself at Chuntok.

Still laughing, the chieftain was already drawing his scimitar. In the distance, Dain heard a woman's voice call out, but he ignored everything except his foe. Lashed by grief and fury, uncaring of his injuries or his inadequate weapon, he did not check before the brandished scimitar, but instead ducked under it and drove his shoulder deep into Chuntok's midsection.

He heard the man grunt as the wind was forced from his lungs. Taller and more muscular, Dain used his weight to topple Chuntok, and as they fell together, he was already striking at Chuntok's vitals with his dagger.

But the chieftain twisted like an eel and blocked the blow with his forearm. They hit the ground, already struggling and gouging as each of them tried to strike a fatal blow.

"*Shagra kee!*" shouted a woman's voice. Something heavy and narrow thwacked Dain across his spine.

The pain nearly stopped his heart. He felt his lungs lose air, and he fell onto his side. He could not move, could not breathe. His back felt as though it had been snapped. Over him an argument raged in shrill Grethori, stopped only by another woman's voice, old and quavery but filled with the force of magic.

"Chuntok!" she said, with unmistakable command. "*Davran kee!*"

Through a hazy blur, Dain saw the red-haired chieftain hold out his palm in a sign of respect, although he glowered through slitted eyes. He slid his scimitar through his belt and picked up the circlets of royalty that had belonged to Tashalya and Ilymir. Grief choked Dain's throat at the thought of his children brutalized and tortured by this vicious barbarian. He felt hatred like a fire burning away his entrails, and he was consumed by the need to strike Chuntok down, to do unto him as he had done. *Great Thod*, he prayed, *grant me revenge before I die.*

The circle of men around Dain parted, and a hideous old crone bent nearly double with age and infirmity came hobbling up to him. Leaning on a carved staff adorned with tiny skulls and bells, she peered down at him, her face contorted with anger.

"Glimmage ah don talbya fend!" Pointing a finger at Dain as she shouted, she glared at him as though he was Ashnod reincarnated and swung her staff at him.

Dain grabbed the end of it, rolled onto his knees, and jerked the old woman off her feet before any of the men could react. A terrible cry of rage issued from their throats, but by then he'd yanked her close enough to pin her struggling, frail body and hold his dagger to her throat. Carefully, gritting his teeth against the pounding agony in his head, he stood up and held her as a shield.

Howling and cursing, the men circled him, brandishing their weapons but not attacking. He'd already figured out that she must be a *sheda* and was vitally important to her tribe. He could cut her throat in an instant, thus wreaking the revenge he'd prayed for, or he could use her for negotiation. It was hard to force down his anger, hard to make himself think when his head hurt so badly and all he wanted was to destroy these fiends.

Baring his teeth, he tightened his hold around the *sheda* and circled so that he faced the chieftain. Chuntok was clearly furious, his cruel face drawn tight. With his scimitar clutched in one white-knuckled hand, he watched Dain with glittering malevolence.

"I'll kill her," Dain said to him in warning. "If you want to see her die, attack me now!"

Chuntok did not answer. Instead, the *sheda* snarled something. Dain felt magic sting his face as though tiny burning-hot pellets had been hurled at him. He flinched, but it was a paltry spell, too weak to make him drop his hold. He tightened his grasp on her until she squeaked in pain.

That silenced the yelling warriors. They glowered around
Dain, tense and ready to spring at the first opportunity, but he
gave them none.

Swiftly he glanced around, seeking to get his bearings. He
saw another old woman watching nearby. She held a staff in
her white-knuckled hands, and he was certain she must have
been the one who clubbed him just before the *sheda* arrived.
Some of the children and younger women had run up to watch
a short distance away. Their lean, hostile faces held no anxiety, only hatred.

The *sheda* felt suddenly hot in his arms as though she'd
burst into flames. Again, instead of letting her go, he pressed
the blade harder against her throat. The heat abruptly vanished, and he slackened his grip just enough to let her breathe.

She was stiff with rage against him. Up close, she stank of
rancid beyar grease, old blood, and magic. "*You will not escape us,*" said a voice in his mind.

Startled, he nearly lost his hold on her. She tried to twist
free, but he tightened his arm around her middle, lifting her so
that her crippled old feet barely skimmed the ground.

"*Where is my daughter?*" he thought back at her, determined to maintain this standoff until he got Tashalya back.
"*Tell me, quickly!*"

"*You are in no position to make demands, king of the pale-
eyes,*" the *sheda* replied contemptuously. "*She is lost to you
forever. Never will you find her, though you search for a thousand years.*"

And as the old crone spoke, Dain's mind was filled with an
image of Tashalya, her small face tear-streaked, her clothing
torn, her wrists and ankles bound with rope. Held struggling
in Chuntok's arms, she was handed over to a cloaked, hooded
figure wreathed in smoke with hurlhounds panting like huge
dogs at his side. Turning, that individual strode away with little tongues of fire burning in the tracks he left in the dirt. He
lifted a short pale wand into the air. Dain had seen such an object once before; it was a device used by the fire-knights to
travel through the second world.

"No!" Dain shouted, but black smoke billowed up from

the ground, engulfing Tashalya, her captor, and the trotting hurlhounds. When it cleared, they were gone.

"No," he whispered. The vision vanished from his mind, and he found himself still holding the *sheda* prisoner in his arms while the angry warriors surrounded him.

There would be no negotiating for Tashalya, no exchange made. And his anger and heartbreak throbbed through him with such ferocity he no longer cared what he did. The *sheda* would pay for Tashalya and Ilymir, he vowed, intending to kill her, but first he would escape. He wanted more than just simple revenge. He wanted much, much more.

"*Order them aside,*" he commanded her.

She said something, and a growl came from the men. Brandishing his scimitar, Chuntok swore long and venomously in his own tongue.

"*I have promised your death to Chuntok,*" the *sheda* said in Dain's mind. "*He grows impatient for it.*"

"*As soon as you command him to attack, I'll cut your throat,*" Dain threatened.

"*That is not the way of the pale-eyes. That is Grethori way, bold and quick.*"

He nicked her throat just enough to send a trickle of blood running down her neck. Hearing her sharp intake of breath, he sensed her fear for the first time, and liked it. "*We're taking a horse,*" he told her, "*and you will lead me to my daughter.*"

"*She is gone. Never will you find her.*"

"*So you said, but you know where she is. I want the name of who bought her. His name!*"

The *sheda* laughed, the sound raspy and scornful. "*Fool. What good are numes? You have the weakest of eld magic. You are no match for him. Or me.*"

Dain felt his anger swelling into something dark and uncontrollable, and if he had to ride into the very jaws of Ashnod in order to find Tashalya, he would do it. Sweeping outward with his senses, he sought his daughter, but if she remained hidden in this camp, his mind found no trace of her. It seemed the *sheda* was telling the truth . . . Grief sliced through him, but he pushed it aside to shout at the nearest Grethori with such force the man looked startled and retreated.

Swiftly slipping through the circle of men, half-dragging and half-carrying the *sheda*, Dain headed for the horse pen. The *glimmage* came stumbling out of her tent and sank to her knees in his way.

Her torn flesh had mended, and no more did the bones show where he'd attacked her. Her hair, so identical to Alex-eika's glorious color, flowed over the creature's shoulders like a cloak, hiding her nakedness from the avid looks of the war-riors.

That was the distraction Dain needed. He picked up the *sheda* who weighed no more than a child, and ran.

Howling, the Grethori came after him. But Dain ducked into the pen, flung the *sheda* across the nearest pony, and sprang onto its back without saddle or bridle. Leaning down, he slashed through the ropes forming the pen and whooped at the top of his lungs to spook all the ponies into running. The herd stampeded at a gallop, Dain's mount with them, while the men in pursuit of him scattered aside with yells of fear and rage.

A few tried to grab flying manes and vault astride. Some fell flat; one was trampled. Chuntok, however, succeeded in mounting a pony. Holding his scimitar aloft and screaming the dreadful Grethori war cry, he tried to veer his mount to-ward Dain. As the ponies galloped down the canyon through the camp, women scattered out of the way. A thin, redheaded boy came racing out of the large tent where the scalps hung from the trophy pole. Waving his skinny arms and screaming, he ran in front of the ponies in an effort to turn them back. Some of them did, rearing up or doubling back. Chuntok's pony was one of the latter, and the chieftain went flying off the animal's shaggy back while some of the ponies leaped over him and others thundered past him on either side.

Dain's mount also tried to turn back, but with the force of his mind Dain sent the animal onward. Its thoughts were raw with panic: *run/run/run/run*. He used that fear to keep its head pointed toward the open end of the canyon as it swept past the boy. Other ponies followed, racing through thinly spaced trees and plunging down a steep, precipitous trail. Clinging to his mount's mane and longing for stirrups, Dain was completely unprepared when the *sheda* exploded a small ball of spellfire right in his face.

Temporarily blinded and reeling back from the force and pain of it, Dain felt as though his skin were on fire. Only by desperately clutching at the pony's mane did he keep himself from toppling off. But he'd lost his grasp on the *sheda*. She slipped off the pony's back and went tumbling across the ground.

Dain glanced back, expecting to see the frail old *sheda* lying in a broken heap, but she rolled to her feet on the trail behind him and yelled curses, shaking her fist, then laughing in glee.

Dizzy, nauseated with pain, and hampered by spots of light still dancing in his vision, Dain knew that the *sheda* had been his last hope of finding Tashalya. Gant was a vast territory, impossible to search physically and too laden with magic for the veils to be parted there. It was hopeless, he thought in despair.

His pony, as surefooted and agile as a goat, went jolting down the trail while Dain slumped lower over its neck. He longed to rein up until the world stopped spinning, but the warriors would be coming after him, Chuntok especially. He wanted to meet Chuntok again, to fight the chieftain and smash him.

But not until his head stopped throbbing and he'd regained his strength. Better not slow the pony down. Better not give in to pain and the need to rest. Better keep riding despite the bitter cold that numbed his bare skin. Better head for the forest he could see on the mountain slope below and find a stream to hide his tracks. Better ride for his life.

Chapter Twenty-Two

Something hard and sharp prodded Dain awake. He lay in the rocky crevasse where he'd fallen off the pony—minutes ago, hours ago—and crawled beneath a bush before passing out. Now, he felt himself poked again, harder. Certain that Chuntok had finally caught up with him, he dared not even crack open his eyes. Instead, he tightened his fingers on the dagger concealed beneath him, waiting for the right moment.

It came. The third time he was poked, he sprang to his knees and whirled around, slashing hard with the dagger. He missed, because the man on the other end of the spear nimbly jumped back out of reach. In silence, they glared at each other, and the man lifted his weapon into a throwing position, the threat unmistakable.

Light-headed and burning with thirst, Dain blinked at him and slowly realized that this was no Grethori. A small man of wiry build, the stranger possessed a lean face weathered by the elements and mouse-colored hair cropped short. Garbed in soft-tanned leather tunic and leggings, with a rawhide pouch slung across his shoulder, he watched Dain intently.

Freezing, starving, his wits half-scrambled, Dain dropped his dagger in surrender. "I—I—"

The world spun around him; suddenly he was on fire with fever and unable to choke out what he wanted to say. As his vision faded, he saw the stranger coming closer, but there was nothing he could do about it before everything went dark.

He roused briefly to feel himself being dragged by his heels. There was snow around him, soft and clean and cold. He turned his head and scooped some of it in his mouth, but fell unconscious again before he could swallow.

Warmth . . . soothing scents of soil, stone, and roots. Slowly he dragged open his eyes and found himself lying on the ground in a nest of pine boughs, a fur thrown over him and a fire crackling nearby. He was in a shallow cave, dry and swept clean. Through the cave's mouth he glimpsed daylight outside. The glare of it hurt his eyes. He shut them for a moment, and when next he opened them, it was dark, and only firelight illuminated the small cave. An owl was hooting outside, and in the bushes growing at the cave mouth a mouse rustled furtively before growing still.

Dain turned his head fractionally and saw the stranger sitting cross legged on the ground, using a small, sharp-edged stone to scrape hair from a hide stretched across a frame.

Noticing that Dain had roused, the stranger immediately laid aside his work to give Dain water. It tasted cold and very good. Dain gulped it greedily, spilling as much as he drank.

"Easy," the stranger said in eldin. "There is plenty. All you want, and more."

Dain frowned, feeling confused. "You're old?"

"Nay, but you are," the stranger replied, and gave him a fleeting smile.

Dain smiled back. "Three-quarters."

"Aye, well, that drop of human blood must be strong, for you're bigger than most eld folk I know. Wasn't easy, dragging a great lout like you up here to my lair."

Dain sensed that this was an honest man, plainspoken and fair dealing. "I owe you my thanks."

"Aye. Grethori been after you. I watched them yesterday

and the day before, crossing and backtracking. They lost you when you fell into that crevasse."

Dain frowned, groping stealthily under the fur for his dagger.

"I've got your weapon," the man said, refilling the water cup from a skin and supporting Dain's head again while he drank. "A man with fever needs no knife in his hand until he's got his senses. They won't find you here. Be easy now."

Dain lay back with a sigh. "I have to—"

"Nay. There's nothing you have to do right now but lie there," the man said, tapping Dain lightly on his shoulder. "When you have your strength back, you can think about what's to be done."

Dain did not argue. He could feel lassitude spreading through him. "Your name, sir?" he asked with a yawn.

"Corban. And I'm no sir, thanks. I trap furs for my trade, when I can keep the Grethori from ruining my snares. You're lucky, eld. In another week, I'll be heading down from these mountains with my pelts, wintering south during the deep cold. If I hadn't been delayed on my count this year, you'd still be lying out there with the buzzards feasting on your hide."

"I'm grateful to you. My name is . . . Dain."

Corban's keen eyes studied him a moment. "It's not often the tribes take an eld captive. They usually go for Netheran children or women. You've got the muscles of a knight and the manners of a lord," he said, switching to Netheran, and pointed at the pendant of bard crystal hanging around Dain's neck. "Afraid to steal that, weren't they?"

Dain's hand stole up to clutch the crystal, which sighed a faint musical note beneath his touch. "I suppose."

"Aye, very superstitious, the tribes. You're a survivor of the massacre on Tun Peak, aren't you?"

It was a reminder Dain did not want. Images of men screaming and dying flashed through his thoughts. He'd seen Laure, his faithful squire, go plummeting off the trail to his death. He'd seen young Evo cut down, and Omas. *And for what had they died?* he thought bitterly. *The trail was cold long ere we reached the mountains.*

"I didn't see the fight. I could hear it echoing off the peak, and I stayed away," Corban said softly. "If you're thinking of going back to look for survivors, there'll be none."

Dain frowned and said nothing.

"You're lucky to be alive, especially since they took you captive. You've got your hair and your fingers. Be glad."

Dain's gaze shifted away, and he stared bleakly at the shadows cast on the cave wall. What he'd lost was far more precious than a few fingers. The Grethori had taken his son, his daughter, his sword, his men, and his honor. They had even robbed him of his wife, for how could he ever explain what had happened and expect her to understand? Alexeika, so strong, fierce, and capable, had little patience for the weakness of others.

Dain, who'd risen from an orphaned, nameless boy in the Dark Forest to become king of a vast realm, had ceased to know failure. He'd grown assured of his physical prowess, his command of men, and his accomplishments. He'd owned the world . . . or so he'd thought. Now he had nothing, not even clothes for his back, and was utterly dependent on the kindness of a stranger. He told himself that success and high estate were mere illusions, never to be taken for granted. Anything, aye, *everything* could be swept away in an instant.

The easiest course would be to fade away into the wilderness. He could live among the eld folk in exile, if they'd have him, or he could live as a solitary hermit, nameless and forgotten. He wouldn't have to face Alexeika's wrath and hurt. He wouldn't have to see the empty chairs of the two children he'd lost. Thiatcreika had always warned him against man-places and man-ways, but he'd wanted to explore, to see the world and all its wonders. He'd gone willingly into a new life, amazed by all it had brought him, but never had he imagined it would crash to dust like this.

"I've saved a bit of roasted snow-hare if you're hungry," Corban offered.

Frowning, Dain roused himself from his self-pity and realized he was ravenous. The meat was cold and greasy, but he chewed and swallowed with eager appetite. His headache had dulled to a bearable degree, and even cautiously sitting up didn't make it worse. His body was mending, he thought, licking his fingers and drinking more of the cold water.

"I owe you my life," he said to Corban.

The trapper had gone back to scraping the hide. "Out here, one man helps another as needed. Otherwise, he becomes like the tribes."

Outside the cave, an eerie howl lifted on the night wind. Startled, Dain reached instinctively for the weapon he didn't have.

"Easy," Corban said, holding out his hand. "Just wolves. They won't come here."

A little embarrassed by his overreaction, his weak muscles playing out, Dain sank down. He was freezing suddenly, and he reached for the fur cover. It made no difference against the fever, however, and he shivered miserably. "Thought I heard hurlhounds on the hunt," he said.

Corban's brows lifted, but he cocked his head and listened to the howling that had grown more distant. "Wolves," he pronounced at last. "It's good you're that quick, though. Plenty of odd things happen in these mountains."

"When do you take your pelts south?" Dain asked.

"In a few days."

"Have to repay your kindness," Dain mumbled, fighting to stay awake. "I'll work for my keep."

Corban chuckled and slapped his knee. "Work? A knight work? That I'd like to see."

"I don't know much about the fur trade," Dain replied, a little nettled by Corban's gentle scorn, "but as a boy I was apprenticed in a sword maker's forge. I can work, and I'll do it gladly in exchange for being guided out of these mountains."

Corban looked him over thoughtfully, making no effort to hide his reluctance. Dain knew that there were unscrupulous trappers that raided the caches of others when they found them. The fur markets in late fall were busy times in many towns and villages, with bidding wars, underhanded deals, and greedy merchants out to take advantage of trappers ignorant of their scams.

"What were you doing in Grethori country this late in the year?" Corban asked.

Dain met his eyes without evasion. "Trying to get my little girl back from them. They stole her, killed my son, hurt my wife."

"Ah." Understanding flooded Corban's weathered face. He nodded, cleaning his scraping tool between his fingers. "How old?"

"My daughter is six. My son"—his voice broke—"was four."

"Morde, that's an evil thing. You still set on vengeance? You aiming to go after that tribe again if you get the chance?"

Pain and anger warred inside Dain. His hand clenched hard on the cover. "Later, perhaps. Not without weapons or armor. My men—some of them I sent back before the ambush started. They'll be searching—"

"Nay," Corban said. "Not after all this time."

"How long?" Dain asked, startled.

"You've fretted enough. Better rest now."

"But I—"

"I've seen no Netherans about," Corban said. "Your men have gone, if they've any sense, or are lost to ambush. Either way, it's no good you hoping to find them now."

Shivering, Dain accepted the man's common sense. With a sigh, he said, "Then I must go home and face my—I must tell her I failed. My daughter's been sold and—"

"Ah, the poor mite's gone," Corban broke in sympathetically. "She's long gone and not to be found anywhere close by."

"No."

"Well, at least you're smart enough to understand none of these brutes will tell you anything if you catch one. I've seen other men on quests to find their children, wandering around up here until they go mad or die."

Dain nodded, knowing it was futile. Tashalya was in Gant by now, far from his reach even if he dared invade that evil land with his army.

He'd have to go home. He'd sworn an oath to uphold his responsibilities, and he would not gainsay it, no matter how painful it was to return a failure. Facing Alexeika was going to be the hardest thing he'd ever done, but worse than that was the knowledge that somewhere, far away, Tashalya was hoping her papa would come and save her. How long would she believe in him? he wondered, with a flood of guilt. When would her hope finally fade and wither? Would she hate him for failing her?

Tears stung his eyes. He turned his face to the wall, saying no more. And Corban let him be.

Chapter Twenty-Three

Attired in a loose gown of gray velvet trimmed with white ermine, her hair braided in a coronet beneath a white silk veil fastened over it with diamond pins, pearls dangling from her ears, and a gold Circle pendant studded with pearls and sapphires hanging from her slender neck, Alexeika—along with her protector, ladies-in-waiting, and a page carrying a sheathed sword—all swept into the chamber of state where the Privy Council was meeting. To her relief she saw Mirengard still lying across Faldain's throne; she'd feared that it would be removed before she arrived.

However, it was not the small Privy Council that met her entrance with surprise and looks of outrage, but a much larger group. She counted ten richly dressed individuals seated at the long table and realized she'd stumbled into a meeting of the Kollegya. Her first impulse was to retreat, but stubbornly she held her ground and marveled that they dared meet so openly in the king's chamber. A pity Lord Thum, as minister of state, was not present to check their arrogance.

Jonan, resplendent in a new green tunic and short cloak, was standing in the center of the room with his hand resting

on the vellum book of Netheran law. Apparently he had been
stammering his way through a speech when she came in. He
fell silent in midword.

The members of the Kollegya rose to their feet. An air of
hostility and tension filled the room, although a smiling
Vladno Krelinik leaned over to murmur in Fyliks Minshilev's
ear. On the other side of the two archdukes, Prince Tustik
frowned at Alexeika and began shaking his head. Count Unshalin turned red and, thrusting his chair aside so that the legs
scraped the wooden floor, came striding forth to confront her.

"Your majesty, what mean you by this intrusion?" he demanded, his fat gut quivering with indignation. "No one may
interrupt our proceedings. No one!"

For answer, she turned to the page at her heels, drew Severgard from its scabbard, and swung it down, whistling, mere
inches from Jonan. He cringed back with a yelp as the flat of
Severgard's blade smacked loudly atop the book of law. The
wooden stand supporting it rocked from the blow.

Alexeika glared at each of their stunned faces, ignoring
Jonan, who stared slack-jawed at her. "War," she said curtly.
"Declare it against Gant at once, and summon the generals. I
want the armies mustered without delay, ready to march eastward by the end of the month."

"But it will be near the Feast of St. Rodart, and three
weeks after that brings Selwinmas," Lord Litrik protested.
Old and childish, he obviously belonged to this body of men
by inherited right rather than ability. "And to disregard the religious festivities for—"

Unshalin gestured for quiet. His small, piggish eyes glared
at Alexeika. "The queen is exceeding her authority today.
Your majesty cannot order the army to undertake any such action. Nor can you order us."

"And 'tis a good thing, too," Lord Litrik chimed in, "for
ladies do not understand the practicalities of war. By Selwinmas the roads will be impassable."

"Not eastward," she retorted, ignoring Unshalin's attempt
to maneuver her into an argument over authority. She glanced
over her shoulder, where Samderaudin stood unobtrusively.
"And not if some control is exerted over the winter storms."

The *sorcerel* was watching her intently, like a cat waiting at a mousehole. She avoided directly meeting his yellow eyes and turned her attention back to the Kollegya members, who'd all started talking at once, while Jonan shouted shrilly, "No, no, no! I was here before her. I am to be heard first! My claim—"

"What do you claim, boy?" Alexeika asked harshly, turning her angry gaze on him. "Why are you here, wasting the Kollegya's time?"

Jonan's face drained of color. His eyes shifted about for help, but no one spoke, and her question alone hung in the air.

"What do you claim?" she repeated, daring him to make the mistake of a lifetime. "Speak up! Since you dare to assert your business ahead of the queen's, state it now."

"I—uh—I was—"

"His highness," Unshalin broke in smoothly, "was asserting his claim as heir and successor to Nether's throne."

"Was he?" she said coldly.

"I want to be king!" Jonan said shrilly, finding his tongue at last. He glared at her. "It's my legal right according to the laws of succession. Faldain is dead. You can't rule, but I can, and I will!"

She stared at him, unmoved. Her fury had gone cold, like ice in her heart. Across the room, she saw Tustik's hand clench suddenly, then relax. His face, better schooled, gave nothing away as he watched.

"What legal right have you?" she asked Jonan.

He frowned, as though he hadn't expected to be questioned. "Well, I—I—my father was king before Faldain. I should have inherited his throne, when he died, not my cousin."

A sigh ran around the room, and Unshalin's scowl betrayed his disappointment. Jonan's stupidity, Alexeika thought, had already undermined him. She held back a mirthless laugh. *You should have coached this young fool better, Lord Unshalin*, she thought scornfully.

"Your father," she said to Jonan, her voice a lash of contempt, "was king, not by right, but by treachery. He poisoned Queen Nereisse, and among his many crimes was the attempted murder of Prince Faldain and Princess Thiatereika. He seized the throne wrongfully and held it through a blood-bath that nearly destroyed this realm. If that is the *only* basis for your claim, boy, then you stand on the crumbling foundations of treason, betrayal, and dishonor."

"I am Faldain's cousin!" Jonan said, rallying better than she expected him to. "I am his closest male relative, and that makes me his heir no matter what my father did. My grandfather was a king, too, and I have royal blood and—and a noble lineage."

"Agreed," she said mildly, and watched him puff up in triumph. "A pity you have chosen the same path of dishonor and treason as your father, by trying to wrest the throne for yourself when Faldain still lives."

His mouth fell open. "Only your majesty makes that claim," he said, his voice shrill again. "We—I—was there. You weren't! I saw the battle. I saw Faldain struck down. We brought his poor, battered body home with all the honor we could give it, but you won't accept the truth. You want to keep me from the throne, but you can't! I am king!"

For a moment her rage was so strong she tightened her grasp on Severgard and took an involuntary step forward. Eyes bulging in alarm, Jonan cringed behind Unshalin, who lifted his hands in placation.

Samderaudin glided forward, intervening, and pointed at Jonan. "Lies!" he announced. "Lies! You were so great a coward that the king made you and your escort turn back. You were not present at the battle, or you would be dead. Lies!"

Jonan flung up his head, his nostrils flaring, his gaze held by the *sorcerel's*. He trembled visibly and his large hands clenched and unclenched at his sides. "I know what happened," he said, his voice tangled with rage and stubbornness. "I saw Lord Miest find the body."

"A body," Alexeika said. "Not the king's. We've been through this before. You waste our time, Jonan. You may withdraw."

He turned on her with a snarl of fury, the desire for violence contorting his face. She braced herself, with Severgard ready in her hands, but Sir Pyron stepped in front of her with his weapon half-drawn. Unshalin gripped Jonan's shoulder and murmured urgently in his ear. Jonan shook his head, and Unshalin spoke to him again.

Scowling with obvious reluctance, Jonan bowed his head and shuffled across the room, where he flung himself in one of the chairs and slumped there, pouting. He was the only person in the room sitting in her presence.

Vladno poked him hurriedly, but Jonan refused to budge.

His rudeness was a deliberate offense. At that moment Alexeika wanted to order this recalcitrant oaf hauled out and flung over the cliff for assuming a privilege that was Faldain's alone. Teetering on the edge of fury, she knew she could not afford to lose command of her emotions, not there, not then. Beckoning to her page, she swiftly put Severgard back in its scabbard and gave it into the lad's keeping lest she be tempted to strike Jonan with it.

"You cannot sit in the queen's presence," Vladno was saying to him. "Get on your feet, you dolt. She has dismissed you. How far do you mean to insult her?"

Jonan gripped the arms of his chair stubbornly. "She has insulted *me*," he said sullenly. "I should be king. It's the law."

Exasperation crossed Vladno's handsome face. "Law or not, at least stand in her presence. Have you no inkling of what manners are?"

Jonan sighed and slowly got to his feet. Alexeika stared at him with disgust. After all she'd done for him, and more to the point, after all Faldain had done for him in sparing his miserable life, worrying about him, and trying to protect him from those who meant him harm, this churlish behavior was unforgivable. Tustik, she thought, had been right all along.

Unshalin bowed to her. "Your majesty, please permit his highness to stay. His manners may be deplorable, but he *is* the heir, and as such has a few rights of—"

"He is *not* Faldain's heir," she broke in, knowing the time had come to strike. Up till then, she'd been acting to save her husband's throne because she loved him. Now, she intended to save the throne in order to survive. If Faldain lost power—as she'd already lost *him*—then she would have nothing; her children would have nothing. If Faldain remained king, at

least she would keep her position, titles, and wealth. Such
things meant little to her and nothing compared to his love.
But with his love gone, she intended to lose nothing else. She
was seething in a maelstrom of fire and ice, rage and cold determination. She had no intention of retreating nobly into
exile, effacing herself quietly to live in obscure poverty. She'd
lived hand-to-mouth for too many years to go back to that.
And she'd be damned before she tamely let these pompous
fools put Jonan on the throne and forced her to depend on his
largesse for her household expenses.

With that in mind, she met Unshalin's gaze steadily with
her head held high. "The king has never expected Jonan to
grovel in gratitude to him, but he does expect loyalty." From
the corner of her eye, she saw Jonan flush. "As do I."

"It is not a matter of loyalty, your majesty," Unshalin said
with an exaggerated sigh, "but of legal right. Prince Ilymir—
may Tomias guard his soul—is gone. That leaves—"

"—the child which will be born in the spring."

Uproar filled the room, with everyone talking at once.
Among the group, Tustik stared at her in open delight before
he swiftly mastered his expression. Vladno pursed his mouth
with disappointment. Jonan's mouth hung open. Unshalin
eyed her with disbelief.

"Allow me to be the first to offer your majesty felicitations," he said without enthusiasm. "Since the king made no
announcement before his departure—"

"There was not time," she broke in. "And in the circumstances, it was not an appropriate occasion for such news."

"Of course," Unshalin said doubtfully. "Forgive me, but
this seems to be a most convenient occurrence, timed solely
to block Prince Jonan's—"

"If the baby will be born in the spring, I am sure you can
calculate that he has not been conjured up in the last hour,"
she said with asperity. "If you mean the timing of my announcement is convenient, it is not. I would naturally prefer
that the king announce our—our happiness." Annoyed by that
tiny break in her composure, she clenched her hand at her
side. "But events have forced me to act contrary to traditional
conventions and make the announcement myself. I would pre-

fer this news to remain within this circle, and not be spread publicly until Faldain's return."

"And if the king does not return?" Vladno asked.

She was unprepared for how much that question hurt, despite her efforts since parting the veil to block all feeling. Momentarily overwhelmed, she hesitated while battling for self-control.

"There is no need for her majesty to answer such a painful question," Tustik said. "The succession is assured, providing the child comes to term and has a safe birth. All will be done to see that the queen is kept protected and comfortable to achieve both."

"But if the child is not male," Unshalin said, "then we—"

"In due time," Tustik cut him off, with an elegant gesture of one thin hand. "In due time. That lies in the will of the gods."

Alexeika shifted her gaze to meet Samderaudin's yellow eyes. He was staring at her with such intensity she knew he was willing her to look in his direction. *He knows what this child will be*, she thought with sudden conviction. An involuntary chill ran through her, and although she longed to ask him if she carried a son, she resisted the temptation. She'd announced her pregnancy to gain time, and she'd achieved that goal. If Samderaudin told her the child was a girl, all would be lost. She could not afford to gamble more than she already had. Not now.

Archduke Minshilev, silent until this moment, abruptly cleared his throat. "The question ought to be whether this coming child is worthy of inheriting the throne. The royal children have thus far displayed distressing tendencies and erratic qualities of magic that are inappropriate. Prince Jonan— whatever his shortcomings—is at least human."

Appalled silence fell over the room. Alexeika wished she had not taken her hand off Severgard. Her heart was thumping hard at the insult, so deliberately and cruelly spoken, and she guessed that this man, this member of the powerful Kollegya, must be her most vehement critic, the one who had opposed her influence over Faldain and sought to drive her into a more traditional woman's role.

She turned to him slowly, her body rigid with anger.

"Fyliks, really," Lord Litrik was saying with an uneasy frown. "That's too harsh. A mother still grieving over the tragedy of what's happened—really too much."

"Her majesty violated the privacy of this meeting," Minshilev said without apology. "She has been strident and unseemly, carrying a sword like a man, dictating orders and battle strategies like a man, arguing legalities like a man. If this is her chosen behavior, then let her also hear the plain-spoken truth like a man without pretty compliments and euphemisms deemed appropriate for a lady's ear." He turned back to Alexeika. "Have I uttered any untruths in what I said, your majesty?"

She was still bitterly angry, but her initial shock at his attack was fading, and she could think again. She drew on memories of her father, knowing how he would have dealt with such a bully.

"If the gods permit me to bear another son," she replied steadily, "he will possess his father's qualities, as Prince Ilymir did. The royal princesses have demonstrated the gifts of their eldin heritage, but since they have no place in the succession, I do not see any grounds for Archduke Minshilev's objections. As for Jonan's qualities, I think we've seen sufficient display of them this morning. He shows distressing inclinations toward treason and insurrection, both of which should be checked at once rather than"—she shot a glare at Count Unshalin—"encouraged."

A murmur ran around the room, and Jonan's scowl intensified. She could not feel sorry for him, for he'd brought this on himself.

"Comparisons are wasted effort," she continued. "At least let this new child come into the world before you criticize him."

"Well said!" Vladno applauded. "It's against Writ to prejudge. Whether our king comes home or must be ransomed, the succession is no longer in question. Let us be grateful, my lords, and move on to other matters more pressing."

"War with Gant," Alexeika said, giving him a nod of thanks for his support. Having quashed the matter of Jonan, she went back to her objective for revenge. "The Gantese are taunting us, provoking us in border skirmishes. Let us deal them a heavy blow before winter closes in."

Unshalin frowned. "Your majesty should bring this matter before the Privy Council. We were discussing matters of the treasury before—"

The door burst open without warning, and Lord Thum du Maltie strode in. Splattered with mud, snowflakes still dusting his red hair, he looked tired and heartsick. One swift glance about the room made him frown as he dropped to one knee before her.

"Your majesty," he said, "I rode back as soon as the terrible news reached me. Please accept my sympathy, which is joined with the concern of all the chevards of upland Mandria. They were in session with me when the news came, and they have charged me with messages of their complete support, including offers of men, supplies, even ransom money. By now I assume Matkevskiet has dispatched a force into the Kransval Mountains to seek the king's liberation?"

His voice, clear, honest, and direct, its Mandrian accent crisp, filled the room, which had gone utterly silent. Alexeika allowed herself to savor the relief of his loyalty and support for a moment before she spoke. "No," she said. "The general has sent no troops at all."

Thum sprang to his feet. "What? Why not? Why the delay? The king's safety is paramount. If he's—"

"My lord," Tustik broke in quietly, "come and join us. Allow us to explain all that has transpired that you may understand the matter completely." He paused and sent Alexeika a courteous lift of his brows. "If we may have your majesty's permission to proceed?"

In the politest way possible he was asking her to depart. His courtesy enabled her to smile slightly and incline her head. "Please do so. The queen is grateful for having been received by the Kollegya. She expects war to be declared without delay."

Turning about with dignity, she started out, and paused only to extend her hand graciously to Thum. "The queen is well pleased to see you safely back."

Although his gaze held puzzlement, he bowed over her hand. "I'll do all that I can," he murmured.

Without reply, for she could not possibly explain that she no longer feared for Faldain's safety, she gathered her little entourage and left the chamber of state. Not until she was well away down the passage, past a little knot of curious onlookers, idlers, and pages, did she halt and turn her back to everyone while she pretended to study a rotted place on a tapestry. Her eyes were too blurred with tears for her to see anything. She felt exhausted, as though she'd run a long distance, and all she wanted to do was retreat to a private corner and cry.

But she couldn't do that. She refused to cry for Faldain, no matter how much her emotions gnawed at her.

Behind her she could hear Lady Emila and Lady Buni whispering excitedly to each other about the baby. Already they were laying plans for her seclusion—her imprisonment, she thought in frustration. What she wanted to do was ride with the army toward Gant, but it would not be permitted. She would not be allowed to take any risks now that might injure the child she carried. Forced to sit quietly and fold her hands, she would have nothing to distract her from her raging thoughts or the memory of what she'd seen in her vision. Tormented, she suffered a degree of agony she'd revealed to no one.

"Your majesty," Sir Pyron said in warning.

She heard a slight stir behind her and Lady Buni's gasp. Swiftly trying to find her composure, Alexeika turned around and found Samderaudin and Vaunit standing side by side before her.

To face one *sorcerel* at a time was difficult enough. Two emitted such an aura of potent magic that she took an involuntary step back from them. Already she guessed why they had approached her, but she wished they had chosen a less public place for this confrontation. In annoyance, she gestured for her ladies and page to step out of earshot, then shot Samderaudin a look of accusation.

"I know the truth," she said curtly. "You need not trouble to keep secrets from me in future."

"Better the queen had remained in ignorance."

That wrung a harsh laugh from her. "Better for whom? Faldain? Oh, yes, I daresay it would be."

"The queen has been warned before not to part the veils. Always she makes mistakes and suffers. Why does the queen not learn this lesson?"

"Because I wanted the truth. You kept it from me, pretending that all your visions were dark. And you as well," she added, shooting a glare at Vaunit. "Even the *sorcerelle* participated in this conspiracy of silence. Do you think I'm so weak I cannot endure the truth, however painful?"

"The queen has sought pain and found it," Samderaudin replied. "But has the queen found any truth in what she saw? No, she has not."

Alexeika wanted to grab this crumb of hope he offered, but she did not trust him. She had no intention of being misled again. "Are you saying my vision was in error?"

"It is not enough to part the veils. The queen can do that well. It is in the seeing that all can be misunderstood."

She met his gaze coldly and kept her voice very, very low so that no one could overhear them. "Did Faldain lie with that Grethori female?"

"He did."

"Did he sport with her?"

"Yes."

She felt as though she'd been stabbed. She had no breath. For a moment little gray dots danced before her eyes, and she was cold as though all the blood had been drained from her body. "Then what have I *not* seen?" she forced herself to ask. "What do I *not* understand?"

Samderaudin stared at her a long moment. Although no expression showed on his smooth face, she gained the impression that he was angry. "Until the queen is willing to listen, nothing can be explained."

"Exactly," she snapped.

Without another word, she moved forward. The two *sorcerels* parted to let her pass, and she did not look back.

Chapter Twenty-Four

Sleeting ice pellets rattled the trees and clattered on the snowy ground. At the crossroads near the foothills of the Kransvals, Dain and Corban took shelter beneath the snowy branches of a pine tree and spoke their farewells.

"You've been a good friend," Dain said, giving Corban his hand. "I owe you my life."

"And you've repaid the debt by helping me haul out my pelt bales," Corban replied. "I couldn't have dragged them all on the travois without your muscle."

Dain shrugged. "It's not enough—"

"'Tis plenty," Corban insisted. "I'll be a rich man when I've traded. And there's a share for you, if you'll stay to collect it."

"Nay, I must go," Dain said, conscious of an urgent sense of time running out. "I'm needed home."

"You won't get there in this weather," Corban said worriedly. "Best you come with me to stay with the Widow Tander. She runs a good inn, and you might hire on as a hostler to earn your keep till thaw."

Dain shook his head. "My way lies east."

"There's a time for stubbornness and a time for good sense. You're not well yet. You'll never hike far once your feet freeze and your fever comes back up. And if this muck turns into a blizzard—"

"We've argued this too many times," Dain said. "Farewell. If ever our paths cross again and I can repay your kindness, know that I'll do it."

"You'll repay me by taking refuge in yon market town and keeping safe until this season is over." But as he spoke, Corban pressed a pouch of dried meat into Dain's hand. "This will supply you a day or two."

Thanking him, Dain tucked the food into his pack, which contained a waterskin, strikebox, extra snow-hare pelts to tuck into his footgear for additional warmth, a trap for snaring game, and a supple old beyar hide for sleeping in. He wore clothing made of tough danselk hide, and the dagger he'd taken from the Grethori warrior was belted around his waist. With no beard to protect his face from the brutal cold, he'd fashioned a mask and hood of fur. He drew them on, lifted his hand to Corban, and set forth.

It was a bleak, gray morn, and the sleet came pelting down mercilessly. He set himself a steady, ground-eating pace, refusing to think about how far it would take him to walk fifteen leagues in this weather, especially since his fever was likely to come up in the afternoon and render him shaky and helpless. Just as Corban had never trusted him enough to reveal the location of his fur caches in the mountains, so had Dain never revealed his true identity, or discussed his intention to walk to the nearest garrison and get the help he needed there. With a swift horse and an armed escort, the rest of the journey to Grov was possible in a matter of days.

All he had to do was reach the garrison. So simple a plan in theory, but far from easy to execute. The wind was cutting through his clothing and already making him shiver. He quickened his pace, only to feel himself flag a little. Frustrated, he slowed down, knowing he must not overtax his strength. This damnable fever wore him down too much.

A quick healer who'd lived his life immune from ordinary ailments thanks to his eld blood, Dain found himself unable to

shake off the remnants of the *sheda's* evil magic. This strange
fever continued to fester in his chest wound and in the newly
closed scar across his temple that ached when he overexerted
himself. Corban thought he simply needed rest, but Dain understood that no ordinary remedy would do. His only hope of
recovery lay in finding an eld healer or in drinking pure water
from the Chalice. But until then, he must accomplish this
journey, no matter how difficult.

Topping a slight ridge, Dain glanced back at Corban, who
still lingered at the crossroads, watching. His lean, gray figure
was barely discernible in the freezing mist and sleet. They
waved briefly before Corban turned and trudged away. A
sense of lonely solitude enclosed Dain. He had neither protector nor friend now. It was up to him to make it. Bending his
head against the wind, he resumed walking.

Wrapped in heavy lyng furs, a thick beyar rug across her lap,
and a heated stone warming her feet, Alexeika was driven in
a sleigh across the wide parade ground at Drev garrison some
leagues from the Nether–Gant border. A light snow was
falling over the mass of Netheran troops. More of the army
was located at Grad and Tomblisk, the easternmost outposts,
but Drev was as close to Gant as Alexeika was permitted to
travel. Even so, her presence here at all was extraordinary.

She'd come because she and Lord Thum considered it vital
to raise the army's morale. The king's continued absence incited constant rumors of his death, and Nether's enemies were
taking advantage by stirring up more and more trouble. Alexeika knew that her visit would mean much to these knights,
especially before they marched into battle. Furious debate had
raged in the Privy Council, of course, for it was unheard of for
a pregnant queen to leave official seclusion, but she was here
just the same.

Having arrived last night after a miserable journey hindered by icy roads, howling snowstorms, grim accommodations, and her sudden physical discomforts, she'd dined with
the officers. Her pregnancy was visible now, for in the last
fortnight she'd swelled greatly, and the men seemed to find

her condition both an embarrassment and a fascination. High-born ladies did not exhibit themselves in this way, and unless men were married, they never saw the changes in a woman's body. Their behavior to her was constrained and uneasy, yet she could see them take heart from such tangible proof that she carried their next king. She'd brought them something to fight for, and she understood the value of that even if the Privy Council did not.

At the center of the parade ground, her sleigh halted. She gazed at the straight rows of mounted knights arranged for inspection. How magnificent they looked, with swords and spurs gleaming, their armor polished, their war chargers pawing the ground eagerly. The officer who'd been assigned to escort her was splendidly turned out with a sword scabbard of islean fur, gleaming boots, silver spurs, and a fine cloak of quilted wool lined with fur. Handsome and bursting with the honor of her company, he reined up his horse beside her sleigh and pointed out the regiments with crisp efficiency.

"Your majesty understands strategy very well," he said in admiration, after she asked several questions about numbers, deployment, and battle signals. "I've never before met a lady so well informed."

"The queen is always well informed," she replied curtly, for she was in no mood for compliments. The sleigh seat hurt her back, her feet were swelling despite the cold, and she felt very tired. However, she summoned a smile for the man. "If these knights fight as splendidly as they look, they'll trounce the Gantese speedily."

The arrival of General Radbril cut off what the officer might have replied. A coarse-featured man, his face heavily pocked above his thick beard, the general wore a canar pelt draped across his breastplate and a tall fur cap. Thick gauntlets embroidered with his family crest protected his hands. His horse was a magnificent stallion, dappled gray so that he seemed to blend into the falling snow.

"Your majesty honors us," the general said gruffly.

She gave him a gracious nod. "The men look splendid. Are they ready?"

"They are. We plan to march out at daybreak if the weather holds. Your majesty arrived just in time."

It hadn't been until last night that she'd learned how close the timing was. Still relieved that she'd made it there, she smiled at him calmly. "When this battle is over, I want the men to be able to say they fought for their new king before he was born."

Radbril's eyes darkened, and he clamped his mouth in a tight line. "I would to Thod we had King Faldain here now on his darsteed, with Mirengard in his hand. That's what these men need to lead them against Nonkind, your grace. A real king, not the hope of one."

The image of Faldain in full armor, roaring out his orders to a field of cheering men, filled her mind vividly. At once she closed off the thought, finding it unbearable to think of his valor, his handsome looks, his strength, or the way he could smile at her with that little quirk at the corner of his mouth and set her pulse racing. Frowning, she reminded herself to think of him as lost, never to return, or she would not be able to function at all. The pain and bewilderment of his betrayal continued to cut through her as sharply as the night she'd parted the veils of seeing. She did not believe she would ever recover from it.

She had left Mirengard still lying across Faldain's throne to hearten the courtiers and remind them that Faldain remained their king, but she no longer spoke of his return. In her mind, the only hand that would lift Mirengard from the throne would be her new son's. Until then, she had to carry on, doing whatever was necessary to keep this turbulent realm together.

Accordingly, she held her head high and met the general's gaze with hers like steel. "These men, if you've trained them well, can meet anything, even Nonkind, and bring Nether a proud victory."

Radbril bowed. "I thank your majesty."

"The king has always had the utmost confidence in his generals," she went on, "as do I. We are convinced that Gantese agents were behind Prince Ilymir's murder. That is why I have come here to urge these knights to do their best."

"Revenge," the general said, nodding. "Aye, the men understand *that*. With your majesty's permission, I'll share your remarks with them."

"Of course."

Their eyes met with perfect understanding, and she stood up for a moment on her aching feet to lift her gloved hand in salute to the men. They remained at strict attention, and the silence on the field was deafening. Seated again, Alexeika ordered her sleigh driven down the entire line and back again. When she left the parade ground, she heard an order ring out, and cheers rose up in her wake.

The sound of them made her eyes sting with tears. She knew, of course, that the men were not cheering her but instead their king and country. She'd accomplished her goal in heartening them, and that was all that mattered. It was vital that they win a victory, not just because she wanted to bring harm to Gant in retaliation, but because both the army and the people needed to learn that they could function without Faldain. The succession could continue smoothly even if he never came back. The realm would not fall back into chaos, civil war, and despair.

Huddling deeper into her furs as the sleigh picked up speed and the cold wind stung her face, she clenched her gloved hands tightly inside her fur muff. Setting aside her personal hurt, she could not understand why Faldain had chosen to abandon his people and his responsibilities at such a critical time. He'd done more than damage her belief in him; he'd broken his people's trust. He'd left Grov vulnerable to revolt in the palace. He'd opened the door to all kinds of political mischief. Bad enough that he was no longer her husband, but he'd ceased to be her king. And for that, more than anything, she could not forgive him.

Chapter Twenty-Five

Jonan was sitting in his room, aimlessly tearing off little strips of parchment, wadding them up and tossing them at the window. It was snowing outside, and the palace grounds were blanketed in white. Bored with waiting, he thought about smoking some tyneweed to pass the time.

The door slammed open without warning, startling him so much he jumped to his feet and knocked his chair over with a crash. Count Soblinsk entered, looking resplendent in a fine dark brown tunic and a small fur cap on his bald head. He carried a rolled-up document and was tapping it impatiently in his hand.

"Are you ready?" he asked without greeting. "Come! There's little time."

Jonan stared at him, both astonished and suddenly afraid. "You don't mean it's really going to happen."

"Of course it's going to happen!" Soblinsk said impatiently. His eyes were gleaming with excitement. Still tapping the document, he bounced up and down on his toes. "Everyone is in place. The opportunity we've been waiting for is finally at hand."

"Oh. Do I really have supporters?" Jonan asked.

Soblinsk uttered a short laugh. "How many times must I assure your majesty that you do?"

"But I haven't done anything for them."

"You will. All that's for the future. There are plenty of Netherans who've disapproved of Faldain's pagan, blasphemous ways. *You*, sire, will lead Nether back to piety and righteousness. You will install the Chalice in the cathedral under the suitable guardianship of proper church officials, and you will clean the *sorcerels* out of the palace. Tomias be praised that this day is here at last. Ever since our ignominious defeat at the hands of Faldain, I've worked for this. He brought a foreign army against us at the Battle of Grov. Did your majesty know that? Mandrians." Soblinsk nearly spat the word. "He's thrown aside everything Muncel worked so hard to accomplish, but he's finished. A new day has dawned."

Soblinsk's excitement and jubilation increased Jonan's sense of alarm. What had begun as a simple plan was rapidly growing very complicated. Initially, all Jonan had to do was assert his claim to the throne and wait for the palace officials to grant it on legal grounds. But Alexeika had thwarted that by announcing her pregnancy. Although disappointed, Jonan had been prepared to bide his time until the baby's birth and gender determined his future. But Soblinsk refused to wait, and when the queen departed for Drev, the count wasted no time constructing an elaborate plan that Jonan feared was far too risky. He had the feeling of having grasped the tail of a serpent, and now, although he was afraid to hang on, he dared not let go.

Wheezing and light-headed, Jonan suddenly felt the need to relieve himself. Desperately, he said, "It can't be today. I'm not well. I can't—"

"Your majesty, things have gone too far for you to back out now," Soblinsk said forcefully. His black eyes bored into Jonan. "We've gambled on you, risked our necks in putting this together. All for you!"

"I—I know," Jonan stammered. His head was buzzing, and he was sorry he'd made the count angry. "I just never thought it would be like this, and I don't—"

"Do you want to be king?" Soblinsk asked fiercely. "Do you?"

"Yes."

"Then you must take the risk! In Thod's name, do you think the queen will relinquish power now that she has it? She's planning to set herself up as regent and rule through her child. Damne, the very idea of a woman ruling over us is more than improper. It's unthinkable! You don't want that, do you?"

"No, of course not. But she might have a girl, and then we won't need to worry."

Soblinsk glared at him. "I've waited too long to depend on even odds."

"What?"

"Don't you understand?" Soblinsk asked. "The queen is your enemy. She's determined to rule just to keep you off the throne."

Jonan blinked. "Me? I thought she wanted to—"

"Your majesty, I know you think of her as a benefactress, but she hated King Muncel. She grew up among rebel forces trying to oust your father from his throne. Treason is in her blood, sire. And she blamed your good mother for the death of hers. She has every reason in the world to despise your majesty."

Hurt and resentment swelled inside Jonan. He thought of how she'd snapped at him that night, and believed what Soblinsk said.

"And now she's gone off to war, when modesty and decorum demand that she seclude herself." Soblinsk cleared his throat. "This will be her undoing, for even now, a dispatch, beautifully forged and announcing both defeat of Nether's army and Queen Alexeika's death, is coming here by messenger. We must be among the courtiers when it arrives."

Jonan gasped in shock. "She's dead?"

"No," Soblinsk said impatiently. "I know not how the battle goes or whether she is anywhere near it."

"Then how can such news come?" Jonan asked in bewilderment.

"Men are waiting to ambush any real couriers on the eastern road. The messenger who will soon arrive is in my employ. The news he's bringing is false, stating that the queen and her unborn child have perished."

Blinking, Jonan stared at the count and tried to understand. "This is a lie," he said finally.

"Of course. A bold and daring lie."

"But people will find out the truth when she returns, and then—"

"By then you'll possess the throne. An order for her arrest will be issued, and she'll be accused of treason in claiming a false pregnancy and trying to stop your rightful succession after Faldain's death."

"But can I do all that?" Jonan asked.

"Of course! As king, your word is law. Your commands must be obeyed."

"I don't think Prince Tustik will believe this trick because he hates me, and he doesn't trust you."

"By tonight, Tustik will be imprisoned and silenced." With a cruel smile, Soblinsk held up the rolled document. "This is his arrest order, already prepared. He can do nothing to stop us."

Jonan opened his mouth, but he could think of no more protests. Soblinsk seemed to have planned for every contingency.

"Come now. Your majesty must hurry. The guards on duty in the gallery have been bribed to shout acclaim for you as soon as the announcement is made. When that happens, the courtiers will believe all the palace guards have given their support to your majesty, and they will follow suit. Now please, sire, be of good heart. This will work! All that's needed is boldness and courage."

Jonan felt as though an iron band was tightening around his throat, choking off his air. His knees were water. He stood there, staring at Soblinsk, and suddenly darted behind the privacy screen for the slop pail.

As soon as he emerged, Soblinsk hurried him from the room. "Quickly! There's no more time to lose. The midday prayers are over by now. The courtiers will be assembling in the Gallery of Glass to gossip and lay their plans for celebrating Selwinmas. All you have to do is watch for my signal."

"But I—"

"You will hold Mirengard aloft for all to see, and you must hold it well, like the king you are. Then sit on the throne and do not leave it. I'll see to the rest."

Jonan nodded, but the thought of handling Mirengard especially worried him. "But if it burns my hand, and I drop it—"

"You won't drop it," Soblinsk said with authority. "Our lives from this moment forward depend on your majesty. You will not fail those who have been loyal to your father and to you all these years. You," Soblinsk said intensely, pinning Jonan with his gaze, "are our king!"

Gulping, Jonan dared say nothing else. Soblinsk had been so patient and loyal an adviser that Jonan knew he had little choice but to play his part.

Together they strode down the passageway, heading for the main section of the palace. With every step, Jonan felt as though he might collapse, but somehow he kept walking. His breathing was labored; his lungs felt so rigid with fear they couldn't expand. Feeling little beads of sweat popping out along his hairline, he prayed that he could remember all that Soblinsk had told him to do.

Halfway up the majestic staircase, Jonan and Soblinsk turned into an alcove off the landing, where an officer of the guard was waiting. The man saluted, his gaze flicking over Jonan briefly.

"All is in place?" Soblinsk asked softly.

The officer nodded curtly. "The men are ready."

"Good. You have it?"

The officer produced the famous sword of Nether's kings from beneath his cloak, taking care to hold it by its scabbard. "We had a little trouble subduing the men guarding it in the chamber of state, but we managed."

"Wait for us in the Hall of Kings," Soblinsk commanded, and the officer hurried away.

Handling the sword with caution, he avoided touching the hilt as he swiftly threaded the scabbard onto Jonan's belt.

Thod above, please do not let me faint, Jonan prayed. His heart felt as though it had doubled in size and was trying to pound a hole through his ribs. Mirengard hung incredibly heavy on his hip. He wondered if he could even lift it when the time came. Mesmerized and afraid of its magic, he gazed at the glittering hilt jewels.

If only it would give me courage, he thought. In sudden self-honesty, he knew he was nothing a king should be. He was no leader of men, no warrior, no strategist. But Thod had seen fit to give him royal blood and the heritage of a king. Who was he, as Sofina had once said to him, to go against his destiny? He just wished he didn't feel like a helpless leaf swirling on the surface of a stream, being swept along faster and faster by events he could not control.

Abandoning protocol for once, Soblinsk grasped him by his shoulders and gave him an encouraging shake. "Stand tall," he said, and twitched a fold of Jonan's cloak forward to conceal the sword. "Hold your hand thus on the edge of your cloak to keep it in place," he suggested, curling Jonan's stiff fingers around the fabric. "Good. Remember that you were born to be king and this is the greatest day of your life. Seven years of patience and hard work are culminated at last. May Tomias bless us both."

Making the sign of the Circle, Jonan felt he should speak, but his tongue seemed stuck to the roof of his mouth. Everything had taken on an unreal quality, as though he walked through a dream—nay, a nightmare.

Suddenly they were in the grand passageway, and Jonan did not remember how he got there. As he and Soblinsk walked past knots of merchants, diplomats, and courtiers talking, a few glanced Jonan's way, but most ignored him. That stiffened his spine as nothing else had today. *When next I walk here*, he promised himself, *they will all bow to me*.

Even at that hour, when gray skies and swirling snow clouded the tall windows, and burning candles provided the only glitter reflected in the huge mirrors, the Gallery of Glass held a magnificence and beauty like no other room in the palace. The noise of conversation was loud, almost drowning out the zithren music being played in the background. Ladies were tittering behind their hands, their heads close together. A pair of dashing young lords in elegant attire were setting up a game of quick-fingers and calling out for others to join or lay bets. Servants moved unobtrusively about, filling braziers with hot coals beneath the tall windows to counteract the icy drafts, or serving sweetmeats, comfits, and mead.

Suddenly hungry, Jonan gazed with longing at a tray being carried past him. When he reached for a comfit, a sharp look from Soblinsk stayed his hand.

"Go forward," Soblinsk murmured, and gestured.

Jonan focused his gaze on the runner of carpet beneath his feet, following it to the throne. The throngs of people did not part for him, and many turned away from Soblinsk in hauteur.

Jonan scowled at these slights to his friend, but Soblinsk seemed not to care. The count stayed close, steering Jonan through the crowd as together they made their way to the far end of the room and stopped near the edge of the dais.

Carved of wood, the throne's tall back was draped with a white beyar hide, somewhat rare. A darker beyar hide served as a rug. An iron ring was still bolted to the floor where once Jonan's father had kept a half-tamed lyng chained while he gave audiences. Jonan remembered the huge predatory cat lying there, its tail twitching back and forth as though it might spring.

"Stand here, facing the room," Soblinsk whispered to him, scattering the memories.

Jonan felt as though he'd become a huge block of wood. He watched Soblinsk gaze slowly about the long room, taking measure of the bribed guards positioned at either end. Feeling horribly self-conscious, Jonan swallowed with difficulty. Every idle glance cast his way made him certain Mirengard would be noticed. His hands were sweating. He tried to remember to breathe steadily and deeply in order to hold down his panic.

On the opposite side of the room, Sofina appeared and smiled at him. She stopped next to Lord Thum, looking pretty in a gown of a soft rose, her golden curls visible beneath a filmy veil that gathered in graceful folds on her shoulders. Jonan marveled at her courage in talking to the minister of state. Lord Thum was powerful and influential; he could order their arrest for treason if he grew suspicious.

"Your majesty," Soblinsk whispered, "please don't stare with your mouth open. You've gone as white as your linen. What's wrong?"

"Sofina is with Lord Thum!" Jonan gasped out in alarm.

"Of course she is. I told her to hold his attention with conversation," Soblinsk said calmly.

"But he can ruin us!"

"Not so loud," Soblinsk said, looking about sharply. "He suspects nothing."

"The m-minute I d-do what I'm supposed to, he'll order us arrested."

Soblinsk's dark brows drew together. "He has no authority save by the order of the king. As soon as you take the throne, Thum is finished, and can give no order. Besides, these guards are loyal to you."

"Oh, yes." Jonan sighed in relief. "I forgot."

"Stop thinking so much and just concentrate on your part," Soblinsk said pleasantly, although his teeth seemed to be gritted. "I assure you I've overlooked nothing. Do what you're told and leave the rest to me."

Wheezing a little, Jonan nodded. He wished it were all over with. He did not think he could endure much more.

"I am going to talk with Archduke Minshilev," Soblinsk said, and held up his hand before Jonan could protest. "We can't both stand here. It would look strange. Wait for my signal. I'll give it *after* the courier makes his announcement. Watch me and no one else. Is that clear?"

After Soblinsk moved away into the crowd, no one came up to speak to Jonan, and he began to feel a perfect fool. Surely he looked suspicious, standing there alone as he was. Because the throne was located near one of the tile stoves, the warmth at this end of the room made him far too hot under his cloak.

Sweating heavily, he started to fling off the garment; then realized just in time that he could not do so without revealing Mirengard at his side. Horrified at how close he'd come to making a fatal mistake, he clutched his cloak tighter around him and stood there trembling.

"Are you ill, Jonan?" Vladno asked. "You look like you're

ready to faint. Or don't you understand that when you are indoors, standing within a few feet of a stove, you needn't wear a cloak?"

The lady clinging to the archduke's arm giggled, and Vladno smirked with the mockery that Jonan so detested.

"I'm not ill," Jonan said curtly. "I wear my cloak because I want to."

"Of course you do. Oh, and I saw you come in with Count Soble."

"Soblinsk."

"Ah, yes. Lives in a swamp, I believe. One of the old traitors that supported the tyrant. Why do they hang about the court? It's pathetic, the way they hope for sinecures and positions that are impossible."

Jonan frowned. "He's—"

"You'd do well not to befriend such a man," Vladno broke in sharply. "He's never been officially received, and his presence here is an affront. I'm going to speak to the chamberlain about having him put out. Aye, him and that ripe bit of tartlet he calls his daughter."

"Take that back!" Jonan said furiously, advancing on Vladno. "You will not insult the lady!"

"Are you championing her?" Vladno asked with a lift of his brows. Surprise and a touch of pity filled his face. "Morde, Jonan, she's no lady but clearly a—"

"Make way! Make way!" came a shout.

Conversations died around the room, and people parted as a road-stained courier came striding in. He paused in the middle of the room and looked about swiftly. Ice coated his mustache and eyebrows, and the snow layering his cloak and fur cap had not yet begun to melt.

Forgetting his anger with Vladno, Jonan held his breath as Lord Thum met the courier. The archduke, urged by his companion, moved away from Jonan to a position where he could see better. Jonan stood rooted in place, his pulse pounding so hard in his ears he could barely hear what was said.

"My lord," the courier said hoarsely to Thum, "I come from Drev."

"Good news of the battle, I trust?"

"Nay, my lord. The battle is lost. We took a defeat."

A roar of consternation went up. Women cried out, and men angrily shook their heads.

"Shameful. Shameful!" Count Unshalin's loud voice said over the general hubbub. "To lose to Gant. It's unthinkable!"

"If our king had led them, we'd have a victory," elderly Count Estev said in a quavery voice. He lifted a frail fist. "We need our valiant king!"

Prince Tustik pushed his way through the crowd to the courier. "How bad are the losses?" he asked quietly. "Have Gant forces advanced into Nether?"

"My lord, the army is in disarray, but there is worse news. The queen is dead."

Craning his neck, Jonan saw Thum's face turn white. Tustik shut his eyes and lifted a hand to his face. Across the room, people began calling out to Thod, clutching their Circles, some weeping openly. Others stood stunned, while, out in the passageway, servants wailed. Breathing hard, Jonan groped beneath his cloak for Mirengard's hilt, felt a tingle shoot through his fingers, and jumped as though bitten. His fear came rushing back, and he knew he could not hold the sword.

"This is the end of us, the end of Nether," old Count Estev was saying tearfully.

At that moment one of the guards stationed near the door called out, "Long live King Jonan!"

Another guard echoed him. "Long live King Jonan!"

Silence fell across the gallery, and belatedly Jonan happened to glance at Soblinsk, who was gesturing.

Jonan gasped and reached under the cloak as he turned and stepped onto the dais. He stumbled but managed to catch his balance. When he gripped the hilt of Mirengard, he felt a jolt of pain shoot through his hand all the way to his elbow.

He cried out, but somehow managed to draw the sword. The pain was excruciating, making sweat break out across his face. He struggled to lift Mirengard but couldn't hold it aloft. Indeed, it was all he could do not to fling it away from him.

"King Jonan!" the guards cheered.

The stunned courtiers looked at each other and began to

make slow obeisance. A triumphant Soblinsk pushed his way forward. Sofina stood with her hands clasped together, beaming radiantly. And as he gazed out at the faces with his hand on fire and his heart racing, Jonan tasted glory.

I really am the king, he thought in amazement.

Soblinsk pointed at the throne, and Jonan belatedly remembered the rest of his instructions. He turned, letting Mirengard's tip drag on the floor, and had just started to sit down when a deep, unmistakable voice called out, "Sit on that throne, whelp, and you die."

Someone in the room screamed.

Jonan whirled around and found himself staring at Faldain, who had appeared behind the throne as though by magic. He did not notice the private door still standing ajar in the wood paneling. All he could see was Faldain, towering head and shoulders above him; Faldain, looking gaunt and haggard as though he'd walked back from the gates of perdition; Faldain, garbed in sumptuous dark blue velvet trimmed with lyng fur, jewels glittering across his tunic and on his hands, his black hair sleek and gleaming, his gray eyes like chips of ice in a face without mercy. Pale of visage and terrifying, he looked like a ghost to Jonan, a ghost from the second world come to stalk and haunt those who had turned against him.

In panic, Jonan dropped Mirengard with a clang on the floor, but he was too terrified to run.

Advancing implacably on Jonan, Faldain stretched out his hand. "Give me that sword."

Certain he was going to die, Jonan stood there with his mouth open, desperately gasping for air.

"Pick it up, Jonan," Faldain commanded.

Jonan's hand was throbbing still. He glanced down at Mirengard's shining length, the blade brightly polished, the hilt jewels glittering in the candlelight, and he knew that as soon as he handed Faldain the weapon he would lose his head.

Trembling all over, he wet himself. Shame made him weep, and he held out his hands in supplication. "Please," he gasped. "Please!"

"You would be a king, Jonan," Faldain said mercilessly. "A king must have a weapon. Pick it up."

"I—I—forgive me, but I can't!"

"Did it burn your hand?"

Jonan nodded.

"And you held it anyway."

"I—I had to."

Faldain stopped less than a stride away. His gray eyes bored into Jonan's. "Why?"

"I thought you were dead, sire! I'm your heir. I had to hold the sword in order to prove myself, but I . . ." He let his voice trail off under Faldain's gaze and wiped his nose with his sleeve. "I thought you were dead."

Faldain's gaze bored into him. The room at Jonan's back had fallen deathly silent.

Jonan continued to cry, for he'd known something would go wrong. He'd known he shouldn't take such a huge risk. And now, he was done for.

"Kneel," Faldain commanded.

Certain this was the end, Jonan stared at him fearfully. His knees would not hold his weight, and he sank down, bowing his head.

"Pick up the sword, and hand it to me."

"I can't touch it. It burned me."

"Will you refuse the king's command?" Faldain shouted.

The candles burning near them went out, and the room seemed to shake for a moment. Jonan heard a queer sound overhead. Glancing up, he saw one of the globes of king's glass trembling on its chain as though it might shatter from the force of Faldain's anger.

Panting, Jonan forced himself to touch Mirengard. The sword's magic repudiated his hand with such heat he cried out and sat whimpering.

"Do you not know that as long as the king is alive, Mirengard will let no other wield it?" Faldain asked.

Jonan's mouth trembled. He wept harder and nodded.

"And still you proclaimed yourself king. What is that, Jonan?"

"T-treason, sire."

"Treason," Faldain said harshly. "By your own confession.

Did you know that years ago when you were a child in the dungeons I was advised to execute you?"

"Please," Jonan whispered. He flung himself flat on the floor and tried to grasp Faldain's foot for mercy. Faldain shifted himself out of reach.

"For years, I have been your guardian and protector, Jonan. And this is how you have repaid my forbearance."

"Don't kill me. Please, your majesty," Jonan pleaded. "Please! I—"

"Pick up the sword and hand it to me."

Jonan's eyes were burning with tears. His fear overwhelmed him, and yet he could not disobey that voice like iron. Slowly he forced himself to pick up Mirengard, this time by the blade rather than the hilt. He cut himself, and the pain was swift and intense against the throbbing burn in his palm. His blood dripped on the bright steel as with trembling arms he lifted the weapon to the king.

Faldain's pale hand gripped the hilt with surety and confidence. The king swung the weapon aloft as though it weighed no more than a straw, and the blade sang through the air. The courtiers cheered, and Jonan closed his eyes in anticipation of his beheading.

"Take off the scabbard," Faldain commanded.

Astonished, Jonan opened his eyes. He gawked at his cousin, wishing Faldain would stop tormenting him and get this over with.

"Are you deaf, Jonan? Take off the scabbard!"

Hastily with fumbling fingers, Jonan obeyed him and handed it over.

"On your feet," Faldain said.

Hope began to trickle through Jonan's terror. With widened eyes, he staggered upright and faced Faldain. "You aren't going to k-kill me?" he whispered.

"Am I a barbarian, to run you through in my own palace before the witness of ladies and gentlefolk?" Faldain retorted scornfully. "You will be put to trial, Jonan, and you will name all who have helped you in this infamy."

By then, Agya warriors and more guards were streaming into the gallery. The bribed guards tried to flee, but were quickly overcome. Jonan glanced over his shoulder for Soblinsk, but did not see the count. Astonished at how quickly his adviser had abandoned him, Jonan realized he was on his own. Although he'd escaped execution at this moment, his ordeal was far from over. The thought of being tortured nearly made him plead for mercy again, but he knew it would avail him not.

Lord Thum and Prince Tustik were approaching the dais. Thum was grinning. "Well done, sire! Your timing was impeccable. Had I not known to expect you, I would have jumped a foot."

"You knew the king had returned," Tustik said to him in astonishment, "and you did not tell me? Lord Thum, I must protest this cruelty in keeping us ignorant."

"It had to be done," Faldain said. "From the moment I met Thum's agents on the road and learned of the plot planned against me, I pledged all involved to secrecy and had myself smuggled into the palace." He turned to Jonan. "I arrived last night, barely, it seems, in time to stop you."

A look of horror was slowly spreading across Tustik's thin face. "How much did your majesty overhear before you entered the room?"

"None of it save that paltry cheer for *King* Jonan."

"Please," Jonan blubbered. "Oh, please—"

"Then your majesty doesn't know," Tustik said, wide-eyed. "Oh, merciful Thod, I know not how to repeat the news about the queen."

"What news?" Faldain asked with a frown. "Where is she?" Before Tustik could answer, he turned on Jonan. "If you've harmed her, by Thod's wrath I'll—"

"She's dead," Tustik broke in. "The word just came by messenger from Drev."

Bewilderment and grief crossed the king's face. Faldain stood as though stunned, turning even paler than before, and Jonan thought he might swoon. But he held himself together and, after a moment, said in a voice no stronger than a whisper, "What took her to Drev? How can this be?"

Tustik started to answer, but a gesture from Lord Thum stopped him. The minister of state's hazel eyes, more hostile and cold than Jonan had ever seen them, turned on Jonan. "Perhaps this traitor would care to answer the king's questions?"

Horrified and mute, Jonan shook his head.

Never shifting his gaze from Jonan's face, Thum began to explain about the war, and how the queen had deemed it necessary to visit the troops until Jonan felt he could bear it no longer.

"It's a lie!" he burst out. "A lie. The message is false. We planned it so in order to seize the throne today. She isn't dead."

Faldain's head tilted back with an expression of raw relief, and he passed his hand across his eyes.

Hope dawned in Jonan. His cousin would be merciful, Jonan told himself. Faldain always forgave a transgression, for he was a kind and generous man.

"It was just a trick," Jonan said, anxious to please now. "I don't even know the real outcome of the battle."

Thum was nodding as though he'd suspected the truth all along, but Tustik was staring at Jonan wrathfully. A tide of color surged into his bearded face, and his fist suddenly knocked Jonan to the floor. "You fiend!" he shouted. "You damned, sniveling, wretched fool!"

Jonan's face felt numb. He lifted his hand to his jaw, probing cautiously as he scrambled up. "How dare you strike me? I am the heir to the throne! I deserve—"

The tip of Mirengard touched his chest, and Jonan's terror came rushing back.

"You are a traitor," Faldain said coldly. "And condemned for it." He stepped back and gestured to his men. "Take him to the dungeons."

"No!" Jonan screamed, but two of the Agyas grimly seized his arms and marched him out. "Not the dungeons!" he shouted, struggling and trying to plant his feet, but they kept him moving.

Out in the passageway, an irate crowd of guards, onlookers, and servants milled about. Several individuals rushed at Jonan to strike him and spit on him. The Agyas shouted in an effort to clear their path, but to no avail.

Suddenly Jonan felt himself shoved bodily against the wall. As the Agya on his right grunted and sagged, Jonan found himself staring at Soblinsk, wild-eyed and holding a bloody dagger.

The other Agya guard attacked, but Soblinsk parried the blow and yanked Jonan out of the way. "Run to the Hall of Kings!" he ordered, and went on fighting.

Without hesitating, Jonan plunged through the crowd. Shouts went up as men tried to grab him, but they hindered each other, and Jonan kicked and shoved his way clear. Behind him came a death scream, but he dared not look back to see if Soblinsk lived or died. Ducking his head, he ran for his life.

Shouts and the thud of running footsteps told him he was pursued. With terror giving his long legs speed, he darted along the passageway, leaped down the stairs, and made his way for the ancient Hall. The second part of their plan had been to secure possession of the Chalice immediately after Jonan was proclaimed king. According to Soblinsk, this would solidify Jonan's position and guarantee that he stayed on the throne.

Now, with disaster falling all around him, Jonan simply understood that if he got hold of the Chalice, he could bargain his way out of the palace alive.

Flinging himself into the Hall, he found the place unlit save for a single burning torch. The officer who was supposed to be there had vanished. Gloomy and cold, the Hall could prove to be a trap if he did not figure out the way into the secret chamber. Hearing louder sounds of pursuit, Jonan knew he had scant minutes.

Desperately, he plucked down a sword from the wall and held it awkwardly in his hand as he searched behind the paneatha for the control lever that would open the trapdoor. In his haste, he knocked over the paneatha, and its gilded icons went flying across the floor. He hardly noticed his desecration of the holy objects as he pushed and pulled every piece of carving on the wall.

Finally, just as the doors were slammed open, he found the right place. With a rumble, the trapdoor slid open. Forgetting the torch, Jonan hastened down the steps into the secret cham-

ber. His foot slipped, and he went tumbling, to land on the dirt
floor at the bottom with a jolt.

Gasping and groaning, he rolled himself over and climbed
awkwardly to his feet. He'd dropped the sword, but there
wasn't time to hunt for it in the gloom.

The chamber around him was small, almost like a cave. He
saw the altar within the circle of white stones and felt his heart
lurch at all the pagan effects on top of it. What was he doing
there, he wondered frantically. He'd just wanted to be happy
and liked. He'd never meant to take things this far. Where
were the men Soblinsk said supported him? Why did no one
come to protect and help him?

Longing to give himself up, but knowing he did not dare,
Jonan looked around fearfully until he saw a pillar of black
stone at the rear of the room. And on it stood the Chalice.

Awed by the sight of it shining pale and holy in that otherwise unlit chamber, Jonan regained his determination. The
Chalice was his only hope.

"Get him!" came a shout, along with the sound of footsteps
hurrying down the steps.

Jonan ran to the Chalice and swiftly made the sign of the
Circle in respect. "I'll guard you!" he whispered to it. "I'll put
you in the cathedral where you belong. Cardinal Winnder will
give me sanctuary."

As he spoke, he reached with both hands to lift the Chalice down. For a moment the vessel felt cool and clean in his
hands. Certain it would heal his burned palm and hoping it
might even infuse him with strength and courage, Jonan
turned at bay to face the guards.

"Stop!" he cried, and they halted near the altar.

In the gloom, he could barely see their faces. But their
menace was clear enough. The faint light glinted off their
weapons.

"Defilers!" he shouted at them. "You bring death and
swords into this holy presence." He'd forgotten all about the
weapon he'd dropped and lost. "Get back, and let me pass! I
am the keeper of the holy Chalice now. I—"

Light and fire exploded around him. Blinded and nearly
deafened, Jonan dropped the Chalice and stumbled back. He

was overwhelmed with heat, an intense heat that seared him right through his clothing. Then he smelled burning cloth and burning flesh, and realized he was on fire. Screaming, staggering, and unable to see, he blundered into the wall and beat at himself, trying to put out the flames.

"Thod have mercy!" he screamed, but the fire went into his mouth, choking him. He collapsed, writhing in agony, and only dimly grew aware of hands grappling with him, hands rolling him into a cloak and smothering the fire while icy cold water was doused over him.

But the flames were in his lungs and heart, burning him from the inside out. He tried to scream, but it was too late. There was only the all-consuming pain, then eternal darkness.

PART IV

Chapter Twenty-Six

A large stone hurtled across the chamber at Tulvak Sahm.
Glimpsing it from the corner of his eye and caught by surprise, the *sorcerel* barely had time to lift his hand. The stone
veered away from him, missing him by a hairbreadth, and
smashed into the wall. Bits of rubble and dust fell onto the
brightly patterned carpet. Slowly, trying to master his anger,
Tulvak Sahm left his stool and turned to meet the child's gaze.

For a moment there was silence, broken only by the hiss of
fire in the braziers and the soft, rattling sigh of the tiny
shapeshifter perched on Tulvak Sahm's shoulder.

Tashalya's blue eyes were bright and icy with defiance.
Shackled by one ankle, the little girl was dirty and unkempt,
her once fine clothes in tatters, her dark hair hanging un-
combed and matted around her face. She glared at him in
open hatred.

He glared back, so annoyed he was almost tempted to slap
her. Not that it would avail him to do so, for he knew she
would only unleash worse behavior in retaliation. Ever since
she figured out how important she was to him, she'd lost most
of her fear. During lessons she might be a termagant, scream-

ing insults and refusing to cooperate, or she might sit meekly absorbing what he had to teach her, only to turn the lesson or skill against him later at an unguarded moment.

As she'd just done. He'd been transfixed by the horoscope he'd been casting, fascinated and a little puzzled by the new change in what the stars foretold. Busy making notations for further study, he'd lost track of everything else—including Tashalya. Had his reflexes been fractionally less quick, she could have cracked his skull with that stone. Hurled with all the power of her ruthless mind, it had been a deadly missile intended to kill rather than annoy. She was getting quite strong and skillful. His eyes narrowed to slits. She was getting dangerous.

"That was unwise," he told her.

Her chin lifted with the quick, rebellious pride he'd been unable to quench. "I will get you yet, demon-eyes."

"If I die, so will you die," he said.

Her expression did not change. She said nothing.

"Do you want to starve to death in this cavern, alone?" he asked. "Thirsty and hungry, alone in cold darkness?"

"I'll get away."

Tulvak Sahm reached up with his taloned forefinger to stroke the breast of his little shapeshifter. It moaned faintly and leaned against his neck, its venomous jaws parting in pleasure. "But perhaps you would not have a chance to starve. My pet would eat you first, and make you Nonkind."

Her eyes widened, then she frowned so furiously he knew he'd frightened her. But it wouldn't last. Tulvak Sahm turned back to his casting table, but although he gazed down at the chart, for a moment he did not see it. Instead, he found himself experiencing unexpected frustration. Never before had he attempted to train a more promising pupil. Never before had he encountered one so stubbornly determined to defy and thwart him. By this stage in the training, the lure of the magic usually entranced a pupil into eager obedience, but thus far Tashalya had resisted the darkest threads of his magic. Perhaps she was simply too young to be corrupted as yet. He'd found no way to befriend her or seduce her trust. Nor had he been able to trick her often. She learned with brilliant ease, and her potential was even greater than he'd at first believed.

She was, he told himself yet again, growing far too dangerous to keep. But the challenge intrigued him, and he was determined to conquer her.

He stroked the shapeshifter again, sending the faintest trickle of magic through his finger until the tiny creature was almost drunk on it, then he murmured and sent the shapeshifter flying across the chamber to land just inches from where Tashalya crouched on the floor. Shaking its leathery wings, it hopped at her, making her flinch, and screeched.

She screeched back, imitating its cry, but Tulvak Sahm sensed her fear beneath the show of bravado. Smiling to himself and knowing the shapeshifter would keep her distracted for a while, he went back to his work.

A voice tickled the inside of his mind. He frowned, turning away from his charts, and gave unspoken assent before leaving the heated chamber with its sumptuous draperies and carpets to duck into a smaller room. This one was a bare cave devoid of furnishings and comforts. Moisture glistened down one stone wall, collecting in a tiny, bottomless pool near the back. Somewhere, in the dark distance, Tulvak Sahm could hear the faint drip of water. The air smelled cold and dead.

He waited, tucking his hands into his wide sleeves to mask his impatience at this interruption, and a moment later mist and smoke filled the small space. A fire-knight emerged, bringing a glimpse of flames behind him that vanished as the cloud dissipated. He stood before Tulvak Sahm, garbed in armor made of thin slices of obsidian. His gauntleted hand rested on the hilt of his sword; his other hand held a short wand for traveling through the second world. Smoke curled through the visor slits of his helmet, and he brought with him the stink of ashes and sulfur.

Recognizing him by the patterns in his mind, despite the fire-knight's shielding to keep his thoughts hidden, Tulvak Sahm felt a spurt of anticipation. Had Ashnod forgiven him? Was his return to the dark god's favor to be sooner than he'd hoped?

"What brings Lartk to me?" he asked.

For answer the fire-knight lifted his hand and traced the letters of a single word in midair from tiny, dancing flames: FALDAIN.

Tulvak Sahm lifted his head with a sharp inhalation of breath. "Faldain is dead, killed by my minions."

"Not dead," Lartk answered, his voice a scratchy growl. "Lives."

"Impossible!" Tulvak Sahm said, spreading wide his hands. But already the veils were parting between his fingers, and he saw a vision of Faldain alive and walking about a richly appointed room in conversation with a red-haired man. Faldain looked gaunt, and there was the shine of spell fever in his pale eyes, but he was unmistakably alive. Fury speared Tulvak Sahm. He clenched his fists, ending the vision with such force, the cave ceiling cracked overhead with a small rumble of shifting stone, and little trickles of dust rained down.

His mind flashed to the Grethori *sheda* and the bargain they'd struck. "Betrayed," he whispered, his eyes narrowing to slits. "She'll pay for this."

"The Chief Believer wants an accounting," Lartk said hoarsely.

The threat made Tulvak Sahm stiffen. "I have been repudiated by Gant," he said formally. "I need not account for anything."

Lartk drew his sword slowly and extended it so that Tulvak Sahm could see swirling patterns of golden sparks running along the blade. "Lartk has been empowered to combat you, if necessary. Give the accounting and be spared."

"A fire-knight against a *sorcerel*?" Tulvak Sahm sneered. "I can crush you like an insect."

"Lartk is under orders. What has been done against Faldain? Why his son and heir killed? Why him nearly killed?"

"He should have died," Tulvak Sahm muttered, curling his long fingers. "I paid well for it."

Slowly Lartk lowered his sword but did not sheathe it. "Why?"

"He robbed me of my position, I—who had been privy to Nether's deepest secrets and able to pass them on to Believer agents, I—who exercised the strongest influence over Nether's king. Faldain took that away, and the Chief Believer blamed *me*!"

"For this you seek his death?"

"Yes!" Tulvak Sahm hissed. "I seek his destruction, him and all his house. I seek his suffering and annihilation. Mere revenge is not enough!"

Smoke blew through the slits in Lartk's visor. "All this have you done without instruction."

Tulvak Sahm uttered a harsh laugh. "I know the Chief Believer once wanted Faldain to be rendered Nonkind and kept under his control. But that failed, and is it not better to have Faldain broken and dead, and all of Nether in chaos?"

"But you have failed," Lartk said harshly.

"I am not finished yet!"

"You have failed, and you have aroused the wrath of Faldain and his mate. War has been declared against Gant, and already battle has been joined. Never before have Netherans fought in their season of great cold, but they fight now. We have had to retreat, shamed by their ferocity. They blame us for deaths of children and attempted death of king."

"They were supposed to blame the Grethori tribes," Tulvak Sahm muttered. "I took great care to lay a misleading trail."

"Not misleading enough. The deception did not work, and much trouble have you caused."

"And I will continue to give Faldain trouble until he is finished," Tulvak Sahm said.

"It is for Chief Believer to say when Gant will attack Nether, when Gant will strike at king."

"If the king had died, the Chief Believer would praise my name," Tulvak Sahm said angrily.

"But Faldain lives. And you did not know."

The *sorcerel* muted his rage, for at heart he was appalled by his mistake. He had been too confident in trusting the *sheda* to do what she'd agreed. Occupied with Tashalya, he hadn't bothered to check on the Grethori after seeing Faldain struck down in battle. He had seen no need.

"Back you are to go to second world," Lartk said, and lifted his sword.

"Wait!" Tulvak Sahm flung up his hand, but released no power. He was not yet willing to fight Lartk, for despite his confidence, he knew such a battle would leave him mauled. It might even destroy his lair. "In Ashnod's name, I do not deserve such a fate."

"Lartk does not judge. Lartk executes orders."

"But you must explain to the Chief Believer that I can yet guarantee Faldain's death."

"Faldain is protected by the Chalice of Eternal Life. He cannot be reached by *magemons* or *sorcerels*."

"But he can be lured beyond the Chalice's area of protection. And when he is, he can be destroyed." Tulvak Sahm bared his fangs and beckoned. "Come and see his weakness."

Lartk followed him into the larger cave and stared a while at Tashalya, who was hurling tiny fingers of fire at the shapeshifter, which darted and snapped at them in a game. Tulvak Sahm barely concealed his astonishment. The wretched child was *playing* with his familiar. He had counted on her ingrained fear of Nonkind to keep her in bounds, but she had surprised him once again by reacting in an unexpected way.

"What is this?" Lartk asked finally.

At the sound of his ruined, guttural voice, Tashalya glanced up and gasped. She scuttled back against the wall and stared wide-eyed and alert.

"This," Tulvak Sahm said proudly, "is Princess Tashalya, firstborn of Faldain. Tashalya," he called, switching to Netheran so she could fully understand what was said, "behold your first look at a fire-knight."

"Gantese," she whispered, and her blue eyes narrowed at Lartk with undisguised hostility. Suddenly she stood up straight, fists clenched at her sides. "My father fought a fire-knight named Quar and defeated him! My father humiliated the Chief Believer and escaped Ashnod! If he were here, my father would defeat you!"

Tulvak Sahm braced himself to defend her life if Lartk attacked her, but a strange, raspy noise came from the fire-knight. After a moment Tulvak Sahm realized Lartk was laughing.

The fire-knight pointed at the child. "Good courage," he said in approval, still speaking Gantese. "Does not fear Lartk."

Slowly Tulvak Sahm released the tension in his muscles. "If Faldain is told where to find her, he'll come to the lure."

"Good. Lartk will take child to Chief Believer to make trap."

"No!" Tulvak Sahm said sharply. "She stays with me. She is mine."

Tendrils of smoke thickened around Lartk's helmet. "Is good you caught her, but now she goes to Chief Believer."

"No, I want the trap to be set here. Faldain will come here alone, but he won't ride into Gant without the entire Netheran army. Does the Chief Believer want Gant invaded that way?"

Lartk tilted his head to one side thoughtfully. Turning on his heel, he strode back into the smaller cave where he was just a shadow in the dim light. "You will make this trap quickly—"

"No, not yet," Tulvak Sahm said. "I need more time."

"Why?"

"I am training Tashalya to be a *sorcerelle*. She is not yet corrupted into accepting Ashnod."

"How long?"

Tulvak Sahm thought swiftly. He knew that he could afford no more mistakes. If the Chief Believer chose to unleash several trios of *magemons* against him, he could perish in the battle, and he did not want that. But if he succeeded in destroying Faldain, he would be received back into favor.

"I will set the trap when the cold season ends."

Lartk brandished his sword. "Too long!"

"No! Faldain cannot journey here through blizzard and gale. And I must finish turning the child to our ways."

"Why?"

"Because," Tulvak Sahm said angrily, "before he dies, I want Faldain to see his precious daughter worshiping the glory of Ashnod. Even as he dies, he will suffer."

"Better he not die," Lartk said. "Better he become Nonkind as Chief Believer always intended."

"Then I shall do that," Tulvak Sahm said. "I swear it."

Lartk inclined his head and sheathed his sword. "I will tell all you have said to Chief Believer. His orders will I bring to you, and you will obey."

"I don't—"

Lartk spoke a single word that appeared in midair in flames, and the cloud of smoke and mist reappeared. Without hesitation, Lartk stepped inside it and vanished, leaving only a smell of sulfur behind him.

Thoughtfully, hoping the Chief Believer would agree to let him handle things his way, Tulvak Sahm returned to the larger cave, but as he entered its warmth and light Tashalya said shrilly, "My father isn't dead! I just read your thoughts, and you've been lying to me."

Not giving him a chance to respond, she screeched at the shapeshifter, and the small creature launched itself into the air, flying right at Tulvak Sahm's face with a slash of its talons. The *sorcerel* reacted instinctively, hurling fire from his fingertips that exploded the shapeshifter into a small cloud of noxious-smelling ashes.

Tashalya shot him a look of blazing triumph and laughed. "Poor little pet. It loved you, and you killed it."

She went on laughing that false laughter of mockery and contempt. Appalled at what he'd done, at what she'd tricked him into doing, Tulvak Sahm felt his wrath gathering into a fiery ball inside him. He curled his hands into claws, shaking with the effort to control himself. After a moment he turned and left her, for only his fear of Ashnod's wrath kept him from destroying her on the spot.

Chapter Twenty-Seven

Across the city of Grov, bells were ringing in celebration. With less than a week before the feast of Selwinmas, a victory in a major skirmish against Gant, and the safe return of their long-absent king, the people were rejoicing openly in the streets. Nobles and prosperous merchants traveling about in horse-drawn sleighs tossed coins to the poor with extra generosity. Pious folk streamed into Helspirin Cathedral and smaller chapels to begin a series of prayer and ritual. In the central square, mummers in vivid costumes performed the Miracle of Selwin before crowds of excited onlookers. Pilgrims, many of them eldin, flocked to the venerable Tree of Life outside the city. They formed circles around the massive tree and sang hymns and chants older than time. Serfs and citizens alike trekked up the hill to the palace gates, gathering there in the snow to cheer the king's name.

Inside the palace, servants bustled about, stringing garlands of greenery over doorways in the eld tradition. Fragrant boughs of firs and pine perfumed the air. Merchant princes brought costly gifts for the king and dispensed largesse among the courtiers in hopes of fat new trade contracts for the coming year.

The courtiers, busy with fittings of new finery ordered for the feastings and banquets about to commence, spent lavishly on clothing, jewels, and the selection of expensive gifts to exchange with friends and family. After such an intense period of mourning and uncertainty, the king's return and the swift stamping out of Jonan's rebellion had brought an upsurge of relief and gaiety. They were, perhaps, a bit giddy in their readiness to rejoice and anxious to disconnect themselves from any appearance of treason while the king's agents still combed the palace.

As for the king himself . . . he vanished from view, retreating to his private apartments behind heavily guarded doors, and all save a select few were denied access to his majesty.

Awakened by a stealthy sound nearby, Dain jerked upright, reaching for the dagger beneath his pillow, and found himself confronting an equally startled Thum in the gray light of daybreak.

His friend's freckled face slowly stretched into a cautious smile. " 'Tis only I, sire."

Ruefully Dain smiled back and relaxed, tossing the dagger aside. "Your pardon, old friend. I forgot where I was."

"Understandable, I'm sure, considering what you've been through. I did not intend to wake you—"

"Of course you did." Yawning, Dain rubbed his face and shivered. For the past three days he'd slept hard, waking only to eat and talk briefly to Thum or Tustik. He'd asked Thum to notify him the moment Alexeika returned. Realizing that must be why Thum was here at this hour, Dain raked back his hair and looked eagerly at the door. "The queen—"

"Aye," Thum said with a smile. "She arrived at dusk yesterday."

Dain frowned. "Why wasn't I informed? I gave specific orders—"

"Easy, sire," Thum said calmly. "No one forgot your instructions, but her majesty was weary from the journey. She went straight to her apartments to rest."

"Oh, of course." Again Dain looked at the door. He longed to see her. There had been times, during his struggle out of the snow-enclosed wilderness, when he thought he would not survive to see her again. And even once he staggered to the garrison and found aid, then later encountered Thum's men who were searching for him, the journey home had been one of urgency, frustration, and hardship. Caught twice by blizzards, they'd nearly perished of the cold, and only the thought of returning to Alexeika kept Dain going. Now he flung aside his blankets. "Why does she tarry in formality, waiting for my permission? Bid her enter at once."

With a frown, Thum put out his hand to keep Dain in bed. "Priest Dazkin is here, not the queen," he said.

Disappointment filled Dain. He shivered. "Oh."

"You're cold, sire," Thum said, pulling the covers around him. "Dazkin wanted to be sure of your majesty's health. He thinks that perhaps your majesty needs another drink from the Chalice."

As he spoke, Thum turned and beckoned. Two individuals emerged from the shadows and advanced to the bed of state. Behind them, Dain saw a sleepy servant, roused no doubt by the sound of voices, arrive with a burning candle in his hand, but was turned back by the protector on duty.

Dazkin, garbed in his blue robes, folded his hands together and bowed low to Dain. "If your majesty will permit, I have come to repeat the ritual."

Still shivering, Dain wrapped himself more tightly in his covers. "Let that servant back in to build up the fire."

"Sire, the room is warm," Thum said quietly. "'Tis your fever that makes you cold."

"And your majesty's illness that keeps you abed when by now you should be rested and hale once more," Dazkin chimed in. He gestured at his companion, who had hung back in silence. "Will your majesty permit my friend to also attend you?"

Dain squinted at the man through the gloom, and his nostrils caught a whiff of sky and forest. He smiled. "Eld, you are welcome here."

The eld came forward and gestured in the eldin way of respect. He was slight of stature, his pointed ears barely visible beneath a white cap of hair that curled and moved about as though stirred by wind.

"This, majesty, is Nilainder, Guardian of the Tree of Life."

"We have met," Dain said in pleasure. He returned the eldin gesture of greeting and saw Nilainder smile briefly. "But seldom do our paths cross. Are you a healer?"

"I have some talents," Nilainder said modestly, "but I am not an acknowledged healer."

"You understand the situation?" Dain asked, fighting off sudden fatigue that made him long to sink down. "The spell, some foul Grethori—"

Nilainder raised his slim hand, and Dain did not complete his sentence. "I understand," he said in his soft voice. "If we are permitted to now attend your majesty?"

Dain, secretly worried because the first drink from the Chalice had not been sufficient, nodded and allowed Nilainder gently to press him down onto his soft pillows. The eld's hand was cool and dry against Dain's brow. His touch was immensely comforting, and Dain sighed without being aware of it.

Thum, concerned and watchful, stood aside while Dazkin began to utter a soft-voiced prayer and opened a small wooden box heavily carved with interlocking circles. When Dazkin fell silent, Nilainder, who had not removed his fingers from Dain's brow, traced the newly healed scar on Dain's temple and began to hum.

It was a soothing, wordless song of health and life, goodness and decency. Half-closing his eyes, Dain began to hum in harmony with Nilainder's song, and let the eld draw out his shame, heartbreak, and rage. Memories of the *glimmage* swirled briefly in his mind and faded. The humiliation at how he'd been tricked ceased to sting. He knew he would never forget what had happened among the Grethori, but the festering effects of the spell were fading quickly. Nilainder's song changed, and Dain fell silent. Nilainder used words now, and they conjured up an image of a long wooden splinter, a splinter filled with the rottenness of Grethori magic and evil. And as he sang, the splinter was extracted from Dain, hurting him until he lay tense and sweating. Gritting his teeth, he made no sound, doing his best not to fight Nilainder's effort, and at last it came out of him.

He felt it go with a relief so overwhelming he nearly

moaned. A dark shape hovered over him for a moment; then Nilainder spoke a sharp word of command, and it drifted like a tiny dark cloud toward the window. "Let it out," Nilainder whispered.

Thum rushed to open the window. A gust of icy air blew into the room, and the cloud vanished. Thum slammed the window shut and bolted it. "Great Thod," he choked out. "What was—"

"Please be quiet, my lord," Dazkin said.

Dain's head was swimming, and he felt strangely as though he were floating, but Nilainder's grip on him tightened, lifting him, while Dazkin took a glass vial from the wooden box and poured it into a cup of pure eldin silver. Praying over it, he put it to Dain's lips.

"Drink, majesty, and be restored," he murmured.

The water was clean and cold, so pure and sweet of taste that he gulped it too fast and nearly choked. Vaguely he was aware of Nilainder's soft words soothing and encouraging him. Strength flowed back into his limbs. The pain left him, and he no longer felt cold and weak.

Draining the last of the holy water, he smiled and looked up at them.

"Ah, yes," Dazkin said, smiling back. "That is better."

"The fever is gone," Dain said, and sent Nilainder a look of gratitude. "The spell is no longer on me."

"No," Nilainder said wearily, "it is gone. Were I a true healer I could have destroyed it."

"That you removed it is enough," Dain told him.

Nilainder looked at the window. "Let the wind blow it far from here, where it can fasten its evil on no one else." He bowed to Dain. "Forgive me for the pain. A true healer would have spared you that."

"A small price to pay," Dain said. "I am grateful, Nilainder. And to you as well, Priest Dazkin."

The priest, having put away cup and vial and closed the small box, smiled. "I would the first drink could have accomplished all this, sire. Now we must go. These matters are not for those who are arriving to attend your majesty."

And indeed, faintly in the distance Dain could hear the

sound of approaching voices and footsteps. He sighed, aware that with his health restored he could fend off the normal routines no longer. As king, he was not permitted even to get up and dress without procedure and custom.

Dazkin and Nilainder were ushered to the private door by Thum, who then returned to Dain's bedside just as the main doors opened and the lords of the bedchamber streamed in. They were quiet, their eyes big with curiosity, but when they saw that Dain was awake, they relaxed, smiling, and began to chatter among themselves.

None of them were permitted to address him directly at this stage in the proceedings. The master of the bedchamber approached with a bow, and asked Thum, "Will his majesty arise this morning?"

With equal formality Thum turned to Dain, who nodded fractionally. Thum turned back to the master of the bedchamber. "It pleases the king to do so."

Retreating, the master of the bedchamber gave the signals, and servants entered, one bringing fresh wood for the stove fires, another bearing a tray of food, another bringing a basket of petitions, a fourth laden with gifts from various courtiers, and so on. The royal valet threw open the clothes chests and began to lift out selections, while in the bathing chamber fires were kindled to begin heating water.

Lord Omas, looking thinner than of old but hale, to Dain's joy, arrived to relieve the night protector. Bowing to the king, he shoved forth a scrawny old man who served as the official taster. With his stomach growling, Dain waited while the taster sampled every dish of his breakfast and even his mead. Omas grunted in satisfaction and gestured for the man to withdraw.

Dain set to eating, enjoying the food with new appetite. For the first time in weeks, he felt marvelous in body and well rested. Chewing, he gestured for Thum to commence his morning reports.

"The investigation is proceeding," Thum said. "More arrests were made in the night. We've caught perhaps forty implicated thus far, and my agents are combing Grov in hopes of catching more. The plot seems to have been centered primarily inside the palace. And under my nose," he said angrily. "I should have been paying more attention."

"While you were in Mandria?" Dain asked, and reached for a dish of stewed millet sweetened with honey. "Or while you were advising the queen to lead a battle against Gant?"

Thum's hazel eyes narrowed. "Your majesty is remarkably well informed."

"Not well enough," Dain said. "I did not expect to be abandoned by the men I sent with Jonan to safety. Nor did I expect to return to insurrection."

"Jonan was responsible for both. That young fool," Thum said in angry disgust "After all you did for him, to turn against you at the first opportunity."

Dain had no regret to spend on his cousin. With a grunt he shoved the tray aside. "A pity he did not live to name his co-conspirators."

"Will your majesty order a funeral?"

"Nay!" Dain said with such vehemence the gossiping courtiers paused to look at him. He lowered his voice. "Have him buried next to his mother in Traitor's Field, and let that be an end to it."

"The leader of the plot was apparently a man named Soblinsk."

Dain nodded grimly. "I remember Tustik warning me against the scoundrel. He seems to have gained influence over Jonan speedily."

"He was killed in the fight. The woman with him, masquerading as his daughter, has vanished. We'll find her," Thum promised. "These old traitors are hard to stamp out, but eventually we'll get them all."

Dain was not so sure. He frowned a moment, wondering why Alexeika still had not come. In the past, whenever he was away, she always came through the private door, blushing and eager to welcome him home. Even if the room was full, as it was now, she usually peeped in long enough to send him a smile.

But of course, he told himself, she'd no doubt been informed that he'd returned without Tashalya. This time, he would have to go to her.

"Sire?" Thum said, interrupting his thoughts. "Are you growing fatigued? Are you still unwell?"

Dain glanced up to see the fresh worry in his friend's eyes. "No!" he said briskly. "I'm well, I assure you." Then he dropped the false brightness from his tone and scowled at his fists. "How can I tell the queen?" he asked in frustration. "How can I tell her that they sold Tashalya to a Gantese agent? How in Thod's name do I get her back from *there*?"

Dismay filled Thum's face, and he stared at Dain with compassion. "Oh, sire."

"I would rather have seen the child's slain body hanging among the trophies in that Grethori camp than think of her at Sindeul. By now she's in the clutches of the Chief Believer, probably being tortured, corrupted, or rendered Nonkind."

Racked with anguish, he bowed his head. Thum moved swiftly to block him from the sight of most of the courtiers, and unobtrusively squeezed Dain's shoulder.

"I'm sorry," he whispered. "I am not yet a father, but what you and Alexeika have gone through this autumn is more than flesh and blood should have to bear. My prayers have been with you both."

Closing his eyes against stinging tears, Dain nodded and struggled to master himself. He could not break down here, he told himself. He had to appear to be strong, no matter how much he grieved and suffered inside.

"I'll send word to my spies along the border," Thum said softly. "'Tis mortal hard to infiltrate Gant itself, but I'll try to pick up what word I can. Perhaps . . . Samderaudin can help."

Hearing the slight hesitation in Thum's voice and well aware that his old friend still belonged to the Reformed Church and disapproved of the *sorcerel's* presence at court, Dain straightened up with a nod. "Thank you," he managed to say.

Thum's hand dropped from his shoulder, and he turned about as the master of the bedchamber approached once more.

"If his majesty has finished eating, water for his ablutions is now ready."

Dain, who had spent the years of his youth breaking the ice skim atop a water pail before washing up, sighed and tossed aside his covers. At once, a lackey hurried up with his dressing robe, and the master of the bedchamber himself threw the garment around Dain's shoulders.

Ignoring these ministrations, Dain gave Thum a nod. "Do what you can," he said. "And have someone inform her majesty that I will come to her within the hour."

Later, when she received him, Alexeika looked more beautiful than ever. Softly rounded by her pregnancy, her dark hair coiled out of sight beneath a veil of pale pink silk, she wore a gown of a matching color, loosely fitted and extremely becoming. White ermine trimmed its bodice, and diamonds glittered in her ears. Her eyes, the color of the sea on a cloudy day, looked enormous in the pale oval of her face.

When Dain walked into her sitting room past the curtsying ladies-in-waiting and other attendants, she rose from her chair and made her obeisance to him. Her little dog barked and ran excitedly back and forth between them, wriggling and panting. Alexeika straightened, and her gaze seemed to be drinking Dain in.

Breathless at the sight of her, surprised anew at how beautiful he found her, and glad to be home, he smiled and reached out his hand. "I have missed you, beloved."

Her grave expression did not change, but something hardened in her eyes, and she hesitated visibly before grasping his hand. Her fingers felt icy cold in his, and with shock he realized that she must know all that had occurred.

"Your majesty," she said with cool formality.

Pain, guilt, and disappointment were tumbling through him. He frowned slightly and released her hand. Conscious of the people staring at them, he hesitated, unable to find the words he needed to say.

The constraint between them was like a wall. He had never known such awkwardness in her presence since they'd wed. He hated it, hated himself, and gathered his courage slowly.

"Alexeika—"

"She is not with you. You did not find her."

In a way, it was a relief to discuss Tashalya. He allowed himself to be deflected, and told himself that perhaps it was only her disappointment about the child that he sensed and nothing else. "I did not find her," he admitted quietly.

Alexeika closed her eyes with a sharp grimace of anguish.

Dain glanced at the others. "You may all withdraw," he commanded.

They hurried out, agog with curiosity but not daring to linger. Dain couldn't understand why Alexeika had received him so publicly when she knew they had intimate matters to discuss. Impatiently waiting until the door finally closed behind the last person, he swung back to her.

"I found the tribe that took her. I fought the man who killed Ilymir," he said, and realized he was trying to defend his failure with a pathetic list of his deeds.

"Did you kill the savage?" she asked harshly.

He sighed. "No."

Her face grew pale and tight. "You swore you would bring Tashalya home," she said, still using that flat, cold voice.

"I know. They had already sold her to a Gantese agent."

"You've never broken your oath to me before," she said.

He met her eyes and found them without mercy. "No," he agreed softly. "Come thaw, I'll ride into Gant if—"

Her fist smacked into her palm. "Oh, do not speak such foolishness! If she has been taken to Sindeul, there's no way to get her back. The Chief Believer will use her against you in some vile way, force you to make some treaty that puts Nether back into the darkness with it."

He could not bear to see her so hurt and angry, yet he dared not approach her when she was like this. "Alexeika, we'll think of something. Thum's men will seek any information they can learn. I'll consult with Samderaudin—"

"He won't help you. He'll say he can't find her, and when he parts the veils, the seeing will be dark," she said bitterly.

"I'll find a way."

"Make me no such promise," she said, her face puckering. "Do not swear to something you cannot do."

"Alexeika—"

"I've lost all of them now. I felt so rich, so blessed. I was happy, Faldain! Was it a sin to be happy with my life? Now the nursery lies empty, with all of my precious ones lost to me. When this babe is born, who is to say he won't meet a similar fate?"

She looked so fierce and anguished he dared not take her in his arms and hold her. Miserable, he wished he could give his kingdom to undo the last few weeks. Then something she'd said finally penetrated his thoughts, and he frowned at her.

"Empty?" he said. "What mean you?" A terrible fear clutched him. "Not Mareitina, too?"

Alexeika would not meet his eyes. "Mareitina has been taken away by the eld healer you sent for. He said she had to leave us, that she could not live among us."

"Who told you that," Dain asked sharply. "I will send for Nilainder at once and—"

"He took her. He brought an eld healer here, and they took her," she said bleakly. "I didn't want to give her away. Why should I have to lose her, too?"

Rubbing his brow, Dain began to pace back and forth. He understood that from her birth Mareitina had been more eld than her siblings, and he'd been aware that probably when she grew older and lost some of her dependence on Ilymir and her mother that she would choose to go and live among the eld folk. But she was presently too young for such a wrenching separation. Surely Nilainder had not told Alexeika it would be forever.

"A misunderstanding, I'm sure," he said. "I'll speak to the guardian and deal with the matter. You—we haven't lost her, beloved."

Alexeika appeared not to hear him. She was staring at the far wall, her gaze bleak and distant, her hands folded quietly over the mound of her belly. He hesitated, thinking that he should leave her and not upset her further. Being pregnant made her tearful and unsettled enough without him adding more bad news to her burden.

And yet, he knew that if he did not force himself to tell her everything, then he would never tell her. Already his guilt was a burden he could hardly bear. If he kept this secret, it would lie between them forever, driving them farther apart.

But if he told her when she was in this mood, he reasoned, he might lose her forever. She was going to be terribly hurt.

"Alexeika," he said and stopped, for his courage was deserting him.

"Yes?"

"Alexeika, while I was held prisoner in the Grethori camp, I was tricked—"

"Are you confessing about the woman?" she interrupted stonily. "I know you have been unfaithful to me. You need not labor through an explanation that is shameful to you and a source of pain to me."

He blinked but did not ask how she knew. "It was a spell—"

"Yes," she broke in again. "I know about their lust spells. Did you lie with her on the Adauri stone under a full moon? Did she wear painted designs on her naked skin? Was she beautiful?"

He closed his eyes, for this was much worse than he'd anticipated. "She was made to look like you. I was injured. I didn't realize the truth until it was too late."

"Strange that a woman can resist such a spell if she has sufficient will, but a man cannot."

"She looked like you! I thought she was you until the spell broke." He frowned, his fists clenching as the horrible memories spilled over him anew. "I don't know what kind of—of creature it was, Nonkind or something worse, but it wasn't even a real woman, just something made of magic and loathsome." He made himself look up. "I'm sorry, more sorry than I can express. When I discovered what it was, I tried to destroy it, but I couldn't do even that."

Silence stretched between them. She was frowning fiercely, her lips clamped together while tears slid down her cheeks.

He hated to see her cry. His strong, valiant Alexeika, who could withstand almost any kind of trouble and had more courage than most men—no, he did not want to make her cry.

"Beloved," he whispered, trying to take her hand. Glaring at him, she backed out of reach. He sighed. "I know I have failed you, our daughter, and our marriage. It was not intentional. I did my best, but this time it was not enough. I know you're disappointed and hurt. I hope you will forgive me."

She dashed the tears from her eyes. "Of course," she said, not looking at him. "Of course."

"Alexeika—"

She whirled around to put her back to him. "My pregnancy is official. May I have the king's permission to retire into seclusion?"

He stared at her in anguish and did not know how to get through the barrier between them. "Alexeika, please. I need your understanding."

"But you have it!" she said angrily, still turned away from him. "I understand you very well. Now may I be secluded? If I do not withdraw from court life, I will offend your subjects. I have offended members of the Council already in trying to keep your throne for you."

"I owe you my deepest gratitude for what you've done in my absence," he said. "I knew I could rely on you."

She walked over to an ornately gilded and inlaid desk and from a drawer pulled out the royal seal and the Ring of Solder. She held them out to him. "I have kept these safe."

At the moment he cared not a skannen for either of them, but he took both objects. "Alexeika,"

"You see, you trust and rely on me," she said in a voice too light and false, "but I, it seems, cannot feel the same about you. I found a way to fulfill my obligations, despite the cost. You—"

"I swear to you that I was tricked."

Her eyes flashed with rage. "Oh, forget the cursed woman for a moment! You would not even warn me that the Kollegya wants my complete withdrawal from all political matters. Tell me, sire, once you accede to their demands, when am I to see you? During supper banquets? By appointment? In public audiences in the Gallery of Glass?"

"That isn't—"

"My influence over the king is considered unseemly and inappropriate," she said as though quoting someone. "Why didn't you tell me? How long have they been pressuring you to put me aside? And how many other secrets do you keep?

You promised, when I agreed to wed you, that you would let me be a part of your life. You said you wanted my counsel, my help in ruling your kingdom."

"I do! I always have."

"I wonder. Since you have not seen fit to defend me to them—"

"Alexeika, you know the power of the Kollegya. They make life a misery at times and—"

"Then why don't you take away their power? You're the king, not their lackey! All you need do is exercise your authority and squash them."

It exasperated him that she'd chosen to drop their personal issues to discuss political ones. "I have chosen to rule not as a tyrant, but with order and according to law."

"The Kollegya is not part of Netheran law!"

"But its existence stretches back over a hundred years. The tradition of it—"

"Is nothing if they thwart you and render you weak at every opportunity. Unshalin supported Jonan's claim to the throne. Are you aware of that?"

"But I am sure he was merely supporting the legalities of the succession—"

"You could change the laws of succession if you chose. You could make it possible for Tashalya to succeed you, if you were brave enough to make new laws."

He looked at her bleakly, wondering if she realized what she was saying. Tashalya was in all likelihood gone forever. But he couldn't say that aloud. He could barely stand to think it.

"New laws can wait until more of the kingdom is rebuilt," he said wearily, having scant interest in this argument. "There's too much to do—"

"Oh, yes, there's always more to do than can be done. You have to choose what you will make important. And you're so determined to preserve everything from the past that you've jeopardized the future."

"A little at a time, Alexeika. Too much change too quickly—"

"And what has your caution accomplished? Had Jonan

managed to suborn more than just a handful of guards, you could have been slaughtered in your own throne room! You listened to the Kollegya when they urged you to use Grethori auxiliaries, and look what happened! They've no business holding such power, not when they're such fools! On and on it will go, as long as you do not put your feet on the neck of the Kollegya and teach it to serve *you*, not the other way round."

After all these years, she still had a tongue as sharp as a blade. His eyes narrowed as he sought to suppress his temper. "We can quarrel about this later. It's us I want to—"

"You are the king, and I am your consort," she said impatiently. "We cannot be separated from anything that involves the realm."

"Don't be so pompous. You know that isn't true. We're people first, Alexeika, man and woman, husband and wife, parents. We've lost our children, and we need to find a way to deal with our loss together."

"I have done my grieving alone," she said coldly. "I buried Ilymir alone. I gave Marcitina to the eldin alone. I have waited and waited for Tashalya to come back while you have been gone, and all that time I have been alone."

"That's not fair," he said angrily.

"Fair? Nay, sire, there's nothing fair about any of this."

Her voice cracked with strain, and, abruptly, she buried her face in her hands, sobbing as though her heart would break. He could keep away from her no longer. Cautiously, he gathered her into his embrace, but she stood stiff and unyielding in his arms.

"Please," he whispered, wanting back the woman who'd delighted in his touch. "We have a new child coming. Let us mend this rift and try to go on as best we can. Please, Alexeika. I have done my best, but I'm not a perfect man. It's time you accepted that and stopped holding me on a pedestal the way you did your father. Even the general was probably not as perfect as you believe."

She jerked away from him, white-faced and glaring, and slapped him across the face. "I suppose you expect me to forget them?" she said furiously. "Forget my son—"

"Our son."

"Forget Tashalya? Think of what she's suffering right now. Think of how she must still be hoping her papa will come and save her. You risked your life and your realm once to rescue a golden-haired foreigner you barely knew. Can't you do at least the same for your own daughter?"

"I—"

"Well, now the long cold is on us. You have all winter to think of what you will do," Alexeika swept on, heedless of his pain. "But when thaw arrives, I expect you to scrape together what honor you have left and at least keep your promise."

Her cruelty and inconsistency left him stunned. "And if I can't do it?"

For a moment she looked stricken and lost. "I don't know," she whispered, and fled into her bedchamber with a slam of the door.

Alexeika hardly knew what she was doing as she shot the bolt. All she could think about was getting away from him. How could he talk of failure and forgiveness and expect her to agree to such rubbish? How dare he try to hold her in his arms, as though she would lose her senses enough to forget what he'd last held? Unable to bear his description of his adultery, unable to listen to his plea for her understanding, she'd lashed back at him any way she could. He, the highest-born individual in the land, still felt himself somehow inferior to the Kollegya, still refused in some measure to be the king he could be. And she found herself torn between her anger and disappointment and the desire to stroke the lines of worry and defeat from his dear face. She had never seen him beaten before, and it frightened her. She did not want to believe her Faldain could be anything less than the heroic, honorable man she'd always thought him to be.

Hadn't she lost enough, she thought angrily. Must he now break down all she revered in him?

There was silence on the other side of the door. He did not call to her. After a few moments she heard him leave. Tears stung her eyes, and she wished she had not left things like this. Although he'd hurt her in so many ways, the cruelty she'd just shown him gave her no satisfaction. She had not been raised to be vindictive or unfair, but Faldain deserved punishment.

It was as though something larger than herself had taken charge of her. She was surprised by the depth of her rage and alarmed by how viciously she'd attacked him. She wanted to unbolt the door and go after him in an effort to work out all that divided them. She wanted to be back in the shelter of his arms. It had taken everything she had moments ago not to give way. She wanted to be with him so terribly. But too much had happened. She could not believe he expected a simple apology sufficient to mend her broken trust. And thus she stood where she was, awash in misery but too stubborn to bend, and every beat of her heart hardened it more.

Chapter Twenty-Eight

On a cloudless spring day, with sunlight shining over the pines and sending snow melting into streams, the *sheda* stood in the center of camp, shaking her staff and chanting as the *glimmage* strained to give birth. A bright yellow-and-red robe covered the flat Adauri stone, on which the *glimmage* lay. Cloth ties restrained her from thrashing too much. In recent weeks, as the spell grew older and weaker, she'd begun to fail. It had taken all the *sheda's* magic and determination recently to keep the *glimmage* alive, and now, although the birthing was early, there was no choice but to bring the dragon-child to life before the spell failed completely.

Pain pierced the *sheda's* abdomen, and she doubled over, moaning aloud as the *glimmage* arched and struggled. Two of the *mamsas* hurried over to support the *sheda* and keep her from falling, while the rest continued to chant. Glazed with sweat, the *sheda* lifted her head and saw the crowning. When the babe slid forth into a *mamsa's* waiting hands, the *sheda* screamed the birthing cry that the mute *glimmage* could not utter and broke the spell. The *glimmage* crumbled to dust on the filthy robe.

Shouts of excitement rose up from the watching tribespeople, but the *sheda* wasted no time expressing her joy, for this was the critical moment. The baby was not yet anything save a squirming, semiformed lump of pink flesh, slick with birth fluids, and dangerously vulnerable.

Swiftly she slashed her wrist with a ritual knife and let her blood flow over the newborn. Lifting her fingers to the sky, she called down the force of the wind and joined it to the strength of the ground. From the eagle soaring over the mountain peaks, she called forth fearlessness. From the wolf roaming in a nearby canyon, she called forth cunning and strength. From the trees swaying in the breeze, she called forth endurance. From the fossilized droplets of dragon's blood in her necklace, she called forth ferocity.

Weaving words and magic together, she infused the child with these potent elements until arms and legs began to form, then small hands and feet. As the baby kicked vigorously, her chanting intensified until the head took shape. Small eyes opened first, glaring and wild, then the nostrils and mouth.

It squalled furiously, while she wove an additional spell to render it male, hurrying now to complete him. Had there been time to carry the child to full term, she could have given him the magic more slowly and carefully.

Then the task was finished. Swaying, she felt herself dangerously close to collapse, yet a sense of triumph strengthened her. Closing her eyes, she gave thanks to the gods for the knowledge and skill necessary to bring the deliverer to life.

"Is it done?" Chuntok asked.

She opened her eyes to find the chieftain staring at the baby with wonder and a touch of fear.

Good, the *sheda* thought. *Be afraid, for he will grow up into the most fearsome leader this world has ever known.*

Summoning the dregs of her strength while a *mamsa* hastily bandaged her wrist, she shook her staff until the bells and tiny skulls jingled. "It begins," she said proudly, casting a protection spell over the child to safeguard him from Chuntok's jealousy. "Behold our deliverer!" she cried out to everyone in the camp. "He will lead all the tribes in a vast horde, and all pale-eyes will he kill or drive forth from our territories, to trouble us no more. He will stride the world. His eyes will be as fierce as the sun. And all will fear his name."

Wailing, many of the people knelt, but Chuntok remained on his feet. Scowling, he shot a glance at his son.

"Wonder not," the *sheda* said to him with a cackling laugh. "Your boy will be named chieftain after you. There is time for you both to know a warrior's glory and a warrior's death before this child grows to manhood."

Chuntok frowned at her prophecy, but because he was a man and proud, he voiced none of the questions that were so obviously teeming in his mind. "What will you call this deliverer?" he asked instead.

She tilted her withered old face to the sun and drew in a deep breath. "The gods have willed his name to be Anoc."

"Anoc," the women of the camp murmured.

Wrapped in a swaddling cloth, the baby was held up for all to see.

"Who will serve as his wet nurse?" one of the *mamsas* asked, and three young women stood up eagerly.

The *sheda* shot them a look of contempt before pricking her finger and shoving it between the baby's toothless gums. He fussed a moment, and then began to suck her blood. Smiling, she cooed to him, aware that he drank her magical powers as well as her life force. She would feed him all of herself until she died, but by then he would be able to survive on his own.

So had it been foretold. So would it be done.

In the royal palace at Grov, a spring thunderstorm crashed and boomed until the very turrets shook and the windows rattled. Sheets of rain flooded the steps, courtyards, and gardens. Water gushed off the roof and gurgled through the stone gutters. Out in the deer park, lightning struck one of the trees and brought it down with a crash of flaming sparks. But the downpour swiftly put out the fire, and no harm was done.

Pacing back and forth in the vast bedchamber of state, Dain sought to remain calm while Alexeika labored in the huge bed to bring forth their child.

She screamed, and his heart seemed to stop, but a sudden flurry of activity from the physician and his attendants told Dain that the birthing was nearly over. He held his breath, not daring to come closer, while Tustik, Unshalin, and Thum all stood near the bed as witnesses of the royal birth. Tustik was expressionless; Unshalin looked slightly green; Thum seemed both fascinated and embarrassed. The baby loosed a feeble wail, then suddenly cried with force. A nursemaid wrapped it in a white cloth, cleaning the muck from its red face. Tiny fists waved furiously.

Swept with relief and delight, Dain went forward, to be met by a grinning Thum.

"Your majesty has a son!" he said gladly. "Accept my congratulations."

Dain nodded, finding himself speechless.

While Alexeika was attended to, the baby was brought to him. Holding the warm, squirming bundle, Dain found himself gazing down into a pair of vivid blue eyes set in a round face with a pointed chin. A tuft of black hair stood straight up atop the infant's head.

The baby stared up at Dain, studying him in turn, and Dain sensed his vigor and keen intelligence. Smiling, Dain found himself eager to watch this new little life unfold and explore.

"My son," Dain murmured, as the baby furrowed his brow and yawned. "Welcome to this world. Whatever befalls you, know that you are blessed of Thod and loved by your parents. We rejoice in you."

Gently he kissed the baby's cheek and gave him back to the nursemaid, who carried him to Alexeika. She lay exhausted, her dark hair lying tangled on the pillow, her eyes glowing with pride.

She looked up at Dain and smiled, and for that moment all was as it had once been between them. He took her hand and kissed it, thinking of past occasions when they'd shared joy over the births of their children. Because it was always his custom to shower her with gifts, he now slipped a necklace of vivid enameling studded with sapphires into her fingers and smiled at her.

"Alexeika—"

Her gaze, however, went to the baby, and she gathered her son close to her breast, cooing and murmuring to him. Dain watched them tenderly, grateful to see her happy once more.

"My deepest congratulations, sire," Tustik said. "May I instruct the chamberlain to arrange the celebrations?"

Nodding, Dain found Alexeika's gaze on him. His heart leaped, but with a frown she swiftly looked down. The door between them shut once more. Although his hand clenched at his side, he made sure nothing showed on his face, especially with everyone watching. Recently, as Alexeika neared her time, he'd believed that perhaps her anger against him was softening a little.

A fortnight past, he had met with the eld folk and brought Mareitina home for a visit. Their blond daughter had outgrown some of her chubbiness and looked hale and happy. Her large blue eyes seemed to find the palace and all in it strange, as though she'd forgotten her home, but she clung to Dain's neck with her old sweetness, whispering, "Papa, Papa." When he'd taken her to her mother, Alexeika had lit up with such joy he felt certain they could become a family again.

Alas, Alexeika shared her delight only with Mareitina, and when Mareitina had asked to go home to the forest as soon as she saw the new baby, Alexeika grew remote once more.

Dain's remaining hope was that the baby would reconcile them, but he saw now that it was not to be so. She would use the infant as an excuse to shut him further away.

"And the name of the child?" Tustik asked as though he'd noticed no constraint between the royal couple.

With an effort Dain forced himself to smile at the old man. "Ah, how sly you are, lord prince. You think you will trick me into revealing his name before the banquet, but such tactics will not work."

Tustik smiled, his black eyes shining with amusement, and bowed to Alexeika. "Your majesty," he said to her, "I rejoice at this blessing Thod has seen fit to grant you."

"Thank you," she replied, her voice tired but content. Her eyes drifted closed, and she slept.

Next to Dain, the physician cleared his throat, and reluctantly Dain turned away. He could have stood watching over her and the baby for hours, longing for one and delighting in the other, but he walked with the physician to a private corner.

"Sire," the physician said softly, "did the potion I mixed for you have no effect?"

Dain had no intention of telling the man that he hadn't drunk the foul-smelling stuff. There was no remedy against what tormented his dreams, but the physician—arrogantly confident in his skills—refused to accept that.

His dreams came every night, usually fearsome encounters with Nonkind and Grethori or old battles in which friends and loved ones were slaughtered. Sometimes he jerked awake in the darkness with Tashalya's screams echoing in his ears. He'd lost more weight, to the despair of his tailor, and beneath his eyes were dark circles of strain.

"Sire," the physician said a bit more sharply, "did you not hear my question? I was asking if the potion had given you ease."

Displeased with the physician for showing more concern for him than with Alexeika, Dain frowned. "How fares the queen?" he asked.

"Her majesty does very well," the physician replied. "She enjoys splendid health, and this birth was not as difficult for her as the last."

"The twins made her suffer cruelly."

"This is a fine, healthy boy, but her majesty should stay in bed for several days and not tax her strength too quickly."

"Are you suggesting the celebrations should be delayed past the usual time?" Dain asked in concern.

"No, I believe that might cause the people unnecessary worry," the physician said slowly, as though his words held another meaning. "Many have already expressed concern for your majesty—"

"There is no need for concern about me. I do not sleep well, 'tis all."

"Your majesty has been saying that all winter, but insufficient rest can cause many ills. How long can your majesty grieve and blame himself for what he could not have prevented?"

Dain's gaze grew cold. "You overstep yourself, physician."

"Forgive me, your majesty. I spoke only from concern."

"Let us confine our discussion to the queen's health."

The physician sighed. "If perhaps the banquet and naming ceremony could be delayed an extra day, that would allow her majesty to enjoy the festivities in better fettle."

"Of course." Nodding, Dain turned away and found Count Unshalin waiting to speak to him.

Portly and pompous, Unshalin bowed. "My felicitations, sire. His highness looks to be a healthy, stout little fellow."

Aware that Unshalin would have preferred the child to be a girl, therefore leaving Dain without an heir of his body, Dain inclined his head with a courtesy he did not feel. "You are very kind. Thank you for serving as an official witness."

Never mind that Alexeika had protested vehemently against having Unshalin in the room. Never mind that Dain had deferred to Unshalin's prominent position in the Kollegya. He'd done it because he wanted no whisper, no rumor against this birth. Every protocol had been followed to the letter, and although it would not spare his son from future criticism, at least it was proven that the baby was a boy and honestly born.

Dain was walking away from the count when without warning a cold feeling of foreboding passed through him, robbing him of breath and causing his knees to buckle. He threw out his arm and caught himself against the wall, but not quickly enough to avoid notice. They all came running to cluster around him. Omas and Thum reached him first.

"Sire!" Thum said in concern, gripping Dain's elbow. "What ails you? Omas, fetch a chair for his majesty. Someone, bring him wine."

"I'm all right," Dain said irritably, shaking off Thum's hand as he was persuaded to sit down.

The physician clasped Dain's wrist and shook his head. Afraid they were going to awaken Alexeika with their noise and fussing, Dain pulled away from him. "You will attend the queen, not me. I tell you I'm fine. I require you not."

The physician backed away, as did everyone save Thum

and Tustik. They stood over Dain while a servant came hurrying with the wine. Omas intercepted the cup, sniffing its contents and pouring a tiny measure into a thumb-sized beaker to taste it. Only then did he hand the goblet to Dain.

The wine tasted dry and sour, withering Dain's tongue. He took only a single swallow before thrusting it away.

"Drink it down," Thum urged him worriedly. "It will strengthen you against swooning."

"Morde," Dain muttered. "I am not about to swoon."

"Must you argue and pretend we did not witness your faintness?" Thum asked with sharp exasperation. "Drink the wine."

"Your majesty is extremely pale," Tustik said.

"Please, sire," Omas pleaded.

Dain drank another swallow and grimaced. "I like this not. 'Tis as sour as Thirst cider."

The men exchanged glances, and Omas said softly, "That's good vintage from southern Mandria, as sweet and fine as ever I've tasted."

"Then you drink it," Dain said. "I'll have no more of it."

"Shall I send for Dazkin?"

"No," Dain said sharply. "I've no need of him. I—" He broke off as another queer, cold sensation passed through him. With a blink he abruptly found himself in a forest of tall trees barren of foliage. The wind sighed in mournful gusts, blowing so cold it seemed to freeze his veins. There was no snow, only bare dirt. 'Twas a desolate place. He stared around in amazement, wondering how he came to be here.

"Papa!"

It was Tashalya's voice, frantic and faint.

"Papa, help me!"

He turned about, staring in all directions, his heart thudding painfully beneath his ribs. Then he saw her, running through the trees with her dark hair streaming out behind her. And he began to run, too.

He tried to call her name, but his throat was frozen and mute. Although he quickened his stride, he could not catch her. Something dark and indistinct chased her, and in alarm he tried to warn her.

But still he could utter no sound. As though somehow she sensed his presence, she halted and whipped around to stare in his direction. Waving, he headed for her, but something unseen tripped him, and he went sprawling hard across the barren ground.

The jolt knocked him out of the vision, and he found himself back in the chamber of state, disoriented and panting for breath. His body ached as though he'd traveled through the second world and come back in the blink of an eye. Frowning, he stared down at the Ring of Solder on his hand. It was not glowing with power and felt cool and normal on his finger. Whatever had just happened, he thought in a daze, had not occurred because of its magic.

"Sire?" Thum was saying urgently. "Dain!"

Rousing, Dain saw his minister of state kneeling before him. He started to speak, but suddenly the effort seemed beyond him. *Tashalya*, he thought in despair, *why can't I find you?* Thinking he was going mad, he lifted his hand to his aching head and rubbed the scar on his temple.

"Your majesty should rest," Tustik said. "Too much excitement for today. It has been said that a birthing can be harder on the expectant father than on the mother."

Rather surprised that Tustik, usually the most serious of men, was actually making a joke, however mild and out-of-date, Dain summoned a wan smile for him. "There may be truth in that."

"Shall I escort your majesty to the winter bedchamber?" Omas asked.

"Yes, his majesty had better go," Thum said before Dain could answer. "He needs some sleep."

Sleep, Dain thought with scorn, rising to his feet before anyone could assist him. *Sleep had become the enemy.* And now his dreams tormented him even when he was awake.

He wanted to stay with mother and child, but he knew his attendants would not leave him in peace with his family, and if they kept fussing over him, they might wake Alexeika.

Wistfully, he stared at her sleeping face. *If only we could talk*, he thought, longing to run his fingers through her silky hair and touch the warm smoothness of her skin. He missed her as his friend and companion. This coldness and formality between them hurt him more than any loss he'd ever faced. Nothing he did or said reached her heart, and he had nothing left to try. If only he could have brought Tashalya safely home, Alexeika might have forgiven him the rest. As it was . . .

Sighing, he turned about and saw Omas and Sir Pyron standing near the door with their heads together. Omas was talking, while Sir Pyron kept shrugging. As soon as Omas saw Dain looking his way, he left Sir Pyron and came to take his usual place at Dain's side.

Aware that excited courtiers were gathered outside in the passageway, Dain departed instead by the private door and took refuge in his study, where he seated himself at the fancifully carved desk that had been his grandfather's.

The clerk on duty—scrawny, chinless, and always nervous—dropped a scroll case and managed to stammer out congratulations. Dain nodded and picked up a list of appointments for the day. "This has changed," he announced, crumpling the parchment. "Have Samderaudin come to me at once."

Thum put his hands on the desk and leaned forward to scowl at Dain. "You should rest."

"I've had all winter to rest. Now there's too much to do." Impatient for his friend to go, Dain looked up into Thum's worried eyes. "When I grow tired, I'll stop. My word on it."

Thum shrugged. "Nothing I say seems to persuade you."

"That's right," Dain said briskly. "Ah, Samderaudin," he said, surprised by the *sorcerel's* swift arrival. Lightning flashed outside the window with a violent boom of thunder, and rain rattled the glass violently.

Thum shot the *sorcerel* a startled look and, clutching his Circle, stepped aside to let Samderaudin glide up to the desk.

Samderaudin's yellow eyes looked at no one save Dain. "Your majesty saw the vision?"

"Vision?" Thum echoed. "What—"

Dain had no intention of discussing the matter before his friends. Gesturing at Thum and Tustik, he said, "You may withdraw, my lords. Consider yourself free until tonight's festivities."

Given their dismissal, they had no choice but to bow and retreat in obvious reluctance. As soon as the door closed behind them, Dain rose to his feet. "Lord Omas, please go outside."

The large protector scowled, but obeyed without protest.

Alone with Samderaudin, Dain frowned. "How do you know about my vision?"

"I, too, guard the king in my own way," Samderaudin replied. "Does your majesty understand what was seen?"

"Of course I do!" Dain said eagerly. "A waking dream . . . or a vision . . . or a visit." He frowned. "Was she in my dream or I in hers?"

"Both, perhaps. It is as though you parted the veils of seeing and stepped through to another place."

"I don't understand."

"You have done so before."

Dain thought of the night years ago when he'd been in Savroix-en-Charva, dreaming of meeting Tobeszijian on the beach, and in the morning found his leggings wet and sand on his feet. "Aye," he said warily. "But it can't be the same. I remained here physically this time. I only looked into another place."

"How you got there is less important than why."

"Agreed. I heard her call to me in my dreams a few nights ago, but this time I *saw* her. I nearly reached her. I think, if I hadn't tripped, I would have—"

"As I sensed," Samderaudin said with disapproval.

Staring at him, Dain felt sudden suspicion. "Do you now dare to spy on my dreams?"

"I was not there," Samderaudin replied. "I merely sensed your danger."

"Did you halt me?"

"Yes."

Furious, Dain shot around the end of his desk. "You dared interfere! You—"

"I sensed danger around your majesty, and I acted to protect you. That is all."

"*All!*" Dain shouted, then hastily lowered his voice so

Omas wouldn't come into the room. "I nearly had her. A few more steps—"

"What would you have done?"

Dain was so angry and frustrated he couldn't find words.

Samderaudin stared at him coldly. "If Tashalya truly walks through your dreams, then there is a chance to rescue her. It means that she has grown stronger in her absence, strong enough to reach through the magic that conceals her from my searches. I wish you had talked to me of this when you first dreamed of her. We could have perhaps been prepared for what happened today."

"Can you find her now?" Dain asked quickly. "Has she been concealed all this time in the second world?"

"No. She could not endure it long. Do not confuse the second world with the place of dreams. They are not the same. She is a clever child, but what she does is dangerous and can harm her if she is not careful."

"And if her captors realize what she's doing?" Dain asked worriedly. "What will they do?" Fretting for her, he began to pace back and forth. "If only she thought to tell me where she is. If necessary I will ride there with my army and—"

"You have become a moth, throwing yourself at a flame because you can see nothing else," Samderaudin said. "Heed me, Faldain. Your army will avail you not in this matter."

"'Twas a place of dead trees and bare ground," Dain said, so busy trying to recall such a region that he barely heard what the *sorcerel* said. "I've never seen a forest like it."

"The world of dreams resembles none other."

"The next time she calls to me, I *will* reach her. If I can actually grasp her hand—"

"No, Faldain. You cannot do what is necessary. You lack the knowledge."

"But—"

"How would you return?" Samderaudin asked.

"The way I always do."

"It is one thing to return from your own dream. It is less easy to exit the dream of another. And how would you bring the child with you?"

"Tell me."

"No. This is not a task for you."

"Who, then? You?"

Samderaudin nodded.

Dain began to feel cold and uneasy. With narrowed eyes, he shook his head. "Tashalya is my responsibility. Teach me what to do."

"You lack the skill and the knowledge to do what must be done."

"Teach me."

Samderaudin snorted. "The cry of ignorance. 'Teach me!' As though the imparting of knowledge and skill can be accomplished in a moment. Could you wield a sword the first time you held one? How long do you think it would take for you to learn the lessons necessary? This stubbornness will not help Tashalya."

Dain stared at him. "Then what is to be done?"

"Let me walk in your dreams and—"

"No!" He turned away. Revulsion was crawling beneath his skin, making him shudder. "'Tis not possible. I refuse."

"Then you condemn Tashalya to whatever fate her captors intend."

"Morde!" Dain said in a fury. "For months I have asked your help, and you gave me none. I have waited all winter for Lord Thum's agents to bring me some hint of where she is, and they've discovered nothing. And now, when at long last I have a measure of hope, you block my path."

"You are the one refusing help," Samderaudin replied without expression. "Exactly what is it that you fear?"

Dain stiffened, ready to deny it, but when he met the *sorcerel's* gaze he found he could not utter the lie. He looked away for a moment and on impulse reached out to deliberately touch his mind to Samderaudin's. Fire seemed to spark behind his eyes, and he staggered backward as though struck. When his head stopped buzzing and his vision cleared, he drew in an unsteady breath and sank into his chair.

"That was unwise," Samderaudin said coldly. "Were I not in service to you, I might have killed you for that."

Dain said nothing, and, after a moment of silence, Samderaudin tilted his head. "I did naught but defend myself against your touch. You have proven nothing. Because I have the power to do harm does not mean I will use it."

"I do not want you wandering freely in my mind. I want no one in there again."

The *sorcerel's* brows drew together, and he stared at Dain a long time before gliding over to the window and bowing his head in thought. "This," he said finally, "I did not know. For years, you have shielded your thoughts very skillfully from me. Your secrets, it seems, go deep."

Angry that he'd inadvertently revealed too much, Dain scowled. "My secrets are my own. Let that be enough."

"It is unwise for a king not to confide in the *sorcerel* who serves him. Who violated you?"

"Cardinal Noncire of Mandria," Dain said. His mouth went dry at the memory of that ordeal, when Noncire's mind had broken into his, smashing and hurting in an effort to force the location of the Chalice from his mind. Only by pretending to give up the hiding place of the Chalice and thereby tricking the cardinal into releasing him had Dain saved himself from total madness. He'd never talked to anyone about it, not even Thum, who'd found him afterward. He found he could not discuss it now. Raking his hands through his hair, he said unsteadily, "It was . . . I cannot endure that again."

Samderaudin continued gazing out of the window. When he spoke, his voice was surprisingly gentle. "The rape of the mind is as cruel and bestial as the rape of the body. But to willingly share the mind with another is not—"

"I can't do it." Dain lifted his fists to press them against his burning eyes. He was ashamed of his panic, of the old feeling of terror, which had come clawing out of his memories. "You don't know how it was."

"Perhaps I do," the *sorcerel* said softly. He turned to look at Dain. "When I was a child, and just discovering what I might become, I fell into the clutches of a dabbler in the dark arts. He was no *sorcerel* but just an incompetent determined to appropriate my gifts by force. He hurt me most cruelly, accomplishing nothing else, and threw me in a ditch to die. But I did not die. Instead I went mad."

Samderaudin spread wide his hands. "I lived in rage for

years, unable to trust anyone, unable to stand training, unable to cope with my raw talents, which continued to grow."

Dain stared at him in amazement, seeing Samderaudin for the first time as a person. "What changed you?"

"Like a mad dog, I was stoned and driven out of every village I came to. At last I wandered into a place where the terrified peasants tried to hang me. But again I did not die, and a *sorcerelle* found me, cut me down, and healed my mind. After that, I was able to commence my training. It was hard to trust, hard to let go of old cruelties, but necessary for growth."

Dain frowned. He understood why Samderaudin had told him this story, but his fears were too ingrained to be overcome by one small tale. Perhaps Samderaudin had only invented such a past to gain sympathy.

"Ah," the *sorcerel* said softly, "still you doubt. You have become a king by acclaim, but at heart you remain a starved, mistreated half-breed. You doubt yourself as you doubt others. You cannot entirely feel at ease with all the good fortune that has come to you because you wait for it to be taken away. That is no course for a king."

"Enough!" Dain said angrily. "You may withdraw."

Samderaudin did not budge. "If I were not right, you would have no anger. How many times have you urged me to speak to you plainly, without riddles? Now, I grant you what you wish."

Dain scowled, still fuming, and did not reply.

"Wounded pride is the indulgence of a fool," Samderaudin said. "You are not a fool, Faldain, nor are you a coward. Without my help, how will you save your daughter?"

Dain's anger died, leaving him awash with conflicting emotions. From childhood, he'd been raised to abhor *sorcerels*, and not until he came to Nether had he learned to tolerate and use them. Samderaudin was asking him to submit himself in complete trust, to put himself at the *sorcerel's* mercy. And yet, Tashalya mattered more than anything else.

He swallowed hard. "What must I do?"

"When next you sleep, let me enter your dreams," Samderaudin said quietly, his yellow eyes intent. "Do not fight or re-

sist my presence. I will watch. If she comes, I will bring her
forth."

It was the first real hope for his daughter he'd known in
months. An ache filled Dain's chest. "I don't know if I can
keep myself from fighting you," he admitted.

Samderaudin nodded. "You let Tobeszijian share your
body during the Battle of Grov. It is not much different."

"It's very different," Dain said sharply. "He was my father."

"Whom you never knew until his ghost began to haunt
you. Come, Faldain. What does it matter if I learn your secrets? Is that too high a price in exchange for Tashalya's recovery and perhaps the queen's renewed favor?"

Dain looked at him sharply, resentful of that last remark,
but as he met the *sorcerel's* eyes he knew Samderaudin had
astutely perceived the truth of his motives. Shame burned in
Dain's throat. "Aye," he said hoarsely. "I confess I have come
to that. Does it show so much?"

Samderaudin said nothing.

"Very well," Dain surrendered. "For Tashalya's sake, I'll
put myself in your hands."

Chapter Twenty-Nine

Three evenings later, on the night Dain was to display his son to the court for the first time, the Hall of Kings looked festive, with garlands of flowers hung from the smoky old ceiling beams. Torches flared bright. Long rows of tables stretched the length of the room. Already the courtiers, arrayed in finery, were gathering. The buzz of happy conversation filled the air. The night would finish the initial round of celebrations, but the following week would bring the new prince's christening following a procession through Grov to Helspirin Cathedral, then onward to the Tree of Life. There would be largesse thrown to the people and a public feast in the central town square, with more banqueting planned for the palace. Gifts for the occasion were already arriving, and the Gallery of Glass was being decorated especially for the event.

It should have been a joyous time, but beyond his great pride in his new son, Dain felt only a wish to have the celebrations finished. However, that night the queen was to be present, and he had hopes of enjoying the banquet. If nothing else, it might temporarily distract him from the disappointment of no further contact from Tashalya. Whether her ab-

sence from his dreams was due to Samderaudin's presence—
disturbing to Dain despite the *sorcerel's* care—or some other
reason hardly mattered. She'd not returned.

As Dain and his entourage came down the passageway toward the Hall, he heard a flourish of trumpets announcing his
arrival. Ahead through the open doors, he glimpsed people
hastily assembling themselves, while the chamberlain tapped
his staff on the floor for quiet.

The queen, flanked by her ladies-in-waiting and attendants, emerged from the antechamber where she'd been waiting. The sight of her lifted Dain's heart. She looked happy
tonight, lovelier than ever, with a faint bloom of color in her
cheeks and a smile still lingering on her lips from what someone had been saying to her.

Their eyes met. His smile brightened, but hers faded. She
curtsied with deep formality to him. Sighing, he offered his
arm, and she placed her fingers atop the back of his hand. Neither of them spoke. They might have been strangers as together they walked the length of the Hall to the head table and
were seated, side by side, with their protectors positioned behind their chairs. Prominent officials of state and church
joined them. As the courtiers took their places at the lower tables, lutes and zithrens struck up sprightly music.

Servants began carrying in the food. Soon, the Hall echoed
merrily with the babble of talk and laughter. More platters of
food were brought to replenish what was eaten. Flagons of
wine and mead filled the cups. Toasts and jokes and speeches
resounded through the room. Various lords of the realm fre-
quently ambled up to the head table to toast the new prince or
to compliment the queen.

It pleased Dain greatly that most of the attention tonight
was showered on Alexeika. Gowned in a gray-green dress that
made her eyes look luminous, her dark hair coiled beneath her
veil, the new necklace glittering at her throat, Alexeika smiled
at the company and inclined her head graciously to every
compliment. Dain watched her with pride, a lump of emotion
in his throat. He thought she'd never looked more beautiful.
He had told her so, but she'd only given him that same prac-
ticed smile that she was now bestowing on the courtiers.

Sighing, he gave his gritty eyes a surreptitious rub.

"Are you unwell?" Alexeika asked softly.

It was the first remark she'd initiated to him all evening. Startled, Dain felt like a starving dog thrown a crumb and shook his head. "Just tired."

"You dozed through this afternoon's concert. I fear the poor minstrel was greatly disconcerted by your indifferent reception to his efforts."

The minstrel, Dain recalled, had caterwauled through a dreary new composition consisting of dull verses and a lackluster tune. "Very restful," he said. "I should perhaps engage him to sing me to sleep each night."

"Yes," she agreed, but did not quite smile at his sally. "Your men said your slumbers are poorly. Nightmares?"

Had she still been a wife to him, she would have known. And with her arms around him to comfort him, the dreams would not have been so dreadful. "Aye, nightmares," he said ruefully, shoving his barely touched trencher aside. "'Tis nothing new, is it?"

She studied him a moment with the shadow of a frown between her brows. "Is the food not to your taste?"

"I've eaten enough."

A servant refilled his cup before he could wave the man off, and her frown deepened. "I see you've learned to like drink more than food."

He leaned back in his chair to hide how much her unfounded scorn hurt. "Ah, the first barb of the evening. I wondered when it would come."

Color rose in her cheeks. Her eyes blazed at him a moment before she turned away.

Angrily he resisted the impulse to hurl his cup at the wall. He was no drunkard, and well she knew it.

The chamberlain sidled up to him with a bow. "Your majesty, the children have arrived."

Relieved, he looked behind him, where a private door was opening to reveal attendants and nursemaids. Mareitina, her golden curls undulating gently on her shoulders, looked big-eyed with apprehension. The baby was swaddled tightly in a velvet cloth embroidered with the royal crest.

By then Alexeika had noticed their arrival and was smiling. "Mareitina's here, too," she said in pleasure. "Oh, Faldain, please see if you can coax her out to stand beside my chair."

He rose to his feet, and at once the talk and laughter died down. The music ceased abruptly. Smiling, Dain beckoned to Mareitina, but she shyly hid behind her nursemaid's skirts.

He walked over to her and took her small hand. "I'm glad you came to see the feast, precious," he said softly to her, keeping his voice gentle. With his mind, he soothed her nervousness as he might any skittish animal.

She looked at him with blue eyes that understood what he was doing. "Don't, Papa," she said clearly. "I don't want to go any farther."

"Not even to stand beside your mother while I make my speech?" he asked coaxingly. "Remember how you chose your dress to look pretty with hers? Wouldn't you like to be seen with Mama, just for a few minutes? It would make her very happy."

Mareitina looked dubious. "I don't like those people staring at me."

"They won't be staring at you. They'll be staring at me and your new brother," he said.

"That's almost not true," she said.

He swallowed a sigh, aware of the crowd's impatience beating at his back. "You're right," he admitted and smiled at her. "You would please Mama very much. I won't make you stand beside her for long."

"Does Mama love him"—she nodded at the baby—"more than me?"

The nursemaid drew in her breath sharply. Ignoring the woman, Dain said, "No, not at all. Mama let you go to the old folk, didn't she?"

Mareitina smiled broadly, revealing a missing tooth. "I like it there a lot. When can I go back?"

The child's eagerness to leave them sent a pang through Dain, but he understood. "Soon," he promised.

"You said as soon as I'd seen my new brother. I've seen him. He isn't like Ilymir at all."

"No, he will never be like Ilymir."

She came to him and put her arms around his waist. "I still love you, Papa, but I want to go back to the forest."

He picked her up, burying his face against her fragrant neck for a moment, the fullness of her skirts billowing over his arms. "I've told Nilainder," he told her softly as he carried her into the glaring torchlight where all could see her. "He said the eld folk will be coming for you."

"Can't you take me back?" she asked pleadingly. "Tomorrow? On your fastest horse?"

Melting before those blue eyes, he hated having to say no. "I can't leave the palace right now. The eld folk must come and fetch you this time."

Turning to face the assembly, he smiled to the crowd. The head table had been carried away, leaving only their chairs, so that all present could see the royal family without hindrance. Standing at the edge of the dais, Dain whispered at Mareitina to wave. Her face was buried on his shoulder, but he kept coaxing her until at last she lifted her small hand and waved briefly. A ripple of pleasure passed through the courtiers. Pleased, Dain set her down so that she could stand beside Alexeika.

Beaming, Alexeika put her arm around the child and murmured in her ear so that Mareitina smiled and gave her mother a kiss. The courtiers applauded her, and Dain took the baby from the arms of his nurse.

The sleeping child's rosy lips were pursed slightly. His cheeks had plumped out, and the tuft of black hair still stood straight up despite obvious efforts to tame it.

Holding him proudly, Dain recalled another feast five years ago when the nursemaids had carried in the twins. That had been a joyous night indeed as he lifted tiny Ilymir, wrapped in this same velvet cloth, and proclaimed him to the court. Now, awash with memories, he hesitated and glanced at Alexeika.

He could tell she was thinking similar thoughts, for her eyes glistened with unshed tears as she stared up at him. She did not smile, as she would have once, and he forced himself to face his subjects.

"Lords and ladies of Nether," he said, projecting his voice across the Hall, "I present to you my son and do hereby proclaim him my heir—"

A ball of spellfire flashed without warning, sending up a pillar of black smoke. Two hurlhounds appeared, causing people to jerk to their feet with screams and cries of alarm. Some at the rear of the Hall darted out the door, calling for help, but the guards who rushed inside halted as Dain swiftly raised his arm for caution. Thus far, the hurlhounds had not attacked. He did not want to provoke them.

Wearing collars of blazing fire around their necks, the monsters growled and whined, with venom dripping from their panting jaws. Their red eyes sought potential prey, but they did not move from the place where they'd appeared.

Alexeika was on her feet, her face white as she pressed Mareitina tightly to her skirts. Dain turned and handed off the baby to the nearly hysterical nursemaid, and took the sword Omas pressed into his hand. In turn, the protector accepted a weapon one of the guards plucked off the wall and tossed to him. Cursing that he wore not Mirengard, Dain reached into his pocket for salt.

"Everyone, stay calm," he commanded. "Make no sudden movements. Captain, can you and your men reach the salt basin near the paneatha?"

"I'll try, sire."

"Take care."

The room seemed frozen as the guard edged cautiously along the wall. Some of the women present were sobbing. Men whispered prayers or curses. Cardinal Winnder held aloft his jeweled Circle, but a glance from Dain held him silent.

Worried for Alexeika and the children, Dain ignored his thudding heart and signaled unobtrusively to her. "Alexeika," he said softly, "slowly back away."

She'd already gathered up her voluminous skirts in one hand, while with the other, she kept a firm grasp on Mareitina. Although she was still extremely pale, she'd fought hurlhounds before and knew what to do. Carefully, she tried to retreat, but one of the hurlhounds looked at her and growled. At once she halted and shot Dain a glance of alarm.

He was watching, prepared to spring into action if either or both of the monsters attacked, but he did not want to start a battle if it could be avoided. Some force was obviously holding the creatures under control.

Thum's young wife was weeping. He stood with one hand on her arm, the other clutching his dagger grimly. "Sire," he whispered, "if we—"

"How you all stare and tremble," said a voice that came from nowhere. It was a deep voice, flat with hatred, and as Dain looked for the owner of it, a robed individual shimmered into existence beside the hurlhounds.

Tall and gaunt, with strangely slanted eyes that seemed to glow with fire, the *sorcerel* lifted himself to hover in midair before Dain. Jewels glowed in his ears and around his long fingers. He stank of ashes and dark magic.

"I am Tulvak Sahm," he announced. "Behold me, King of Nether. I am your sworn enemy."

Dain did not remember the name, but he recognized this *sorcerel's* visage. Tulvak Sahm had stood behind Muncel at the Battle of Grov, and deserted his king and master while Muncel lay dying. Murmurs rippled through the Hall, for clearly others remembered Tulvak Sahm. Prince Tustik, in particular, stood rooted in place, white-faced, while his eyes blazed hatred.

This, Dain realized, must be the enemy who'd thrown such evil against him and his family. Suddenly everything made sense. No one could have given the Grethori spellfire save a *sorcerel*. No one could have wrought a spell to bind Mirengard to another sword during combat save a *sorcerel*. This one.

Rage swept him, and he gripped the borrowed sword more tightly. In no mood to discuss Tulvak Sahm's motives, he did not waste time asking why. "Where is my daughter?" he demanded.

"Do you really want your little hell-cat spawn, oh mighty king? Will you pay the price of her ransom?"

"Name it."

Tulvak Sahm laughed. "What? No hesitation? No sense of caution? Do you not fear my price?"

"Name it," Dain repeated through gritted teeth.

"The Chalice of Eternal Life!"

Exclamations of horror rose up. Winnder began gobbling a protest.

Stunned, unable to believe it, Dain stared at the *sorcerel*. "You—"

"That is the price!" Tulvak Sahm shouted. Tiny bits of flame burned in the air, and the hurlhounds threw back their heads and howled. "Three weeks hence, bring the Chalice to the Field of Skulls in Nold, and put it into my hands."

"In Thod's name, your majesty," Winnder pleaded. "Refuse!"

Dain ignored him. He was frowning at the *sorcerel*. "Why the delay?" he asked harshly. "Why not demand it now?"

More shouts of protest rang out, but Dain never took his gaze from Tulvak Sahm. "Do you think I am likely to walk into such a trap?"

The *sorcerel* bared his filed teeth. "Three weeks is necessary for you to ride that distance. Bring the Chalice to the Field of Skulls, if you want your daughter back."

"How do I know you have her, or that she's—"

Tulvak Sahm gestured, conjuring forth a second cloud of smoke. Tashalya appeared from it, stumbling slightly as though unsteady on her feet. Filthy and tattered, she looked around as though she could not believe what she saw. When her gaze landed on Dain, she screamed, "Papa!"

She tried to hurl herself forward, but Tulvak Sahm held on to her.

The sight of that taloned hand digging into his daughter's shoulder was too much for Dain. Forgetting all his intentions, he jumped off the dais and charged the *sorcerel* to free Tashalya.

"Sire, wait!" Omas shouted, running after him.

A hurlhound leaped between Dain and Tulvak Sahm. Dain swung his sword, but the ordinary steel blade glanced off its black, scaled hide. The second hurlhound knocked him down from the side, while people screamed and scattered out of the way.

"Faldain!" Alexeika shouted, as both hurlhounds closed in.

Half-winded and sprawled on the floor, Dain flung salt at the beasts, driving them momentarily back and giving himself time to get to his knees. He jabbed short and hard, managing to wound one monster. It staggered aside, shaking its head with splatters of steaming, black blood. Growling and ignoring Omas, who was hacking at it from behind, the other beast sprang for Dain's throat. Struggling to fend off the monster leaping past his sword, Dain desperately thrust his left fist into the creature's slavering mouth. The Ring of Solder, glowing white in the presence of evil, sent it flinching back with a yelp.

Someone yelled a warning, but Dain was already scrambling to his feet to meet a fresh attack from the first hound, still streaming blood but far from finished. Panting hard, his tunic ripped, his left hand bloody and stinging from venom, Dain flung more salt at it, but Tulvak Sahm burned the salt away in midair before it landed on the hurlhound. The beast gathered its powerful haunches and leaped, and Dain swung the sword with all his might against it.

At that moment Samderaudin arrived and roared out a curse. Green fire shot from his hand to engulf the hurlhound. It exploded into ashes with such force that Dain was staggered. Dizzy, his head ringing, he fought to keep his balance. By then Omas had reached his side and steadied him, shouting curses of his own.

"Get Tashalya," Dain gasped out.

Before Omas could act, Samderaudin flew at Tulvak Sahm, hurling more fire, but Tulvak Sahm turned the flames back against Samderaudin. The clash of magic shot sparks into the air, and smoke boiled around them.

Shaking off Omas's supportive hand, Dain pushed forward in an effort to reach his little girl.

"Papa!" she screamed, but Tulvak Sahm caught her around the middle and hoisted her off her feet. She fought and thrashed to no avail. "Papa!"

Dain leaped for her, and his hand just grazed her outstretched fingers as Tulvak Sahm rose with her into the air.

Vaunit entered the Hall, and Samderaudin called out a command to him in a language Dain did not understand. Vaunit raised his arms and uttered the first words of an incantation, but with his eyes blazing, Tulvak Sahm hurled a bolt of magic that slammed the younger *sorcerel* against the wall.

"Three weeks!" Tulvak Sahm shouted at Dain. "Or she'll be made Nonkind." And he and the hurlhounds vanished with her.

Chapter Thirty

Stunned by what had just happened, Alexeika slowly realized that the danger was past. The air still stank of Nonkind and magic, but the evil *sorcerel* and his monsters were gone. *Taking Tashalya with them.* She began to tremble. To have the child so close, almost within their reach, only to lose her again was too heartbreaking to endure.

At her side, Mareitina was crying. Alexeika gave the child a quick hug and kiss, sending her away with an ashen-faced nursemaid, before turning to Faldain. The king was kneeling on the floor a short distance away, breathing hard, his head bowed. Men hurried to surround him while more blue-cloaked guards streamed into the Hall, shouting orders and pushing people back. The captain at arms came striding up, scowling, his hand on his sword hilt. He gave Alexeika a brief nod, but went to the king's side and began a report she could not overhear in the hubbub.

Omas was bending over Faldain, talking urgently, while Chesil came running with a salt basin. Although the king was now blocked from her view by those clustered around him, she heard his yelp of pain, bitten off.

Worried and determined to make sure they took proper care of him, she picked up her skirts and started off the dais toward him, but Sir Pyron blocked her path.

"Stand aside," she commanded urgently.

"Best get back," he said gruffly. "Orders are for the Hall to be cleared at once."

"But I belong with his majesty."

He crowded her in the opposite direction she wished to go. "Best use yon door and avoid this crowd. Best get yer majesty safe to quarters."

"Don't be absurd!" she said sharply. "Tulvak Sahm is gone. We needn't run to safety now. I must speak to the king."

"His orders," Sir Pyron said, shooting her a brief glance of sympathy. "Wants the place cleared at once."

As she opened her mouth to argue, she overheard the cardinal's voice raised hysterically, "And the Chalice right here in the palace. Right *here* within that demon's reach, had he but known it. If he could get so close, bringing those vile monsters into the Hall of Kings, there's no real protection for any of us."

A little finger of alarm froze inside Alexeika's heart. Although she despised Winnder's cowardice, 'twas a valid point he was making. She could not help but glance at the paneatha, thinking of the Chalice's presence beneath this very floor. How could Nonkind endure such proximity to it? Over the past few years, they'd all relaxed their tight vigilance against Nonkind, believing the Chalice would keep such creatures away. But if they'd been mistaken, if the darkness was gaining strength, then what was to become of them?

"Yer grace!" Sir Pyron was saying with exasperation, for she had not budged.

Thum hurried over. "Your majesty, the king has commanded everyone to go."

She looked into his hazel eyes with urgency. "What is Faldain going to do? I must speak with him. I have to know his decision."

"You will be informed," Thum said crisply. "Please do as he asks."

Fuming at being treated like an ordinary courtier, she obeyed at last. There'd been a time when Faldain would have kept her close by, allowing her to voice her opinion. Now, with their daughter's life at stake, he ignored her as though she did not matter.

Raging, she refused to go tamely to her apartments and instead took herself to the chamber of state, where she paced up and down and wondered why he did not come. The Privy Council would have to meet, she thought impatiently. Faldain could not take a step these days without consulting with his advisers. So where were they? Why had they not assembled here immediately?

The door opened, and she spun around eagerly, but it was only Tustik and Unshalin who entered. They stared at her with equal surprise and obvious dismay.

"Your majesty should not be here," Prince Tustik said softly.

"Where should I be? Waiting in my chamber like a commoner?" she flashed back. "She's my daughter, too, and I demand to know the reason for this delay. Why isn't something being done?"

Tustik and Unshalin exchanged a glance. "His majesty must be examined for Nonkind poison," Tustik replied. "That takes time."

Feeling as though the wind had been knocked from her, she opened her mouth, but it was a moment before she could speak. "I thought his wound a minor one. Are you saying—"

"I do not know. Please, will your majesty not withdraw?"

Her eyes flashed at him. "You dare dismiss the queen, lord prince?"

"I ask the queen to not add more troubles to those already before his majesty."

Humiliation scorched her face, for he was right, and she knew herself to be in the wrong. Wordlessly, aware of Unshalin's barely concealed smirk, she swept out with her head held high and her ears roaring.

This time she did go to her chambers, where she found Chesil waiting by the door. Slender and exotic-looking in his crimson Agya clothing, Chesil always used to smile at her with admiration. Now his slanted eyes held only coolness.

"Majesty!" he said. "I am to inform you that the king will come to you within the hour."

"Yes, of course," she said furiously. "After he has consulted everyone else. Why does he bother at all to tell me of his decision? Clearly I am not to be permitted any say—"

"Am I to tell his majesty that the queen denies him audience?"

Her brows drew together in outrage. "How dare you?" she choked out. "I have offered no such insult to him. Do *not* put lies in my mouth or presume to speak for me."

Chesil compressed his mouth. "Then what am I to say?"

"You can tell him that I am displeased at being put last."

"Your majesty put yourself there," he muttered as he turned away.

She couldn't believe he'd said such a thing. That was twice tonight she'd been dealt insolence. At a time like this, when her child was in mortal danger, how could men she'd considered friends turn on her this way? What was wrong with them?

Her entourage stared, and Sir Pyron edged closer, but she needed no one to defend her. "Chesil Matkevskiet! Come back," she commanded.

Chesil hesitated as though he was considering ignoring her order, then he swung around and faced her.

The defiance glowing in his eyes annoyed her more. "You are not permitted to criticize me—"

"Then who is to do it?" he broke in with Agya hauteur, and gestured at her ladies and attendants. "Will any of these lapdogs say the truth? No!"

"That's too far," Sir Pyron growled.

"No, I have not gone far enough." Chesil tossed his head so that his hair beads clacked and swayed. "I am not afraid to tell the queen that she has driven the king to the limit of his endurance. Our king, the bravest warrior in all this realm, and she seeks to break his proud spirit and noble heart."

"'Tis his guilt that does so," she countered angrily. "If it eats at him, he has no one to blame but himself."

"Do you not blame him enough?" Chesil asked in disgust. "What in all this is his fault? Did he incite the auxiliaries to treason? Did he not risk his life in going after them, and endure capture and torture at their hands? And now, does he not waste away before our eyes, worried over all that besets him until he is unable to eat, unable to sleep? Do you think this man is made of iron, never to crumble? Tonight, he fought Nonkind without thought of his safety, fought them without armor or magicked steel, and you blame him for not prevailing against hurlhounds and *sorcerel*. I see it in your majesty's eyes, the anger, the blame. *Aychi!* Who can please such a spoiled and arrogant woman?"

Sir Pyron drew his sword. "That be enough, Agya dog! Apologize, or I'll see yer guts strung around—"

"No," Alexeika said, holding up her hand. "Let him be, Pyron."

"But—"

"Let him be." She felt as though Chesil's accusations were darts piercing her flesh. She was on fire from them, and suddenly all she wanted to do was hide somewhere. But that was wrong, she told herself. The fault was on Faldain's side, and now he played the suffering martyr and gained his subjects' sympathy. If Chesil got away with insulting her in such fashion tonight, more criticism and insolence would follow. She knew she had to stop it now, but she could not bring herself to order his punishment. Instead, she only wanted to get away from him, from everyone.

"You have given me the king's message," she said coldly to Chesil. "You may go."

Without waiting for his response, she turned and entered her apartments. Once there, she dismissed her gossiping attendants, and, in the dim glow of a solitary burning lamp, she paced back and forth until her still-sore body drove her to sit down. She had no tears to shed. She could not find any sort of order or clarity in her mind. Never one to tolerate waiting, she longed to take action, but there was nothing for her to do. She had been put aside. Where once she had been first, now she was last. Thod only knew what Faldain's advisers were urging him to do. Would they be intelligent enough to recognize that the prize offered was obviously a Gantese trap? As for Tashalya, the bait now dangling in that trap . . . Alexeika felt her heart burning for her little girl.

The hour came and went, without Faldain's arrival. She dozed at last while the lamp sputtered low, and was awakened by a soft knock. She sat up, confused for a moment, and saw Sir Pyron admit Faldain before retreating outside and shutting the door to leave them complete privacy.

She started to rise to her feet, but he gestured for her to remain seated as he crossed the room and dropped into a chair. Wordlessly, he bent over, propping his elbows on his knees, and buried his face in his hands.

In the silence she studied him, and was startled to see a few silver hairs glinting among the black. His left hand and wrist were bandaged. He had not bothered to change his raiment, and his ripped and crumpled tunic was blood-splattered and reeked slightly of Nonkind.

She'd intended to let him speak first, but the silence was stretching out too long. She wanted matters over with. "What has the Council decided?" she asked.

He straightened, scrubbing his face with his hands, and leaned back in his chair to stare bleakly at nothing. A tiny muscle leaped spasmodically in his jaw. "I do not know," he answered. "I told them the responsibility was mine, and I left them."

His voice was flat, conveying nothing.

Impatient at having to pry everything from him, she frowned. "Well, what have *you* decided?"

"Nothing." His pale gray eyes shifted then and sought hers. "Of course it's a trap."

"Yes."

"I am sworn to protect the Chalice with my life. I cannot surrender it. Neither can I sacrifice my daughter." Looking puzzled, he shook his head. "I know not what to do."

She drew in a sharp, furious breath, but before she could speak he said, "That's why I have come, to let you decide. You're her mother. You brought her into this world. Whatever you command, I will do."

Resentment flared through her. "What is this?" she asked incredulously. "What game do you play?"

His eyes looked dead. "No game. You could always think more clearly than I. Whenever I remember how my fingers touched her hand, my wits go numb, and my head buzzes. I am caught, doomed in the clutches of this *sorcerel* as I have been since last summer. Everything I do is the wrong thing. Every action I try is a mistake. Tulvak Sahm has yanked me hither and yon like a puppet, intending me to fail at every turn. As I have done."

"But—"

Faldain gestured, closing his eyes. "You decide. You instruct me, and I will obey."

"Do you abdicate your sovereignty?" she asked angrily. "How convenient of you, when things are difficult. You are not being fair!"

His eyes opened to meet hers. "I know," he agreed softly. "But I cannot fight this—this evil and you, too. I—I think you will tell me that Tashalya should be sacrificed because the Chalice must never fall into Gantese hands. You are still strong enough to tell me that, Alexeika. I—I love her too much to make the choice."

Tears shone in his eyes, and as she listened to him with shock and dawning horror, Alexeika felt the sting of her own emotions. His face blurred for a moment, and when she blinked her vision clear she saw defeat and exhaustion in his face. When, she thought in amazement, had he grown so haggard? What were the new lines carved in his countenance? She stared at him as though she'd not seen him in months, and all the while she was thinking that never before in all their years together had he come to her in surrender. In private, they had always been equals. But now, she could see that she'd beaten him into this shadow of what he once had been, and it appalled her.

Swept with sudden shame, she asked herself if she'd been so cruel and heartless a judge. Aye, she had. In the lamplight, she stared at the scar gleaming pink and puckered across his temple. She'd never let herself look at it closely before, for she wanted to feel no sympathy for him. But now she stared, and it spoke of the serious wound he must have suffered in fighting the Grethori. For the first time, Alexeika forced herself to consider whether she could have withstood the *sheda's* magic had she been wounded so terribly. He'd been tricked. He hadn't ceased to love her. He hadn't willingly broken his marriage vows in order to stray. He'd been enspelled by a magic that was incredibly strong, and briefly he'd succumbed to it.

Although some hurt would always remain, she believed he hadn't betrayed her of his own free will. It was the *sheda* she should have blamed, not him.

Relief flooded her, and with it came genuine forgiveness. She realized that she'd been hurting herself as much as she'd tried to hurt him. Her anger and resentment the past few months had served to drive a wedge between them deeper than anything attempted by the Kollegya. Worse, she'd been the one who made him doubt himself, until he feared his own powers of judgment and decision.

"What have I done to you?" she murmured. Dismayed, she went to him and placed her hand against his cheek. "Faldain, I'm sorry. I know none of this has been your fault. I've been so wrong. So very wrong."

He reached up and pressed his face against her waist, and she held him tightly, giving him comfort the way she would a child. She could feel his bones sharp and hard beneath his clothing, and as his frame shook she realized that he was crying silently against her.

She cried, too, and began to rock him in her arms. "We'll find a way," she whispered, trying to reassure herself as much as him. "We'll find a way."

Chapter Thirty-One

The Field of Skulls was a legendary battlefield from the mists of antiquity, still spoken of around campfires with reverence and awe. According to dwarf lore, on the Field of Skulls had been fought one of the final wars of the gods. Giants strode the land then, along with other creatures no longer to be found outside of tales. So many warriors fought and died on this ground that their bones, white and picked clean, still blanketed the soil. Despite the passing of centuries, nothing grew there. The pine forest stopped abruptly on all sides, and not even weeds encroached.

Riding slowly along the edge of the old battlefield in the pearly light of dawn, Dain kept his nervous horse from shying away as he stared out across the desolate place. Many of the bones had crumbled to pale powder, but others remained intact, especially the skulls. The air felt dense and compressed, and old spell tracings still crisscrossed the ground. Feeling the hair standing up on the back of his neck, Dain swallowed hard and kept his senses alert for trouble.

"This is a bad place," Omas rumbled at his side. He had his Circle out, wearing it openly atop his hauberk, and his brown eyes were darting from side to side. "I never believed it really existed, but Thod's teeth, this is no place for mortals to walk."

"No," Dain agreed.

He glanced over his shoulder at the army of men riding in his wake, men half-seen and quiet like ghosts in the gloomy light. Having circled the field to make sure no trap was waiting, Dain set about creating his own. Since the night of the banquet, he'd had no further contact with Tashalya, neither dreams nor any sense of her. Knowing there was no honor in Tulvak Sahm, Dain believed that even if she still lived, she would not be permitted to survive their next meeting. She had served her purpose, and he had no hope of saving her. Accordingly, he'd set up his battle strategy with the intention of killing the *sorcerel* and as many of his men as possible. As he divided and positioned his forces to the best advantage, his mind felt raw and hot, unable to think of anything save delivering death.

The forest grew thin along the boundary of the field, but a short distance back the trees closed in thick and dark. Because he did not expect Tulvak Sahm to come alone, and if the *sorcerel's* allies were Gantese, they would arrive from the east, Dain concealed his knights on the north and south sides of the field. With luck, they'd be able to press the Gantese from two directions, without putting the rising sun in their own eyes.

Furnilov, the commander at arms, passed along quiet orders, and without much talk the Netherans readied themselves for battle, fitting on their helmets, loosening their swords in their scabbards, whispering their prayers over their Circles and amulets. They'd been given their instructions the night before. They understood that they might be called on to face almost anything. The place grew quiet, broken only by the occasional restless stamp of the horses or a bridle jingle beneath the soft snapping of Nether's pennons in the freshening breeze. Neither birds nor insects sang in this place of death.

Dain's heart was beating quick and fast beneath his gold breastplate embossed with the hammer and lightning of Nether's kings. Barely repaired in time for his hasty departure, with the dents made by the Grethori tribesmen not quite smoothed out, his hard armor no longer fitted as well over his chain mail as it once had. Although his appetite had improved twofold since his reconciliation with Alexeika, the hard ride to arrive well in advance of Tulvak Sahm's ultimatum had kept his body honed lean.

Like the best commanders, Dain had come to the appointed battleground early. He had scouted the lay of the land. He had plotted his strategy. Two nights ago, Samderaudin had shot up an arc of rainbow-hued sparks in the direction of the nearby Charva River, letting any Gantese sentries know the Netherans were there. But of course if Tulvak Sahm watched them through the veils of seeing, he needed no such signal. Vaunit was responsible for screening Dain and his knights from being spied on through visions, but who knew if such efforts were successful?

So they waited for Tulvak Sahm to come. Dain hoped it was soon, for he felt restless and edgy in this evil place, eager to finish this battle of revenge. The protective magic laced through his armor was thrumming. In its scabbard at his side, Mirengard glowed white, and the Ring of Solder felt hot around his finger. Because Dain had sensed no Nonkind in the vicinity, he suspected some dormant power lingered on around them.

A chill of dread shivered down his spine, for he was convinced that the Chalice's presence could raise these bones and bring back to life, or at least partial life, thousands of slain warriors such as the first world had not seen since the dawn of time. *Take care*, he warned himself, all too aware of the risk he ran. *You are tampering with things best left alone.*

He bent his head a moment to gather his courage and pray. Throughout the journey, he'd tried to prepare himself for whatever he was about to face. Now that the moment was almost upon him, he found himself sweating and distraught with wild hopes that she might still be alive and back soon in his keeping. *No*, he thought harshly, taking command of himself once more. *This is a day of trickery, not honor. Be strong.*

Looking up, he breathed in deeply, trying to draw reassurance from the forest and sky, even from the river coursing a short distance away. But for once, his eld side failed him.

There was nothing he could feel from nature while his heart throbbed for the slaughter to come.

Oddly, at that moment, he found himself wishing that he sat astride his darsteed, but when the creature had died a few years ago he'd never ordered another one captured. Perhaps, he thought bleakly, it had been a mistake to shy so far away from his own few magical talents, depending instead on others.

"Something comes," Samderaudin said softly.

Dain drew his sword quietly, for now he, too, heard the distant sounds of horses and darsteeds. A moment later the wind shifted, and he smelled the decayed, foul stink of Nonkind.

Holding ranks, his men drew their weapons. Their tension beat across Dain's senses, and with a frown he closed himself to their emotions in order to concentrate.

Then came the louder rumble of galloping horses, and as the sun lifted above the horizon a cloud of dust rose into the air. Heedless of what they trampled, the Gantese forces rode partway across the Field of Skulls before halting.

Dain lowered his helmet visor with a grim snap, and did not think the Gantese would enjoy what he was about to unleash.

"Damn them," Omas breathed beneath his mustache. "Damn them to perdition."

Dain exchanged a glance with Furnilov on his right, touched the heavily wrapped bundle tied to his saddle to be certain it was well secured, and kicked his horse forward. He moved out of the trees into sight, Samderaudin and twenty handpicked men with him. The rest of his army remained concealed in the trees. If Tulvak Sahm was aware of their presence, he had as yet given no warning.

As the dust settled over the Gantese forces, Dain squinted against the spreading sunlight to estimate their size. Not as many as he'd expected.

"Three hundred to our five," Omas muttered, "unless they've got more hidden away."

Dain halted, for he was having trouble forcing his frightened horse forward. Bones rolled and shifted loosely beneath his mount's prancing feet, and he kept a tight fist on the reins. *Calm/calm/calm/calm*, he commanded the animal.

"Ah," Samderaudin breathed, riding up alongside him.

A number equal in size to Dain's small party moved away from the main body of Gantese and trotted forward. Dain counted five fire-knights and a dozen or so Believers besides Tulvak Sahm. When one of the fire-knights lifted his arm, they halted perhaps forty strides from Dain, leaving Tulvak Sahm to advance alone another twenty before he stopped.

"Do you have it?" he called.

The tension grew stronger. Dain could feel Samderaudin ready to pounce. The *sorcerel's* magic, which shielded Dain's mind from Tulvak Sahm's attempts to probe it, crackled inside Dain's skull, making him itch restlessly. He stared at Tulvak Sahm, taking care not to look the villain fully in the eyes, and untied the bundle from his saddle.

Lifting it in the air, he said, "I have it."

Tulvak Sahm's eyes darted suspiciously. "I sense no power. You are a fool if you think to trick me."

A wall of magic that shimmered like heat on the desert appeared before him. Tulvak Sahm raised his hand, but although sparks flew along the surface of the wall, it did not dissipate.

"What nonsense is this?" he asked furiously. "If you are so afraid of me, why have you come at all?"

"Just a precaution," Dain replied. He spurred his mincing horse forward until he faced Tulvak Sahm just on the other side of the shimmering wall. He could feel the humming force of the magic Samderaudin was expending. It made his hair stand on end and crackle. His horse was snorting, standing hunched and ready to bolt.

"I have brought what you asked for," Dain said. "Where is my daughter?"

"Close by."

It was a lie. Dain could not sense her presence at all. Anger and grief surged through him. Despite his readiness for betrayal, actually going through this charade was proving to be far more difficult than he'd anticipated. His emotions did not want to cooperate with his mind, but somehow he forced himself to concentrate on the bargaining.

"If she is not brought forth," Dain said harshly, "we'll make no deal!"

"You dicker like a peasant," Tulvak Sahm sneered. "Where is the word and honor of a king?"

"Here!"

Shaking off the cloth wrappings, Dain lifted the false Chalice high. The spell Samderaudin had placed inside it shot from the top with a shower of golden sparks. Behind Dain, Samderaudin spoke a low, sharp word that seemed to crack in the air, and some of the bones on the ground began to stir and rattle. A skeleton rose upright and took a jerky step. A second skeleton joined it. A simple spell of illusion caused swords to appear in the skeletons' hands.

Some of the Believers called out in wonder, pointing, while the fire-knights sat impassively. Dain held his breath, for would his gamble pay off? Would this ploy fool Tulvak Sahm?

The wall of magic continued to shimmer between the *sorcerel* and Dain. Tulvak Sahm stared at the Chalice still held aloft in Dain's hand while the power flowed from the mouth of the vessel and shimmered down over the standing skeletons. He remained suspicious, Dain saw, but greed began to shine avidly from his eyes, gradually winning over doubt.

"My daughter," Dain said. "Now."

Tulvak Sahm gestured, and from behind one of the Believers a small figure slid off the horse and trudged forward, picking a slow path over the bones and avoiding the lashing barbed tails of the darsteeds. Dain's heart jerked, but he held himself firmly under control. Her presence was far more than he'd hoped for, but it could still be a trick. *Beware*, he warned himself. *Beware*.

She came up beside Tulvak Sahm's mount and halted. Her head was bowed, concealing her face beneath the unkempt hair. *Was she Nonkind?* Dain could hardly bear to ask himself the question. He wouldn't know until he touched her.

Slowly, taking care not to disperse the spell making the false Chalice shine with radiant magic, Dain dismounted.

Tulvak Sahm did the same. They faced each other grimly

for a moment before the *sorcerel's* hand gripped Tashalya's shoulder. She flinched with a small gasp of pain.

A muscle in Dain's jaw leaped. *I shall slay you for all you've done*, he vowed.

The shielding wall hummed and crackled between them. Tulvak Sahm was peering at him intently, no doubt trying to read his thoughts.

Dain forced himself to think about nothing at all. The time had come. "Now," he said, without looking over his shoulder.

Samderaudin allowed the wall of magic to drop.

"Let her go," Dain said.

The *sorcerel* gave Tashalya a little push, and she started forward, walking slowly instead of running. Dain watched, holding himself with iron control as he let her take a few steps closer, a few steps closer. He dared not let himself believe Tulvak Sahm really intended to let her go, and yet . . .

"Stop," Tulvak Sahm said, and the child halted with a ready obedience that renewed Dain's suspicions. His Tashalya would have flown to him like the wind . . . unless her spirit had been entirely broken by this villain. Tulvak Sahm gestured impatiently. "Hand the Chalice to me, Faldain of Nether."

The triumph and arrogance in the *sorcerel's* face only intensified Dain's desire to run him through. In that moment he hesitated.

Tulvak Sahm smiled. "Ah, at last I discern an honest thought in your mind despite the shielding of your *sorcerel*. Hatred is a bitter drink, is it not? I have grown surprisingly fond of the taste." His smile vanished abruptly. "Hand it over."

"The last miscreant who dared hold the sacred vessel perished from holy fire," Dain said in warning.

"A fate for fools who do not know how to handle an object of power," Tulvak Sahm said, gesturing. "I shall not ask again."

"As you wish."

Dain tossed the false Chalice to him and sprang forward to grab Tashalya in his arms lest Tulvak Sahm pull her back. She clung to him fiercely, crying against his shoulder.

"You came," she whispered brokenly.

He pressed her close, drawing a swift breath of thanksgiving, but there was no time for more.

The *sorcerel* had caught the Chalice deftly, taking care not to touch it with his bare hands. Just as he loosed a triumphant laugh, Samderaudin allowed the skeletons to crumple back to the ground and unleashed a ball of spellfire in the midst of the Gantese fighters.

"Now!" Dain shouted, running for his horse. He tossed Tashalya up in front of the saddle, stepped into the stirrup, and swung astride. Drawing his sword, he lifted it high. "For Nether!"

It was the signal his knights had been waiting for. They poured from the trees and thundered across the field, brandishing swords and war axes. Wheeling his horse around, Dain was about to hand Tashalya off to his squire so that she could be taken safely out of the way, when she suddenly started struggling in his hold.

"Be still," he said to her.

At that moment his horse neighed in terror and reared. Struggling to control his horse, Dain tightened his sword arm around the child, but she shimmered in his grasp and changed into a shapeshifter. With a screech, the thing struck at him, sinking its venomous fangs into the mail gorget protecting his throat.

Cursing, he fought to get the creature off him while it beat him with its black, leathery wings and lashed him with a barbed tail. Omas shouted something, and sliced off one of its wings with his sword. Black blood splattered across Dain's armor. Shrieking, the shapeshifter snaked its head away from Dain's throat and tried to fly at Omas. Instead it wobbled to the ground, unable to fly with one wing. Leaning recklessly out of the saddle, Dain plunged Mirengard through its body, exploding it into ashes.

"That filthy trickster!" Omas swore. "Did it wound you, sire?"

"Nay!"

There was no time to deal with the sudden shift from relief

to horror, no time to think about Tashalya at all as the battle was joined.

A fire-knight came charging right at Dain. Omas closed with him in a furious clash of weaponry, while Dain turned and took on a Believer in red mail. Mirengard hummed and sang in his hand, and he made short work of his opponent.

A short distance away, a howl of rage rose over the din, and the false Chalice went bouncing and rolling across the ground.

Dain grinned inside his helmet with scant satisfaction. *Betrayal on both sides and likely victory to neither*, he thought bitterly.

"Sire!" Omas bellowed over the noise. "To your right!"

Just in time, Dain wheeled around and parried the blow of a fire-knight's black sword. Mirengard was glowing white, and sparks flew as the two weapons clashed together. Disengaging his blade, Dain sliced through the fire-knight's armor, sending thin disks of obsidian flying. Reeling, the fire-knight uttered a string of curses that popped fire all around Dain's head, and swung in response.

Protected by his magicked armor, Dain filled his mind and spirit with Mirengard's war song. The sword's magic supplied fresh strength to his muscles and lungs. Slicing upward, he cut off his opponent's fighting arm. With a hoarse cry, the fire-knight went tumbling off his mount, and Dain spurred his horse forward to meet the next foe.

A pillar of flame shot up before him, however, and Dain's terrified horse bucked to one side, trying to bolt with him before he brought it back under control.

Levitating himself into the air above the battle, Tulvak Sahm uttered another scream of rage, and hurled shooting flames at Dain.

Samderaudin's green fire intercepted the evil *sorcerel's* attack, but when he was nearly scorched in the crossfire of their magic, Dain ducked and spurred his horse out of the way.

"You will pay for this!" Tulvak Sahm shouted after him, descending to the ground. "I would have kept her safe and taught her as my own child, but now she'll go to the Chief Believer!"

Rage exploded inside Dain. He reined up, wrenching his horse around, and charged back to the *sorcerel*. Yelling, he swung Mirengard with the intention of cutting off Tulvak Sahm's head.

Smoke billowed around the *sorcerel*, and Mirengard sliced through nothing. Swearing with frustration, Dain swung again, but the magicked sword bounced harmlessly aside and was nearly twisted from Dain's hand.

"No!" Dain shouted. "You will die. I have sworn it!"

Chanting terrible words that smoked and flamed in the air, the *sorcerel* spread wide his hands. "She lives yet, you fool!" he shouted viciously, and stepped into the black smoke. "But you have lost her forever!"

"Sire, no!" Omas roared.

Unheeding, Dain had already launched himself from the saddle in a flying tackle, knowing only that he could not let Tulvak Sahm escape him. The smoke blinded him, but his outstretched hand grasped a fold of Tulvak Sahm's robe just as the *sorcerel* vanished from this world. Dain's hand felt as though it had been torn loose from his body. Shouting with pain, he swiftly summoned the power of the Ring to his aid.

"Tashalya!" he yelled, focusing his mind on the child.

Golden sparks spewed around him, and he felt himself buoyed up in midair for a moment. Then he was sucked into absolute darkness.

Chapter Thirty-Two

It seemed as though Dain hurtled through a black tunnel forever. This journey through the second world was longer than any he'd taken before. He could see nothing, and a screaming wind buffeted him, deafening him so that he could barely hear even his own thoughts.

Tashalya. He focused on the child, letting nothing distract him, for he dared not lose concentration for an instant.

Without warning, he hit something solid. The tremendous jolt snapped his teeth together and jarred every bone in his body. The barrier gave way, and he tumbled out of the darkness into a cavern. Rolling over and over across sharp, porous black stone that cut and scraped him mercilessly despite his armor, he came to a halt and lay stunned.

It was very hot. The light around him glowed strangely orange as though lit by a gigantic fire. Although the cavern was not immense, the ceiling of it rose high in a conical shape. Far, far above him, steam boiled and gathered in a cloud. He could hear a rushing, burbling sound nearby, and when he raised himself on his hands and knees he saw a gigantic idol carved of polished red stone standing astride a stream of molten lava coursing through the cavern. Hissing and boiling, more of the lava spewed from the open jaws of this hideous colossus, streaming into a large basin before flowing onward through a channel. Smoke poured from the nostrils of the idol, and its outstretched arms were draped with garlands of skulls strung together on chains.

Sweating and panting to breathe in the hot, ashy air, Dain struggled to his feet while he sought his bearings.

A child's scream sent him whirling around with his heart in his mouth. He saw Tashalya, bound and struggling, being carried toward the idol. For one horrified moment, Dain thought the men who carried her intended to throw her into the lava stream as some kind of sacrifice, but instead they turned aside and laid her atop an altar. Tulvak Sahm, his back to Dain, walked toward her, calling out something to the Believers who were tying her down.

Hope lifted in Dain's heart, for he had not come too late, but there was little time in which to save her. Gripping Mirengard, which by some miracle he had not dropped in the second world, Dain rushed at Tulvak Sahm from behind. But just as he reached the *sorcerel* with sword upraised, Tulvak Sahm whirled on him with a shout, and Dain was knocked off his feet by an invisible force.

Winded by the blow, he blinked tiny gray dots from his vision and rolled slowly upright.

Tulvak Sahm was staring at him with outstretched hands. "Welcome to the sacred presence of Ashnod, mortal!" Turning toward the idol with his hands still spread high, he shouted, "Behold, great master! I have brought Faldain of Nether as I promised."

"Papa!" Tashalya cried, thrashing with all her might. She snapped at the hands of a Believer like a mad dog, and with a yell the man struck her.

Furious, Dain went for him, but suddenly several fire-knights came running from the shadows. Brandishing swords of black iron, red eyes glowing through visor slits in their helmets, they surrounded him swiftly. Dain halted in a half crouch, his gaze shifting from figure to figure. Ten of them, he counted, all highly dangerous and hard to kill. He sucked in a breath and fought off a sharp feeling of despair.

Tulvak Sahm stepped between him and the altar, blocking Tashalya from his sight. "You fool," the *sorcerel* said with contempt. "Such careful plans and strategies . . . did you think I could be so easily tricked?"

"Aye," Dain replied, believing Tulvak Sahm was making his claim in bravado, hiding the fact that for a few minutes he'd truly thought he had the Chalice. "I did. Were you planning to use the Chalice to raise an army from the Field of Skulls to serve you?"

Tulvak Sahm's brows drew together, and Dain knew his guess had struck home. "Enjoy your triumph, for it is small," the *sorcerel* said. "The real trap has now closed around you. Tashalya is not my offering to the dark god. *You* are. She is mine to keep."

Bleak understanding poured over Dain. At last he could see the clear connection of events, all designed to bring him to this place, to the doom that Vaunit had foretold.

As Tulvak Sahm moved to one side, Dain gazed at his daughter in despair. She was lying quietly, her pale blue eyes fixed on him with trust and the obvious belief that he would save her. *How*, Dain asked himself frantically. He'd come there by using his third—and last—journey with the Ring. He stood surrounded by the enemy, cut off from his friends, and hopelessly outnumbered. When he glanced around, he saw no exit from the cave. Even if he managed to free Tashalya, and they ran for it, he doubted he could escape before they were recaptured.

Doomed, he thought, and met his daughter's eyes once more. Their bright, indomitable courage shamed him for his moment of despair. He told himself that while he remained her hero, he must not let her down, impossible odds or not.

With that new determination came an idea. He might be finished, but Tashalya wasn't. He possessed a way to ensure her escape, and swiftly he sent up a silent prayer to Thod for the courage to use it.

"Papa, be careful!" she called.

The warning made him swing around, but the fire-knights

behind him were not attacking. Instead, they parted to let the Chief Believer approach. Having seen the monster before, Dain did not recoil, but revulsion crawled through him. Although the Chief Believer had the vague body shape of a man, he was made of fire that blazed around the edges of his stone-disk clothing. A necklace of skulls hung around his neck, and he carried a long scepter with a huge clear crystal at one end.

Memories overtook Dain. At Sindeul's palace years ago, he had faced the Chief Believer and nearly perished. He remembered gazing into the scepter's crystal and seeing the faces of tormented souls entrapped within it. He had escaped only because he carried the god-steel sword called Truth-seeker. Now, with Mirengard singing and humming in his hand, he did not know whether a mere magicked sword, even one eldin-forged in purity and justice, could prevail against this foe.

"Great lord and master!" Tulvak Sahm called out eagerly. "I have delivered Faldain of Nether to you, as I swore I would. Hereby do I prove my loyalty to Ashnod."

The Chief Believer's blazing eyes turned on Tulvak Sahm. "Where is the Chalice of Eternal Life?"

The *sorcerel* scowled. "Not even for the child would this mortal dog surrender the Chalice, master."

When the Chief Believer said nothing, the *sorcerel* bowed and retreated behind the altar. Tashalya stirred and whispered something to Tulvak Sahm. He murmured a reply, touching her hair briefly as he spoke.

That little interaction, both familiar and intimate, filled Dain with jealous disgust. Before he could shout at Tulvak Sahm to take his hand off Tashalya, however, the Chief Believer opened his mouth, and shot a thin flicker of fire right at Dain.

Although it did not quite reach him, the very breath seemed to be sucked from Dain's lungs. He swayed, choking and gasping, his hand at his throat.

The desire to kneel nearly made his knees buckle, but he realized it was the Chief Believer's will trying to command him, and he stiffened his limbs in defiance.

"Faldain of Nether," the Chief Believer said. His voice

held no inflection or life. It was like listening to something without a soul. "Our business remains unfinished. This time, thou shalt not escape."

Dain lifted his chin and found breath enough to speak. "You could not hold me before. What has changed?"

Another flicker of flame shot from the Chief Believer's mouth, and in silent answer he pointed his scepter at Tashalya.

Despite the heat that had soaked him with sweat, Dain felt chilled.

"She holds thee as nothing else can," the Chief Believer said in his terrible voice. He gestured at his minions. "It is time for her to eat fire."

Horror shot through Dain. He started for the altar, but the fire-knights shoved him back.

Tulvak Sahm placed his taloned hand protectively upon Tashalya. "Master, the child belongs to me. I seek only the reward to continue training her into a powerful *sorcerelle*."

"Morde!" Dain swore furiously, smashing Mirengard against a fire-knight helmet. "She doesn't belong to you! She's my daughter, and I'll—"

Flames from the Chief Believer struck Dain to the ground. His cloak caught on fire, and he jerked it off, rolling free before collapsing, panting and trembling, with his face pressed against the stone floor.

"Master," Tulvak Sahm was still pleading. "The child will serve Ashnod well as a *sorcerelle*. Permit me to finish her training."

"She intrigues the dark god," the Chief Believer replied. "She will eat fire. If she survives this test, she will walk beside me and know the honors that only Ashnod can bestow."

Picking up Mirengard from where he'd dropped it, Dain struggled to his feet. Grimly he headed for the altar, knowing that he had to get Tashalya out of there immediately.

This time a single fire-knight stepped into his path in clear invitation to combat. Without hesitation, Dain swung Mirengard. The fire-knight closed with him swiftly, and they fought swift and hard.

In moments, smoke was boiling from beneath his opponent's helmet, and Dain redoubled his efforts, pressing the fire-knight back as he struggled to maneuver closer to the altar. Through his visor slits he glimpsed the two Believers dipping a long-handled ladle into the lava flowing from the idol's mouth. Chanting some litany that made his ears hurt to listen, they came back. The lava boiled and bubbled as they carefully ladled some of it into a smoking stone cup. The thought of them pouring that death down his daughter's throat sent him into a frenzy, and he drove his opponent hard, breaking the fire-knight's defenses and smiting him to his knees. Turning, Dain ran for the altar, but before he reached it, the Chief Believer hurled flame at Mirengard.

Although brilliant white light flashed from the blade, it was not god-steel, nor could it withstand such magic. Suddenly the sword grew so intensely hot that Dain dropped it with a cry of pain. His armor was likewise hot, burning him through his mail shirt and quilted undertunic, and the Ring of Solder shot agony through his left hand. Desperately, Dain tried to sing of ice and snow, but his attempted spell was crushed by the Chief Believer's power.

"Lartk!" the Chief Believer commanded. "Bring him down."

Unarmed, Dain lifted his hands in surrender, but the biggest fire-knight stepped forward and knocked Dain sprawling with his heavy, black sword. If not for his magicked armor, Dain likely would have been cut in half. As it was, he found himself aching for breath, feeling as though his ribs had caved in, and unable to roll fast enough to dodge another blow.

"Papa!" Tashalya shouted. "No, no! Don't hurt him!"

Groaning, Dain tried to crawl toward Mirengard, shining white and radiant on the ground, but Lartk planted his boot on Dain's back, pinning him down.

Tashalya started shouting in a language Dain did not understand, but the violence and threat were obvious in her clear voice. The curses were nothing she should know, he thought in dismay. What she was saying sounded evil. It was filled with a power she should not have.

And in response, something rumbled in the cave.

Frightened for her, Dain shouted, "Tashalya, no!"

The rumbling continued, as a small quake shook the cavern. One of the Believers staggered to keep his balance and nearly dropped the cup of lava. Turning on him with a wrathful shout that made the air smoke, the Chief Believer gestured at the altar, and the cringing Believer hurried to Tashalya.

Still pinned beneath Lartk's boot, Dain heaved with all his strength and managed to roll away. Scrambling to his hands and knees, he lunged for Mirengard, but Lartk kicked it over to the base of the altar out of reach.

By now Tulvak Sahm—his protests apparently silenced— was propping Tashalya up and clamping her head still as he forced her mouth open. All the while he was talking low and urgently to her while the Believer lifted the cup of lava to her mouth.

Jerking free of Tulvak Sahm's grasp, Tashalya screamed.

Dain found his feet, shoving one of the fire-knights aside with his shoulder and fending off another ferociously. Desperately, he ran at the cup-bearing Believer and grabbed him from behind, knocking the cup to the ground and splashing the lava across the second Believer. Screaming, that man went reeling back.

A heavy blow across Dain's shoulders drove him to his knees, and the world spun a moment. He clung to the altar to keep himself from falling completely. Blinking hard against the blackness that dimmed his vision, he told himself he must not pass out.

Tulvak Sahm came to him and yanked off his helmet.

"Take care," the Chief Believer said. "Hold Faldain, but do not damage him further. His time is next."

Roughly his captors dragged him upright on sagging knees. Although the fire-knights wore gauntlets, he could feel the heat of their hands almost scorching him through his clothing. Time was running out. He understood that very soon the Chief Believer would cease to toy with him. Before then, he had to get to Tashalya.

Sitting atop the altar, Tashalya looked more furious than frightened, although Dain knew that often she used anger as bravado to hide her fears. He tried to smile at her in reassurance, but she scowled ferociously.

"Let my papa go," she commanded, "or I'll hurt you. I can do it."

Lartk uttered a horrid, rasping laugh in reply.

Tulvak Sahm gestured to her. "Tashalya, no—"

Her small face knotted with concentration, and the fire-knights gripping Dain suddenly cried out in unison and released him. Astonished, he nonetheless seized that tiny moment of opportunity to fling himself at her. "The Ring, Tashalya," he said, pushing it onto her finger. "Use it. Hurry!"

The glowing Ring of Solder was far too large for her, but she clenched her small fist around it. "How?"

Growling, Lartk yanked Dain away from her so hard he was sent staggering.

"Think of Mama, nothing else," he called frantically, and smiled at her with all his love, knowing this was the last time he would ever see her. "Go!"

She drew in a deep breath and closed her eyes.

"Get the Ring!" Tulvak Sahm shouted. "Take it from her, you fools. Hurry!"

A Believer gripped her arm roughly, but Tashalya vanished in a shower of golden sparks that puddled and shimmered on the altar before sliding off it in little rivulets that melted away. Panting with relief, Dain tried to assure himself that she had the courage to make it through the second world.

Without warning, a fist slammed into his jaw, and he staggered sideways, sinking to his knees. Tulvak Sahm gripped his hair cruelly, yanking back his head. The *sorcerel's* eyes were blazing with fury. "You fool! You've ruined everything I planned for her. She—"

"My daughter," Dain shot back, "is not yours to plan for, or to torture."

Tulvak Sahm struck him again, bloodying his mouth and making his head ring. But Dain lunged at him, despite the fire-knights hanging on to his arms, and might have succeeded in breaking free, only something queer seemed to be happening to him. The strength drained from his limbs. It grew harder to breathe or marshal his thoughts. He struggled up, only to sink down once more, bracing himself on his hands. *Must kill Tulvak Sahm*, he thought groggily. *Must fulfill my vow.*

"Release him," the Chief Believer commanded. "He belongs to the dark god, and Ashnod's will is his."

The fire-knights obeyed at once, stepping back from Dain, but Tulvak Sahm's face remained contorted with rage. With a bolt of magic, he slammed Dain to the ground with such force the world went black a moment.

As Dain slowly regained his wits, he heard the *sorcerel* shouting, "He has taken the child from me, and I—"

Flames shot from the Chief Believer in all directions. "Thou darest disobey the will of Ashnod! Blasphemer! Is thy will greater than mine, or greater than the dark god's?"

Tulvak Sahm cowered before him, lifting jeweled hands in supplication. "Forgive me, master. Forgive me!"

One word did the Chief Believer speak, but it cracked through the air and made the cavern shake. Tulvak Sahm tried to flee, but some unseen force held him rooted. Shouting, he cried out again for mercy before his voice was abruptly silenced. Fear filled his eyes.

Advancing on him, the Chief Believer reached out a flaming hand and dug fiery fingers into Tulvak Sahm's chest. The *sorcerel's* mouth opened in a soundless scream, and his robes caught on fire as the Chief Believer pulled out his heart and held up the black, pulsing organ before tossing it into the lava flow.

Tulvak Sahm's eyes widened. He tried once more to speak; then he simply crumbled to dust.

Too weak to move, Dain stared at what remained of the enemy who had taken his son's life, altered his daughters forever, and caused untold grief and suffering. It did not seem to be punishment enough.

"Hatred," the Chief Believer said. "Ah, I feel it in thee, Faldain of Nether. It is good that thou art coming into my power with hate. I have waited long to command thee. Thou knowest Ashnod's will for thy future. Ashnod is patient, but Ashnod will be served."

Dain's eyes widened, and his heart began to pound. He remembered all too well how Ashnod intended for him to be rendered Nonkind, to serve the dark god forever as a mindless, soulless puppet. He wanted to break free of the Chief Believer's spell and fight his way out, but he could not overcome the lassitude that held him prisoner.

"No," he whispered defiantly. "I won't serve—"

"Thou hast no choice," the Chief Believer said, and held out the crystal end of his scepter. "Here will thy soul reside, trapped for all time. It is Ashnod's will, and Ashnod's will do we serve." Stepping back, the Chief Believer gestured to his minions. "Prepare him."

As they lifted Dain atop the altar a surge of panic engulfed him. They laid him on his back but did not bind his legs and wrists. There was no need, for he could barely move. With his heart hammering and his mouth dry, he struggled to keep his courage.

It was said among the dwarves that a good life reached its end without regrets, but all Dain could think about were the things left undone, the ambitions and projects not yet achieved, the children he would never see grow up, the wife he would never again hold in his arms. There was still so much to do, and he understood, too late, how in his efforts to be a just and careful king he'd erred too often on the side of caution. On some level, he hadn't truly believed in himself, and because of that lack of self-confidence and his resolve not to repeat his father's mistakes, he had instead let others influence his judgment too much. He'd felt secretly inferior to his nobles, a stranger in his own realm. Under it all ran the stupid little fear that someday they would discover he wasn't really a king at all, but instead just a bastard eld orphan of no lineage or rights. His good fortune and tremendous success had seemed to be a dream at times rather than something he truly deserved. And to his shame, he had not always stood firmly enough for what was right against the stubbornness of his people, and then excused them for their barbarity and ignorance. He'd been too much a reed and not enough a king. He had not been a bad sovereign, but neither had he been a great one. And Nether needed greatness if it was ever to reach its full potential.

The Chief Believer thrust the end of his scepter into the little pile of dust that had once been Tulvak Sahm. As he stirred it, something began to take shape until a slick, amorphous gray thing writhed and slithered obscenely on the floor.

Gazing at it, Dain felt his heart lurch in his chest. "Soultaker," he whispered. It was what he feared and dreaded more than anything else. To die, yet live as one undead, never to reach the third world of spirits. They were going to render him Nonkind, damned for eternity to exist as an abhorrent, stinking, empty husk. He would be evil, as they were evil.

Shuddering, he tried with all his might to fling himself off the altar and crawl away. But he remained trapped under the Chief Believer's control, too weak to move. He could not save himself.

"No," he pleaded. "No!"

Fire flickered from the Chief Believer's mouth. He pointed, and Lartk picked up the squirming soultaker and placed it on Dain's chest.

"Now, thou shalt become one of us," the Chief Believer said. "Ashnod's will is done."

Chapter Thirty-Three

The Tree of Life, ancient and gnarled, its spreading branches so old and heavy they were themselves the size of lesser trees, stood leafed out in tender green foliage against a pale blue sky. Spring clouds, fluffy and soft, floated overhead, and the morning sunshine felt warm and good on Alexeika's shoulders. Said to have been worshiped by the eldin of ancient days, long before humans formed the first Circle, the Tree of Life had suffered neglect, ruin, and near destruction, yet it had survived as Nether had survived.

Standing outside the gates of Grov, the tree marked one boundary of the ground where the Battle of Grov had been fought, and where Faldain had first been acclaimed victor and king of his people. Although once the meadow had been open and desolate, now countless saplings had sprouted up around the tree, growing rapidly the past few years into a young grove that would in time become a sacred wood. Pilgrims journeyed there from every corner of the realm, and the eldin guardians tended the tree and grove, shoring up the lowest and heaviest branches of the tree to keep it from split-

ting, protecting tender sprouts and seedlings from those who
sought to carry away a souvenir.

It was there among the slender, swaying young trees that
Alexeika walked slowly with King Kaxiniz and Nilainder
while an excited Mareitina skipped ahead, waving to some
of the other eldin who had come here. Aware that Kaxiniz
was Faldain's grandfather and had paid them great honor by
venturing forth from his forest refuge so close to the sprawling, teeming Grov, a man-place all eldin abhorred, Alexeika
sought to offer him full honors of hospitality.

"You are welcome to stay within the palace gardens," she
was saying. "I realize you would not wish to come inside the
palace, but Faldain has restored many of the plantings and
flowers that his mother loved."

"Faldain has honored his mother well," Kaxiniz replied.
His long silver hair curled and stirred restlessly on his shoulders. His serene gaze seemed to see through her as though
he beheld all her secrets. As he trod the tender spring grass,
tiny flowers sprang up and unfurled in his footsteps. "Your
offer is gracious, Alexeika, but we will not linger here. The
meadow beyond this grove has been spread many times with
violence and atrocity. Your gardens have experienced the
same."

She frowned at sharp memories, and he clasped her hand
in apology. "I say this not to cause you grief. Behold this
wood around us, so new and wonderful. This is the true circle, Alexeika. Life following death following life. A simple
concept, too simple for many man-minds, but true just the
same. After loss comes gain. You have lost a son, but you
have gained a son. You have lost a daughter—"

"Forgive me," she broke in, unable to remain respectfully
quiet, "but I have lost two daughters."

As she spoke, however, there came a flash of vivid light
as though lightning had struck from a cloudless sky. Alexeika flinched instinctively and cried out. The next moment
she caught her breath and straightened. That's when she noticed a huddled little figure on the ground before her.

Wonder filled her, and she could not believe her eyes.
"Tashalya?"

Almost unrecognizable in filthy rags and matted hair, the child scrambled up and launched herself against Alexeika's skirts, hugging her tightly and sobbing.

Joy made Alexeika laugh, but she was weeping, too. Swiftly she knelt to embrace her daughter. "Oh, darling, my precious girl!" she said, smoothing back Tashalya's rough hair. She ran her fingers over Tashalya's dirty face, smeared now with tears. "You're real. You're here. Oh, I'm so glad to have you home."

Tashalya abruptly pushed herself back. Her small face was ashen, and she was shuddering. "You have to help him. You have to hurry. He saved me, and they're going to kill him!"

"What?" Alexeika gripped her arms and tried to calm her enough to make sense. "Slow down, Tashie, and tell me what's happened."

"Papa's going to die!" Tashalya shrieked. She opened her clenched fist to reveal the Ring of Solder. "He sent me home, but they have a soultaker, and he's—he's—"

She burst into tears.

Horror coiled inside Alexeika. She thought of Faldain surrounded by his enemies, perhaps dying, perhaps already rendered Nonkind. "I knew it was a trap," she whispered. "He had to go, but—"

"Save him!" Tashalya screamed hysterically. "Save him! Save him!"

Feeling hollow and unlike herself, Alexeika rose to her feet. Their reconciliation had been all too short before he had to ride forth to the Field of Skulls, most certainly to face terrible danger. She'd been anxiously counting the days until his return, praying he would be successful and would return safely home.

"Severgard," she murmured, trying to think. "If I use the Ring, I can go to him."

"No," Kaxiniz said. He spoke briefly in eldin to Nilainder, who nodded and hurried away. "Solder's Ring is not for you to use, Alexeika."

"I have to do something! If they take his soul—"

"We shall go," Kaxiniz said. His silver-hued eyes had

grown stern. "Faldain has done much for the eld folk, as much perhaps as Solder First. This debt will we now pay."

She stared at him in hope and worry. Somehow, she couldn't quite match these gentle, plant-tending people before her with the old tales of eldin warriors. Persecuted for generations, the eldin had withdrawn and secluded themselves until they'd become more mystery than anything else. Yet within the old king's calm silver eyes, she now saw steel.

"Please," she whispered. "If you can save him or help him in any way, please hurry." As she spoke she reached down to Tashalya, who was now crouched on the ground, weeping as though her heart would break, and started to remove the Ring of Solder from the child's hand. "Take the Ring and—"

"No," Kaxiniz said. "Solder's Ring is not for us." He knelt by Tashalya and briefly touched his fingertips to her face. Tashalya lifted her drenched blue eyes to his and, with a tiny sigh, fainted. Gathering her up, Kaxiniz handed her to Alexeika. "Poor child," he said softly, stroking her tangled hair. "Take special care of her, for she will never be as she was."

By then the other eld folk came hurrying up. Kaxiniz spoke to them briefly, his voice calm but brisk. "Farewell, Alexeika. We will do all we can, if we can reach him in time."

"But how do you know—"

"The child has told me."

"But how will you—"

"Pray hard," he said, and moments later they were gone as though they'd never been.

Alexeika held her unconscious daughter, who was skin and bone beneath the dirt and seemed to weigh no more than a bird. Tashalya's head lolled back over her arm, and Alexeika gazed at her unconscious face worriedly. Mareitina, frowning and bewildered, came up and clung to Nilainder's hand.

"Where did they go, Mama?" she asked over and over. "Why didn't they take me? Where did they go?"

A nursemaid arrived, flustered and out of breath, urged on by Sir Pyron, but Alexeika barely noticed when they took Tashalya from her arms. Her attention was elsewhere, hoping desperately that it was not too late for Faldain and fearing . . . fearing . . .

"Mama!"

"Hush, Mareitina," she said, rousing herself to silence the questions. "They've gone to help Papa. They'll come back as soon as they can."

Oh, merciful Thod, she prayed desperately. *Please let them reach him in time.*

In Ashnod's cavern, Dain lay helpless on the altar, struggling to breathe in the intense heat while his mind screamed with fear. The soultaker landed on his chest with a soft plop of squishy flesh. Gray, hideous, shapeless, and grotesque, it should have immediately squirmed its way straight to his throat, but instead it began to writhe frantically, moving in an aimless little circle until it rolled off him and landed on the floor. There, its movements became jerky and spasmodic. Abruptly it crumbled back into dust.

The fire-knights and Chief Believer all stared at it a moment.

"Magicked armor!" the Chief Believer said.

Dain closed his eyes in momentary relief and sucked in some deep breaths. "Run out of little monsters?" he taunted weakly.

The Chief Believer ignored him. "Lartk! Remove his armor at once."

Dain stiffened and tried to fend off the fire-knight who approached him, but the Chief Believer's will held him pinned. Lartk's gauntleted hands reached for the buckles at Dain's side, but sparks flew against his touch, and the fire-knight flinched back.

Flames shot from the Chief Believer into Lartk's back, driving the fire-knight to his knees. "Remove it."

Tendrils of smoke blew out through Lartk's visor. Slowly he hoisted himself to his feet and straightened painfully. He reached again for the buckles, unfastening them despite the sparks and intensifying smell of burned magic.

As they came loose, Lartk yanked the breastplate off Dain and flung it aside with a hoarse cry of pain. Dain closed his eyes, for never had he felt more vulnerable. His sword, armor, and the Ring had all been stripped from him, and the end was coming. Swiftly he was stripped of mail coif, gorget, and shirt as well, leaving him clad only in his undertunic and leggings.

Another soultaker was brought forth. Dain did not see whence it came; it did not matter. All he had left was pride, and he refused to let these villains see him sniveling with fear. *I am no coward*, he told himself fiercely, while his heart raced and thudded against his ribs. *Merciful Thod, give me courage to the end*.

"Why struggle to hide thy fear?" the Chief Believer asked. "Art thou not a mortal? It will please Ashnod to hear thy screams."

When the new soultaker was dropped on Dain's chest, it moved across him rapidly, its gray, flaccid flesh undulating as it squirmed for his throat. A scream swelled against Dain's gritted teeth, but he arched back, refusing to utter it. The soultaker nudged his throat, squirming closer. How clammy and horrid it felt against his naked flesh.

And it began to feed on him. He shuddered as it sucked a hole in his neck above the throbbing jugular. There was no pain, as he'd expected, nothing save a terrible coldness that stole through his limbs, the icy coldness of death. Obscene images and thoughts filled his mind in unspeakable ways. He heard a rushing babble of vile voices uttering blasphemies.

The soultaker burrowed inside him, and spasms rocked his body, sending him to the edge of the altar. His trembling fingers gripped the corner of stone, and one feeble pull was enough to topple him onto the floor.

He hit hard on his side, and his head thudded against the floor with force enough nearly to knock him unconscious, but he did not dislodge the soultaker. How he wished he could have passed out, and thus died without knowing the end of this unspeakable horror, but the soultaker was inside him by then, a part of him. He convulsed again, twisting and slamming his shoulder against the base of the altar. He could no longer breathe. A strange, rasping sound issued from his mouth, but he could not draw in the air he so desperately needed.

Ashnod, he thought vaguely, rolling his eyes in the direction of the idol. *Ashnod's will.*

It was ending. He could feel himself fading as the darkness gathered around him. Creatures of the evil appeared from the shadows, lizards first, then serpents. A slyth, narrow and strangely graceful, slinked into view. It snarled at him silently, sniffing his face before it went away. And the hurlhounds closed in, a whole pack of them growling and pacing restlessly, their jaws dripping venom, their breath foul and hot. There were other things that shambled into view, unrecognizable things that might once have been men.

And the unholy babble of voices filled Dain's thoughts until he felt the last cognizant bits of his mind drowning in the noise.

The Chief Believer came closer, bending down with the scepter pointed at Dain's mouth. "Soon," he said softly. "Very soon now."

Dain looked up at him, and no longer did he see a monster made impossibly of flames but instead a form of grace and shadow with mist instead of vital organs and the mark of Ashnod blazing in him like a beacon.

Astonished, Dain felt something inside him wanting to reach out in reverence to this entity, but it was a fleeting wish driven away by a sudden sensation of pain.

He gasped and jerked. The pain came again, and it felt as though something was being ripped inside him.

"No," he whimpered, trying to roll over. "No!"

"Thy soul is being torn free," the Chief Believer told him. "There is no need for such things as souls among us. Thou seest how we are, what we are. Thou canst embrace the darkness with us now. Release thy soul willingly, and the pain will end. Surrender it to me, and I will comfort and reward thee with the mark of Ashnod."

The pain came a third time, so rending that Dain cried out. His hand flailed against the base of the altar and landed upon Mirengard, which had been kicked there earlier and forgotten.

The sword forged in justice and light . . . it burned him now as he touched it, and Dain flinched away, unable to bear contact with something so foreign and awful. A part of him grieved, dimly aware that never again could he go near things of good or honor. *I am lost*, he thought in despair.

Something odd caught the corner of his vision. As he stared beyond the gathered horde of Nonkind creatures, he glimpsed a pale, shimmering mist that gradually cleared to reveal a group of eld folk. Their raiment shone strangely white in this dim, ashy place. Fairlight shone from their fingertips and in their eyes. Softly, so softly that at first he thought he only imagined it, they began to sing.

A cry of rage came from the Chief Believer, the sound loud and discordant enough to drown out the faint song of the eldin, but Dain had heard enough to find his courage again. His fingers groped blindly and closed around Mirengard's shining blade. This time he welcomed the agony it brought him. He had little time, only a few last heartbeats as his soul was pulled away, but the final remnants of his will refused to die in this filthy way, consumed by evil and rendered into evil. One mortal blow from this magicked blade, and he would die with his soul preserved.

"Tarry no longer! Render up thy soul!" the Chief Believer roared.

Dain struggled to lift the sword. "I . . . am not . . . Nonkind!" he gasped out, and plunged the blade deep into his side.

White magic like molten fire poured into his body. It filled him and engulfed the soultaker. The monster screamed, and Dain screamed with it. As it perished, Dain knew a swift instant of peaceful release.

Free, he thought; then white light flashed everywhere, consuming all the darkness that he'd become, and he knew nothing save one last flickering wish to reach the third world's eternity.

He awakened to the sound of someone singing, soft and low. The melodious, gentle refrain had no words, only tune. It lulled and soothed him, and he thought, *So I did reach the third world after all. Thod is good.*

A baby whimpered, and the singing stopped a moment. "There, there. Hush, little one," said a familiar voice.

Dain opened his eyes. At first he found himself looking only at blurred shapes and dazzling light. He squinted and turned his head slightly, and someone said excitedly, "He's awake!"

His vision cleared, and he found himself staring up at Alexeika. Wearing a gown the color of sunshine, her dark hair hanging over her shoulder in a loose braid, she held the baby in her arms. Tashalya and Mareitina crowded between her and Dain, jostling the bed in their eagerness.

"Hello, Papa! We thought you would never wake up," Tashalya said.

He stared at them all in wonder, still unable to understand what had happened. Glancing around, he saw that he was lying in the vast bed of state. Sunlight shone in through the tall windows across the room. The sight bewildered him. Had he dreamed all that happened?

Frowning, he tried to raise his hand to shield his eyes, but felt a pulling in his side painful enough to make him wince. *Ah*, he thought, *that was real enough.*

Alexeika pushed his hand down by his side. "You must not do that," she said gently, gazing at him with love and tenderness. "You will make yourself bleed again if you open the wound."

By then, he'd discovered a constrictive band around his throat. Memories of the soultaker abruptly returned to him, and he frowned. "Am I not dead? How came I here? I thought—"

"King Kaxiniz saved you," Mareitina said importantly, bouncing up and down on her toes to see over the top of the tall bed. "He found you, Papa, and he saved you."

Tashalya clamped a hand on her shoulder to make her be still. "He did not," she corrected her sister. "Papa saved himself. Kaxiniz came for him afterward and brought him home."

Mareitina's bottom lip began to tremble. "You're supposed to call him *King* Kaxiniz. You have to use his title with respect."

Tashalya shrugged. "Grandfather, then."

"He doesn't want us to call him that. He says it's a man-word."

"Only Papa is king," Tashalya retorted. "There can't be two kings in Nether. Not at the same time."

Listening to them bicker convinced Dain that he was indeed home. It had been a long time since he'd heard childish argument around him. The very absurdity of it felt good. "I owe the eld folk. I must talk to Kaxiniz and thank him," he said. "I don't understand what happened. How did he find me in that awful place?"

Alexeika bent and kissed Dain lightly on the lips. Some of the tears spangling her eyelashes moistened his cheek. "The eld folk went after you. I know not how, but they brought you home. Healer Voxtanimir said that had you not had the courage to turn Mirengard on yourself, they could have done nothing for you. Oh, Faldain, 'tis good to have you safe."

Little fingers tapped his hand to take his attention away from Alexeika. "Papa," Mareitina said, "Tashalya has been away, but so have I. And I can talk of greater wonders than she can."

"No, you can't," Tashalya said angrily. "I could make the whole palace fall down if I wanted. I could break all the mirrors in the Gallery of Glass with one word."

"Tashalya," Alexeika said in gentle rebuke. She sent a quick frown at her elder daughter. "Don't you have something of your father's to return?"

Tashalya, pale and thin beside the rosiness of her younger sister, glowered a moment with resentment darkening her eyes. "Why?" she protested. "He can't use it again, and I can."

"Whether he can use it or not is none of your business. Only the king may wear the Ring of Solder," Alexeika said sternly, patting the baby in her arms as he began to fuss. "Do as I have bidden you."

With a formidable frown, Tashalya put the Ring in Dain's hand. Sighing, he let his fingers curl around the pale, milky stone. Its use had been designed for the protection of the Chalice. Twice had he used it for its correct purpose. The third time, he had not. But Tashalya's life was worth the sacrifice, he thought, and smiled tiredly at her.

"You've talked to Papa enough," Alexeika said, signaling for a nursemaid to take the baby. "Kiss him and run along."

"Me first," Mareitina said with more assertiveness than she'd ever displayed before. "I'm leaving to go back to the forest, so I get to kiss Papa first." She gave him a messy smack on his cheek. "I love you. I'm glad you didn't die. I hope you will come to the forest and see me soon."

"Yes," he murmured, missing her already as she skipped away.

Tashalya stared at him, and her eyes had grown intent and stony. "Papa," she asked, "where did you hide the sword called Truthseeker?"

Startled by so unexpected a question, he wondered uneasily how she knew about it. He'd never talked about that mighty sword made of a god-steel forbidden to ordinary men, a sword he'd carried and gave up before he became king. Truthseeker was best forgotten . . . and left hidden. Remembering how easily sometimes this child used to read his thoughts, he frowned and swiftly thought of harlberries kissed by frost and ready for picking.

Her eyes flashed with annoyance, and she stamped her foot. "More secrets!"

"Run along," Alexeika said, shooing her away. She settled herself beside Dain and smiled at him. "Why do you frown, beloved? We have come through a hard time, but it is over. Both you and Tashalya are safe, and I am so very grateful."

His sense of unease faded, and he found himself full of things he wanted to tell her. "Alexeika, I intend to abolish the Kollegya and—"

She placed her fingertips across his mouth. "Hush. Rest."

"But—"

"I am glad to hear it, but you can be king a few days hence when you are better. Right now, you are only my husband and my love. Let that be enough."

He settled deeper into his pillows with her hand clasped in his. And smiled. And slept. And grew well.

The royal intrigues of
The Ring, The Sword, and *The Chalice*
trilogy continue in

The Queen's Gambit

0-441-00997-2

by

Deborah Chester

*The throne was her destiny—until
Princess Pheresa lost her groom,
Mandria's heir, to dark magic.
Now her fate is uncertain. Her enemies are
strong. And her only ally is the last man
she would ever choose—and the one
man she should never love.*

**Available wherever books are sold or
to order 1-800-788-6262**